NEVADA BARR

WINTER STUDY

AN
ANNA PIGEON
NOVEL

D0038325

EAN

ISBN 978-0-425-22695-7

9780425226957

50999>

"Chilling . . . Barr's visceral descriptions of the winter cold nicely complement the paranoia that follows the appearance of the mythic monsters at play."

"The environmental quotient in Barr's novels is always high; the facts about wolves are fascinating, as are descriptions of frigid landscape, alternately beautiful and horrifying. There's plenty of drama, too, as Anna finds herself alone and in danger more than once, but what many readers return to this series for is Anna herself, strong, funny, perceptive, and well aware that she is a small part of a dynamic, ever-changing natural world."

"A new Anna Pigeon mystery is a treat for fans of the series who expect the best from Nevada Barr and get it with this strong 'closed door' whodunit in a wintry outdoors setting. As Anna digs into the lives of the scientists and their aides, she uncovers dark secrets and blackmail, hidden agendas and ties to a cold (pun intended) case. Readers will enjoy armchair trekking with Anna as she seeks the truth allegedly of a killer wolf stalking humans."

"A locked-room mystery, one with a room twenty miles long and no walls . . . Fans of the Anna Pigeon series have waited patiently for the return of their wiry heroine, gray-streaked red braids, plentiful scars, and all. Anna is most certainly back, and we're glad to see her."

"Barr does best in the northern parks and here is no exception. In the locked room of the frozen national park, Anna Pigeon has to explain unnatural phenomena, keep Homeland Security from destroying scientific work, and try and find the murderer. All of which she does just as gracefully at fifty as she did at thirty-something in *Track of the Cat*. Let's hope that we don't have to wait three years for the next Anna Pigeon book. This is a series that hasn't lost it." —ReviewingtheEvidence.com

"Nevada Barr's legions of fans will be almost certainly more than pleased with *Winter Study*, which features Anna Pigeon at her resilient best in an action-packed adventure with plenty of thrills and lots of tense moments for the charming and plucky park service ranger."

—*BookLoons*

TITLES BY NEVADA BARR

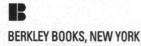

WINTER STUDY

NEVADA BARR

BERKLEY BOOKS, NEW YORK

THE BERKLEY PUBLISHING GROUP
Published by the Penguin Group
Penguin Group (USA) Inc.
375 Hudson Street, New York, New York 10014, USA
Penguin Group (Canada), 90 Eglinton Avenue East, Suite 700, Toronto, Ontario M4P 2Y3, Canada
(a division of Pearson Penguin Canada Inc.)
Penguin Books Ltd., 80 Strand, London WC2R 0RL, England
Penguin Group Ireland, 25 St. Stephen's Green, Dublin 2, Ireland (a division of Penguin Books Ltd.)
Penguin Group (Australia), 250 Camberwell Road, Camberwell, Victoria 3124, Australia
(a division of Pearson Australia Group Pty. Ltd.)
Penguin Books India Pvt. Ltd., 11 Community Centre, Panchsheel Park, New Delhi—110 017, India
Penguin Group (NZ), 67 Apollo Drive, Rosedale, North Shore 0632, New Zealand
(a division of Pearson New Zealand Ltd.)
Penguin Books (South Africa) (Pty.) Ltd., 24 Sturdee Avenue, Rosebank, Johannesburg 2196,
South Africa

Penguin Books Ltd., Registered Offices: 80 Strand, London WC2R 0RL, England

This is a work of fiction. Names, characters, places, and incidents either are the product of the author's imagination or are used fictitiously, and any resemblance to actual persons, living or dead, business establishments, events, or locales is entirely coincidental. The publisher does not have any control over and does not assume any responsibility for author or third-party websites or their content.

WINTER STUDY

A Berkley Book / published by arrangement with the author

PRINTING HISTORY
G. P. Putnam's Sons hardcover edition / April 2008
Berkley premium edition / April 2009

ISBN: 978-0-425-22695-7

BERKLEY®
Berkley Books are published by The Berkley Publishing Group,
a division of Penguin Group (USA) Inc.,
375 Hudson Street, New York, New York 10014.
BERKLEY® is a registered trademark of Penguin Group (USA) Inc.
The "B" design is a trademark of Penguin Group (USA) Inc.

PRINTED IN THE UNITED STATES OF AMERICA

10 9 8 7 6 5 4 3 2 1

For Mr. Paxton.
He dedicated his life to rescuing people.
The most recent was me.

ACKNOWLEDGMENTS

Winter Study is real and has been ongoing for over fifty years. The value of the research is inestimable not only in the detailed work done from winter to winter but in the patterns that can only unfold when a project is maintained over periods of time which are meaningful to the natural world. There's little space and much work to do during these weeks on the icebound Isle Royale. Had Superintendent Green not extended to me the generosity of the park and the forbearance of a good manager, I wouldn't have been able to write this book. Thank you, Phyllis.

And thanks to the Forest Service pilots in Ely, Minnesota, who took the time to share stories with me and who delivered me, along with food, to the island in January.

Most especially, thanks to the Winter Study team: Rolf Peterson, John Vuceti, Beth Kolb and Donnie Glaser. They are the heart and soul of this book. They had the kindness not to throw me out in the snow when I was whining about the cold; they answered endless e-mails with questions about what a wolf smelled like and how fat a fat tick was and who ate what and whom. Had Rolf not taken the time to work through the manuscript, researchers everywhere would have been rolling their collective eyes at the errors I made. The four of them shared not simply the knowledge they had but the spirit that motivates what is good in this book.

FOREWORD

In July 1970, when I was a neophyte graduate student just beginning fieldwork at Isle Royale National Park, a stranger invited me to lunch at the Windigo Inn. He must have thought I knew something, or at least was poor and in need of free food. The cafeteria adjoined a house of the erstwhile Washington Club, a turn-of-the-century private organization that predated the establishment of Isle Royale as a national park. (Over a decade later, I helped burn down the house in winter, tidying up the place and helping it revert to forest.) The stranger, a balding and very tanned man dressed in a stylish recreational outfit, explained how he had traveled the world over but he believed Isle Royale was simply the finest place on Earth. I recall thinking I was lucky indeed—this man spared me the need to look any farther.

It must be a similar impression—of splendid isolation—that brought Nevada Barr back to Isle Royale, to write an unprecedented second novel based in the same national park. I was happy to cooperate, as Nevada's signature blend of mystery and nature writing has a wide following. Isle Royale has always been a difficult destination, and relatively few people visit the place, even when open and accessible in summer. To the extent that it is known at all, it is primarily through the writings and imagery of others. A seasoned interpretive ranger at Mesa Verde National Park told me that all she knew of Isle Royale was contained in Nevada's 1994 work, *A Superior Death*.

While Isle Royale has a rich, largely unappreciated history, in the modern era its wolves and moose have put it on the map. As this book goes to press, the scientific effort to document and understand their population fluctuations will be in its fiftieth year. Simultaneously, the worldwide status of the gray wolf has improved remarkably, from vilified vermin to charismatic top dog. No longer confined to wilderness areas far removed from people, wolves now claim as their own many areas of private and public lands, including heavily visited Yellowstone National Park. There are still, however, only four national parks in the United States outside of Alaska, the other two being Glacier and Voyageurs, with a resident wolf population. Providing wildlands for these wolves, as well as other large carnivores, remains a serious conservation challenge.

Another person for whom Isle Royale was the finest place on Earth was Bob Linn, a local park naturalist who participated in the first Winter Studies of wolves and moose at Isle Royale. Bob eventually became Chief Scientist of the Service in the 1960s, presiding over the rocky marriage between science and national park management to which Nevada alludes. Bob hated controversy, but three times he had to take action to help stifle political or bureaucratic interference in the study of Isle Royale wolves. One would think these wolves would hardly have an enemy in the world, isolated as they are from any hint of competitive threat to human interests. Bob marshaled the forces of good to quell threats as they arose, whether inspired by greed, hunger for power, jealousy or just plain orneriness; afterward, he modestly declared that scientists were simply viewed as "loose cannons on the deck." The most serious challenge was certainly when James Watt was Secretary of the Interior under President Reagan; Park Service support was withdrawn and staff was recalled in the middle of the Winter Study in 1983. However, Watt was blameless, as I concluded years later after a rare conversation that demonstrated he didn't even know Isle Royale *existed*, let alone was a national park that he'd been nominally responsible for conserving. So it goes . . .

Nevertheless, to this day the wolves of Isle Royale have survived, the study of them has survived and, elsewhere, the species is thriving in places where wolf recovery at one time was considered most improbable. This is ample testimony to the ability of the human mind to embrace, eventually, the true and unblemished facts about the way the world works and about the role we can play in securing our own sustainable future in it.

For now, enter the white and cold world of Isle Royale and Lake Superior in winter. It is a world that Nevada Barr brings alive with descriptive power through her love of the natural world, her wide-ranging experience in national parks and her curiosity about the sometimes-abstruse ways of wildlife biologists. All this, mixed with the fears, frailties and foibles of her human subjects, makes for a chilling and absorbing account. Finally, one may be well advised to eschew cell phones, and, for the record, it is a bad idea to drink beer in the sauna.

—ROLF PETERSON
January 2008

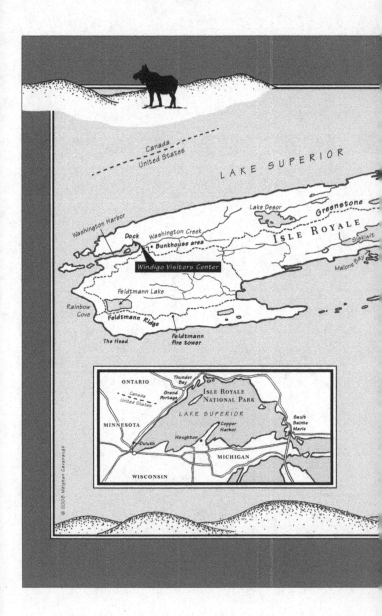

Canada
United States

LAKE SUPERIOR

Lake Desor

Greenstone

Washington Harbor

Dock   Washington Creek
• Bunkhouse area

ISLE ROYALE

Siskiwit

Windigo Visitors Center

Feldtmann Lake

Malone Bay

Rainbow
Cove

Feldtmann Ridge

The Head   Feldtmann
fire tower

ONTARIO   Thunder
Bay

ISLE ROYALE
NATIONAL PARK

Canada   Grand
United States   Portage

LAKE SUPERIOR

Sault
Sainte
Marie

MINNESOTA

Copper
Harbor

Duluth   Houghton

MICHIGAN

WISCONSIN

© 2008 Meighan Cavanaugh

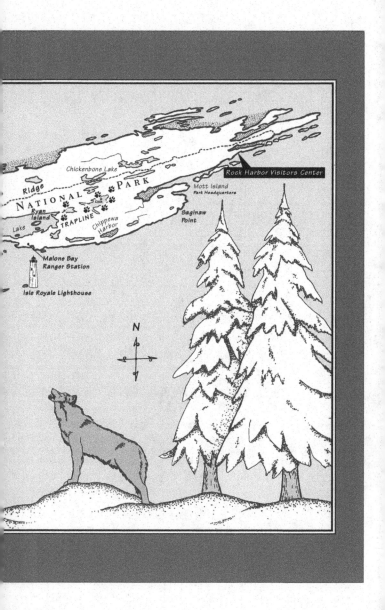

Chickenbone Lake

Rock Harbor Visitors Center

Ridge

NATIONAL   PARK

Mott Island
Park Headquarters

Ryan
Island

Lake   TRAPLINE   Chippewa
Harbor

Saginaw
Point

Malone Bay
Ranger Station

Isle Royale Lighthouse

N

The Beaver was spotless. Anna'd never seen an airplane so clean. Sitting in its heated hangar in Ely, Minnesota, it fairly gleamed from its annual check. Only the deeply scarred floorboards stood witness to the old warhorse's hard duty. Beavers hadn't been manufactured since 1962, and the one the pilot was loading for its weekly provision and personnel trip to Isle Royale in Lake Superior was older than Anna.

But it had taken better care of itself, she thought, with a touch of icy realism. Suited up in brand-spanking-new, fresh-out-of-the-box, felt-lined Sorel boots, insulated socks, ski pants and parka, watching a woman half her age, with legs as long and strong as a yearling moose, move nimbly about in lightweight mukluks and an alarmingly thin winter jacket, Anna suffered a sensation neither familiar nor welcome.

She felt frail, insecure, out of her element. Isle Royale in Michigan had been one of her first duty stations, but that had been years ago. And in summer. A jaunt there in the arctic temperatures of January, when the island was closed to the outside world, wasn't her idea of the perfect winter vacation. Too many years on the Natchez Trace in Mississippi, where a Levi jacket and knee socks were sufficient for a winter wardrobe, had thinned her blood. Her current tenure as District Ranger in Rocky Mountain National Park might bring back her limited tolerance for the cold, but she'd yet to spend a winter there.

She shifted uneasily from foot to foot, feeling the movement of her toes inside the huge boots, the way the many layers of down and fleece muffled her body and wrapped her limbs. New gear: Anna didn't trust it. Nor did she like parties where she had to dress up. The invitation to participate in the long-running wolf/moose study on Isle Royale had come down from Rocky's superintendent, couched in words no woman could resist: "How would you like to snowshoe over rough terrain, collecting blood-fat ticks and moose piss?"

Being a true romantic, Anna had said she would adore it. Rocky Mountain would soon be dealing with the prey/predator issue. Not through any sudden enlightenment of the state legislature, but because the recovery of the magnificent and much-maligned animals had been rapid. Wolves were reinhabiting territories they'd been extirpated from for a century or more.

Anna had reason to know the expected wolves were

already in the park and no reason whatsoever to share the knowledge. At least not till the pups were old enough to fend for themselves. Wolf/moose management was about to top Rocky's list of wildlife issues, and there was no better classroom for studying it than Isle Royale.

"We're set," the pilot said. Anna climbed the two paw-sized steps on the Beaver's wheel pant to get into the high cockpit, no mean feat in boots the size of snowshoes.

"Need help with your safety belt?" The pilot was stiff and edgy, his United States Forest Service uniform so crisp that Anna, accustomed to the rumpled, sweat-stained versions she came across in the field, had, at first glance, mistaken it for a military uniform.

"No," she said shortly. She'd flown on search and rescues, forest fires and animal surveys, more times than she could count before the pilot graduated from high school. Annoyed at herself for being annoyed, she fumbled at her safety harness. She was as awkward a bundle as an Iowa schoolboy waiting for the bus in January.

Pride cometh, she thought wryly as her mittened hands scrabbled on the webbing and her spiffy new balaclava interfered as she tried to bite her fingertips to pull the mittens off. Finally she sat as patiently and helplessly as the apocryphal Iowa lad and let the pilot string her shoulder harnesses through her lap belt and lock the whole mess down.

Then she thanked him politely.

Robin Adair, the long-legged research assistant, sprang

gracefully into the left rear seat, settled herself like a pro, and the plane was pushed from the hangar.

The Forest Service seaplane operation was on the shore of Shagawa Lake, edging the small town of Ely. In summer, the runway was open water. Now it was a lane of hard-packed snow, running north-northeast, between gaudily painted ice-fishing houses put up helter-skelter till they resembled nothing so much as a 1940s trailer park dropped from a passing cargo plane.

In an attempt to quell what was verging on internal whining, Anna focused on the beauty of the boreal forest as the Beaver left the ice and banked, turning east toward Michigan. The day was painfully bright and clear as it can only be in the north, where every particle of moisture is frozen from the air and the sun moves low in the south, feigning evening even at noon. Crystalline amber light honed the edges of the world till shadows of pines, long on the shores of snow-covered lakes, were as sharp and black as fangs drawn by children. Even from an altitude of twenty-two hundred feet and climbing, every track across the dazzle of white showed blue.

Static rattled in Anna's headphones, and then the pilot's voice: "Have you been to Isle Royale before?"

"Once." Anna had the scar to prove it, a six-inch weal of shiny flesh across her abdomen. It still ached occasionally.

When it was cold.

"Did you work there?"

Altitude was making the man downright chatty. Anna preferred him in his martinet mode but dragged herself from the vista of black pine and white lakes to make conversation.

"Ten or fifteen years ago, I was a ranger in Windigo. Boat patrol."

"Wow!" the pilot said. Before Anna could bask in his awe, he finished his thought: "I was in seventh grade then."

So much for impressing the natives.

"Did you ferry the Homeland Security guys out?" she asked, to change the subject.

The "Homeland Security guys" had been sent by Washington to evaluate Winter Study. For fifty years, Isle Royale had been a lab for Michigan Tech, in cooperation with the National Park Service. The park provided money and physical support. In return, the wolf researchers added to the glamour of Isle Royale. Visitors followed the rise and fall in the pack populations as avidly as soap opera devotees. A sizable percentage of the world's knowledge of wolves had been produced by the study.

To remain viable, the ISRO wolf/moose study had two requirements: fifty thousand dollars a year—peanuts as far as research money went—and that ISRO be closed to tourism from October to May, when the wolves mated and denned.

Homeland Security had put forth a resolution to beef up security in all border parks. To that end, they were exploring the possibility of opening the park year-round, to better protect the border from terrorists. If the wolf/moose study—running for over half a century—could be said to be effectively mined out as far as relevant data was concerned, Homeland Security was going to shut it down. ISRO would be opened to cross-country skiers and winter campers. Rock Harbor resort, on the east end, would be revamped for year-round usage, and a smaller hotel built on the east end in Windigo.

The wolf researchers—Anna, NPS seasonals and Homeland Security, in the persons of rented experts from American University—would share a bunkhouse for six weeks. Anna was surprised some enterprising young reality-TV-show producer hadn't offered big money to film it.

The mike woke up, and the seventh-grader flying the plane said: "It was a man and a woman—Homeland Security—the guy was somebody Ridley Murray recommended. They were weathered in in Ely for nearly a week. Hung around the hangar all day, being mad because we wouldn't move the ceiling up. Clouds were right down on the deck."

"I can't believe the park would do this to Rolf." It was Robin from the backseat, her voice-activated mike crackling with more anger than static.

"Rolf Peterson retired," the pilot said.

"The study *is* Rolf." Robin again. From Robin's fierceness, Anna guessed she, like a lot of other young outdoors people, was in love with the charismatic wolf researcher. Not sexual love but romantic love, in the sense that they wanted to grow up to be him, or at least have his life. To a woman Robin's age—twenty-two or -three, at a guess—retirement could look a lot like desertion. Or death.

"Ridley wanted this guy," the pilot said doggedly.

"Ridley Murray was Rolf's student." Robin's voice came back on its bed of cracklings. "Lesser of evils: Ridley didn't want *any* guy."

The mike was live for another moment as if an unspoken thought prolonged its activation, then, noiselessly but unmistakably, it went dead again. Fleetingly Anna wondered what differentiated that quiet open line of communication and the quiet but utterly different isolation that followed. Maybe it was the difference between silence and deafness; some sense deeper than the stirrup and hammer that tells one she is alone.

Embracing the solitude, she watched the frozen miles pass beneath the Beaver's wings and thought of Paul. It wasn't only the Mississippi heat that had thinned her blood. Paul Davidson was the source of the living heat in her life. After her first husband, Zack, had died, Anna had, without even knowing she'd done so, chosen a chill and lonely place to stow her heart, a limbo where it continued to beat, like the heart of a frog frozen in winter mud, to thaw to new life come spring. Paul had been her spring.

There was no warmth like the warmth of Paul's arms around her, no sleep like the sleep she enjoyed when she had her head on his shoulder. He made her feel safe, and, until she'd known him, she'd not realized she felt any other way. Love lent her a dangerous and delicious fragility.

They'd been married four months. They'd been together ten days of it.

Sitting in the right seat of the Beaver, watching the landscape scroll by, she wanted to be with him with a fierceness that bordered on panic. Being a park ranger was a job, not a life; loneliness a choice, not a necessity anymore. It was all she could do not to scream at the pilot to turn the plane around. For a gut-wrenching minute, her career seemed a foolish exercise, a pointless labor for little pay, a cruel hoax that had lured her from her marriage. Being with Paul was the only thing that mattered. She tried to clench her fists, to concentrate her mind, but they only balled into soft paws in the thick down mittens.

A breaking sound in her ears let her know relief was coming, in the form of distraction, and she welcomed it. Robin spoke again, the edge of anger in her voice a refreshing antidote to Anna's weakness.

"Ridley recommended the Homeland Security guy from this list they sent the park, but nobody who knows anything made up the list."

Nobody who knows anything. Anna'd been around research projects enough to know that meant an NPS person. There was a strange and mutually hostile love affair between scientists and the parks. Years back, the Park Service abdicated the role of science in the parks and opened it up to outside researchers. Researchers tended to look on the parks as their private laboratories and the Park Service as an annoying necessity at best and interfering ignoramuses at worst. A professional hazard of research was the tendency to narrow-mindedness. Often researchers lived for the one thing they studied. Anything that did not serve that study was viewed with scorn. The wolf/moose study on Isle Royale had decades of homesteading by researchers, most of whom came back year after year, six weeks in winter, six months in summer.

"Word came down from Washington. Terrorists." Robin snorted, and Anna was surprised such a delicate sculpted nose could produce such an excellent snort. "If they're from the Middle East, creeping across the Canadian border in the dead of winter to paddle to the island, they're going to freeze their little terrorist butts off."

Word had come down from Washington.

After 9/11, Homeland Security dumped money on the NPS. Everybody loved it. It was like Christmas, till they noticed the money was earmarked for law enforcement. Like Popeye's arms, the LE divisions were puffed up in classic steroidal fashion, the interpretive programs relegated to the leavings.

Now D.C. sent down the "Interpretive Theme" for the year, and campfire programs—from the Everglades to Death Valley to the Kenai Peninsula—had to focus on pollution or endangered species or bioterrorism—whatever the folk in Washington thought was important at the moment. Never mind that the public wasn't interested, or that the theme didn't suit the park.

Free money was never free.

"Lake's wide open," the pilot said.

Anna looked at what she'd thought was the gleam of ice on the approaching shore of Lake Superior. Open water. In a colder winter, a pair of wolves had crossed an ice bridge from Canada and set up housekeeping on the island. The lake freezing solid from Isle Royale to the Canadian shore was rare; it hadn't happened in over thirty years. She watched as water replaced land beneath the wings and Isle Royale began to take shape on the horizon. In the joy of seeing the island from the air, she forgot about Paul, the cold and the antagonisms of mere mortals.

Washington Harbor reached out a welcoming arm, and the airplane flew in low and slow. Water, catching the iridescent blue and amber of the sky, riffled between narrowing banks of evergreens, black with shadow. Blue turned to white as ice formed in the shallower water, ringing Beaver Island in a necklace of diamonds. At the level of the treetops, and hugging the bank to avoid the worst of the crosswind, the pilot lined up on the expanse of white between the tiny harbor island and the docks at Windigo.

The weekly arrival of food and people from the outside world was apparently quite an event. A snowmobile, surrounded by four figures so muffled in layers of clothing that they looked like bags of dirty laundry, was parked on the ice east of the dock. As the airplane slid gracefully from the sky, one of the bundles turned its back, dropped its insulated trousers and mooned them; a pale butt exposed to the elements. Anna laughed. The pilot ignored it.

As the propeller came to a stop, bearded faces with fur-rimmed hoods peered up at them, and Anna was put in mind of Cro-Magnons first sighting a metal bird from the gods. The pilot shut down the engine, unbuckled his harness and slid from the left seat. Robin Adair, light as a snowflake in a Christmas globe, drifted from the rear seat to the harbor ice. Anna pawed open her harness buckles and maneuvered her oversized boots out one at a time, thrust her down-padded rear end through the door and clambered awkwardly down the itsy-bitsy steps on the wheel pant. Ninety minutes sitting in the cold had done nothing to add to her natural grace and she clumped to the ground with all the dignity of a garbage bag tossed into a Dumpster.

Wind, razor-sharp and just as cruel, cut across her cheek as she turned to the troglodyte welcoming committee. A wall of parka-puffed backs greeted her.

Robin's voice cut through the whistling silence: "Holy smoke!" She spoke in the hollow whisper of a celluloid citizen seeing the mother ship. Anna toddled to the end of the wall of flesh and goose feathers. Through the dense night of trees on the ragged shore, a huge dark shape moved erratically.

"A windigo," Robin breathed.

The Algernon Blackwood story of the Ojibwa legend that rangers told around the campfire to scare the pants off park visitors flooded Anna's mind. The windigo was a voracious and monstrous cannibal that feasted on human flesh and souls on the shores of northern lakes, where no one could hear the crying of its tortured victims.

Anna was not given to superstition, but the summer she worked on the island the story had given her the creeps for a few nights. Robin's pale, pinched face and hollow voice brought them back.

The creature in the trees was immense, larger than a horse, and moved in painful lurches. It appeared to shrink and expand in an unnatural way, and it took Anna a tense moment to realize the animal was not drifting in and out of supernatural realms but falling to its knees and fighting its way up again. It stumbled clear of the masking trees and onto the lake ice, hooves ringing loud against the rimed stones.

"Watch out," one of the bearded men said. "Not all moose are Bullwinkle."

Anna shaded her eyes against the glare. Where the moose's antlers should have been were freakishly twisted horns with gobbets of diseased-looking flesh, pustules the size of hens' eggs, six or more inches long, and dependent from a bony structure grown wild as coral, cancerous and out of control.

Head swaying in wide, low arcs, as if the deformed antlers tugged at its sanity and drove spikes deep into its brain, the animal lurched toward them. In the harsh light reflecting from the ice, the grotesque growths looked pink and alive. Sixty yards from where they stood, the moose went to its knees. Dark eyes, full of anguish; it raised its massive head and cried, a tiny bleat like that of a newborn lamb. Then its chin fell to the ice and it didn't move again.

In sci-fi movies, when a plague was loosed on mankind, it invariably produced a growth unfettered by gravity or plan; warts and goiters to cause a makeup artist to wriggle with delight. This windigo was as cursed as any Hollywood extra, dying for eighty dollars a day.

"What's wrong with it?" Anna was startled at the anger in her voice.

"It's rare, but it happens when an old or malnourished bull hasn't enough juice to grow a set of new antlers for breeding season," replied the youngest looking of the beards. "At least we think that's part of it. The Ojibwa thought these moose were taken by the windigo, possessed by evil."

"We should put it out of its misery." This from the tallest and bulkiest of the Cro-Magnons.

There was a note of excitement in his voice that bothered Anna almost as much as the crumpled monster on the ice.

2

"I'm Ridley Murray," said the man who'd explained the twisted antlers. All Anna could see of him were his eyes, deep hazel, with thick dark lashes. His voice was alto rather than tenor, but he didn't sound weak or womanish; he sounded gentle. Anna liked him instantly; always a red flag in her book. Judgment of character wasn't one of her strong suits.

"I'm the lead researcher," he told her. "This," and he waved a mittened hand in the direction of the large man who'd evinced the desire to kill the windigo moose, "is Bob Menechinn, Homeland Security." Ridley's voice was bland almost to the point of insolence. Almost.

"Pleased to meet you," Bob said and offered Anna his hand. He resembled the actor John Goodman. Even without down padding, he was a big man, well over six feet, and had the fleshy, plastic face Goodman was so deft at morphing from benevolent goodness to bloated evil, as a role required.

"Anna Pigeon, Rocky Mountain," Anna said.

"It's dead," Robin called. While they'd introduced themselves, she'd scooted quickly and easily over the slippery surface to where the moose lay. The fourth Cro-Magnon was with her.

"Adam, would you get the camera and an ax?" Ridley asked a lanky individual wrapped in the most disreputable winter gear Anna had ever laid eyes on. His parka had at one time probably been a uniform khaki but had been smudged, drizzled, splashed and spotted by so many substances the original color showed only under the zipper flap. Ripstop nylon had proved unable to stop the incursions of sharp objects. Sleeves and body sported tears sprouting feathers, and his cuffs looked as if they had been caught in a paper shredder.

"Will do," Adam said and loped off toward the snow-mobile, joints loose, back straight, a scarecrow in an arctic Oz.

Anna, Bob and Ridley shuffled over the ice to join Robin and the remains of the windigo.

Robin was on hands and knees by the deceased animal. Ridley clapped a hand on the shoulder of the man Anna'd not yet met. "This is—"

"The only sane, and by far the handsomest, man on the island." The man swept back his hood as if to show Anna the extent of his beauty. His hair was snow white. Awry from being smashed, it stuck out everywhere it wasn't glued to his skull. His beard was close cropped and white to the point of iridescence. Reflections flashing off lenses in round wire-rimmed glasses obscured his eyes.

"Robin has been after me for two seasons," the sane and handsome man went on, his smile showing small straight teeth that would have suited the face of a beatific child or a feral badger, "but the poor child has had to settle for—what's his name, Robin?"

"Gavin," Robin said. Anna couldn't tell if she was flattered or simply bored by the pseudosexual attention. At any rate, she seemed used to it.

"That's right, Gavin, a callow boy, and tall enough to be my father. Jonah Schumann at your service," Jonah said to Anna.

Ridley Murray showed no irritation at Jonah's interruption or at being relegated to, at best, the second-handsomest man on Isle Royale but watched with a slight affectionate smile on his face as one might watch a favorite uncle.

"You want to tell her about antlers, Jonah?" Ridley asked.

Jonah ducked his head in graceful declination. "Let's see if I've taught you anything," he said.

"Antlers are grown over the summer to impress females when mating season comes in the fall," Ridley told Anna. "They're expensive. Enormous amounts of food and minerals and energy go into growing them."

"Size does matter," Jonah interjected solemnly.

Ridley laughed. "Older moose, or animals that are too worn down—maybe the winter's colder or there's not much fodder—can spend the last of their reserves growing antlers. If they pull it off, they get the girl, but they usually die the next winter."

Anna thought of old men and Corvettes but had the good sense to keep her mouth shut.

"The deformity is called a *peruke,* French for 'wig.' This is one for the record books. I've never seen one this extreme. Shoot, I've never seen one alive, just photographs."

"Everything he knows is from my book on the crepuscular deviations of caddis flies in ungulates," Jonah said gravely.

With a stiff-backed arrogance that could have indicated a big ego or chronic lower-back pain, Bob Menechinn squatted at the animal's head. Momentarily he lost his balance and grabbed a twisted antler to steady himself. Ridley flinched.

"Careful of the antlers, Bob," he said evenly.

"Whoa! This is the mother lode. Lookie," the biotech said as she deftly pulled a small ziplock bag out of the army rucksack she'd off-loaded from the plane. "Ticks. This old guy was about drunk up. How many you figure?" she asked Ridley.

He surveyed the carcass. The moose's ribs showed stark from starvation. The flanks were caved in, the hide patchy with bald places where he'd scraped against trees to free himself of the pestilence of winter ticks. "Jeez. At least fifty thousand, maybe sixty," Ridley estimated. "This boy was a regular Red Cross blood bank."

Robin plucked a thick tuft of hair. Half a dozen fat

ticks clung to the roots. She put the little colony into the plastic bag, zipped it and put it back in her rucksack. Anna hoped the baggie was one of the fancy double-lock kind.

No one spoke for a moment and silence settled like snow. A sound, both distant and immediate, didn't so much break the silence as join it, the call of a gray whale beneath fathoms of seawater. Anna looked to Robin to see if she'd heard it too. A reflex from the bad old days, when windowpane acid had slammed into her brain so hard for years she'd been careful not to remark on odd phenomena lest she be the only one experiencing them. She'd thought she'd left that particular paranoia behind. The retro twitch must have been triggered by the weird black-and-white world, with its windigo and Cro-Magnon tribe.

And cold so vicious and unrelenting, it felt personal.

She tried to shove her hands in her pockets, but they were too fat to fit.

"The ice is singing," Robin said. "It's always moving, shifting. Sometimes it cracks like a gunshot. All kinds of sounds."

Anna blocked out the fact that Jack Frost was gnawing her bones and opened to the song: far off, underfoot, a murmur of instruments not yet invented, hollow lutes and soft drums, the warble of birds without throats just beyond the threshold of hearing, as if it came into the mind on some other wavelength. In Texas, the wind sang in that same way when the rock formations were just right. Music so deeply ingrained in the world, Anna felt if she could listen long enough and hard enough, she would learn a great truth.

Before enlightenment was achieved, the snowmobile came shrieking back down the hill from the bunkhouse. Dragging a trailer—a lidded aluminum box the size of a coffin set on skis—the machine raced over the lake and came to a stop beside the moose's body.

"Adam Peck," Ridley said as the driver turned off the engine. "He missed our meet and greet."

"Hey," Adam said affably. He looked to be in his forties, and, when he pulled down his muffler to speak, Anna noticed he hadn't a beard but a lush mustache of the kind seldom seen anywhere but in pictures of Civil War heroes.

He sprang off the snowmobile with the sharp suddenness of a switchblade knife opening and lifted the trailer's lid.

"Camera," he said, like a surgical nurse might say "Scalpel."

Robin began taking pictures of the moose from all angles. The buzz of a scientific find—or an audience at a freak show—began over the size and peculiarity of the antlers, the number of ticks, the marks of starvation on the body.

Due to moose predation, balsam fir, the favored food in winter, was almost gone from the island, and the once-thriving herd—nearly fifteen hundred when Anna had been a ranger on Isle Royale—was down to around three hundred animals.

"Will hunger make the wolves more aggressive?"

Menechinn asked. He'd been watching the recording process, with his arms folded across his chest and his chin buried in his neck scarf.

"It will," Robin said.

"I've never seen an increase in wolf aggression that was tied to food availability," Ridley said. "Only to sex and turf."

"There's always a first time," Adam sided with the biotech.

Ridley shrugged. "Are we ready for the ax?" he asked Robin. "We need to take the head," he explained to Anna. "It's a perfect example of the *peruke* deformity. If we leave it, the critters will get it." Already ravens were calling the good news of the slaughter to each other and cutting up the pale sky with ink-stained wings.

"Here." Bob Menechinn held out a hand for the ax. "I'll do it. Man, it would be something to have that on your wall, wouldn't it?"

"Step back," Ridley warned them, ignoring the offer. "This is going to be messy."

Ridley wasn't much taller than Anna, five-eight maybe, and slight, but he swung the ax like a man long used to chopping his own wood. Hefting it back across his shoulder, he swung it in a clean arc, the strength of his legs in the blow.

The axhead buried itself in meat and bone behind the moose's ears.

Anna'd thought it would be the way the guillotine was depicted in the movies; a single chop and the moose's head would roll free of its body. Except, with the antlers, it couldn't roll. With the long, bulbous nose, it couldn't roll. Moose were not beasts designed for a beautiful life or a dignified death.

Ridley put his mukluk on the thick neck and yanked on the ax. With a sucking crunch, it jerked loose, and blood flew like a flock of cardinals over the ice.

The head lolled. Great, dark eyes stared upward; the executed watching the executioner botch the job.

"He looks stoned." Bob laughed. "Or is it a she?"

Ridley's ax hit the animal between the eyes.

"God dammit," he whispered, took a deep breath and swung the ax again, severing the head but for an eight-inch strip of hide that Adam quickly cut with a mat knife he produced from somewhere in his ragtag clothing.

Ravens were landing before they'd finished wrapping the moose's head in a tarp. They hopped and scolded; their feast was growing cold. Bolder birds dashed in to snatch bits of flesh from the open neck wound; easy pickings, with no tough hide to tear through. By the time the carcass was consumed, all manner of smaller creatures would have had a good dinner; maybe the meal that would give them the strength to make it until summer, when the island provided in plenty.

With the severed head wrapped in black plastic and stowed in the snowmobile trailer, Anna and the others shuffled back to the Beaver and finished transferring gear and food into the trailer around the moose head. Because of the size and awkward shape of the antlers, the trailer's lid had to be propped partly open. Adam driving, Bob behind him, and Ridley, boots planted

wide on the rear runners like a musher with a mecha-
nized pack of dogs, headed up to the bunkhouse.

The Forest Service plane took off, leaving the ground
in a surprisingly short time and disappearing around
Beaver Island as the pilot used the length of Washington
Harbor to get up to altitude for the flight back to Ely.

The sounds of internal combustion machines, simultaneously anachronistic and a reassuring reminder that
Winter Study team was not marooned on an icebound
island in the time of the mastodons, grew fainter. Anna
wanted to hear the ice singing again, but there was
nothing but the quarreling of ravens.

For a moment, she, Robin and Jonah stood without
speaking, eyes on the sky where the USFS plane had
gone. Then, as if moved by the same impulse, the way a
flock of birds will suddenly change directions, they
turned and followed the track left by the snowmobile.
Ungainly in bulky clothes, boots unsure on the slippery
surface, Anna felt like a toddler. Robin, doing a kind of
Texas two-step, the soles of her soft mukluks never leaving the surface of the lake, shuffled expertly along.

Partway back to the dock, a supercub was tied down,
a tandem-seat fabric airplane used since before World War
II for air reconnaissance, search and rescue, hunting—
any job that called for flying low and slow and being able
to land anywhere the pilot had the guts to set it down.
This one was a classic, down to the fat brown teddy bear
painted on the tail, and skis where wheels would be in
summer. Lines, dropped through holes cut in the ice and

held there by lengths of two-by-four, were gripped by the ice when the hole froze again, making as firm a tie-down as any hook set in concrete.

"That's my airplane you're admiring," Jonah said. "She'll let you pet her if you kiss her on the nose first."

Jonah was the team's pilot. *Old*, Anna thought. *Moon*, was her second thought as she realized that when the Beaver was coming in on final approach it was Jonah's pale old behind that dared the frigid air to welcome them in proper style.

The glare went off the lenses of his eyeglasses and showed Anna eyes the palest blue she'd ever seen, the color of the sky with a high, thin overcast. They'd probably taken on the tint from too many years staring through the windscreens of airplanes. Jonah Schumann had to be seventy. Seventy-five, maybe.

Jonah looked as if he could see her doing math in her head and said: "I normally don't offer my lady's favors to strangers such as yourself, but she may have been traumatized by recent events. The old gal is pushing fifty, and it would be a comfort to her to have the company of a contemporary." His eyes twinkled through the deadpan seriousness of his words.

Anna laughed and realized she'd not introduced herself. "Anna Pigeon, Rocky Mountain." Reflexively they both thrust out their hands to shake in the approved manner, but with the mittens and gloves they were more like two old declawed bears pawing at each other.

"Nice butt," Anna said.

"Thank you," Jonah replied gravely. "Many women and some men have told me that. You have already met my fiancée." He was looking at Robin, with her sweet, unblemished face perfectly framed by long, straight brown hair. Anna had a balaclava with the drawstring pulled till only her eyes and nose showed and, around that, to keep the cold from creeping down the collar of her parka, a wide thick scarf. The only concession to the cold Robin had made was a wool Laplander's hat, the kind with a pointy top and silly earflaps.

"In your dreams, Jonah," Robin said.

"She's shy," he confided. "It embarrasses her that she would marry me just for the sex."

Robin ducked her head and looked inland. "I'll walk back by the Nature Trail," she said. "I need to stop and take a look at the weather." With that, she was two-stepping toward shore, slender and graceful in her mini-malist wear.

Anna's twenties came back in a hot flash: the flattering but endless and, finally, exhausting sexual references and jokes, the mentioning of body parts, the sly looks, the double entendres. She'd thought that sort of thing had gone down beneath the nineties tsunami of lawsuits and political correctness. Maybe it had just gone under-ground, or, maybe, it would not be dead till every man of her generation and the generation before her was rot-ting in his grave.

She and Jonah shuffled on toward the dock and his little airplane. On the ice to the right was a waist-high pile of snow with a shovel stuck in it. "Ice fishing?" Anna asked. "Pretty grim pastime without an ice-fishing house. I hope it's voluntary."

"That's our well," Jonah said. Then: "Doggone it!" He hurried over to the hole chopped in the ice. "The little bastard is trying to poison us. He's done it before." Jonah snatched up the shovel. On the side of the excavated snow and ice was a patch of yellow. "Fox," Jonah said. "A pesky, pissy little red fox whose mother was no better than she should have been." Shoveling up the tainted snow carefully, he tossed it as far from the well as he could. "I tell you, this little fur ball is potent. One drop of his urine got in the well a while back. *One drop* and our water reeked of fox for two days."

"Reclaiming his territory," Anna said.

"Very broad-minded of you, Ranger Pigeon. Wait till you've had café au fox piss." Grumbling, he began using the tip of the shovel like a gargantuan scalpel, incising spots of yellow. Anna looked back to where the moose with its cloak of ravens lay on the ice. Blood spatter from the ax formed three lines out from the pool where the animal's head had lain. The sight was not gruesome, not ugly. Ravens were so black they seemed cut from construction paper and pasted on the reflective white of the snow. Blood was still the bright cheery red of life. The composition was set off by the inky lines of leafless trees against the blue of the sky. Stunning in its simplicity, the tableau put Anna in mind of a Japanese painting she'd seen: *Death of a Samurai*.

"What are you going to do with the body?" she asked.

Jonah jammed the shovel back into the snow pile. "Nothing. There's nothing we could do even if we wanted. Used to, before the warm-and-cuddlies got up in arms, we'd shoot a moose once a winter. Middle pack always knew and always showed up. One year, the rules were changed, but Middle pack showed up right on schedule anyway, like they had a watch that read: MOOSE TIME. No free moose meat. They never came again. I don't know how they know things, but they do."

"Think they know this is here?" Anna asked.

"See that raven?" Jonah pointed to a sharp cut of black flying toward the western shore of the harbor. "He's going to tell the pack supper's on."

Anna believed him. She'd been around animals enough to know humans might know how much Jupiter weighs and where stars come from, but they remain in total ignorance about what the cat in their lap is thinking or who their dog tells their secrets to.

They heard the snowmobile returning and, stiff in their bundling, rotated toward it. "We'll load up on water, then head back up," Jonah said. "You sure you don't want a ride?"

"I'm sure." Without the distractions of dead ungulates and fox piss, she remembered how cold she was. If she didn't move soon, she would freeze where she stood.

"Stay away from the dock," Jonah called after her. "Ice is always rotten around docks."

Anna waved an arm to let him know she'd heard. Though she'd been hypnotized by its singing and delighted in the canvas it created for the blood-and-bird painting, she wouldn't be sorry to be on solid ground. The thought of getting wet, when the temperature was near zero and the wind brisk, scared her.

There was no negotiating with thermodynamics.

3

W alking up the bank from the lake, Anna felt like a one-woman band. What snow the wind had not scoured from the Earth was so desiccated it didn't crunch beneath her boots, it squeaked as if she walked on beads of Styrofoam. Fur and fleece rasped over her ears, nylon ski pants whistled as they rubbed cricketlike with each step. The racket made her think of Robin Adair and her friendship with winter. She and Robin spent a couple of hours together, eating breakfast and killing time, till the Forest Service pilot got the call that the clouds over Isle Royale had lifted. Though Ely and Washington Harbor were on the same parallel and not more than one hundred fifty miles apart, the lake made its own weather, often completely unrelated to what the mainland was experiencing.

Over eggs and bacon, Anna learned Robin was born

and raised on the St. Croix River in Minnesota, that she would have made the junior Olympics in cross-country skiing if she hadn't been invalided out on a knee injury. Robin had been in love with winter her entire life. Winter was her favorite season. Either the woman had antifreeze in her veins or winter succumbed to her shy beauty and returned her affection. What else could explain the fact that she alone seemed comfortable in less than a walrus-sized amount of down blubber and moved as a wraith—or the apocryphal Indian—through the north woods?

All by herself, Anna constituted a public disturbance.

Where the dock met the shore, she stopped. The ranger station was gone. In its place was a picnic area designed with the inherent poetry of an RV-storage garage. The old, red rambling ranger station had been cramped and dirty and full of mice, but Anna missed it. The parks were never supposed to change; they were supposed to house memories of better days, keep them intact: nobody filled in the creek where one used to hunt crawdads or built a Wal-Mart in the field where the reading oak had grown.

An unpaved road curved to the west by the fuel dock and up to the seasonal employees' housing area. That was as she remembered it, but four huge orange fuel tanks had been put at the turn.

Huge.

Orange.

She decided to take the trail through the woods.

Twenty yards in, she saw what had become of the old

ranger station. It had been replaced by a much-larger structure that housed a Visitors Center as well. Cranky as the cold made her, she could find no fault with it; it was beautifully done, and, with a boatload of tourists arriving every day in the summer from Grand Marais, when it rained the poor wretches would now have a place to seek shelter rather than sitting along the edge of the dock making pathetic attempts to keep dry beneath unfolded island maps.

Above the new V.C. was the original concessionaire's store: an unattractive brown wooden rectangle full of junk food, mosquito repellent and fishhooks. In the fall of her season on ISRO, two bull moose had fought in the picnic area by the door. Their antlers were so heavy, they could do little more than sway them at one another, rarely making serious contact. If moose felt the same about their antlers as old men did about their Corvettes, the windigo on the ice must have nearly died of shame.

A quarter of a mile farther uphill, she stepped out of the trees into the clearing where the seasonal employees were housed. The place she had lived in—fondly known as the "Mink Trail" due to its plethora of mice and the weasels that came to dine on them—was gone. Beyond it, trees had been cut down and earth disturbed. In preparation for the threatened winter resort? Anna wouldn't put it past an overeager concessionaire to finagle it through NPS channels prematurely.

The bunkhouse where the Winter Study team would live for six weeks had smoke coming from the chimney.

Anna hurried the last hundred feet. Designed for multiple occupants, the living space was laid out around a central room with a woodstove at the west end. Racks of drying socks and boots and shirts screened the heat from the fire. The three sofas, like in any self-respecting suburban home, were in a C shape around a television set. Along the back wall were computers and radio equipment. An old upright piano served as a bench for two laptops. To either side of the common room were small semiprivate apartments, with two bedrooms, a bath and a kitchen.

Trying not to look obvious, Anna headed for the nearest bathroom, shedding her parka as she went. The door was closed, and she knocked softly before pushing it open. A blast of icy air met her. The window over the commode was open six inches, and the toilet, shower and sink area were filled with milk, orange juice, potatoes, cheese, onions, butter and a dozen other perishable food items.

No electrical power; this was the Winter Study team's refrigerator. She turned and started toward the bathroom in the mirror-image apartment on the other side. Halfway there, she could see three large, round plastic containers with spigots on the sink counter.

"Our well," Jonah had said of the hole chopped in the lake ice. There was no running water.

No flush toilets.

"It's by the woodstove," a soft voice said, and Anna realized she was not alone. Hunched in front of a computer was a small woman in gray sweater and cargo pants, on her feet the indoor version of Mrs. Steger's moose-hide mukluks, available only in Ely and only from the store owned by übermusher Will Steger's wife. The woman's bland face was pleasant enough, and the brown eyes, small behind the thick glasses of the truly near-sighted, moderately welcoming. "There." She pointed toward the stove.

Anna looked where she indicated. Beside the wood-stove, half hidden behind a rack of worn dish towels and industrial-strength winter boots, a toilet seat leaned against the wall. It had been lovingly decorated with bright red kissing lips and holly, WINTER STUDY painted on it in what looked like crimson nail polish.

"Thanks," Anna said, trying to look as if she'd not been foolish enough to hope for indoor plumbing.

"The outhouse is through the kitchen door a ways," the woman said helpfully.

Anna caught up the ring of porcelain—or, more likely, plastic—on her way toward the northernmost kitchen, the one the study used. The toilet seat was warm from the stove. Evidently even the hardiest of souls required some few comforts.

JONAH FIRED UP THE GENERATOR and informed Anna they would have power each evening till lights out at ten. Anna bunked with Robin on the refrigerator side. She divested herself of her layers and dressed in Levi's and one of Paul's old sweatshirts. On her feet was the one luxury she permitted herself to stuff into the two small-to-medium soft-sided duffels she was allowed to bring, fuzzy slippers, a sedate black but frosted with yellow-and-white cat hair. She joined the others in the working kitchen.

Bob Menechinn was enthroned at the Formica-topped table in the chair nearest the wall, a glass of the boxed red wine, ISRO's *vin ordinaire,* in his hand. Robin sat opposite him, quiet and smiling. The woman who had shown Anna where the bathroom facilities were hovered between Bob and the door to the outhouse as if, at any minute, she would make good an escape.

Menechinn smiled at Anna appreciatively. "You clean up nice, Miss Pigeon." The woman behind him shot him a look of alarm, quickly quelled, and Anna wondered if the woman stood where she did to be ready to protect her turf, in the person of Bob Menechinn.

"Have you met my able assistant, *Doctor* Kathy Huff?" Bob said, affecting a drawl that made his words seem to linger in the air after he'd spoken. Smiling with a bon-homie that wrinkled his bulldog cheeks, he winked. Dr. Huff looked at her feet.

Maybe Menechinn was proud of his helper's doctor-ate. Maybe she was shy. Maybe he mocked her and she was hurt. Maybe they were lovers. The undercurrents were lost on Anna. She was too hungry to care.

"What can I do to help?" she asked the kitchen in general.

Adam peeled and chopped. Ridley cooked. Robin

was allowed to make a salad, but only after begging for the honor. Over five decades of tradition was squeezed into the small kitchen: jobs were not up for grabs; one had to be grandfathered in for every task. Realizing the study's dinner rituals were as full of social land mines for the uninitiated as the kitchen of a kosher chef on the eve of Hanukkah, Anna sat down out of the way and watched.

It was the first time she'd seen her housemates divested of layers and hoods, gloves and down pants. Ridley was as she had envisioned him: a smallish man with wiry muscles and surprisingly broad shoulders. His hands and feet were small and would have suited a dancer, had he gone in a different direction. At thirty, he was a full professor at Michigan Tech, married and now the lead researcher on one of the country's most prestigious studies. His hair was fine as a baby's and curled down between his shoulder blades in a loose ponytail held by a rubber band. Ridley would have been beautiful but was saved by crooked teeth and a mouth too wide for his face. Had he gotten early orthodonture, he would have been a pedophile's dream as a kid and a students' heartthrob when he grew up.

Except for Robin, Ridley was the youngest member of the team, but his authority wasn't questioned—at least not by the Winter Study people. On the ice, he and Bob had swayed what passed in Homo sapiens for antlers at each other. Neither seemed intimidated. Bob might have Homeland Security's ax, but Ridley was at home on the island as Bob Menechinn was not. Like

Anna, he seemed to suffer from the cold, and she got the feeling he was more comfortable with women than men.

Adam struck Anna as the natural alpha of the group, but he apparently didn't mind taking orders from Ridley. He was younger than she'd first thought, in his late thirties. Like Ridley, he wore his hair long, keeping it in a braid. Silver was beginning to weave through the dark brown plait. Anna loved men with long hair, a hangover from her college days. It suggested a wildness that appealed to her. Adam's suited him. His scarecrow body was ridged with muscle and his hands scarred from work. The nineteenth-century mustache gave his gaunt face a dramatic appeal, the hero of a western saga or a soldier making a last charge into the valley of death.

Adam maintained the machinery and the physical plants. From the talk, Anna guessed he was a perennial seasonal; one of the men and women who worked a northern park in summer and a southern park in winter. They had little in the way of material things, living with long-distance and commonly broken relationships, no children, no savings, no house. The lifestyle seemed glamorous till one hit forty; then, by the alchemy of age, it was touched with failure and sadness.

During the course of the meal, Anna began to be initiated into the rules and regulations of Winter Study. Rules written nowhere except in stone. She learned the red rag was for dishes, the gray for wiping countertops. One did not wash with the wiping cloth nor wipe with the washing cloth. It had "just evolved" that way, Jonah told her, and she understood that it had calcified into law and would remain thus until one or the other of the rags—or the team—disintegrated with age.

No one but the pilot could remove the cozy from the bowl containing brown sugar and then only with much discussion of "Mrs. Brown's" disrobing and how that might or might not affect those attempting it.

She learned that the researchers had two modes of dinner conversation: mocking the Park Service, most particularly the law enforcement end of it, and talking nonsense, the ringleader of the nonsense being Jonah, the audience Ridley and Adam.

By the end of the meal, which was excellent—that or the calories one had to burn just to stay warm leant savor to it—Anna realized that this style of communication, or, more to the point, noncommunication, allowed them to live together in greater harmony than meaningful exchanges would have; an American backwoods version of the privacy once maintained in the Orient by elaborate ritual courtesy.

In another setting, Anna might have taken offense at the scorn heaped on the rangers and management of Isle Royale. Being law enforcement and, with her new position at Rocky Mountain, at least nominally management, the mean-spirited gossip should have offended her. In principle, it did and, like the ongoing sexual teasing of Robin, grew tiresome, but it didn't hurt her feelings. There was a habitualness about it that transcended insensitivity or insult. Like the other rituals, it had evolved over the years, and they carped with much the same lack of devotion as illiterate Catholics mouthing a Latin mass.

Anna was happy to sit without speaking and let it wash around her. She couldn't remember being so hungry. The helpings she was given—and the seconds she took—were double what she was accustomed to, yet she was as excited about the dessert as any of the men and had to restrain herself from asking for more ice cream.

When the meal was finished, Ridley and Adam thanked Jonah for a fine dinner. Anna hadn't seen the old pilot do anything, but, not wanting to be rude, she thanked him as well. Jonah hauled one of the two large metal containers of hot water that lived on the woodstove and poured the double sinks full. He and Ridley began pulling on yellow rubber gloves as Jonah joked about his favorite subject; this time it was Ridley he pretended was madly in love with him and was lecturing him about unwelcome visits to his room in the night. Neither was gay—Anna would have bet on it—it was simply another game that had taken root so long ago no one was sure why they still played it.

She offered to do the dishes, which she thought was mighty big of her, but was met with uncomprehending and none-too-friendly stares. Precisely what custom dictated who a chief bottle washer was, she didn't know, but, wanting to help, to thank them for the meal, to ingratiate herself—or whatever it was she felt a need to do—she insisted.

Confused rather than appreciative, they abandoned her to it. The only one who remained to help or keep her company was Dr. Huff.

"Do you want to wash or rinse, Kathy?"

"*Katherine*. Rinse." That speech brought the sum total of words the woman had uttered since the toilet seat introduction to about twelve. She made Robin seem like a motormouth.

As the steam rose and the pile of dirty dishes diminished, to make conversation Anna asked Katherine what her doctorate was in. Again, there was the odd ducking flinch and the furious blush. Katherine wasn't much older than Robin, not yet thirty, yet her skin had the opacity associated with women considerably past menopause. The blush didn't prettily pink her cheeks but dyed them the color of new brick.

"I haven't got it quite yet," Katherine admitted. Moisture blanked her glasses, and Anna couldn't read her eyes. "I'm all-but-dissertation. Bob—Dr. Menechinn— has my thesis. Then it goes to committee. It's on the wolves in Wyoming. The alphas have started mating with more than one female in the pack."

"They must be becoming habituated to humans," Anna said.

They had progressed to the flatware, washed last, and dumped into a long-handled deep-fat fryer set in the rinse water for that purpose—another rule, and one Anna would have bent had not Jonah appeared behind her and Katherine with the implement and the instructions at the proper moment—when Katherine whispered: "God's nightgown."

The archaic oath made Anna laugh. The look on Katherine's face made her stop. Religious awe or deep-seated horror drew the skin around her eyes tight. Her jaw had gone slack.

"What is it?" Anna demanded.

Katherine pointed at the small window over the sink. Her hand was shaking so bad tiny bubbles from the dish soap floated free and rose on the warm air. When Anna tossed the flatware into the rinse, steam had blanked the window. Undoubtedly shattering half a dozen traditions, she wiped it clear with the red dishrag.

Silver light from a three-quarter moon caught ice crystals on the snow and rime on pine needles and tree branches. In the superdried air, the light was so pure the world beyond the glass glowed with it, and Anna could see with surreal clarity. Whatever Katherine had seen was gone. Or had been imaginary.

Hands dripping, Katherine turned and ran to the common room.

Anna ran after her, drying her hands on her trousers. Katherine squeezed behind the television set, cupped her hands against the glass of the picture window and pressed her face to the glass. Anna did the same.

Delineated by moonlight and snow, seven wolves trotted across the compound. Heads low, they came single file, long legs and big paws carrying them effortlessly over the patchy snow. Anna'd seen wolves in captivity, seen wolf pups, but to see seven adult wolves in the moonlight, wolves that moved through the night the way they were meant to, the moon catching their fur until they were frosted with silver, their shadows black on the ground, was pure magic.

Then they were gone, the last tail swallowed up by the shaggy line of birch trunks at the edge of the clearing.

"Wow!" Anna whispered inadequately.

"They've never done this. Never. Not even close," Ridley said. "Something's got them stirred up." He'd crowded so close behind Anna, she felt his breath on her hair. He must have noticed the moment she did. He backed away awkwardly.

The others began to move and talk. Katherine remained immobile. Her face had the same rapt look that had scared Anna over the dirty dishes. In a child, she would have termed it awe. In a woman grown, it was the aspect of true love beholding the object of adoration.

"I didn't think they came around people," Bob said.

"They don't," Ridley replied. "Three times in the last fifty years, we've found wolf tracks in the housing area. Not a pack, tracks of a single wolf. Every time, there was a dead wolf in the carpentry shop, either dissected or about to be. They stay away from us and we stay away from them. We try and keep it that way. In wolf/tourist run-ins, wolves always come out the losers. The island is too small to destroy or transport a wolf without damaging the population and screwing up the study. Something stirred them up," he repeated.

"The windigo," Robin said. It sounded as if she wanted to believe in a windigo more than moose meat. People loved their ghosts, demons, fairies and angels. Anna didn't. For her, stark reality was magical, mysterious and sufficiently deadly. She didn't need to put monstrous faces on starvation and cruelty, or wings and feathers on hope.

"I thought windigos were strict humanitarians," she said. "Don't they just eat people?"

"Everybody loves junk food," Jonah said.

"They smell the blood of the moose," Bob said. "Their sense of smell is acute."

"Exactly." Ridley's word was agreeable but the tone was not. The lead researcher evidently didn't like an axman from Homeland Security educating him on wolf traits. "They can smell over a thousand times more efficiently than humans. And they can smell humans. We must reek like a paper mill to them. There is any number of ways the pack could get to the moose. Why come so near us?"

"Do you think the other packs will come?" Robin asked.

"They shouldn't." Ridley moved to the piano bench and began pulling on high-waisted woolen ski pants, snapping the suspenders over his shoulders.

"If they do, it could get ugly," Adam said, and Ridley shot him a look, a widening of the eyes and downturn of the lips that Anna associated with social conspiracies, like listening to your best friend lie her way out of detention.

"Pack wars," Robin said somberly. Anna figured it out. They were trying to scare the pants off the Homeland Security guy.

Pack wars were not uncommon, but there was sufficient territory for East, Middle and Chippewa Harbor packs so they didn't clash too often. When they did, it was hit-and-run, not the full-scale slaughter humans had perfected.

Ridley took mukluks from the drying rack beside the woodstove and sat down again to put them on. The anesthetizing influence of a wolf sighting wearing off, it dawned on the group what he was doing.

As one, they scrambled for their boots and coats. Cursed with new gear, Anna was last out the front door. The rest were halfway across the housing complex. Uplifted by the excitement of watching a pack of wild wolves devour a kill, she wasn't bothered by the cutting wind from the northwest as she duckwalked quickly down the slippery steps in her ungainly boots and started across the clearing.

Suddenly she stopped. A whiff, a hint of something freakishly bad, evil and death and old fish distilled into a toxic perfume, was borne on the wind. Tilting her head back, she sniffed. It was gone. She smelled nothing but the clean, vicious perfection of winter.

The Ojibwa's windigo was heralded by the stench of rotting corpses, the rotten stink of a cannibal's breath, and the distillation of hopelessness. The cannibal spirit came on the wind from the northwest.

For someone who had eschewed the supernatural not

ten minutes before, Anna felt a distinctly unnatural chill along the back of her stomach and up both sides of her spine.

She waited and watched the black of the woods in the direction from which the wind blew. The line of shadows that marked the trees hid anything that might have been there.

4

Despite the pack's dramatic arrival, the wolves settled down in lupine domesticity around the unexpected gift of the moose carcass. Anna could have happily burned her calories just keeping warm and watching them, but the second day of the pack's visit Ridley put the team back to work. Robin had gone cross-country with her rucksack and plastic baggies to seek out ever-more-marvelous bits of frozen excretions and effluvia. Adam was building a snowmobile shed. As far as Anna was concerned, he had the worst of the work. Construction at seven above zero struck her as a miserable way to make a living, but he'd acted as if he was looking forward to it.

She landed the plum job. Jonah was taking her up in the cub to see if they could find Chippewa Harbor pack.

Flights in the supercub were jealously guarded. From the scuttlebutt, Anna knew there'd been guests of the study who'd never managed an invite to fly. She doubted she'd have been so lucky had Ridley not had so many wolves close to home to play with.

Four hours immobile in a two-seat fabric airplane with a heater that did not deserve the name was a recipe for misery, if not frostbite, and Anna had not come prepared. In borrowed knee-high, insulated boots that looked more like robot prosthetics than shoes—Ridley's size nines—and more layers than a winter onion, she watched uselessly as Jonah walked around the airplane checking for damage, standard operation for preflight. At first, to be companionable, she'd attempted to follow him, but in the oversized boots she moved like an arctic clown on Quaaludes. The characterization was completed, she suspected, by a bright red nose.

On the far side of the harbor, beyond the little airplane, wolves lounged around the moose carcass like fat house dogs around a hearth. "Won't we scare them off?" she asked.

"There's not been a wolf on this island in three generations—that's in dog years; ten years old is an old wolf—that hasn't had an airplane buzzing around from the time he was a pup," Jonah said and began unwrapping an orange, oil-stained down comforter he kept around his lady's nose when she was earthbound so her engine wouldn't turn into a block of ice. "The sound doesn't bother them. Most don't even look up. I think they live the simple life: food/no food, threat/no threat, sex/no sex. In the no food, no threat, no sex category, the cub and I aren't worth a passing glance.

"Get the tie-down, if you will."

Anna clowned over to where the wing was tethered to the ice and was amused momentarily by the image of the supercub taking off with the frozen harbor dangling cartoonlike from the tie-down lines beneath the wings. Loath to remove her gloves, she had barely loosed the knot by the time Jonah had untied his side and come around. Because she'd learned to do it on ISRO with boat lines, she carefully laid the rope in a coil.

The cub had clamshell doors, a hexagon cut laterally and opening up and down. Jonah let the lower part of the door down and held the upper against the high wing. "Hop in. I fly from the rear seat."

Hopping was not an option. Anna clambered into the front seat and manually arranged her great booted extremities so they wouldn't interfere with Jonah's operation of the ailerons, then lay there helplessly gazing at nothing. The supercub was a tail dragger and, on the ground, sat nose high, the windscreen pointing at pale gray sky.

The plane jounced. Jonah had gotten in. A prisoner of survival gear, turning around to look was in the same category as hopping. "Here," Jonah said, and a headset was thrust over her right shoulder. "You know how to use one of these things?"

"I do." High-tech communications in an old super-cub struck an odd note. It seemed as if the small-plane industry had not kept pace with electronics. But, then, nothing had kept pace with electronics. Anna put on the earphones, adjusted the mike and then continued staring at a blank sky while Jonah went through his checklist.

The engine fired smoothly and the plane began to taxi, skis sliding over the ice. The nose blocking the view forward, Anna looked out the side window at the pack. Ravens inked the snow in ever-changing kaleidoscopes of black and white. They ranted and teased, flying at the wolves' heads, then stopping in a sudden outthrust of wings inches out of reach of the wolves' jaws. Suddenly the radio-collared female whipped out of feigned sleep, and where there'd been a bird there was only a few feathers and new drops of blood, bright and jewel-like, on the snow. Neither wolves nor ravens turned a head as the supercub roared by.

The engine revved up to a determined bellow and the cub picked up speed. The tail lifted off the lake and the horizon came down; Beaver Island was approaching with considerable speed, and Anna unconsciously braced herself for collision. Then they were airborne, banking around Beaver and flying down Washington Harbor. Forgetting the mike was voice-activated, Anna laughed aloud with the gust of pure expanding freedom.

"I feel it every time," Jonah said.

The NPS was Anna's favorite bureaucracy, but a bureaucracy all the same, and it had endless safety regulations. Aviation safety experts had come up with the mind-boggling discovery that many crashes were caused by the airplane colliding with the ground and passed rules about how low and slow was acceptable. Jonah Schumann exhibited a fine indifference to the rules. Anna could almost feel the treetops tickling the airplane's canvas belly.

She loved it. Except for the cold and the racket, it was like flying in dreams.

"East pack has been hanging around Mott Island, but we haven't found Chippewa Harbor pack yet," Jonah said in her ears.

Isle Royale was forty-two miles long and no more than twelve across at its widest point. It was hard to believe a group of seven or eight big animals could stay out of sight from air surveillance, but they did. Wolves traveled long distances, and slept a lot during the day. It wasn't unusual to "lose" a pack for a week or more.

"We'll head up toward Malone Bay, see if we can scare anything up," he said. Malone Bay was about halfway between Windigo at the west end of the island and Rock Harbor at the east. Malone Bay was one of the backcountry outposts; the ranger was inevitably dubbed the "Malone Ranger" because of the isolation.

Anna settled into the joy of flight, of being up where there was air to breathe instead of sequestered in a smoky bunkhouse, of seeing the island in a glory of white and black.

The bed of Lake Superior had been gouged out by glaciers. Isle Royale, made of tougher material, was scored and slashed but remained above water. From the air, the colossal shredding was evident; ridges ran the length of the island, and smaller islands, long and thin as scratches, stood offshore separated from the main island by deep channels. Hikers unfamiliar with the topography frequently underestimated the difficulty of traveling through country boned with sharp stone ridges and crosshatched with swampy valleys.

As they flew toward Malone Bay, Anna caught glimpses of the Greenstone Trail, a ribbon of white weaving in and out of the trees.

"This goes any lower or we get any wind, we'll have to head back," came Jonah's voice in Anna's ears. She looked from the trail to the sky. The cloud ceiling, high and solid looking in Windigo, was lower, the clouds darker. Situated in a cold basin of water, the island's microclimates were pronounced and unpredictable.

Anna didn't want to go back; like Peter Pan, she wanted to fly to the second star to the right, then straight on till morning.

An expanse of white unfurled inland from Lake Superior between the airplane and the cloud mass. "Siskiwit Lake?" she asked. Siskiwit was the largest lake on Isle Royale.

"Siskiwit," Jonah confirmed. "Hey!" He banked the cub so suddenly that Anna lurched to one side and banged her elbow on the Plexiglas window.

On the clear expanse of ice, seven black figures made a fan-shaped pattern like the wake of a boat behind a larger dot. A pack of wolves had chased a moose out of the trees and onto the open area of the lake, an old bull by the look of it. Jonah closed the distance quickly and flew low and to the side so Anna could get pictures.

"Chippewa pack, I think. I guess it could be East. Holy moly, look at the blood! You'd have thought the ticks would have drunk so much there'd be hardly enough left to fill a thermos," Jonah said with more glee than Anna thought seemly. "Looks like what you'd get if you crossed Jackson Pollock with Bloody Mary."

Channeling the Pillsbury Doughboy, she lifted the camera and pushed her body closer to the window as the plane banked and circled for another pass. The wolves had been on the moose for a while, harrying it in hopes it would die of a thousand cuts or exhaustion. Reading the tracks, Anna could see how the battle had unfolded: the line of hoofprints from the northern shore of the lake to dead center; behind, the single-track wolf paw prints spread out among the trees—the pack pushing the moose to open country. Once on the lake, the wolves' tracks fell into close formation behind the hoofprints, keeping back from the sharp hooves and bone-breaking antlers.

"They're going in," Jonah shouted in her ear.

A wolf lunged, battening onto the narrow haunch of the moose. Trying to throw off the beast locked on its rump, trying to keep the pack in front of it where it could use its front feet to defend itself, the bull spun around, the center of a tornado of gray-furred predators. Blood spattered in a mutant circle thirty or more feet in diameter. In the trees, the moose would have slammed the wolf on its rear into rocks or tree trunks, tried to smash it with brute force. On ice, the moose was at a disadvantage.

Blood and beasts tangled in a macabre snow angel,

then the moose broke off and bolted for shore, the wolf still hanging off his haunch. A second wolf drew down, long and lean, and streaked across the snow, then lifted into the air, struck the moose's other rear leg, bit down and hung on. The moose, with this burden of death, fell to its knees. The rest of the wolves began to circle. To Anna's surprise, the bull struggled to its feet, three wolves on it now. Twice more it fell and twice more rose and fought on.

"Can we land?" Anna asked.

"I don't trust the ice. Nobody's checked the thickness yet," Jonah said. He brought the supercub lower for the last act of the moose's life. Three wolves on its back, the others made side rushes, cutting at the tendons in its legs. The moose stayed on its feet another ten yards, then stopped.

As if he was not being savaged by wolves but had chosen, like Chief Joseph, to fight no more forever, he folded his long legs neatly beneath himself and sank onto the ice. Wolves closed in, tearing at the moose's sides, ripping out entrails in a wild display of color on the white canvas of snow.

Anna breathed. Till that moment, she'd not been aware she wasn't. The savagery and death didn't sadden her. As the wolves fed, she didn't feel anger toward the predators, nor did she feel sorry for the prey. What moved her was the stunningly beautiful dance of life and death. The bull was old. Tough as he was, he probably wouldn't have lasted the winter and, if he did, he wouldn't live to mate next rutting season. Today he had died as he was meant to, gone down fighting with a respected enemy, his body nourishment for the next cycle of life. The wolves would stay with the kill till they had consumed it; nothing would be wasted. Ravens and foxes would feed. Come spring, fishes would get the bones.

The cub banked and climbed, and Anna lost sight of the dinner party. "Did you get some good shots?" Jonah crackled in her ears.

"Damn." Anna heard a breathy chuckle in return.

"Greenhorn," he said without malice. "We got to head back. Look at the horizon east there."

The horizon had solidified into a dark wall. Clouds touched the surface of the lake. Both water and air were the color of slate. A mile or so out, whitecaps snapped to life on black water.

Jonah radioed Ridley to let him know about the kill and that they were returning to Windigo.

There was a moment without response, then Ridley came back: "Robin saw fresh tracks along the Greenstone Trail. It wasn't Middle pack; they haven't moved. If you're looking at Chippewa Harbor pack, then it's not them. It's either East pack or a lone wolf. Could you swing by and check it?"

East pack was so named because the east end of ISRO was its territory. Wolves were warriors; they protected their turf, and the fights were vicious and often to the death. East pack that far from home would indicate a major disturbance in the population, proof of Ridley's assertion that "something stirred them up." A lone wolf wouldn't. On ISRO, only the alphas mated. Maturing animals would often leave the pack to seek another lone wolf with whom to start a new pack. Occasionally they joined a rival pack. Most often, after a month or two, they came home humbled. Wolves, like other sentient beings, had their own minds. One female had been noted to move, apparently with ease, between all three packs.

"Roger. We're nearly there," Jonah replied to Ridley. To Anna—or himself—he added: "A couple of minutes out of the way. We'll make it." As if in answer to his effrontery, a gust of wind, running ahead of the heavy weather, nudged the cub.

Jonah dropped the airplane down till they were flying two hundred feet above the Greenstone Ridge. They were traveling at airspeed of eighty-five miles per hour, slow for most airplanes but incredibly fast for humans, creatures designed to go no faster than a horse can canter. Trees and rock outcrops flashed by, their nearness enhancing the sense of speed. Anna enjoyed the rush.

They followed the trail for three miles but saw no tracks, then a fist of wind rocked the supercub and Jonah said: "This bird's for home."

Anna watched the ground. Jonah watched the sky. She saw a dark shape where dead grasses had been mashed. It looked like a moose bed, but, lying in the makeshift nest, partially hidden by the lower branches of a stunted spruce, a dark shape was curled up.

"Wait," Anna almost yelled into the mike. "I think I saw something. Make another pass."

"Not today," crackled back over the headset. "Pilots are a dime a dozen. Old pilots are rare as hen's teeth."

Anna didn't argue but she wanted to.

"What'd you spot?" Jonah asked.

"I don't know what it was," Anna said. She tried to look back but gear and seat belt trussed her as neatly as a straitjacket. "It looked like a great big dog."

The shape, the black silhouette curled nose to tail, had looked like a wolf. A monstrous wolf, more than half again as big as the biggest alpha she'd ever seen.

5

That night, the bunkhouse ran out of water. Since Middle pack had come to Washington Harbor, Ridley had banned the use of the snowmobile for all tasks, including hauling water up from the well. Wolves might be impervious to Jonah's supercub, but a snowmobile was an unknown quantity.

At first light, Anna positioned herself on the dock to get a final look. Robin was collecting along the Greenstone Trail. Adam had gone with her. Anna, Katherine, Jonah and Bob stood shoulder to shoulder, like cattle in the wind, watching the Middle pack as the angry whine of the snowmobile grew louder. The alpha female's head came up first, then the others; not one by one but in concert.

Ridley on the snowmobile broke free of the trees and the pack was on its feet.

Then they were gone.

Anna found herself laughing. They didn't turn tail and run the way Taco, her old dog, did when squirrels chirred at him. They dissipated like mist burning off a pond in autumn.

"Children of the night," she said.

"Let's go," Katherine begged.

"Let's do it." With Bob's permission, Katherine was off, trotting down the slippery dock and onto the lake, shuffle-sliding her way toward what remained of the moose.

"Mmm-mm." Jonah smacked his lips. "Fresh steaming wolf scat and lots of it. For a wildlife biologist, it just doesn't get any better."

Apparently carnivore excreta being of little interest to him, Jonah stopped at the ice well to help Ridley refill the plastic water barrels. Anna and Bob joined the gnawed carcass and Katherine. "Will the wolves hang around?" Bob asked.

"They may come back tonight, but I doubt it," Anna replied. "They got most of the meat."

"I'm going to take a look at their trail," Bob announced. "Want to come?"

Anna shook her head. Bob seemed nice enough, but he was too big. With his height, bulldog jowls and thickening middle, he made the bunkhouse feel cramped. Add six inches of cold-weather gear and he was huge, a yeti. It made her claustrophobic.

"Don't get eaten," she said to be personable. After

a hard, lean winter, if a wolf ate Menechinn it would probably flounder and die like a horse in a granary.

"The axman never gets eaten by the wolf." Bob grinned and turned away. The trees took him bite by bite.

For a while, Anna watched Katherine, absorbed in her work.

While convinced that wolf poop was a fine and desirable thing, without the actual furry beasts around it, Anna found her interest flagging. The front that had chased the supercub home had settled in. Wind gusted with malicious intent, and the weather site on Ridley's computer predicted snow. On the hill behind the bunkhouse was a vintage wooden weather station, the kind that had served parks and mom-and-pop airports for eighty or more years. The slat-sided wooden box housed a barometer, minimum and maximum thermometers and a thermometer designed—with some dipping into water and spinning—to give windchill. The NPS had given Robin the task of checking it daily.

The scientists thought this the height of absurdity, one more example of Park Service ineptitude. The machinery for weather recording had moved on while the NPS clung to the old ways. Still, when the stations were gone, it would be one more link broken from when the world was a more mysterious—and less endangered—place.

"Think it'll snow?" Anna asked to keep her mind off the hoarfrost forming on her eyelashes.

"I hope so," Katherine replied. "It makes it easier to map the packs' movements. You can follow their tracks from the air."

Watching Katherine scooping frozen urine-soaked snow into ziplock baggies and packing up wolf scat, Anna was surprised to note she no longer looked mousey or hangdog at all. For the first time, Anna saw the fine bones in the nose and the delicately squared chin, the eyebrows, soft brown and perfectly shaped where they showed above her glasses. A flush touched her cheeks. Not the raw pink the wind scoured up or the dull brick of her blushes but a fresh rose hue.

"You're in love with the wolves," Anna blurted half accusingly. She suffered a totally illogical stab of jealousy, as if she alone had the privilege of intimate connection with wild things.

Katherine looked up shyly. A strand of hair escaped from her hood and curved around the swell of her cheek. "I saw one when I was little—three or four," she said. "We had a cabin on a lake just north of the Boundary Waters." She laughed. It was the first time Anna had heard it. "You know Minnesotans, they can live on Lake Superior, but they still have to have a 'cabin on the lake' somewhere.

"We were there one winter, and Momma bundled me out to play." Katherine rocked back till she sat on her heels like an Arab, arms clasped around her knees, and looked through Anna. "The snow was a couple feet deep, but I was so light I could walk on top of it. I felt like I was flying, swooping along above the ground. Then there was this wolf." She laughed again. It wasn't musical but a series of puffs blown out through her nose with the barest of sound, as if she'd learned to laugh in a library with a bat-eared librarian.

"He was doing the same thing. Flying. That's what I thought then. He was taller than me and couldn't have been more than ten feet away. We just stared at each other for a long time. His ears twitched and he blinked. I blinked and tried to make my ears twitch under my hood. Then he turned and walked toward the woods. At the edge of the trees, he looked back over his shoulder, and I started to cry." She sounded wistful enough to cry these many years later.

"I thought he was asking me to go with him and I couldn't."

"Why not?" Anna asked, caught up in the story.

Katherine smiled and went back to her scat gathering. "Momma told me not to leave the yard."

Anna shifted from foot to foot. Her toes were getting numb. "No wolves in D.C. At least not the kind that will refrain from devouring children," she said. Bob was a professor at American University in Bethesda, where Katherine worked on her doctorate.

Wistful beauty burned away in a flash, and, for a second, Anna thought Katherine was going to wrinkle back her upper lip and growl. Whatever soured the young woman nearly to the point of spitting might have been sufficiently interesting to take Anna's mind off freezing to death for another few minutes, but they were interrupted by the squeaky *munch-munch-munch* of boots on frozen snow announcing Bob's return. Katherine's face went blank, her eyes back to her collecting and packaging.

Menechinn emerged from the trees. "Better get Ridley," he said without preamble. "Looks like Stephen King is doing a wilderness version of *Pet Sematary* up here."

"What have you got?" Anna asked.

"Let's wait for Ridley," Bob said and planted his feet as if the sheer force of his will would draw the lead researcher across the ice. Menechinn was either in shock or suffering an attack of melodrama.

"Would you like me to radio Ridley?" she asked politely.

When he answered the call, Ridley echoed Anna almost word for word: "What's he got?"

Anna looked at Bob.

"It's not far in," Menechinn said.

"It's not far in," Anna repeated into the mike. She could hear Ridley sigh all the way from the well and wasn't sure it was over the radio.

"I'll be there when we're finished."

Anna put the radio back in her parka; with mittens, it was more a process of shoving and squashing than pocketing. For a half a minute, she stood with Bob, cooling heels already numb from so long on the ice. Katherine kept her head down, staying busy with her collecting.

Finally Anna headed off toward the woods where Bob's tracks tore up the bank. Katherine pushed up from the scat-dotted ice to come with her.

"Hang on, you two." Bob sounded like a schoolmaster dealing with overeager children. "I don't want you tracking up the area before Ridley gets there."

Idiot, Anna thought charitably as she pretended not to hear him.

Menechinn's find was no more than a hundred yards from shore, near where the Feldtmann Trail joined the Nature Trail that led up to the permanent-employee housing. In a three-foot radius around the body, duff, dirt and snow were plowed up by Menechinn's size thirteens. Mud and blood churned the snow to the unsettling brownish pink Anna associated with wallpaper in old ladies' bathrooms.

"Idiot," she reiterated as she studied the radically compromised scene.

A wolf.

There was no scene. Dead animals did not constitute murder.

Pet Sematary.

"Right," she said, and, careless of where she stepped, she walked up to the animal and squatted on her haunches. It lay on its side, eyes open, tongue—pink and silly looking like a goofball dog's—lolling out of its mouth. Anna pulled off a mitten and touched the tongue. Frozen solid. Scavengers had been at it but not a lot. The animal had been there long enough to freeze but not so long that the body had been torn up. Five or six hours, maybe less. Ridley could make a more educated guess. He knew the island food chain better than she did.

The blood was from the throat. A wolf-on-wolf

killing; on ISRO, nothing else was big enough to take out a wolf. The wolves were isolated by miles of open water for decades at a stretch, and no other large predators had migrated to the island: no puma, no bears, no coyotes, not even a badger. The other wolf—the one who'd left the fray alive—was either very big or very lucky. This animal was a good-sized male, yet he hadn't had time to put up much of a fight. Fur, matted with blood and frozen solid, masked the wound, but it had to have been severe. The wolf looked as if he bled out fast. There was little sign of movement after the neck was slashed.

Anna laid her bare hand on the fur. In the Western world's collective unconscious, wolves symbolized hunger, danger, vicious cunning and cold-blooded slaughter. The flip side was, they were the embodiment of the wild; like the wind, they went where they would, did as they pleased, then vanished into the woods. Touching a wolf—even a dead wolf—Anna thrilled to the echo of primitive, amoral freedom.

"What killed it?" Ridley had come. Everybody had come. Anna stood and moved back.

"Neck wound," Anna said.

"Interpack rivalry," Bob said.

"Could be," Ridley replied noncommittally.

"What else?" Bob demanded.

Anna leaned against the bole of a birch. She loved a good pissing contest when she wasn't on the wrong end of it. Ridley said nothing but crouched over the wolf much as she had. Menechinn gave Anna a conspiratorial grin as if they shared a joke on Ridley. He winked at Anna, then said to Ridley: "You wanted a dead wolf. Now you've got it."

"Now I've got it," Ridley echoed absently. He took off his left glove. With long, sensitive fingers, he pulled back the eyelids, then the lips. Ridley Murray was un-moved by the wolf's death per se. Wolves were not wolves to him, Anna realized. They were subjects of study.

Katherine was not quite so clinical, but she was de-tached and professional. After the story of her first wolf and love torn asunder by parental decree, Anna thought she'd show more emotion.

"Let's get it to the bunkhouse," Ridley said, rising effortlessly to his feet. "It'll need to thaw before we can do much."

"I'll take the pelt and head," Bob said. "I'll have it shipped to American University. You know, for research, a research tool. Our students don't get much of a chance for the hands-on like you folks do." He smiled, turning it on each of them in turn.

Katherine's head twitched up, in a gesture oddly rem-iniscent of the alpha female's, on hearing the approach-ing snowmobile. A shadow passed behind her eyes, and she turned away as if from something obscene. Maybe she wasn't as unmoved as Anna had thought.

Ridley pulled his glove on, his eyes blank under the glare of Menechinn's grin. He looked the way Robin did when she came in at the end of the day; her face

frozen—not figuratively, literally—cold paralyzing surface muscles and skin, as unable to show any expression
as a Botox junkie.

"The head and pelt," Ridley said evenly.

In the minds of the members of the wolf/moose
study team, the island had been their personal domain
for years, intruded on occasionally by the National Park
Service and other ignorant bureaucrats but never con-
quered. Anna waited for Ridley to light into Menechinn.

Ridley didn't take his eyes off Bob for a good ten seconds, then he said to Robin: "Get a tarp from the snowmobile. I want to get it to the bunkhouse before the
ravens find it."

ON THE FLOOR in the unused kitchen down the hall
from Anna and Robin's room, garbage bags were put
down, then newspapers to soak up the fluids. The wolf
was laid on this unglamorous bier to thaw.

"It'll be a few days before we can do the necropsy,"
Ridley said as he handed a fine-tooth comb to Anna and
another to Katherine, then set a box of small ziplock
baggies, the size cheap jewelry is sold in, on the newspapers by the wolf's spine.

"I'll be here to supervise," Jonah said. "Keep an eye
on young Ridley."

"You taught me everything I know," Ridley said
good-naturedly. "Any mistakes I make will be your
fault." It had taken Anna a while, but she'd eventually
caught on; one of the many amusements they'd devel-

oped was the fiction that Jonah was all things: chef, scientist, philosopher and learned professor. Though he was a smart man, Anna doubted he'd gone any further than high school.

"We'll do the external exam now," Ridley said for Anna's benefit. "No smell, for one thing. Once the specimen starts thawing, it'll stink pretty bad."

"At least we've got that to look forward to," Jonah interjected.

"We want to get the ectoparasites off. They are opportunistic and will jump to other hosts if they can. We're the other hosts."

"Like this," Katherine said, and Anna watched as she combed the fur from the roots of the hairs out, much like a mom looking for lice on a child's head. Ridley moved to the kitchen counter and set out a rack of small vials he'd brought from the storeroom off the shared living area. The tubes were held upright by the rack, half filled with clear liquid and tightly stoppered.

"Alcohol," he said. "For preservation."

Anna began combing. She'd thought the fur would be like dog fur, but it wasn't. Where a dog's coat was relatively smooth, hairs all the same length, the wolf's pelt was made of many lengths, and lengths of many textures and colors. From the distance of the dock, the animals had appeared to be rather plain. Up close, the rich color and lush texture of the coat was stunning. Midwinter, times were tough, the wolf hadn't been shampooed or visited a doggie salon in his life, yet the descriptive that came to Anna's mind was "regal," a robe of royalty right down to the extra-long guard hairs around the throat that created a silvery ruff.

The pelt's loveliness was somewhat dimmed by the bloodsuckers it harbored. At least none were embedded. Wolves seemed to possess a natural deterrent to ticks that the moose did not enjoy. Anna didn't have any particular fear of the world's many-legged denizens, but there was something about ticks that had always made her queasy. She was not sorry to drop the little buggers into the certain death of the vials.

The combs dredged moose ticks, lice and mange mites from the thick fur. The combing wouldn't come close to cleaning the parasites from the body. They were sample takers, not exterminators, and Anna knew she wouldn't sleep well for the feeling of crawly things in her sleeping bag.

"That's enough," Ridley said finally. Anna had just culled a fat moose tick from a section of fur on the wolf's belly and was trying to keep it from creeping off the comb till she could drop it in the alcohol.

"Wolves are not at the top of the food chain on Isle Royale," she said disgustedly. "Ticks are."

The alcohol vials were stowed in the kitchen cupboard next to a box of granola bars. Ridley brought in another rack of vials, the glass preservation tubes smaller than those used for ectoparasites. Using tweezers, Katherine plucked guard hairs, careful to get the follicles.

"Ninety-five percent ethanol," she said to Anna as she dropped them in fifteen-milliliter glass vials. "We use that instead of alcohol for the DNA. It keeps the sample from degrading. Well, keeps it from degrading longer. Eventually everything goes."

"We'll have to wait on the teeth and throat," Ridley said. His hands were around the wolf's muzzle, pulling with a degree of force. "Frozen solid."

There was a wrongness in Ridley's hands on the animal's mouth that disturbed Anna on a rudimentary level, the way watching people put a car in gear without fastening their seat belts or wave an unloaded gun in the direction of living things did.

"Rigor or *frozen* frozen?" she asked.

Ridley rocked back on his heels. "When it's this cold, it doesn't make much difference. It takes longer for specimens to thaw out than it would for rigor to go off."

"How long does rigor last in a wolf?" Anna asked.

"I don't know," he said without curiosity. Ridley exhibited a disinterest in anything regarding research animals that wasn't study specific. Maybe a narrow mind was a strength for a researcher; the ability to focus on one tiny thing for a very long time.

"No gloves!" Anna blurted out suddenly. That was the wrongness; Ridley was handling the animal without wearing surgical gloves.

"We'll put them on for the necropsy," he said. "That gets messy."

Anna nodded. There was no need for gloves except to keep one's nails clean. No AIDS, no hepatitis B or other blood-borne diseases. The risk of contamination was nil. A bit of human DNA sprinkled here and there amid the wolf DNA wouldn't interfere with the investigation.

The research, Anna corrected herself.

The wolf's hide had softened in the relative heat of the bunkhouse, and Ridley pulled up the wolf's right eyebrow with his thumb. The dull eyes were gold colored, closer together and more slanted than the eyes of domestic dogs.

"Great eyes," he said as he pulled up the lid of the left.

"Yes," Anna said. "He looks Slavic, as if he hunted the great plains of Russia from the beginning of time."

Ridley stared at her blankly. "They're not eaten," he explained. "Ravens get the eyes first thing, usually." He looked back to the wolf. "No cataracts. Even without seeing the teeth, my guess is this guy is two, three at most. He must have tried to run the pack or gotten himself crosswise with the alpha some other way, then lost the fight," he said, rocking back on his heels. "The rest is going to have to wait till he thaws."

Ridley rose gracefully, his elegant hands held out in front of him like a pianist about to perform. He would wash them immediately with hot water dippered from the stovetop into a basin. The Winter Study team was fastidious about hygiene. Gastrointestinal upsets took on a whole new meaning when the bathroom was a one-holer and the temperature minus twelve degrees.

Anna squatted in the vacated place by the wolf's head. She knew she was making a pest of herself, getting in the way of the scientists and asking what were, to them, foolish questions, but she didn't much care.

A wolf.

She'd yet to get over the wonder of it.

"Wine time," Bob said, glancing at his watch, and followed Ridley toward the common room.

"Generator time," Jonah said. "Since the good Adam, first man on Earth and not on time even once in the ensuing millennia, has not yet returned, firing it up falls to me."

Anna'd not noticed the light going. Her nose was scarcely four inches from the slash in the wolf's throat. She laughed. "I just figured I was going blind."

"Let there be light," Jonah said and left.

Five minutes later the lights came on. Since Katherine showed no indication she was finished, and Anna had nothing better to do, she stayed and watched.

"I've got a new toy," Katherine said, more at ease with the men gone. She lovingly removed a box about the size of two toasters from a duffel bag stacked with other bags and boxes on the unused cot in the corner of the kitchen. "They've been around for a while, but this is of a new generation." With obvious pride, she removed the top half of the Styrofoam packing to reveal a machine that looked like a cross between a computer and an adding machine.

When no explanation was forthcoming, Anna asked: "What does it do?"

"It's a PCR," Katherine said. "A polymerase chain reaction machine. It's brand-new technology." Katherine stroked its plastic face. "American University bought it for this trip. The wolf/moose study is a kind of rock star in animal research studies."

Anna'd known that. In a world where the denizens hyperventilated over the discovery of a new kind of fruit fly larva, wolves would be glamour on paws. It was also the longest-running project of its kind in America and, despite how it seemed at the dinner table, one of the touted examples of how scientists and the Park Service worked and played well together.

"The lab at Michigan Tech does the original finger-printing," Katherine went on as she set the PCR on the counter. "ISRO's samples are sent there. They extract DNA using a Qiagen extraction kit. Then the sample is visualized, using a Beckman-Coul fragment analyzer. They do it at a bunch of different microsatellite loci in the genome."

It would have fallen to Katherine, as Menechinn's graduate student, to teach the basic classes. Anna felt a twinge of pity for her students. Katherine's mind moved in higher stratospheres of science, and it sounded as if her trips back to Earth had been infrequent.

"You lost me at 'Qiagen,'" Anna said.

Katherine looked sheepish, oddly juxtapositional to the technically precise language she'd been spouting. "Sorry." She bobbed her head in the birdlike way Anna'd noticed her first night on the island, the ducking-under-the-wing gesture when Bob had praised her graduate work.

Katherine took a deep breath and looked into the corner behind Anna's head. "Okay. The Qiagen . . . Okay. No. Okay, let's go to the gel. No. Not yet . . ."

Anna waited patiently as she struggled her way back to total ignorance so she might begin to help Anna understand.

"Tiny fragments of the DNA are taken," Katherine finally said, and her gaze came back to eye level. "From a lot of different places—not on the sample; from different places on the genome from the sample. All these tiny pieces have different weights. The fragments are . . . uh . . . squirted . . . into tubes of gel . . . like Jell-O, you know?"

"I know Jell-O," Anna said gravely.

"Good. Good. So each little piece of DNA is in its own tube, and the tubes are all in a line like . . ." She groped mentally, probably through a bag of metaphors that wouldn't mean anything to anybody without at least a master's degree.

"Like a bowling alley?"

"Yes!" she said gratefully. "Like a bowling alley, but tiny. Very, very small. Small. Smaller than small—"

"Tiny," Anna helped her out.

"Tiny. So each tiny bit is in its own tiny tube of gel in the tiny bowling alley. All in a line like the lanes." She was warming up to the bowling alley and waited till Anna nodded her understanding before she went on. "Then the little bits are pushed down the tube full of gel—the lane—with the same amount of pressure. I mean it's not pressure, it's electricity. It's called gel electrophoresis . . ."

"I get the idea," Anna said. "All the DNA bowling

balls are rolled down their individual lanes with the same amount of force."

"Okay. That will work. The lighter ones go farther along the gel tubes than the heavier ones. When they all stop, you look at a readout; it looks sort of like a shadowy version of the old computer punch cards. A series of marks. Like on television when they lay one DNA readout over the other and all the marks are exactly the same and—Bingo!—you've got the criminal.

"The lab at Michigan Tech has the DNA fingerprints for all of the wolves on Isle Royale. Whenever there's a kill, a biotech or one of the Winter Study guys collects samples from the scat. Over time, they've built up a database on each of the wolves. Those 'fingerprints' are now in this smaller computer. When I put in the sample from the blood or the follicles that we took today," she nodded toward the wolf melting into the newspapers at their feet, "I'll be able to tell where he's been—at what kills—which pack he belonged to, if he'd ever been at another pack's kill, things like that."

In law enforcement, Anna often had to wait weeks for DNA tests to come back, and the kind of detail Katherine was talking about was exorbitantly expensive. Often, up to fifty separate tests had to be run.

"Interesting," she said noncommittally.

Katherine heard the skepticism and cast back over her words to see where she'd gone wrong. When she wasn't guarding, which she did whenever a member of the opposite sex was in the room, she was easy to read. Emotions passed just under the skin the way they do on the faces of very young children, leaving ripples in the eyes and mouth.

"The PCR is a *portable* DNA fingerprinting device," she said.

The machines Anna had seen that tested for DNA markers were huge, computers and other paraphernalia taking up entire walls.

"I first worked with one in the Northwest. Salmon. The fishermen can take only one kind and not the other, but you can't tell which fish is which by looking at them. We used an earlier version of the PCR. The reason it can work is that it doesn't do much. You set it to figure out just one or two things. Like the DNA for the two species of fish. Both fingerprints are known quantities and are already loaded in the PCR's computer. So when you feed it the new sample, all it has to do is compare it with those already on file; it doesn't have to figure out anything.

"What this PCR does is simply show me the readout, what kind of line the balls make; that's that wolf's 'fingerprint.' All the ISRO wolves' fingerprints are in this machine, so the fingerprint I get is compared to the existing fingerprints. Each existing fingerprint represents a wolf and each wolf has been assigned a number. I can look at my readout and see that number such and such left my sample. Or, in this case, *is* my sample. Then I e-mail the lab at Michigan Tech and add my data to theirs. Then *they* can look back in their files and see that my wolf—this wolf—ate a moose, say, at Rock Harbor in the winter of 2005 because somebody collected scat there at that time and its DNA matched the DNA I collected. Do you see?"

She looked so desperate Anna might have said she understood even if she didn't. "I get it," Anna said. "We do it with regular fingerprints. They're run through a national database and, if they match up, we know where our guy was when he left his print behind."

Relieved, Katherine went back to her machine. Anna watched for a while, but it was a one-woman show. Returning to the wolf, she crouched near its head. Fluids were beginning to seep from the corpse as it thawed. Before the animal was anywhere close to room temperature, the bunkhouse was going to smell like roadkill on a hot afternoon.

Until the blood matted and the fur at the throat could be separated, the killing wound—or wounds—was impossible to see. Anna guessed the other wolf got in a lucky hit and punctured the carotid artery early in the fight. That would account for the fact that there were no lesser or defensive wounds—at least none she could see.

The door to the front room banged and Anna rose. "Robin and Adam," she said. Without being aware she was doing it, Anna had been listening for their return. Unconsciously she'd been gauging the level of light, the cold, the freshening wind and listening for the radio. Suddenly angry, she demanded of Katherine, "Did you hear Robin radio in?"

"I don't think Robin carries a radio," Katherine said distractedly.

The woman's interest was gone to scat. Anna left her.

SCAT WAS THE TOPIC OF CONVERSATION at the dinner table. Robin and Adam had not seen Middle pack as it fled Washington Harbor, but they'd come across their tracks. Over dinner—a casserole Ridley had concocted with pasta, frozen peas and chicken—Robin outlined her path.

"We hiked toward Malone Bay. We got as far as the last ridge before you go down to Siskiwit," Robin said in her soft cheery voice.

Eight or nine miles, if Anna remembered correctly.

"Then we split up, and I came back cross-country. Lots of swamps. Downed stuff. I saw moose tracks, then I came across the wolves' trail and followed them back. What scared them off the harbor?"

"We ran out of water," Ridley said in the shorthand of the island.

Anna was still doing the math. *Came back cross-country. Add a couple of miles to the return trip. Nine miles out, eleven or twelve back.*

"We got tons of samples. They're in the kitchen with the wolf."

Twenty miles of rough country, freezing temperatures, carrying a backpack full of shit.

Comforting herself with the knowledge that Robin was nearly a quarter century younger than she and an

Olympic contender, Anna submerged her consciousness in the food. She was just short of shoveling it in, minding her table manners only by an act of will. Calories being units of heat, a concept she'd learned in high school chemistry class, was finally making sense.

"I wish I'd had a camera," Robin said around a mouthful of toast with peanut butter and jam—a side dish served with every meal. "One of the wolves had huge feet. Like twice as big as the others. Then, about halfway between Siskiwit and Windigo, they aren't there anymore. It must have joined the pack on a rocky place. I looked for its tracks all the way back but couldn't find where it had caught up with the others."

"*Twice* as big?" Bob said with a lifted eyebrow and an avuncular smile.

Katherine ducked her head, letting her hair fall over her face in a screen. Robin stared straight into Menechinn's eyes. "Twice as big," she said without a hint of defensiveness. Anna smiled. Olympic training had toughened more than the girl's body.

"That's your work tomorrow," Ridley said. "I'll give you the camera."

"How about you, Adam? Did you see tracks twice as big as a normal wolf's?" Bob asked. He winked at Robin to show there were no hard feelings.

"We'd split up, remember?" Adam said neutrally.

"Why don't you go out with Robin tomorrow," Ridley suggested to Bob. "See for yourself. I'm sure Robin could use somebody to carry the camera."

Robin took a huge bite of toast to cover her smile. Given the chance, Anna guessed she could—and would— hike Menechinn into an early grave.

"No."

Katherine was the one who spoke. Bob, neatly lifted off the hook, gave her a slow smile. She didn't smile back. With everyone looking at her, Katherine lost her confidence. "I need some help," she stammered. "I need Dr. Menechinn to help me with the PCR."

The last words were almost a whisper. "Excuse me," she said and left the table abruptly.

Adam broke the awkward silence that followed. "Mind if I tag along with Robin tomorrow or has somebody busted something I have to fix?"

"Go," Ridley said.

Anna did the dishes alone. After the fit of jealousy, Katherine hadn't come back. If it was jealousy. That didn't feel quite right, but Anna had no better explanation. Whatever the reason, the researcher had hid out with her PCR. She'd identified the samples collected on the harbor ice, but there was all that terrific new poop Robin brought back.

When the washing was done, Anna returned to the common room to find it empty. All six members of the Winter Study team were in the kitchen-cum-morgue crowded around Katherine's PCR. With the thawing wolf, a spare cot and everybody's luggage taking up most of the floor, the six of them were crowded two deep at the counter.

"I don't think this sample came from any ISRO wolf," Katherine was saying as Anna slipped in to see what the show was about. "It doesn't match up with any of the fingerprints Michigan downloaded onto the PCR."

"This year's pup," Bob said. "Not on the radar yet."

Anna weaseled past him. Ridley and Katherine, heads almost touching, were poring over a strip of paper.

"There are other things," Katherine said.

"Every wolf on ISRO descended from the one breeding pair that came across the ice," Ridley told Menechinn. "They've got distinct genetic markers. The obvious one is the mutation of the spine. About half of ISRO's wolves have an extra vertebra. But their DNA marks them as members of a single family. Different from unrelated wolves. This isn't an island wolf. It's wolf DNA but weird."

Anna loved it when scientists talked technical.

Ridley pressed the DNA readout flat on the counter; next to it, he placed another, a known DNA readout of an island wolf, and studied the two together. "It's like wolf plus . . . something."

"The sample got tainted," Bob said.

"Maybe." Katherine was looking not at the readout but out the window toward where they'd seen the pack cross the compound.

She was thinking about the huge tracks Robin had seen, Anna would have bet on it.

6

The following day, the promised snow began to fall. Robin laced up her mukluks, shouldered her army-issue rucksack and headed out to photograph the track of the gigantic hound with Adam. The others slept late and dawdled over breakfast. The wolf pack on the ice had changed the daily habits of the researchers. Usually, when the sky was clear and there was little wind, Ridley would spend the day in the air with Jonah watching and photographing the wolves. When the weather was too bad to fly, there were chores, but not enough to keep them busy.

For most of breakfast, they chewed over the DNA Katherine had identified as alien. The wolf that had left the scat wasn't from the island. At first, Anna hadn't grasped the magnitude of that revelation. Wolves had come across the ice once, had they not? It was only when

Ridley reminded her that the lake hadn't frozen over in nearly thirty years that she understood. A wolf in the wild had to be lucky and strong to live ten years. The wolf who'd left scat along the Greenstone Trail to Siskiwit Lake would have to have been the Methuselah of wolf kind to have traversed the last ice bridge.

This wolf had come to the island in some other manner. Wolves could swim, but they could not swim eighteen miles. That left boat, ski plane, seaplane, canoe, kayak or Ski-Doo. A pup loosed by a misguided do-gooder? A wolf/dog hybrid bred in domesticity, the owner grows bored with it and lets it "go free" on the island? Had a wolf/dog hybrid been raised to be vicious, attacked somebody and, rather than kill it, the owner dumped it at a campground or in the bay?

This last was the most probable. Wolves' reputation as cold-blooded killers of little girls in red capes was unearned. No one around the breakfast table could think of a single recorded incident in their lifetimes or that of their parents. In 2005, a presumed wolf/human killing had been reported, but the attack animal turned out to be a bear.

What there had been were attacks on people by wolf/dog hybrids, kept and bred by dog owners. Like any animal that cannot be fully domesticated, these breeds were volatile. The owners weren't any better. Most obtained wolf/dog hybrids because they wanted a big, scary, mean dog or, worse—illegal but available in all fifty states—a fighting dog. Brutal attacks by these animals had stirred up public opinion to the point that, in many urban areas, it was illegal to own or keep a wolf/dog hybrid.

Jonah tired of saying "wolf/dog hybrid" first and dubbed the speculative animal a "wog."

A wog could have been dumped on the island at any time, but most likely in the last six or seven months. Had the creature been in the park the previous winter, Ridley believed there would have been sign of it, a sighting or scat or the outsized paw prints Robin had reported.

Most domesticated—or even partially domesticated—animals couldn't survive in the wilderness for long, but if the wog was as big as the tracks Robin found suggested, and trained to kill, it might have joined—or taken over—a pack. This could explain why the pack had apparently lost its fear of humans and sauntered through the bunkhouse area. If the wog were big enough and fierce enough, it could have killed the wolf now decomposing in the kitchen, dispatched it so quickly there were no signs of a fight.

"Any alien wolf or *wolf/dog hybrid*," Bob declared, pointedly refusing to use Jonah's word, "would be killed by any pack that came across it."

"What if it was big, really big?" Katherine said.

"It's not one-on-one in a fair fight, Kathy," Bob said with a smile that pushed his cheeks up till his eyes were crescent moons. The smile notwithstanding, the "Kathy" was a clear rebuke. "The pack would kill it."

"Maybe not," Ridley said. "If there was a breeding slot open, the wolf might be assimilated."

Bob snorted. "Pretty hard to arrange," he said.

"It could happen by chance," Ridley said. Anna wasn't sure whether he believed it or was just baiting the other man. "Chance is the only reason we have wolves here at all. A big enough, aggressive enough wog might pull it off."

The breakfast club finally broke up: Ridley to his laptop to work on reports, Jonah to wander the bunkhouse looking for somebody to pester and Bob to the chair closest to the woodstove to read through the daily log, a thick, three-ring binder full of the forms provided for record keeping. The park service was full of such information-gathering tools. For the most part, they were a tedium of pages hurriedly filled in by the lowest-ranking member of any team. On the island, the biotech did it each day. Temperature at sunrise, at sunset, snowfall, comments; office closets were full of these binders, detailing one study or another. As far as Anna knew, Bob was the first person to actually look at one.

For a while, she amused herself in the DNA lab kitchen, watching Katherine pore over her alien sample, running and rerunning it only to get the same answer. When that palled and looking at the wolf, who was beginning to smell, lost its edge, Anna began drifting back toward the common room.

"Anna?"

It was the first time Katherine had spoken in a quarter of an hour and her voice was so low Anna barely caught it. She looked back. The researcher was still bent over her PCR, her back to the room.

"I'm here," Anna said. She, too, whispered though she'd not meant to.

"Tell Robin to stay away from Bob," Katherine said quietly and without turning. Anna waited for further illumination on the subject, but it was not forthcoming.

"Sure," she said. Then, in hopes it would ease Katherine's mind: "She's got a boyfriend."

Katherine acted as if she'd not heard. After a moment, Anna left the kitchen and wandered into the common room. Standing between the door and the stove, she stared at Bob, trying to figure out why anybody would defend that particular chunk of turf.

"Looks like a Christmas card, doesn't it?" he said genially.

She looked out the picture widow. The bunkhouse had a wide deck with a railing. She remembered potluck suppers there the summer she'd worked boat patrol. Now it was three-quarters covered with wood cut by the NPS and stacked there for the use of the Winter Study. The sky was lost in the falling flakes, birch and spruce trees surrounding the cleared area veiled in drifting snow, a muted study in black and white.

Anna pulled on a sweater, stepped into her clogs and went outside. In Rocky Mountain, even in the backcountry, there was sound: a jet high overhead, birds singing, water running, wind through the pine trees, squirrels scuffling in the duff. In Mississippi, life buzzed and chirped year-round. Even Texas wasn't silent; when all else failed, the wind howled and whispered and suggested angry things.

Here, in the thick fall of snow, the silence was absolute. In an indefinable way, even silence was muffled by the slow white flakes.

Anna hated to think of these winters being peopled by lodges, snowmobiles and skiers and beer. Though she'd never come to the island in January again if she could help it, she wanted to know there was a place where silence lived.

Opening the park in winter would effectively shut the study down. The noise and humanity attendant on a winter resort destination would disrupt the wolves to the point the study would no longer be viable.

There was no reason for Homeland Security to send one of their own to evaluate it. The NPS had debated every salient point regarding the study, first with David Mech, then Rolf Peterson and now Ridley Murray. The research was prestigious, high-profile and cheap. People loved the wolves, loved knowing they were around. At every campfire talk, regardless of the subject, the first question was always, "How many wolves are there?"

Pursuing its mandate to keep America's borders safe, Homeland Security needed to plug up corridors used by unsavory aliens. Big Bend in Texas bordered on Mexico, as did Organ Pipe. Glacier, Isle Royale and Voyageurs national parks shared a border with Canada. Many national parks had stretches of seacoast within their boundaries. If Anna squinted and tilted her head, she could vaguely see the logic of souping up security in these areas, but the border parks were a drop in the bucket when one looked at the landmass of the USA. That which was cynical in her suggested the war on terror had gone after the parks because they were high-profile. "Protecting Our Parks" made a much better headline than "Taking Away Your Civil Rights."

But why bring in anybody? And why Bob Menechinn? He was more interested in collecting trophy heads than doing science. Unless he was here to rubber-stamp what Homeland Security wanted stamped. Yet when the agency contacted the park and Winter Study team with a list of possible evaluators, Ridley recommended Menechinn. Was it because Menechinn could be bought? Bought with what money? Professors weren't exactly overpaid. The NPS wouldn't touch a deal like that. Maybe Michigan Tech. Maybe an angel who loved the park had ponied up.

ROBIN RETURNED EARLY. Adam wasn't with her. So dull was the day, Robin's return was heralded with great excitement. She had pictures of the track of the gigantic hound. The camera was plugged into Ridley's laptop, and they gathered around to see if the paw prints were all they'd been advertised to be.

Robin had traveled fast, but there'd been at least a half an inch of snowfall before she'd reached her destination. The light was lousy for photographing tracks, directionless and muted. Tracking was best in the morning and at sundown, when the light was low enough it caught the minute contours of the prints. She'd used a pen for scale—the proper tool was a small ruler, but a pen or a dime was often as good as it got.

Shouldering Jonah aside, Anna leaned in for a better view.

The paw prints did appear significantly larger than those of the other wolves, but, in the diffuse light and with the snow obliterating the edges, it was hard to be sure they had actually been made by as large an animal as they suggested.

"They could have been made when a normal-sized wolf was running. Or this one here." Robin leaned in, and her long hair fell across Ridley's shoulder. He didn't seem aware of it. For all Bob's covert flirting and Jonah's overt silliness, Ridley, the young alpha of this pack, had evidently mated for life. Robin put the tip of a well-shaped finger with cracked skin and a broken nail on the screen. "It could even have been made by a second wolf stepping almost but not exactly in the first one's track. It seemed clearer before, but now I don't know."

"Anna saw something," Jonah said.

Anna'd been thinking the same thing but didn't want to commit herself. "*Thought* being the key word," she said, but all eyes were on her. "On the way back from Siskiwit, I saw what looked like a huge wolf curled under the branches of a tree. It could have been anything, but it looked like a wolf."

"Huge?" Ridley questioned the word.

"Half to twice the size of a normal alpha."

"Wolves here run seventy to eighty-five pounds. Are you talking a hundred-and-sixty-pound wolf?" Ridley asked skeptically.

"Like I said, *thought* is the key word."

"And you thought you saw huge tracks." This was to Robin, and Anna couldn't tell if Ridley believed them or not. He'd donned his scientist's mien and she couldn't read past it.

"I saw them," Robin said firmly, abandoning her earlier wavering.

"Okay," Ridley said, and: "Okay." The second *okay* was more to himself than the others, and Anna wondered what he was giving himself permission to do.

7

Good morning, campers!" Ridley said as they settled down to their oatmeal the following morning. Anna got a bad feeling and shoveled more of the
thick porridge into her mouth.

"Normally we don't trap wolves in winter—too great
a danger of a foot freezing off in the trap before we get
there," Ridley said to the group.

"Not to mention people's feet freezing off," Adam
put in.

"But we've done it before," Ridley went on, ignoring
the aside. "Two years ago, we thought we had a virus
threatening the population and couldn't wait till summer to check it out, and we've had to do it a time or two
when we couldn't get what we needed to do finished in
the summer." He took a topographical map of the island
he had folded at his elbow and spread it out, shoving jam

and peanut butter and milk aside. Anna held on to her bowl and spoon lest it be removed in the sweep.

"I don't know what we've got going this winter, but I don't think it can wait till summer. If somebody dumped an animal here, chances are it won't survive the winter, but it might live to reproduce or just screw up the wolves' patterns. Worst case, it will reinfect them with parvo or some other virus. ISRO wolves have isolation for protection, but they've not been exposed to mainland diseases and have little tolerance for that kind of exposure."

Ridley was rather enjoying the lecture, but Anna sensed beneath it he was nervous about the decision. Customarily there were four experienced wolf researchers on Winter Study. With Rolf Peterson retiring and the extra beds taken up by Homeland Security and Anna, Ridley was having to deal with greenhorns. Ignorant greenhorns.

"You," he said to Robin, "and you," looking at Anna, "and Bob and you, Katherine, will hike up to the Malone Bay area. There's a cabin there you can base yourselves out of, but plan on a couple nights of winter camping." He traced a finger up the Greenstone toward Malone.

Sending Robin made sense: she was an experienced trapper and winter camper. He'd included Anna to assist Robin and further her education in prey/predator relationships. Anna suspected he was sending Bob and Katherine just to get rid of them.

Malone Bay was fourteen or fifteen miles over ridges. The trail was only moderately difficult and stunningly beautiful, with a canopy of trees that suddenly opened to frame views of Lake Superior. Robin could make it in a day even under January conditions. Anna wasn't sure she could, not if she had to carry any significant weight. Katherine would be the slowest and for that Anna was grateful. It was a far better thing to be graciously considerate of a weak link than to have to admit to being one. They would need to overnight on the Greenstone Trail.

Camping in the glow of long summer evenings in the mountains, waking on the shores of a lake to the crisp bite of autumn on the air, sleeping away a hot afternoon beneath an overhang of sculpted rock in a desert creek bed: this was the stuff of heaven. Anna would—and had—walked days, carrying a heavy pack on her back, to enjoy these fragments of paradise.

Dragging oneself out of an always-inadequate down bag, hoarfrost on the tent ceiling shattering into a thousand needles of ice stinging one's cheeks, struck her as a pastime slightly more attractive than wearing a hair shirt, yet still not as much fun as self-flagellation. The only upside she could think of was that, since it was a work assignment, she would not be expected to have fun. "Fun" froze at about fifty-two degrees Fahrenheit.

With the front sitting on the island, Jonah couldn't fly. Everything had to be packed in. A wolf trap, including transmitter and eight feet of kinkless chain, weighed ten pounds. Anna and Robin each carried four. Because of her small frame and lack of backwoods experience, Katherine was given only two; still, her pack weighed in at forty-two pounds, eleven more than was optimum for a woman her size. Bob carried six traps. With the tent and other supplies, his pack weighed seventy-five pounds. He swung it onto his back with a minimum of effort, and Anna was impressed. She was less impressed when it became clear he wasn't accustomed to backpacking. Ridley had to adjust his buckles and straps. Neither man was comfortable with the process. Anna got the feeling that Ridley didn't like to be that close to Menechinn and Menechinn didn't like having his ignorance made public.

BECAUSE OF KATHERINE, they set a slow pace. Freed from the fear she would shame herself by huffing and gasping and throwing herself facedown, crying "I can't go on"—all of which would have been distinct possibilities had she been trying to keep up with Robin—Anna took pleasure in the simple act of breathing out of doors, moving away from "civilization" and into the backcountry.

Ridley had mapped out five miles of trail west of Lake Siskiwit for the trapline. East and Chippewa both claimed the mapped section of the island as part of their territory. Several pack interactions had been recorded in the vicinity.

Ridley and Jonah had had the rare luck to watch one unfold. The photo sequence Ridley captured remained some of the study's most compelling footage. For some reason, a female had been drummed out of East pack. Ridley and Jonah watched the lupine drama play out, with all the pathos of *Troilus and Cressida,* beneath the supercub's wings.

East pack had pursued the female till they cornered her on a finger of land jutting into Siskiwit Bay. Too many to fight, she'd taken to the water. The pack paced her along the shore, twice driving her back in when she tried to reach land. Finally she no longer had the strength to swim and moved to land through the teeth of her former pack mates. They didn't kill her immediately but dogged her, tearing at her back, neck and flanks as she tried to escape. More than once, Jonah and Ridley believed her dead, but then she would force herself up, repel her attackers and run again. Finally the pack, as if tiring of the game—or as a mob stoning a fallen woman will suddenly need a kill—surrounded and savaged her, then fled as if the law was on their tails.

After two more passes, Jonah and Ridley were sure this time she was dead. They were turning for home when they saw a lone male from East pack return. He nosed and pawed the downed female, and, after a while, she staggered to her feet.

On flights over the following days, they saw two bloody beds. The two wolves not only survived but started the island's third pack: Chippewa Harbor pack.

Five years later, the winter of 2005, East pack caught that same female away from her Chippewa pack mates and killed her. The wolves remembered. Anna couldn't help wondering what pack law the female had broken that had a statute of limitations that didn't run out in half a lifetime.

Watching the photographs click up on Ridley's computer screen, Anna had found it hard to believe these intelligent and phenomenally complex animals could be hunted down and butchered so that some fool could have the pelt and head for a hearth rug. But, then, human beings hunted down and butchered one another for stranger reasons.

Two miles up the trail, Robin turned the lead position over to Anna. The young biotech was finding it impossible to hike slowly enough not to kill her companions. Bob Menechinn, probably still smarting from having Ridley buckle him into his pack, pointing out he was the tallest and strongest and best able to protect and serve—an argument that basically boiled down to "has a penis"—wanted to go first. Anna stepped back, content to let him do whatever it was he needed to do.

The third time he led them off trail, she suggested he drop back. She added, "And make sure no one falls behind," to keep the machinery of the team oiled. She then set a pace that would challenge Katherine—they had a lot of miles to cover before the light went south—but, she hoped, would not exhaust her. Katherine was from a sedentary background and carrying a pack too heavy for her. Anna could hear what it was costing her in the push of her breath, yet Katherine never complained. Anna admired her will to endure.

Anna didn't complain either. Her body would complain enough in a day or so. Her pack weighed fifty-three pounds. She weighed one hundred eighteen. Muscle wasn't enough to offset the blunt trauma her joints suffered as she lifted her feet and gravity put them down. Hips, ankles and knees were going to ache like crazy. In her thirties, the aching was gone in less than a week; in her early forties, two. Now she could look forward to nearly a month of groaning every time she stood up.

Since the alternative was to not backpack, Anna gave it no more than a passing thought. What she did think about was her nose. Her nose had become increasingly important. By closing one eye, she could see the tip of it, but, up close, out of focus and viewed through eyes rimmed in frosted eyelashes, she couldn't tell if it was turning white and waxy or not. Frostbite could be gnawing her nose off her face and she wouldn't know it. With increasing frequency, she slid her hand out of its mitten and touched her nose, trying to see if it was warm or cold, if it had feeling, but her fingers were cold and she could never be sure, not positively sure, that her nose wasn't frozen. So, in one or five or ten minutes, she'd give in to the compulsion to go through the whole process again. She was driving herself nuts.

THEY HAD PASSED South Lake Desor and reached the halfway point between Windigo and Malone Bay when Anna suggested they set up camp. The short winter day was nearly gone, and Katherine was worn down to the point hypothermia could set in if she didn't get rest and hot food.

Anna chose a hill where the Greenstone curved gently around what, in summer, would be a tiny meadow waist-deep in wildflowers. In January, it was a flat, white disk of land with white spruce nibbling one edge. Niggardly snowflakes, desiccated by the cold, left a dusting less than half an inch deep. Yellow-and-gray stalks of long-dead grasses poked up through winter's thin skin like old men's chin stubble. White spruce crowded the edges of the open space in a curtain of black, color leached from the boughs by the day's eternal dusk.

Anna's pack was too heavy to shrug out of without the torque twisting her skeleton from its natural state. A kindly rock waited by the side of the trail as if for that very purpose. Sitting on the edge, she let it take the weight, unbuckled hip belt and chest strap and stepped free of the shoulder straps.

Tempting as it was to let the instrument of her torture topple to the ground, she lowered it as carefully as she could, then stood with a groan. Apparently her grace period had grown significantly shorter since last she'd carried an overloaded pack.

Robin followed suit and leaned her pack against Anna's. Bob and Katherine stood dumbly on the trail, two spavined nags asleep in the traces, too tired to think or move without direction. That Katherine did so didn't surprise Anna. She was nearly to that point herself. Only pride and the promise of hot drinks kept her moving. That Bob had reached paralysis wasn't what she'd expected.

Big game hunting, she remembered.

Big game hunters were not known for long, arduous treks carrying heavy loads. There were native peoples for that, and ATVs to carry the carcasses and the conquerors back to the lodge and the wet bar.

Uncharitable, she thought without caring.

She and Robin checked the camp area. As far as they could tell, the little meadow was devoid of hidden evils. Had it possessed a snake pit or hellmouth, Anna would have voted for stopping there anyway. Much as she would have loved feeling superior, she could identify with Katherine all too well. She doubted she had the wherewithal to take up the fifty-three pounds again.

They headed back to spark enough life in Bob and Katherine to get camp set up.

"Stop that," Robin said as they crunched south shoulder to shoulder.

"Stop what?" Not only was Anna not doing anything, she was too tired to think of doing anything.

"Stop touching your nose. You've been touching your nose all day. It's not frozen."

Sheepishly Anna put her hand back into her mitten.

"You're obsessing, aren't you?" Robin asked. The question wasn't judgmental. She asked it like a physician familiar with the symptoms of poison ivy might ask: "You itch, don't you?"

"I guess," Anna admitted. "I keep thinking it might be frostbitten."

"Mine's here," Robin said and tapped her mittened fingertips against her high cheekbones. "I can see them turning dead white out of the corners of my eyes and I picture myself with two holes in my face. Leave your nose alone. You touch it all the time like you've been doing and you'll irritate the skin to where it'll peel. Then you'll really think your nose is falling off."

Anna nodded and stifled the urge to check her nose one more time before she went on the wagon.

Because it was lighter to pack in and their body heat would be consolidated, the four of them were sharing a single dome tent. While Bob and Robin went about pitching it—a task that in moderate weather would have been the work of fifteen minutes but was roughly doubled by the clumsy mandate of winter—Anna settled Katherine on a sleeping pad, for the little insulation from the ground it afforded, and set about boiling water. In a pinch, snow could be melted to drink, but the process wasn't as easy as one might expect. On a freezing day, if snow were packed into a cooking pot and the stove turned up, the pot would burn before enough snow melted to even out the temperatures. Small portions had to be heated slowly till slush formed before the gas could be cranked up. Eating snow was a taboo of which even Anna, with her penchant for avoiding the cold at every opportunity, was cognizant. To convert snow to water robbed the body of so many calories that the heat transfer could lead to hypothermia.

Anna used the water she'd carried inside her parka next to her body. When it was hot enough to pass muster, she stirred in cocoa, twice as much as she would normally use. Backpacking in winter burned three times a person's baseline calorie requirements. To stay warm, a woman Anna's size needed nearly five thousand calories a day.

"Drink this," she said and handed a plastic insulated mug to Katherine. Metalware was useless when the cold got serious.

Katherine shook her head wearily. "No thank you. I just want to sit for a minute."

"You need to drink it," Anna told her. "It'll make you feel less tired."

Katherine took the cup between her mittened hands, and Anna was put in mind of a seal trying to clap with its flippers.

"Hold it tighter than you think you should," she cautioned.

Katherine began to sip.

Anna slipped off her mitten, stopped her hand halfway to her nose, then put the mitten back on.

The tent was up. Robin handed out hot drinks and candy and granola bars while Anna started another pot of water for their dinner of freeze-dried pasta, peas and chicken. Robin unwrapped a block of cheddar, cut it into four pieces and said: "Hors d'oeuvres."

They ate in silence as the light dimmed to nothing. The snow, mean and sparse all day, showed no sign of changing, and Anna was glad. On the Great Lakes, changes in the weather were usually heralded by high winds. The balmy sixteen degrees they'd enjoyed in the heat of the day was going with the light. Had there been wind, what scant warmth the food generated would have been quickly stripped away.

When it was too dark to see the cups in their hands, they put on headlamps and blinked at one another.

"The lights of Marfa," Anna said. Maybe the others knew of the Texas town, famous for its mysterious UFOs. Maybe they didn't. Nobody had enough energy to say either way and she hadn't the energy to volunteer an explanation.

Dishes were scraped and wiped. Washing was out of the question, but since no self-respecting bacteria could survive in such cold the health risks were minimal.

When they'd finished, Robin announced "Jumping jacks!" and Anna feared for the young woman's sanity.

The jumping jacks were to warm them before they crawled into their sleeping bags; calories and layers alone would not suffice.

"Pee," Robin suggested after they'd run around the tent and jumped like mad things for several minutes. "Your body has to work harder keeping extra fluid warm."

They separated in four directions and bared various parts of their anatomies to Jack Frost's kiss.

"No mosquitoes," Anna told herself, trying for a scrap of good cheer.

Then it was bedtime. It wasn't yet seven p.m.

Retiring was a miserable process. Food for the following day's lunch was retrieved from packs; full water bottles were dragged into the tent. To keep these precious items from freezing—or to thaw them out for the next day's use—meant they would spend the night in sleeping bags with the campers. The bags' stuff sacks were turned inside out and boots put in and stowed between the knees to keep from freezing overnight. Parkas and what outer garments wouldn't fit into the bags were piled on top. Thus cocooned, neck scarf and balaclava still on, Anna switched off her headlamp.

"Good night," she said to the black nest filled with her fellow larvae. Even to her own ears, her voice sounded so gloomy that she laughed.

"It'll be okay," Robin whispered. "You'll sleep."

Anna said nothing, but she took comfort.

"Leave your nose alone," Robin said.

The biotech was freakishly intuitive. Anna pulled her hand back under the covers.

"Don't breathe in your sleeping bags." Robin's voice filled the cramped space though she spoke quietly. "It'll make them damp and you'll freeze to death."

Anna quit breathing warm air into her bag.

"Will it happen soon?" she asked hopefully.

8

As challenging as it was to play the Pollyanna glad game with dirty boots and a hunk of half-eaten cheddar snugged between her thighs, Anna was glad for the physical demands of the past day. She was so thoroughly tired that she knew Robin was right; she would sleep. Eventually.

Darkness inside the tent was absolute, thick, pressing down on skin and mind the way it did underground: Carlsbad Caverns, Lechuguilla. Anna remembered that crushing blindness, air so hard with earth and ink that it choked her.

Claustrophobia tightened her skin and squeezed on her lungs. People, flesh, crowded in on her: breathing and rebreathing the air, snuffling, wriggling, adjusting; a filthy monstrous womb and the four of them still-born.

"Enough!" Anna hissed.

An elbow pressed into her side. Robin. Her feet were jostled. Bob. Bob Menechinn took up the lion's share of the space. This was almost balanced out by Katherine, who had squished herself into the corner between tent wall and floor until Robin made her move farther in, where it was marginally warmer.

Cold, as palpable and suffocating as the crowding night, negated the odors attendant on such a pile of humanity, but nothing could negate the ectoplasm—or whatever the stuff was called when people were not yet dead. The lives of the others fluttered and battered in the enclosure as if they were captive birds flying against the bars of a too-small cage.

On the best of nights, tents were not necessarily Anna's friend. She'd woken more than once to claw her way through the opening flap, past the rain fly, to see the sky and breathe new air. This was not the best of nights. Forcing her mind away from crazy places, she readjusted the bagged boots between her knees. Had they been left outside the tent, or even outside the bag, the boots would freeze, Robin said. There would be no getting them warm in the morning.

Who knew boots could freeze? Anna could have gone to her grave without knowing that.

Time passed. The parts of Anna touching the ground cloth numbed. She curled up as best she could with half of North Face's inventory jammed in the sleeping bag with her. The spectral birds began to settle. One by one, pairs of wings ceased to scrabble on her consciousness. The others slept. She tucked her hands into her armpits and tried to focus on a single point of white-hot light in her mind. Shirley MacLaine had done it with some guru or other and gotten so hot, she felt like she was burning up. It didn't do much for Anna. After a time, she drifted into a chilled coma full of aching dreams.

A nightmare wind gusted in her ear: "Anna! Anna, wake up!" The second hiss brought her out of her icy dreams. Her eyes opened to total blindness, her arms were pinioned to her sides and she couldn't feel her legs. She began to panic.

"Listen!"

Robin; it was Robin. Panic subsided. The biotech had hold of her shoulder. She was pressed so close Anna felt her breath on her cheek. It was warm. Anna remembered warm. "What—"

"Shh. Listen," came into her ear on a balmy breeze.

Anna listened.

Beyond the tent walls, the preternatural stillness of a night, frozen into a timeless instant, creaked in her ears. With a mittened paw, she shoved her hat up the better to hear. Silence, thick as an ice floe, pressed against her eardrums.

"There it is again."

Now Anna heard it. Into this concrete quiet came the pad of a soft-footed animal, an animal heavy enough that the snow squeaked under its weight. Faint and ethereal, the sound moved around the tent, then stopped.

Anna's ears rang with the emptiness and she tried to sit up, but Robin was on Anna's left arm and the detritus of Anna's life was tangled around her body.

A thin skritching sound scratched through the black air, clogging Anna's ears. Whatever it was pawed at the rain fly. "Fox," Anna whispered.

"No." Robin's hands clutched and her voice shook. The woman was terrified.

In her short life, Robin had probably hiked nearly as many miles as Anna had in her significantly longer existence. Robin had camped out in all seasons and all weathers. That this night she suddenly got the megrims chilled Anna as surely as the flatlined mercury. She tried to pat Robin reassuringly but ended up hitting her in the face with a great mittened hand. "Sorry," she murmured.

Robin caught her hand and held it. The pawing stopped. There was no *pad-pad-pad* of the animal, curiosity satisfied, going away. Anna could feel it outside the tent, feel it so close to them, had she been able to reach through tent and fly she could have touched it.

They waited.

It waited.

From the huge paw prints Robin had seen and the great curled beast Anna had glimpsed from the supercub, Anna's mind formed a vision, and a jolt of primitive fear shot through her as this monster of the id bared teeth the size of daggers and lunged for her throat. Anna shook the thought off. Claustrophobia and cold were getting to her.

"Shh. Shh. There!" Robin hissed.

Slightly above them came short, sharp whuffing breaths of a creature tasting the air the way a bear might, lips pulled back, nostrils flared, scenting danger or prey. Anna had never heard a canine do it; not fox or coyote or her old dog Taco. The whuffing stopped. The silence was deafening.

Anna pulled off her mittens and fumbled through the jetsam that had been extruded from her sleeping bag until her hand closed around her headlamp. With fingers already clumsy from their short sojourn away from her armpits, she pushed the ON button.

Bob and Katherine were as the dead; so worn out, neither the external noises nor the light woke them. Anna switched the lamp off. Instinct warned her not to make a magic lantern of the tent, with the four of them the shadow players.

Sudden and loud, clawing erupted near the tent flap and Anna squawked, not just at the noise but because Robin had shrieked in her ear.

"What is it?" came a frightened voice. Katherine had woken.

"Nothing," Anna lied. "Probably a squirrel. We may have pitched our tent on top of his dinner cache."

"Too big to be a squirrel," Robin murmured, and her grip on Anna's shoulder became painful. Fear is the most contagious of emotions, and Anna flashed on nights in high school, girls in their pajamas, tales of the escaped lunatic with a hook, the sudden frenzies of fear.

"Would you stop?" she snapped. "We're not doing

Night of the Grizzly here. And I'm not getting out of my sleeping bag and braving the arctic to chase away a fancy dress rat." She wasn't hoping to fool herself or the bio-tech; she was hoping to soothe Katherine and snap Robin out of whatever horrors she was entertaining before they all succumbed.

As if to deny the unflattering characterization, the snuffling came into the black of the tent followed by a low growl that brought up Anna's nape hairs.

"Oh my God," Katherine whispered. "Wolf."

A light beam, sudden and harsh, smacked Anna between the eyes, and a bear-sized shadow raked up toward the tent dome. She screamed like a teenager. So did Katherine and Robin.

Bob had regained consciousness.

"Shh," Robin hissed.

"Kill the light," Anna said. He didn't, but he turned its lens down in his lap.

"What—"

"Be quiet," Katherine said, the first show of rebellion against her professor Anna had noticed. "You'll scare it away."

Robin made a soft sound in her throat, a groan or muted cry. Anna tried to read her face in the dim light of Bob's smothered lamp, but the shadows of hat, scarf and long hair effectively screened her.

Bob was easy to read. His head probably wasn't any bigger than a normal human being's—unless one was speaking metaphorically—but his face appeared immense, meaty, slabs of cheek and jowl dwarfing eyes, nose and mouth. On this wide canvas, fear was clearly writ. The big game hunter didn't like being hunted.

"What's it after?" he asked. He'd meant to whisper, but the words came out in a squeak.

"Food," Robin replied succinctly.

Anna couldn't argue. The chocolate and cheese and other high-fat, high-sugar, high-protein items they'd tucked into bed with them might have been rendered odorless to human noses, but to a wolf they would smell like a deli at lunchtime. For decades, humans and wolves had lived separate lives on the small island. Though ISRO was only forty-two miles long, and trails raked down both sides of her spine and crisscrossed the many lakes and coves, wolf sightings weren't common. Wolves were a private people, a quiet, watchful people. Undoubtedly the frequency of wolves seeing visitors vastly outnumbered that of visitors seeing wolves.

In recent years, that had begun to change. A wolf had been seen hanging around a campground in Rock Harbor on several occasions. A dead wolf washed up on shore in Robinson Bay, apparently drowned. People reported seeing wolves near the lean-tos in Washington Harbor. The wonder of this was that it hadn't happened long ago. Wild animals quickly became habituated to humans when food was involved.

"We're food," Robin said, as if reading Anna's thoughts.

Anna could have smacked her. "Don't be an idiot. When was the last time a wolf ate anybody?" she demanded.

Robin looked slightly cowed, but she said: "Maybe this isn't a regular wolf."

The animal, quiet since Bob had come to life, began frenzied digging, claws scraping loud against the fabric of the tent and the frozen earth.

Bob yelped. Robin, still pressed to Anna's side, screamed. Bob jerked his lamp from his down bag and shined it frantically around the tent walls, a wild, dizzying rush of light. Anna felt as if she was falling into a vortex of hysteria.

"My God," Katherine cried. She grabbed Bob's wrist and steadied the light on a section of tent opposite the entrance flap. The fabric was pounding in and out as the animal's claws raked against it. Big paws. Bigger than a man's fist, and high up the tent wall. The urgent whine of a carnivore closing on its quarry cut through the rapid clawing, then a growl from deep in the chest; the growl of a dog who does not bark but bites.

"God damn," Anna breathed. Her heart thudded against her rib cage, skin prickled, adrenaline poured into her till she was strung out with it. *Night of the Grizzly* no longer seemed so far-fetched. Neither did *The Haunting of Hill House*.

The pawing stopped as abruptly as it had begun. Paws padded away.

Then nothing.

Silence was so complete, Anna realized, not only had the nocturnal intruder ceased its onslaught but the four of them had pretty much stopped breathing. Her hand followed, Anna and Robin feeling there'd been too much sharing, even if they had no idea what had been shared.

"Ketamine doesn't depress the central nervous system," Robin started again. "That's why it's good with animals. They're pretty fragile. The xylazine works as well and wears off quicker, something you need to pay attention to when you're letting them go again."

"Are the trap tranquilizing devices already charged or do we need to charge them?" Anna asked.

"The TTDs are filled with six hundred milligrams of the propriopromazine. All you have to do is clamp it on one side of the jaws. First thing a wolf will do is try and bite the trap. I've never seen a TTD that wasn't destroyed. They always get some tranquilizer into them, but we've found them both out cold and awake and alert. Depends."

Attached to each trap was eight feet of kinkless chain with a vegetation drag on the end that looked like a miniature boat anchor. The drag was amazingly efficient at catching on any bit of vegetation to keep the animal from getting very far while giving it freedom of motion, another stress reducer. Near the drag, affixed to the chain, was a seven-inch-long silver cylinder with a rubber-coated antenna. This was a motion-activated radio transmitter. The metal cylinder protected it from being chewed. When the wolf—or occasionally a marauding fox—pulled on the chain, a receiver in the cabin at Malone Bay would beep to let the trappers know something was on their line and where. In summer, this allowed the researchers to find the wolf before a hapless was cramping. She was hanging on to Robin as tightly as Robin was holding on to her.

She laughed shakily. "Whoa! That was—"

"Shut up," Bob cried and began swinging the head-lamp, clutched in both hands, in crazy patterns, as if the circle of light was an eye through which he could see outside the tent. Shadows rushed and retreated till the space seemed full not only of human bodies and gear but a host of unquiet spirits.

"Stop it!" Anna ordered.

"It's gone, Bob," Katherine said softly.

"Shut up," Bob snarled.

"It's gone," Anna said, forcing her voice to the light and conversational. She found her lamp, turned it on and shined it in Bob's eyes to get his attention. White showed around the irises, and there was a thin sheen of sweat on his upper lip. His fear was phobic; pure terror. The kind that runs amok. "We're okay," Anna said, not sure it was true. She, too, was scared, but she wasn't sure whether it was of the creature outside or that Bob would begin throwing himself around like a panicked bull in a china shop, where her bones took the place of the porcelain.

"Let's all settle down," she said reasonably.

"You fucking settle down," Bob snarled. "You fucking *settle down*! Ridley sends us out to fucking freeze to death because he's bred some freak wolf/dog hybrid that's ripping the shit out of our goddam tent—"

"It's okay, Bob. There's nothing to be scared—"

Katherine was begging, reaching out to touch the back of his hand.

He batted her away and yelled: "Keep your hands off me, you fucking cunt."

"That's enough," Anna ordered sharply. "It's gone. We're all right. Now we sleep." Anger had taken up the space where fear had been.

Bob's eyes cleared marginally. He was coming back to himself from a hunt where he was the trophy animal, but the bone-deep horror remained. Anna saw it and she snorted; a stiff sniff of air through nostrils pinched with cold. Had she been less tired, less chilled, less freaked out by the bizarre behavior of the animal, she would have been able to stop herself. As it was, she saw his fear, and he saw her contempt for it. They all saw it.

As she lay down and turned off her lamp, she knew that was something a guy like Bob Menechinn would never forgive them for. Lying in the frigid dark, she could feel the others listening. She could smell the fear sweat from Bob.

The animal did not come back. And none of them slept.

9

Morning did not come until eight twenty-seven a.m. By then, Anna was desperate to get out of the sack she shared with groceries and laundry. The tent had become intolerable. If she didn't slip out through the zippered fly, she knew she'd claw her way out with greater determination than the wolf had tried to claw his way in. With the first bare hint of gray, she was pulling on socks and boots and layers, not much caring who she jostled or kicked in the process. Their combined respirations had rimed the inside of the tent with ice. Anna's thrashing loosed a tiny avalanche down on her tent mates. She was not sorry.

Quick as Anna was, Robin was quicker. Before Anna'd laced up, the biotech was outside, her mukluks squeaking on the snow as she retraced the path of their visitor. Like a grouchy bear, Anna lumbered from the tent and stood on her hind legs to join her. The light was lousy: dreary, gray-white and gritty; a carbon copy of the day before.

The light would be lousy till it was gone, and lousy the day after that and the week after that, till she got back to the high-country winter in the Rockies or the sweet attempt at winter in Paul's backyard in Mississippi.

"Think happy little thoughts," she sang mockingly under her breath. Discipline would have to take the place of optimism till her body temperature was a few degrees above that of the average corpse.

"Oh, goodie!" Anna heard Robin exclaim.

Scat. The woman had found scat. There was only one sample, and it was not particularly impressive in size or texture that Anna could see, but Robin bagged it happily.

"Not much for tracks," the biotech said as she casually stuck the baggie into her jacket pocket.

They tried the trick of shining their headlamps low and laterally to create a false sun, but Robin and Bob had done a terrific job of stomping around when they'd pitched the tent, and the four of them had continued the stomping with jumping jacks, cavorting to warm up before bed and trips later to answer the call of nature.

If there were wolf prints, they were lost in the crusted mishmash of snow and dead grasses. No prints led in or out of the clearing across the unmarked snow. The animal had probably come into the camp from the trail as they had. Given the choice, wild animals—bears, cougars, foxes, wolves, deer—preferred improved trails just as people did, and for the same reasons.

In the area where the digging had occurred, they found a partial print. Had they not already ruled out foxes in their minds, the print would have. Foxes had tiny catlike feet. The snow and earth had been scored, and the wall of the tent had stress lines running through the fabric where claws had raked it repeatedly.

"Look at that," Robin said. There was no fear in her this morning; she was all business and curiosity. In this competent woman, Anna had trouble finding the squeaky, shrieky teenager of the previous night. "Look at these marks." Robin pointed with her lamp. The light was dirty gold on the gray snow.

Anna squatted down and looked where Robin indicated. To one side of the digging were two clear claw marks, probably made by the first and second digits of the animal's left front paw. The marks were parallel and two inches apart.

"The thing must have been a monster," Robin said. There was a quality to the biotech's voice Anna couldn't place, self-consciousness maybe, like a bad actor pretending to be brave or a brave person trying to empathize with the fear of others. Anna didn't like it.

"This could just as easily have been made by two passes of a real-sized wolf as one pass by a gigantic wolf," she said repressively. Remembering the wild-eyed panic in Menechinn's face the previous night, she scuffed the marks out with the toe of her boot.

"If something's dangerous, don't the others have a right to know?" Robin asked.

"No."

HOT DRINKS AND INSTANT OATMEAL—cold as dirt by the last spoonful—duly consumed, they broke camp. It fell naturally to Anna to take the lead, but before she could set foot on the trail Bob shoved past her. His heavy pack clipped hers and she staggered as her center of gravity shifted. But for Robin's supporting arm, she would have fallen.

He has to reassert his masculinity, she thought without a shred of sympathy. She didn't challenge him; Anna never felt the need to reassert hers.

Despite being condemned to watching Menechinn's butt, after a mile or so on the trail she felt immeasurably better. There was nothing like spending the night in a deep freeze with one's food while unknown forces contemplated one for its own supper to make a woman appreciate the little things. It was good to be upright and moving. It was good to be hiking downhill instead of up. It was good to be carrying three more meals in her stomach instead of on her back. It was heaven to know she'd be spending the coming night in the cabin at Malone Bay, with a fire in the woodstove; an outhouse with a warmed seat, rather than a snow-covered log, for the less glamorous moments of life.

In an embarrassment of riches, the overcast cleared, and, though they paid for it with a drop in temperature, seeing the sun's pale, cheerful face and the blue sky lightened everyone's mood.

Everyone but Bob. Menechinn had returned to his customary jocularity, but there was a razor-edge to his comments: jokes that weren't jokes and double entendres whose single meanings were hard to pretend missing. Katherine took the brunt of it, and Anna felt sorry for her. She was coming rather to like Katherine. It occurred to her to deflect Menechinn's venom onto herself to give the researcher a rest, but she decided against it. Katherine didn't let it roll off her back exactly, but she seemed accustomed to the abuse and handled it better than Anna would have. He made the occasional sideways gibe at Anna, but nothing she couldn't ignore. Fortunately he left Robin alone.

The biotech was a woman of steel; Anna suspected that, if pressed, Robin might leap a tall building in a single bound. Yet her years on the road, competing in countries where she had no one but her coaches and teammates, had left her vulnerable and oddly innocent, a bit of a stranger in a strange land.

Robin might have been able to withstand Menechinn's unsubtle retribution for what they'd witnessed, but Anna knew for a fact that she wouldn't have been able to withstand watching it happen.

EMASCULATION RECOVERY wasn't swift, but by lunch Bob seemed over the worst of it. He quit sniping at his graduate assistant and tied her sleeping bag to the top of his already-overloaded pack. Anna guessed it was his way of making amends and considered dumping hers and Robin's on him as well; see how much the bastard could carry. Had the sun not been out, she might have done it. As it was, she was feeling magnanimous.

Katherine rallied somewhat with the lighter load, both on her back and her psyche, but it didn't last. Anna could tell her joints were causing her pain by the way she pulled on the pack's shoulder straps and tried to ease her steps. Anna's pack was grinding her bones as well, but, like Lawrence of Arabia—at least in the version with Peter O'Toole—she felt the pain but had learned not to mind.

AT THREE THAT AFTERNOON, they reached the rise above Malone Bay. The sun was already close to the horizon and so far to the south that the bay was in shadow. Snow, deeper here by several inches than on the other side of the ridge, was dyed the same battleship gray as the water of Lake Superior, lying cold and still beyond the bay's straitjacket of ice. The sky's winter coat of pale blue had faded till it seemed but a thin sheet of tinted glass between the Earth and whatever lay beyond.

In this colorless stillness were two cacophonous spots of color. On the ice of the bay, a few hundred yards from the dock, was Jonah's red-and-white airplane, her raucous orange down comforter wrapped around engine and cowling, and, on the tiny porch of the cabin, the bright red blade of a snow shovel leaning against the railing.

Blessed as it was by a thick curl of lavender smoke issuing from the stovepipe, the cabin, scarcely bigger and slightly less ornate than a closet in a 1950s tract house, struck Anna as utterly charming. As they started down the gentle grade, the figure of Jonah Schumann emerged from the door and started up the trail.

Jonah met up with them and gallantly offered to take Katherine's pack for the last mile. Anna hoped Katherine would accept and was impressed when she didn't. The old pilot further wormed his way into Anna's affections by telling them he'd flown in canned food, a box of wine, pasta and other delicacies to round out what would have been a bleak diet had they had to subsist on what they'd been able to carry in on their backs.

Adam, who'd cadged a ride on this mission of mercy, had hot Ovaltine waiting when they reached the cabin.

Anna was wearier than she'd bargained on. *The cold*, she told herself as Adam helped her off with her pack.

"Jesus!" he exclaimed as the weight hit him. "Are you crazy or what? I don't carry a pack this heavy. Holy smoke! Iron Woman." He pinched her upper arm, and Anna was gratified.

"Fifty-three pounds," she wanted to say, but boasting had a way of canceling out achievement, and, besides, she was too tired to talk. "Help Katherine," she managed. The cabin was so tiny, six people, four of them in backpacks, were like great Herefords in a pen made for lambs. She had to mill her way past Adam and Katherine to find a place to sit, then she was squeezed into a small straight-backed chair between a doll-sized table and a gas hot-water heater. Bob brushed his butt—a butt Anna had gotten to know far too well over the past nine miles—across her face to help Robin off with her pack. Anna might have taken petty revenge with a two-tined meat fork the summer ranger had left behind, but the offending portion of his anatomy was encased in too many layers for penetration.

Too tired to focus, she let her body sag and her mind slide inward. After Jonah and Adam departed, she would try to get her boots off. With them gone, there might be room enough to bend over.

Above her, the life of the herd went on. Bob was behind Robin, holding on to her shoulder straps as she fumbled with the buckles. "Here, let me help with those," he said warmly and started to reach around her and the pack in a Kodiak-sized bear hug.

"Let me," Anna said acidly and was about to contemplate the effort of rising when Adam turned from where he'd stowed Katherine's pack against wall and bunk and stowed Katherine, as limp looking as Anna felt, on top of it.

"I got it," he said.

Bob snorted.

"Bob, could you help me?" Katherine's voice was plaintive, with a thread of something sharper running beneath—anger or love, maybe both. Bob shouldered his way to where his assistant sat, crumpled.

Anna intended to sit back down but realized she'd never made it to her feet. The mere thought of it had tapped her last reserves. She hoped Robin had the strength and patience to spoon-feed her the remainder of her required five thousand calories. Lifting an eating utensil might be beyond her powers.

Calflike in the corral, she watched dumbly as Adam undid the frozen buckles on Robin's harness. There was definite byplay between the two of them, secret looks and small, quickly extinguished smiles, and Anna wondered if Robin's boyfriend—Gavin or Galen or whatever—was on his way out. Seasonal Park Service life was hard on relationships. Permanent Park Service life wasn't much better.

Life in general was hell on relationships, Anna thought tiredly. She wished Paul was there, wished she was in Natchez. How hard would it be? She could give up rangering—all it seemed to get her was wrecked knee joints and scars—and become a Mississippi housewife. Paul was an Episcopal priest when he wasn't being the sheriff of Adams County. Anna could be a church lady. She liked hats. Anyway, she liked her NPS Stetson well enough. If she believed in God, it would be doable.

Damn.

There was always a catch.

Jonah excused himself to check on the weather. Adam and Robin left shortly thereafter. Bob went out to bring firewood and stack it near the door. Finally there was room to move. Anna roused herself to a little house-keeping, the only kind she was much good at: setting up camp. She began efficiently storing their mountains of gear. In summer, extraneous items could be cached out of doors. In January, anything they wanted the use of, including the wolf traps, had to be kept inside the cabin. The traps had been designed for all weathers. It wouldn't have hurt their form or function to be tossed out in the snow, but working with them would be harder if the metal was cold enough to burn skin.

"Can I do anything to help?" Katherine asked.

Anna had forgotten she was there. "Can you even move after the last two days?" she asked.

Katherine laughed and shook her head. "Surely there's something I can do."

"There's not room to do it," Anna said. She almost added "How are you doing? Are you holding up?" but caught herself in time. Concern and condescension were hard to tell apart, and Katherine's brain was probably as tired as her body. Instead she said: "We won't have to pack like this again. We couldn't count on the weather breaking, so we hauled the traps in. If the weather's too bad for Jonah to pick us up, we'll leave them here." She shot a malevolent glance at the internal-frame pack hanging on the wall at the foot of the bunks. "I doubt if I could do it again. That pack nearly killed me."

She'd said it to make Katherine feel better, but it might be true. She might not be able to take that kind of weight again for a while. The previous season, when she'd been on a twenty-one-day fire assignment in the mountains east of Boise, Idaho, she'd noticed that the difference between the old firefighters and the young ones wasn't in strength or endurance. It was in recovery time. The old guys, the firefighters over forty, were as strong as the kids. She and the others could lift and run and dig with the best of them. But they wore down. The kids were stronger after three weeks of hard physical labor. The grown-ups were just bone tired.

With much stomping, Jonah opened the door and leaned in. "Seen Adam?" he asked. "Weather's souring. We've got to roll."

"I thought he was with you," Anna said.

"He's with Robin," Jonah replied, sounding vaguely ominous. Anna couldn't tell if he was jealous or just worried about getting the supercub up before they got weathered in.

Six bodies crammed in the tiny cabin overnight.

"I'll help you look," she said, grabbed up her parka and shoved her feet in her boots. She didn't bother with balaclava and mittens. She had no intention of being out that long.

The light had dimmed from its paltry glory. A tidal wave of gray was rolling toward shore from the northwest. Above it was the clear silver-blue sky, but that was going to change. Wind was driving the clouds; they would have snow.

"Adam!" Jonah yelled.

Anna walked toward the outhouse. Bob met her carrying an armload of wood for the stove. "Have you seen Adam and Robin?" she demanded.

"He's old enough to be her father," he said.

Anna gave him a hard look. "So are you. Have you seen them?"

Before he could answer, the two missing persons emerged from behind the cabin. They had the excited air of lovers, sharing secret trysts. Or, more apt, a rag-man and tinker, luring the lovely farm girl to sin and degradation. Adam's affectation of a parka and ski pants worn and stained and patched with duct tape in half a dozen places leant his otherwise-honest-looking self a disreputable air.

"God dammit, Adam," Jonah groused. "I'm taking off as soon as I get her fired up. Either you're buckled in or you're staying here." The pilot strode off toward the lake and his lady. Adam started after him.

"Your pack," Anna called. She reached inside the cabin door and snatched up the maintenance man's day pack. "Jesus!" she exclaimed as the weight hit her sore shoulders. "What have you got in here anyway?"

"Give that to me," he demanded harshly.

Wordlessly, Anna handed it over.

"Books," he said and smiled sheepishly. "We'll make another run with goodies if we can," he said. "Hang in there."

With those reassuring words, he started down the slight grade. The supercub's engine purred to life, and he broke into a run, his long legs eating up the distance. Feeling abandoned in an arctic wilderness, Anna watched till he climbed through the clamshell doors.

Adam was up to something. Maybe that something was a twenty-four-year-old biotech. Whatever it was, it bore watching.

10

Despite the tight quarters and the snapping and snarling of animals and humans over the past twenty-four hours, once Adam and Jonah were gone Anna, Katherine, Robin and even Bob began to enjoy one another's company. A night of shared danger—or perceived danger—a hard hike well done, and the reward of heat and food at the end, bonded them as nights in a bunkhouse could never do.

Adding to the general sense of well-being was what Anna's District Ranger in Mesa Verde had liked to call the idiot's delight aspect of camping: after hitting oneself over the head with a two-by-four, it felt so good to stop.

Bob cooked. The big bearish man put on an apron left by a summer seasonal with a taste for frills and bows. Ruffled pinafore straps over his thick shoulders, he began cutting the onions Jonah had brought. His size dwarfed the two-burner stove, his hands made the knife look like a toy and the sash of the apron barely reached around him, but he looked more at ease than Anna had ever seen him. It was as if in a kitchen—even such a kitchen as the backcountry cabin afforded—he felt completely in control, full of confidence, the genuine kind that allows a man generosity of spirit because he needn't constantly put others down or puff himself up to guarantee his place in the pecking order.

As he changed, Katherine changed. She let down her guard. If Bob's armor was arrogance, Katherine's was meekness. Without it hiding her like a translucent burka, she shined. Not a lot, not a shooting star, but she exhibited a sense of humor with a black streak Anna enjoyed. Almost, almost, if she squinted and tilted her head to one side, Anna could see what brought graduate student and professor into a relationship. There was no doubt in her mind that they were in a relationship—or had been—and it was more than merely academics.

By the time they turned out the hurricane lantern to sleep—Anna on the top bunk, Katherine on the bottom, Robin and Bob on the floor—Anna was feeling downright warm and fuzzy.

Maintained by coffee and a breakfast that didn't ice up on the spoon, the camaraderie survived the morning.

Carrying four traps—forty pounds—Anna felt strong and ready as she shouldered her pack after breakfast.

Bob offered to carry Katherine's traps for her, but apparently Katherine felt the joy of not being crippled from the day before as well and insisted on taking her share.

The storm Jonah and the supercub fled the previous afternoon squatted on Malone Bay, settling slate-colored skirts in the hollows and down the hillsides. Three inches of snow had fallen during the night, and more whirled on a scouring wind that erased the track of the cub's skis across the harbor ice and the footprints of the Winter Study team. In the isolated places of the world, nature still retained the power to erase human lives as easily as she did the prints of their shoes. The feeling gave Anna hope that mankind wouldn't sound the earth's death knell quite yet, that Mother Nature wouldn't go quietly and she would take as many of the enemy with her as she could.

Ice on Siskiwit Lake was eight to nine inches thick and blown clear of snow in many places. Wind from the northwest scudded over the surface of the lake with razor-blade cold. The snow had stopped, but the clouds looked heavy with more. A renegade flurry of fat flakes leaped and soared on the gusts of wind, in no hurry to reach the earth. These were not the mean-spirited snowflakes, fine as beach sand in the teeth, that scathed the east end of the island but the lacy flakes that adorned Christmas cards. Their playful beauty made the cold seem less personal. Less deadly. It was a comforting illusion.

Where the wind cleared it, the ice was slick and black.

Anna could see bubbles and cracks that ran like zigzagging white cliffs beneath the surface.

"Leave your nose alone," Robin said.

"What about the cracks?" Anna asked, slipping her hand back in its mitten. She thought she'd gotten past the nose thing.

"There are always cracks," Robin said. "It usually doesn't mean anything. Ice is in flux, expanding and contracting. The cracks are stress fractures."

Usually doesn't mean anything. Anna was only slightly reassured.

Halfway to Ryan Island, famous for being the biggest island in the biggest lake on the biggest island in the biggest lake in the world but still only a froth of evergreens and rocks, they came to the remains of the moose kill that Jonah and Anna had watched from the air several days before. The carcass had been picked clean. What scraps of meat still clung to the ripped hide were being worked on by two ravens. They eyed the human interlopers critically, then, unimpressed, turned back to their work.

The skeleton had been gnawed. One femur and both front leg bones were gone entirely. Skull and antlers had been dragged away from the body and cleaned of meat. Anna two-stepped over to take a closer look. Robin slid gracefully up beside her.

"Hard winter for everybody. Lookie." The biotech pointed, her mittened hand bright and indicative like a Lilliputian tetrahedron indicating wind direction. "The antlers have been nibbled. There's little nutritional value in an antler. Eating it is the animal world's equivalent of boiling shoe leather for supper. Or eating fried pork rinds."

Bob and Katherine caught up with them. Katherine's oversized glasses, perennially steamed, gave her a blind and helpless aspect, but she was a natural on the ice. Her shuffling skate was a match for Robin's. Bob had more trouble. "Pig on roller skates" came to mind, but, still pleasantly full of the breakfast he'd cooked, Anna said nothing.

"Are we going to set traps here?" he asked, looking around as if another area of ice would be different, better, than the one on which they stood.

"Not here," Robin said, and her mouth crimped in a tight line.

Anna didn't so much read her thoughts as share them. Bob knew nothing about trapping, or about wolves. He knew nothing about Isle Royale. Yet he would decide if the study would continue. Only FEMA had proven more inept and corrupt than Homeland Security.

"George W. Bush is the Antichrist," Anna said, apparently apropos of nothing. Leaving her companions to think she suffered from political Tourette's syndrome, she shuffled off.

At the east end of Siskiwit, where the short section of trail from Siskiwit to Intermediate Lake began, Robin stopped. "We start here," she said.

The trapline Ridley had outlined ran from the western shore of Siskiwit, embraced Intermediate, then ran on to Lake Richie and ended at Moskey Basin, about

five miles total. The lakes between Siskiwit and Moskey
Basin were small, part of a scattering of puddles that
dribbled across the island, from north to south, where
the retreating glacier had gouged more deeply. The trapline would cover lakes, land, developed trails and open
runs. Used by both East and Chippewa packs, they would
have a shot at trapping wolves from more than one
pack.

Two wolves in East pack and three of the known
seven in Chippewa pack had been radio-collared previ-
ously. Unless there was a force on the island so powerful
it could alter existing DNA in a living wolf, they could
be ruled out as carriers of the foreign DNA. If they
were caught again, the opportunity would be taken to
check them for parvovirus, weight, general health issues
and statistical information. One of the inestimable val-
ues of the wolf/moose study was that it had collected
mammoth amounts of such data over a long period.
Longevity had been important in earlier times, but,
with the advent of computers, massive quantities of information could be processed in ever-more-illuminating
ways.

Anna had experience with foothold traps but hadn't
used one in years. Katherine was familiar only with old
barrel-type live traps. Bob knew nothing about either.

In her quiet, pleasant voice, Robin explained each step
of the process as she set the first trap. Foothold traps
resembled old-fashioned leghold traps, the spring-loaded
steel jaws with jagged teeth that were famous for causing

animals to chew their feet off to free themselves. The foothold was designed to avoid harming the wolves. The jaws were shallower and had small steel knobs in place of the teeth. The knobs were placed so that when the animal stepped down on the plate and sprung the trap, they would clamp above and between the toe joints to hold the foot fast without tearing the skin or breaking bones. Each trap was supplied with a tranquilizer device, a black rubber nipple two inches long and loaded with oral tranquilizer. The drug was to calm them, to keep them from harming themselves or the trappers, but it was an inexact science. It was impossible to tell how much of the sedative would actually get into the animal's system.

"What drug do you use?" Bob asked.

"Propriopromazine," Robin replied. "It usually keeps them sedated till we get to them. Then we give a mix of ketamine and xylazine to knock them out."

"Ketamine. That's the hallucinogenic that can cause amnesia," Bob said.

"You've worked with ketamine?" Robin asked.

"Have we ever used ketamine?" he asked Katherine.

She turned away as if the question brought up a shameful failure. "I can't remember," she mumbled, and Bob laughed.

"That's what the stuff is known for."

He winked at his assistant. Her face was blank, dead, as if at a secret joke between old lovers, a joke only one of them still thinks is funny. A moment of awkward silence

tourist did—and before the sedative wore off. In winter, it served a more important purpose; sedated, the wolf could lose toes to frostbite or even freeze to death if left too long in a trap.

Robin opened the metal jaws and set the pressure plate, then packed trap and paraphernalia in snow till it was no longer visible. "This trap probably won't fool anybody," she said as she stood and addressed her audience. "There are too many of us and we've been here too long being stinky. The wolves will smell a rat. After you all move away, I'll sprinkle around some clean snow and that might help. It's best to get in and out with the least interruption of the space as possible.

"Do you want me to set the next one?" she asked Anna.

"No. It's coming back to me. I think I'm good."

"Okay." Robin pulled a topographical map from her pack and folded it so the area where they were was uppermost. "You and Bob take the western side of Intermediate. Katherine and I will go around to the east. Lay the first trap here." She pointed to where the trail split on the shore of Intermediate Lake to embrace the perimeter. "When you get to where this little triangle of land sticks out into the water—the ice—you need to cross right here." Robin took a mitten off to better point at the narrow bay where an isthmus curved back toward the main shore. "Put a trap there."

"Why there?" Anna asked. It seemed out of sync with the pattern of following improved trails that Ridley had laid out.

"The wolves have been known to den up on that triangle of land." Robin's voice tightened as if Anna challenged her authority.

"Got it," Anna said.

"Bob, you go with Anna. Katherine, come with me." Anna suspected Bob would rather have learned the art of livetrapping from the lovely young biotech than the crusty old ranger, but life was full of disappointments.

"Help me with my pack," she said. Apparently not too put out at drawing the short straw, Bob complied.

Anna leading, they reached the fork in the trail where Robin had told them to place the first trap. Snow was falling more thickly than it had been, but the wind let up, and Anna was satisfied with the compromise. Given her familiarity with ISRO—and the fact they'd be following lakeshores most of the day—there was little danger of getting lost regardless of how bad the visibility, and snow was warmer than wind.

Setting the trap was harder than Anna remembered. Cold—and the gear needed to protect from the cold—made simple tasks difficult. She had on gloves, but without mittens over them, and handling freezing steel, her fingers were awkward. Having laid the trap on the ground, Anna put a foot on each of the springs to depress them, then pulled the jaws of the trap open. Her left boot slipped and the jaws snapped shut viciously, catching a pinch of glove and skin. Anna yelped as if a finger had been bitten off. She was positive the pinch hurt far worse than it would have had there been a speck

of sympathetic kindness in the elements and half remembered a short story about how wounds festered and
rotted in the arctic. Having pulled off the scant protection of the glove, she surveyed the damage. No blood.
She would live.

Bob turned out to be deft with his hands. Given the
thickness of his fingers, it was a pleasant surprise. He
uncoiled the chain and buried it as neatly as Anna could
have managed. He attached the TTD and stayed out of
the way while she did her best to rehabilitate the area
before they left. And he had insisted that this, the first trap
set, be one that she carried, a ten-pound weight lifted
from her shoulders. All in all, the man was beginning to
ingratiate himself.

The cynical core of her suspected Dr. Menechinn
wasn't ingratiating himself so much as Dr. Jekyll was in
the ascendant. She had seen too much of Mr. Hyde to
expect Bob's goodness and light to last. In the mean-
time, she was only too happy to let him carry heavy objects.

It had taken them twice as long to set the trap as it
had taken Robin, and twice as long again as it would
have taken Anna in the summer. By the time they finished, it was nearly noon. With truncated days and low-
ering clouds, Anna doubted she and Bob would manage
to set all of the remaining traps before they ran out of
light.

"There's where we're going," she said as they packed
up and pointed to a hump of land beyond which lay the
triangular isthmus that marked where the next foothold

trap was to be laid. Intermediate had not been blown clear of snow and the walking was easier. The ice was also considerably thinner than Siskiwit. Ice was often untrustworthy near shoreline and Intermediate was all shoreline.

Long habit of tracking kept Anna's eyes on the ground as they worked their way across the western third of the lake. Fresh snow created a clean palette for the day's news, but creatures were not doing a great deal of stirring. Gusting winds, flurries of snow and the promise of more to come kept them snug in nests and burrows. Anna saw the scratching of small birds and a litter of seed coverings from a cache that had been found or recovered by a squirrel. On a slope running down to the lake from a low rise, she noticed what looked to be the tracks of saucer sleds, the kind used by little kids. It took her a minute to refocus from the image of tots in pointed hoods. Then she laughed. "Otters," she told Bob. "They like to slide in the snow. Look where they've run up the hill just for the fun of sliding down again."

"In winter?" he asked.

"In winter," she assured him. "The park heals in the winter, when people aren't here." She figured she might as well get in a plug for keeping ISRO closed from October to May.

Bob grunted.

The isthmus, comprised of volcanic rock surrounded in glacial rubble, rose from the ice in ragged chunks of stone dusted with white. Desperate earth-starved trees poked skeletal branches through the snow cover, black arthritic fingers reaching for a sky that was the same color as the grave they sank their roots in. Wind bared the rock in places, exposing the tops of granite-colored boulders, till the land resembled a boneyard for formless beasts that had come there to die. Out from the steep shore, ice piled up, six-inch slabs where the water of the lake had risen and receded, refreezing each time.

Using hands and feet, Anna scrambled toward what passed for dry land. Despite the lightened pack, it was hard to keep her balance. A moose had managed it; there were a tangle of hoofprints half filled in with snow. Anna found her center of gravity and a flat place to stand, then turned and watched Bob making his way over the broken ice field. "Take it slow," she warned.

"Umph."

"The next trap we set will be one of yours," she promised as he tottered and fell to one knee.

"God damn!"

He stayed where he was, his backpack rounding up like the hump of a camel kneeling to let a rider mount.

"You okay?"

"My knee," he huffed, but he got himself upright and crossed the rest of the broken ice without incident.

"You're limping," she accused. It was not good to let oneself get injured in the wilderness in the winter.

"It's a bad knee," he said. "How many more traps do we have to set?"

Bob sounded like a little boy who couldn't add and was whining about it. So much for Dr. Jekyll.

"A couple more." Anna started up through the rocks. Abruptly she stopped. In the lee of one of the boulders, half buried in the deeper tracks of the moose, was the print of a wolf's paw.

Maybe.

With the snow drifted in, it was hard to tell, but it was larger than fox and smaller than moose. In spring, she might have assumed it was a calf. Not in January.

"We're in the right neighborhood," she said. Bob limped up and looked at the tracks. "The one on the left," she said. "Wolf, I bet."

"Big." A trace of the fear she'd seen and heard the night they'd been called upon by the wild was in his voice.

The print was beyond big; it was monstrous. "Hard to tell," Anna said, images of Bob, wild-eyed, lamp beam striping the tent walls, transposing over him, charging off through the falling snow, arms waving wildly, foot traps clattering. "Once the wind and snow and drift start, animal tracks can be made to look like almost anything."

"It's crazy to be out here without a rifle," Bob said. He looked around like a virgin in a haunted house. What good humor survived the knee hitting the ice was gone from his face. Anna wished she had an apron or a spatula or some other homey kitchen utensil with which to comfort him. "What are you making us for supper?" she asked to keep his mind busy, then ignored him while he answered.

There hadn't been any wolf tracks on the lake. She

looked at the boulder head high to her left. A furrow cut the snow where something had slid or fallen. The wolf had come down off the rock, possibly following the moose. There was just the single print; it had been traveling alone. The animal that had come to their tent had traveled alone.

"Okay," Anna said. "Let's follow our boy here."

"Are you nuts?" Bob swallowed his fear, but it soured him. "We're losing the light. Let's head back," he said peremptorily.

"No we're not. It's one o'clock, the heat of the day." She could have been more politic, but her mind was taken up with tracking. Moose prints were easy, dimples in the snow eight to ten inches across in two parallel lines. Paw prints were harder, especially without good light. Anna blinked at the unyielding sky, weeping snow static on a gray background. Rocks crowded in, sucking up what little illumination leaked through from a sun gone AWOL.

"It's like living in an old black-and-white TV with bad reception," she said. "I can't see a damn thing."

"Time to start back. We're losing the light," Bob insisted.

"No we're not." Anna found another partial print. The wolf was following the moose or they had used the same route within hours of one another.

"My knee," Bob said. "It's an old injury. I think I threw it out back there on the ice."

Anna found another track. A good one this time, the edges blurred with snow and drift but the clear mark of the toe pads. "Whoa! Take a look at this." She squatted, her back soldier straight to keep her center of balance over her heels.

Bob was following so close he bumped her pack and she pitched forward. "Watch it!" she said. "Look." She'd managed to catch herself without damaging the print. It was immense, huge, beautiful, the track of a magnificent animal. "God, I wish we'd brought the camera."

"We should go back. We need to report this to Ridley—the sooner, the better."

"Radio him," Anna said.

"I got to take a leak," Bob said suddenly.

"Yeah, yeah. Go ahead." Without rising, Anna squinted down the sloping bank. They had reached the far side of the finger of land in a matter of steps. The isthmus wasn't more than thirty feet across. Tracks of wolf and moose, muted and strange with snow and wind, led across the narrow arm of the lake toward the far shore, crossing where Robin had said to set the next trap.

"Perfect." Anna managed to stand without grabbing onto anything.

From her left came moose-sized crashing through what little shrubbery the place offered: Bob dumping his pack. The guy might be a while. Keeping to one side of the faint trail, Anna picked her way down the gentle slope and over the ridged ice where lake met land. Wolf and moose, traveling together or in tandem, the moose tracks close together as if meandering without concern, the wolf's farther apart as if loping after prey.

Ten or eleven yards out—distance was hard to estimate in poor light and a monochromatic world—the tracks vanished as if wolf and moose had been snatched off the surface of the lake by a great carnivorous bird.

"Not possible," she whispered and pulled her focus back to what was directly in front of her. "Hah!" The impossible had not occurred. The snow covering the ice had formed a slight depression. The tracks led into this irregular bowl, effectively vanishing from a distance.

Before coming to Winter Study, Anna had not given ice much thought. She'd seen pictures of arctic floes heaped into mountains, crinkled into badlands and shattered over a white-and-blue no-man's-land. Yet in her mind it remained flat, evened out by God's Zamboni.

On ISRO, she'd realized it was a living thing: changing, moody, struggling, resting, singing. Surrounding this shallow crater, water had oozed up through a circular crack and refrozen, creating a scar, a rugged ridge four and five inches high.

Moose and wolf tracks crossed in the center of the circle, where it looked as if they'd skirmished. "Hey, Bob, you're missing this," Anna called back as she hopped over the ridge.

She landed, and a rifle shot cracked through the silence that had wrapped them since leaving the cabin. Bob was a big game hunter. Bob had wanted his rifle. Rifles could be broken down and carried in a day pack. Bob had slipped away, letting her go, alone and exposed, onto the ice. All this flashed through her mind in an instant of acute paranoia.

She started to look back to where she'd left Menechinn. Another *crack,* a noise like a baseball bat being snapped in half, then the ice began to shift beneath her feet.

11

The sound Anna had mistaken for a rifle report was ice breaking. She felt the shift beneath her boots and engaged all her muscles in the act of remaining motionless. She hadn't punched through a thin place caused by an underwater spring or a rock near the surface; the ice in the depressed area had broken free. If she'd been quicker, she might have jumped to safety after the first *crack*. The second had created an island of ice no more than eight feet in diameter, with her in the center. Around the perimeter, the scar from the old ooze had opened, like the movement of tectonic plates the ice sheared. Water welled up, pouring into the snow in a flush of gray.

If she moved, the free-floating island would tilt and she would slide into the lake. Under the lake. The land spit stretched thirty feet behind her. Another thirty or forty lay between her and the shore in front of her. Possibly the water was no deeper than her waist. Then again, glacial lakes could drop off fifty feet a yard from the shore.

Depth probably wouldn't matter, she thought.

The cold would kill her before she had a chance to drown. Stories of kids revived after forty-five minutes beneath the ice were legend in the north. The shock of the stunning cold produced a phenomenon called a mammalian reflex, causing the body to shut down without dying, the way a bear shuts down to hibernate or a frog to sleep under the mud. Anna was too old to qualify. The courtesy of mammalian reflex wasn't extended to adults.

"Bob!" she called. Tried to call; his name came out on a whisper of air so faint she wasn't sure she'd managed to speak aloud.

"Bob!"

Audible, but only to her ears. The part of her that believed the vibrations of her voice against the air would be enough to tip the balance had shut down her voice box.

For a dizzying second, she saw the ice patch flipping like a coin, her feet going from under her, hands scrabbling uselessly, as she slid into the black death waiting below the ice, the patch of ice rocking back level, shutting her away from the promise of life and light. Iron-clawed terror gripped her insides. Courage drained out as blood from a severed artery.

"Stop that," she hissed. "Die of hydrophobia—how

stupid is that?" Dragging her vision out of the bowels of the lake, she looked for ways to stay alive.

The edge of her iceberg wasn't quite the length of her body away. Too far to make a clean jump, but if she hurled herself forward she should be able to get her arms and shoulders up on solid ice. The shoulders and upper back were key. Her backpack, seemingly light after removing one trap, would be a significant anchor underwater. Mentally she rehearsed the action. Bend the knees, going straight down so the ice wouldn't tilt, push off like a standing broad jumper, throw her arms out like Superman and hit the surface of the lake in a belly slide. Home free.

Unbidden, the movie in her head played past the Hollywood ending. A gap opened behind her. The push of her feet spun the ice. Water the color of ink flicked out a reptilian tongue; the ice plate spun on its axis and reared like a living thing, dropping from under her heels and smashing into the front of her thighs. Gravity and the weight of her pack dragged her back and down. Black water closed over her face. The ice island smashed down, driving her under.

"Bob!" she yelled.

She'd left him on the land behind her and was shouting her feeble pleas to the woods in the opposite direction. Desperate, she turned so her voice would carry. Ice lurched sickeningly under her boots and she screamed.

"Easy, easy, easy," she murmured to herself and the lake. "No need to prance about. Center. Breathe. Still." Talking herself back into balance, Anna wished she'd studied yoga, learned to stay perfectly motionless and balanced for hours.

"Bob," she wailed. As the words flew from her throat, Anna's eyes flew with them till she was in the sky over her own head, looking down on the pitiful creature, bundled up and hooded, crying out in a snowstorm. All she needed was a tin cup of matches to sell to complete the pathos.

The Dickensian image made her laugh. The laugh destabilized her, and the ice slid down an inch or more on the left side. Her soul was sucked back into her body so hard, reality lit up like sixteen million candles, and she was so alive her hair hurt with it. "Whoa!" she breathed, arms out like a child learning to snowboard. Gently she slid her feet wider apart, shifted her weight the slightest bit. The ice did not come back to level. The lip had caught on the edge underneath. Black water pushed out, turning gray as it ate up her world.

Bob had to come, she told herself. He was following her. All she had to do was wait without moving. The ice hadn't shattered; it had broken in a piece. If Bob stabilized one side, took a wide grip and held it so it couldn't rock up out of the water, she should be able to move from the center to the opposite edge without getting her feet wet.

Maybe Bob didn't have to come. The thought floated into her mind as the snowflakes floated onto her eyelashes and shoulders, soft, silently, dead cold.

He'd been stacking excuses like cordwood: knee injury, losing the light, making a report. When he wasn't armed with telescoping sights, beaters and a high-powered rifle, the sight of an oversized animal track scared him. Anna liked to think he was scared because he knew his karma was about as cheery as the inside of a taxidermist's workshop, that word he was a serial killer had gone out through the animal kingdom along with the order to devour him on sight, but she doubted he respected those who died for his entertainment sufficiently to consider them a sentient danger.

Bob might have decided to quietly follow their trail back to the snug kitchen at Malone Bay.

Or maybe he was watching her from the fringe of boulders, waiting for the ice to swallow her. Cautiously she pivoted her head and peered back the way she'd come.

Fat Christmas card flakes she'd so admired earlier in the day drifted in a veil of lace, blurring the shore. A shape hunkered near the water—not particularly informative, given the finger of earth was littered by boulders of all shapes and sizes.

"Bob!"

A shadow big enough to be Menechinn broke away from the others. Anna couldn't tell if he'd been standing, watching, or had that moment emerged from between the rocks.

"Help me!" she hollered, and he moved out onto the lake. Neck aching under the strain, she turned back to stare at the far shore. What was it about Menechinn that made her think him capable of any evil? Of standing by, watching another human being die? Before she'd climbed out of the Beaver onto Washington Harbor, she'd never heard of him. Since then, he'd proven annoying, a little sexist, a little mean-spirited and a little cowardly, but Anna had friends that were meaner, more macho scaredy-cats, and she enjoyed them despite it. Occasionally they annoyed her, but she never seriously considered them capable of acts of craven cruelty.

She risked another look back. Bob was halfway. "Stop there," she said, relieved not to have to shout, to move too much air between her and another solid object.

He stopped. He didn't say anything. Snow leached what drab colors there were woven into his scarf and mittens. The lower half of his face was covered and his eyes were shadowed by the fur of his hood.

"I'm on a chunk of ice broken free from the lake," Anna said, trying to be as clear and concise as possible. "The whole thing is loose. I can't move without tipping it over and spilling myself in the drink."

Still, Bob said nothing, not: "How did it happen? Are you okay? Why did you do an idiot thing like that?" Nothing.

Anna had to turn and face forward before her skull broke free of her spine. The fear boiling beneath her breastbone solidified into a jagged piece of ice colder than the lake. "I need you to kneel there, directly behind me." She pitched her voice to carry. "Put both hands wide on the ice—the piece I busted loose—and don't let it come up when I move forward. Don't push it down; just don't let it come up. Got that?"

Wind sang across the parka's hood over her ears. Beneath her, broken edges of ice grated against one another, the sound of teeth grinding in a nightmare.

"Bob?" She was afraid to try to look over her shoulder. She was afraid he wouldn't be there.

"Answer me, God dammit!" she snapped.

"You broke through?" he asked. Relief that he responded at all, that he'd not left her, was so great, irritation at his slowness almost vanished.

"Yeah. You need to stabilize the floating ice so I can get off."

"Why don't you jump?"

"Jesus!" Anna started to turn; her world tipped, the low edge sinking farther, water rushing up to touch the side of her boot. "Fuck! Jesus. God." Anna got religion all of a sudden. "That's why," she snapped. "Hurry up."

There was no reassuring sound of size-thirteen boots crunching closer.

"I weigh twice as much as you do. If you broke it, I'll go through," he said.

"No you won't. I think it busted along a fault line, or whatever ice gets. It's not thinner here than anywhere else. The whole thing just broke loose when I stepped on it."

Jumped on it, she reminded herself. Should she die, she wanted to be sure she knew who'd been responsible. "I jumped on it," she amended, hoping the confession would give him courage. "If you lie down and slither on your belly, your weight will be distributed over a greater surface area. It'll hold you. You probably don't even need to do that, but it wouldn't be a bad idea. Lay down and . . ." She was starting to babble, as if by keeping a rope of words spinning out she could drag him closer, talk him down like the clichéd stewardess-cum-pilot in old disaster movies.

"That's not a good idea," Bob said. "We'll both go in if I get any closer. Let me call Ridley." He sounded mature, reasonable; he sounded as if she should believe him.

"What the fuck is Ridley going to do?" she said, suddenly more angry than afraid. "He's on the other side of the island in a snowstorm. My legs can't hold out much longer."

Till she said it, she'd not allowed herself to think it, to notice that her muscles, tired from two days' hard walking with a heavy pack on her back, were starting to twitch as she stressed them in her ongoing balancing act. Tiny muscles, seldom used, were being called into play as the infinitesimal weight shifts were executed. They weren't strong. They wouldn't last. When a knee buckled or a leg cramped up, she was going to lose her delicate balance.

"I'll call Robin," Bob said, and she heard him busying himself with his radio. "Hey, Robin," he said. Winter Study didn't bother with radio protocol. With so few people, it wasn't necessary, and their natural contrariness when it came to NPS regulations demanded they eschew it. "Anna broke through the ice. It won't hold me, I'm too heavy, and somebody's got to get closer to her than I can. Where are you?"

"Lake Richie."

While Anna and Bob had set a single trap, she and Katherine had completed their side of Intermediate and moved on to Richie, the next lake in the short chain. They were an hour's walk away.

"Why don't you go ahead and start toward us," Bob said authoritatively. "They're coming," he added unnecessarily.

"I heard."

Bob wasn't going to do as she asked. He had it set in his mind that the ice wouldn't hold him. Or he was afraid that it might not, which amounted to the same thing. Anna fought down the urge to scream and shriek imprecations and obscenities. Sharp, hot tears sprang into her eyes and promptly froze like the Ice Queen's splinter.

Arguing a person out of being afraid—particularly when they wouldn't admit to being frightened—seldom worked, and Anna didn't try to do it now. A tic started in her left thigh muscle above the knee, a flick of the skin the way a horse's hide will flick to shake off flies.

"I suppose I could just balance here till the ice refreezes along the seams," she said sarcastically.

"How long do you think that would take?" he asked seriously.

Anna was going to die and there would be no one but an oversized clown to witness her demise. "Come around to where I can see you, would you?"

"The ice won't—"

"Big circle, Bob, *big* circle, stay as far out as you need to just—" She stopped to let off the steam building in her brain. She'd been about to say "just move your fat ass," etc., etc., expletive not deleted, but, from what she'd observed of Bob Menechinn, he wouldn't respond well to that approach. "Keep well back from me," she said instead. "The ice is solid there."

For a moment, he didn't speak or move, then she heard his boots squeaking over the snow to her left. He loomed into her peripheral vision then, finally, to where she could see him without straining. Pissed off as she was, the sight of him relieved her. He didn't look like he was about to run off and leave her to perish. She had that going for her.

"I need you to go to the shore and get a tree limb, a long one, as long as you can manage."

Bob looked toward the shoreline. Though less than half a football field away, it was murky, dark and out of focus behind falling snow. "Visibility is getting bad," he said. "I'd be afraid I wouldn't be able to get back to you. I don't want to leave you alone out here."

Anna cocked her head the way a Jack Russell terrier will when it's trying to figure out what its master is saying. The visibility was bad, and she knew, as close as they were to the shore, connected by radios, if he went into the trees he could still get turned around and be unable to find where he'd come in off the lake.

"Don't go into the trees," she said. "There'll be something along the shore. Something is better than nothing."

"I don't want to leave you alone," he said. "It would take too long."

His words sounded fine, his voice was even and strong. Still, she suspected his sudden devotedness had more to do with not wishing to go into the spooky old woods alone.

Blinking past the snow and the shards of tears frozen in the inner corners of her eyes, she tried to see who he was, a key to move him. Mockery wouldn't do it. His ego was too fragile. In a way, he reminded her of the psychotics she'd worked with in the lockdown ward where she did her brief mental health internship when she was getting her EMT. Men and women shared a common room, with a television set between the men's ward and the women's ward. Anna'd spent her time there, too ignorant to be of much help to the nurses and too small to be of much assistance to the orderlies, who looked more like bouncers or second-string football players than upstanding members of the medical profession.

It had been a number of years ago, back when "crazy" was as much a medical diagnosis as an insult. The ward wasn't for neurotics; the people who ended up there were desperately ill. Most had lost so much of their world to mental illness and the drugs administered to control it that they didn't care what was said to them. It had little to do with what they heard. Those who could still interact tended to respond instantly, and sometimes violently, if their delusions were challenged. Anna'd always thought it was because somewhere inside they still knew the difference between the reality around them and the one that they forged for themselves, and they believed when the illusion they had of themselves died they would die too.

Sane people weren't a whole lot different; they just didn't drool as much.

Bob Menechinn had a vision of himself. The squeaky, scared man in the tent attacked that vision. That's why he'd had to work so hard the following day to rebuild it. The cowardly Bob, who panicked at the snort of a wolf, wasn't a man he could live with.

At the moment, Anna could muster no pity for him, but she knew she would get nowhere trying to shame him into doing right. Shame would attack the illusion.

The tic in her thigh graduated to a twitch. Soon the muscle would cramp.

"Get the traps out of your pack," she said. Bob was as formless and shadowed in the snow as tabloid pictures of Bigfoot. He went down on one knee and slung the backpack to the ice. As he fumbled with the buckles, Anna went on: "Put the end of the kinkless chains in the jaws of the traps. Don't make a circle; make a line. We've got twenty-four feet, if you link it together."

"I was just thinking that," he said.

Anna watched without speaking as he spread the traps out on the ice and connected them, jaws to tails. She moved her left foot fractionally to ease her thigh muscles. The ice did not shift alarmingly. Maybe the seam was refreezing. *It wouldn't take much,* she thought hopefully. The urge to jump was almost overwhelming. Body and mind craved action. They also serve who only stand and wait was an understatement. Waiting was a purgatory a nonbeliever could not pray her way out of. Trusting in the kindness of strangers was another.

"How's it going?" she asked to take her body's mind off just yelling "Fuck it!" and leaping for the good ice.

He looked up, his hood thick with snow, his shoulders white with it. "Good," he said. "Another minute. Hang on."

The work of his hands had driven thoughts of the oversized wolf from his mind. The linking of the three chains had relieved him of the necessity of getting near where the ice had broken. He sounded manly, strong, stand-up. It was hard to believe not too many minutes ago he was poised to leave her to her fate or, worse, watch while it visited itself upon her. He wasn't afraid now, Anna realized, and that made him brave. Except brave didn't count if one wasn't afraid. Without fear to burn away the dross and transform it from baser metal, bravery was merely stupidity or poor impulse control.

"They should hold," he said and held up the three chains attached to each other by the steel-jawed traps.

It would work, Anna told herself. All Bob had to do was lay one end of the chain to one side of her, then walk the other end around the break and pull till the chain gently eased over her island. She'd pick it up; on the count of three, he'd jerk as she leapt. It would work.

The dull pull of a muscle trying to cramp moved out from the twitch above her knee. If she waited any longer, she would not be able to execute the straight-backed deep knee bend and rise without tottering after she picked up the chain. Inside the Sorels, she flexed toes grown numb from lack of movement. "Let's get going," she said. "My legs are starting to cramp."

Bob hurled a trap at her.

"No!" she heard herself shout. Ten pounds of metal struck her in the chest. Clamping her arms across it, she fought for balance. The ice tilted. Her boots began to slide. White lake and sky rushed past as she fell backward. Her head struck lake ice. Her brain slid forward inside her skull. Her chin smashed into her chest, slamming her teeth down on her tongue.

For an instant, she carried the burden of her life in the balance, trying to decide whether to hold tight to the trap or throw her hands back over her head, get as much of her on the solid surface as she could. The physical world did not slow down while she made up her mind.

The backpack pulled her down.

The ice island tilted.

Water so cold, she felt it only as a blow slammed into the side of her face.

12

The ice did not flip, dumping her like a man in a ducking booth, the way Anna had seen it in her mind's eye. The lake chose to savor her rather than swallow her whole. The ice slab fell away with terrifying slowness, a grinning maw opening at her heels.

She thrust the metal trap from her and threw her arms wide, trying to catch the beast's throat. The island of ice was too wide, and only one mittened hand reached the serrated edge. On her back, a beetle with a backpack as a carapace, helpless to save herself, she was sliding, sliding down, under the ice, pulled by her own weight and the hunger of the lake. Then the lake couldn't wait. The slab under her gave all at once.

Light flashed past, a white streak four inches wide; the edge of the break. Fighting the drag of her pack, she kicked and pawed her way upright and clutched at the surface ice. In sodden mittens, her hands were pulpy, worthless.

Clutching at straws.

A burst of energy that drove a scream from her lips lifted her enough that she managed to get her right arm as far as the elbow onto the surface. Balling her mittened hand into a fist, she drove it hard into the shallow snow and pressed her sodden sleeve against the ice.

Freeze, God dammit. If her sleeve, her glove—any part of her—would adhere to the ice, she might be able to pull herself out. Grabbing the end of the other mitten with her teeth, she pulled. Freezing water crashed against her teeth with the subtlety of brass knuckles. Biting down, she pulled her hand free of the mitten and reached through the fractured water to press it to the ice by her elbow. Flesh might freeze faster than fabric.

"Bob!" she screamed. "Where the fuck are you?"

Hell would freeze over.

The sleeve of her coat was sticking, freezing to the good ice.

Carefully she dragged on the arm. She could see herself moving infinitesimally closer to the edge but was losing feeling. Cold was killing her body while her mind watched. A quarter of an inch; an eternity.

Ice canted steeply toward a white sky. Flakes of snow, scarcely differentiated from the universe they fell through, showed clear for an instant, like magic, like the pictures in the mall that flashed from two dimensions to three with a flash of the mind. Then the sky grew too steep.

Her hand was not in front but above her. She hadn't grabbed the solid ice; she'd grabbed onto the edge of the floating island and it was rotating with her weight. Through frost-rimed eyelashes, she watched each thread of her sleeve as it pulled free of the ice. Her pack was battened on her back, dragging her down, hungry like the lake was hungry. Sentient and indifferent.

Frantically she wrenched her gloved hand from its last tenuous connection with the ice and pounded on the buckle of her chest strap. The push-button release opened and the strap came free. The pack lifted, drifted from her.

She had won; she would make it.

Straps followed the pack toward the bottom of the lake, tugging down her arms, pinioning her elbows to her side, prying the end of her sleeve from its tenuous marriage with the ice, her hand from where it battered ineffectually at the buckle of her hip belt. Water closed over her. The narrow margin of sky receded as she sank. She forced her eyes wide to keep the light in them. Cold burned her sclera like acid.

Kicking with more force than she'd believed she had in her, she moved upward. Half a foot, a foot, the light grew stronger.

The Sorel boots filled with water. Her feet moved as if through freezing mud. Then she couldn't move them at all. Wriggling eel-like, she tried to struggle out of the bondage of the shoulder straps, but her coat had swelled with water, the fabric stuck to the webbing. Desperately she pummeled at the release on her hip. Anna fought till her last gasp of air put the last of its oxygen into her blood and her lungs began to push against her rib cage, shoving the panic of their need through her bones and into her heart.

The hip belt released, and she used the last of her air to kick for the surface. Then she stopped. Fell back and down and back. The drag on her hips gone, but the pack still holding her fast to her upper arms, pulling her head-first toward the bottom of the lake.

The light grew watery and faint. Anna watched as her feet floated up past her eyes.

The cold that had hammered into her face and neck soaked through the layers of clothing. At first, it seared her flesh, then it didn't. Icy fingers crept up her legs, down the neck of her parka. Her feet were gone to it already, she couldn't feel them.

One arm came free of the confining straps, the hand with the bloated mitten. Anna watched it as it drifted out from her body. Above it, the irregular half-moon shape of light was no bigger than the palm of her hand.

Oddly detached, she watched it shrink to the size of a half-dollar. A gentle bump stopped her fall. She rested on the bottom of the lake, the moon of light feeble in the liquid sky. Quiet surrounded her. Her breathing stopped, her heart starved and pounded throughout her body, a frenetic drumbeat in a deaf world. The water was so clear she could see gravel on the lake bed, a vestige of weeds as unmoving as if sculpted in stone.

Dropping arrow straight from the world above was a single line, inked black against the gray of the water. At its end, a *D* was written in crushed script. The foothold trap on the line of kinkless chain. She had wanted to trap a wolf with it, wanted to stroke its living fur and feel its breath. *Cruel to want that,* she thought. To frighten such a grand creature that she might be close to it.

Water was clearer than air; she could see each individual link in the chain she had carried so far. She marveled that an entity as fierce as the lake could be so completely still; not a ripple showed its power yet it had swallowed Anna as neatly as a trout swallowing a fly. The lake had slipped away into silence. And the water was so clear, soon, Anna believed, soon she would be able to breathe it.

The trap was an ugly thing, a reminder of the metal rampage humanity with its mines and forges and industry had loosed on the world. Anna didn't want it to be in her eyes when she drew the lake into her lungs and took her first breath in this new world. As she mustered the energy to turn her head away, the foothold trap leapt; a quick jerk upward, then fell again, the way an angler's bait pretended life to lure greedy fish.

Anna wondered if she was a fish yet.

The line jerked again. Lazily she reached for it, wanting to make it be still, make it part of the lake with her. Her fingers fumbled. The trap swayed away. Slowly it drifted back. She threaded her hand and wrist through it and pulled, a tiny pull, maybe not a pull at all.

The crescent of light dimmed. Her brain was shutting down. The pounding from her heart eased to a soft rush, waves breaking lazily against sandy beaches. Bands of pressure within her lungs pressed outward, attempting to break through to the air.

When she was asleep, she would breathe in the lake.

Ophelia.

HOOKS CAUGHT IN HER MERMAID MOUTH, cutting the flesh and trying to drag her from the sea. Anna tossed her head from side to side. Fishes chewed at her face; she felt the ripping but not the pain. A hammerhead shark rammed into her chest and the air blasted out of her.

And in again.

"Annnhhh. Annnh."

Breath out and in and vomiting, her lungs caught fire, her throat burned with charred flesh.

"Annh. Annnh."

Hot lead spewed from her scalding her tongue, blistering her lips.

"Annhh. Anhhh."

The noise maddened her, and she knew she was crying as she descended to hell in fire and ice. Her eyes would not open, as in dreams of blindness they had been sewn shut. Screaming, she forced her lids wide.

She was out. She was on her side, one arm stretched over her head. Her right eyeball was so close to the ice, she could see crystals moving by in fits and starts. The endless embrace of the lake was being scraped off. A machine gun battered through her head. Her teeth were chattering.

"Annnh."

Anna had not made that sound. Fish did not speak. Fish got fried over hot coals. She was looking forward to that.

"I've landed four-hundred-pound marlin that were easier to reel in than you." This was grunted. Anna had been caught by a bear. Too bad. Bears ate their fish raw.

"Are you alive?" The bear pawed at her and she was rolled onto her back.

"Hey, Bob," she said when she saw his red, sweating face.

"Are we going to have to get naked in a sleeping bag together?" he asked.

"Throw me back in," Anna croaked.

13

Bob was a hero.

When Anna had gone under, trap and line snaking after her, he'd stomped on his end of the chain to stop it. For a nanosecond, he waited to see if she would resurface.

"Nanosecond" was Bob's assessment of the time. Anna was fairly sure it had been at least five minutes, never mind that she could only hold her breath for two, and that was under ideal conditions.

The ice was paper thin, Bob told Robin and Katherine, and he'd tugged on the chain so Anna would be able to see it, then pulled her from the lake bottom.

Anna was sufficiently grateful to have been saved from a watery grave that, for a while, she forgot it was Bob who'd put her there. She chose not to remind him of this because he had raised not only her from the dead with nothing but brute strength and determination but her pack as well, trailing behind her by a single shoulder strap.

She remembered nothing of their return to the cabin but knew without a doubt she would have died if Bob had not taken quick action. He'd cut her free of the backpack, stripped her wet coat from her, wrapped her in his own parka and carried her back to Malone Bay.

Clad in dry clothes and propped on the bottom bunk in a sleeping bag, a fourth cup of hot Ovaltine in front of her—the first she'd been able to hold all by herself—Anna listened as Bob again told Robin and Katherine how he'd run the two miles.

"Flat out," he said. "I knew she was going to die."

Anna doubted he'd managed to sprint the whole way, but he had covered the ground rapidly. And he was right: she was going to die and now she wasn't.

"You saved my life, Bob," she said. "Remind me to buy you a beer sometime."

He grinned hugely, tucking his chin back into his neck. Anna's words had been meant to sound grateful and they did. She was. There was no arguing with the feats of strength he had performed. The man was powerful and she was grateful to him. Grateful. For some reason, she had to keep reminding herself of this, and felt small and mean because of it.

Bob Menechinn mystified her. One moment, he was a coward shaking in his boots, a streak of yellow down his back so bright it shone through his thermal undershirt. The next, he was carrying a damsel in distress miles through a storm to safety. Anna had long known that everyone has a panic button. Those who are considered brave are simply people lucky enough to wander through life without theirs getting punched. She'd known men who would scale precipitous cliffs, only to fall apart when a water snake slithered into the tent; women who marshaled the combined forces of Boy Scouts and church camps but would faint at the sight of their own blood.

As near as she could figure, Bob had two Achilles' heels: he was terrified of wild beasts who were better armed than he and women who knew he was terrified. Watching him bask in glory, Anna wondered if that was why he loved hunting—killing them before they killed him—if that was why he kept Katherine under his thumb.

Fear made some people brave and some dangerous. Bob was in the latter category. Because he was strong, he'd not been afraid he couldn't carry Anna a couple of miles. He'd also known fishing her out with trap and line would not put him in any danger. And there was no risk of failure. Either he'd succeed or the witness to his humiliation would be dead.

Anna took a sip of the oversweet Ovaltine. The drink was hot, the cabin so warm the others had stripped down to trousers and T-shirts. Anna was packed in goose down and surrounded by plastic bottles filled with water heated on the stove, yet the core of her was still on the bottom of Intermediate Lake.

"I was looking for tracks up in the rocks when I heard that ice crack," Bob embellished his tale. "I was on that ice like a man shot out of a cannon. What a noise! I didn't think anything but a Remington could crack like that. Anna was trapped, yelling, 'Bob, Bob,' and the ice was so thin I couldn't get to her. Man," he said and shook his head.

"God, I'm sorry," Robin said to Anna.

"Not your fault," Anna told her.

"The ice on Intermediate is good. You shouldn't have broken through."

"It happens," Anna said. Then, to make Robin feel better: "I jumped."

"I can't figure out what made the ice break like that. It should have been fine. You were where I said to place the trap?"

Anna nodded and took another sip of Ovaltine.

"It makes no sense. I am so sorry. You could have died."

"Nah," Anna said. "Bob's making it all up. We formed a polar bear club and he chickened out at the last minute."

"Don't joke," Robin pleaded. "You really could have died."

Robin was obsessing and Anna didn't know how to stop her. As a young woman leading her first backcountry trips, Anna had felt the same way a few times when people in her care, following her instructions, were endangered. She hoped she hadn't carried on as much as Robin was. The biotech was three pews short of banging her heart with her fist and crying, *"Mea culpa, mea culpa."*

"Lots of things don't make sense," Anna said reasonably.

"It couldn't have broken." Robin shook her head, her hair swinging in the silvery light from the window over the small dining table. The sun had creaked out, making an appearance between fronts. They had been without showers for days, during most of which they wore hats and hoods crammed on their heads, yet Robin's hair was shining, silken.

"Go figure," Anna said aloud. She didn't bother to explain she was remarking on the hair. "Go figure" was one of those contentless statements that mean whatever the listener chooses to believe they mean.

During Bob's regaling, Robin's breast-beating and Anna's slurping of hot drinks, Katherine had been unusually quiet. She was retiring by nature, but since Anna had been dried, warmed and declared officially among the living Katherine had not uttered a word. She'd not congratulated Bob on his bravery or marveled at his Samson-like strength; she'd not asked Anna what it was like to die or live. Like the Cheshire cat, she had slowly disappeared, till all that remained was the reflection of the window's light on the rim of her spectacles. Wordlessly, making eye contact with no one, she'd drifted from the stool by the door to the straight-backed kitchen chair tucked next to the water heater to a footlocker jammed into the space between the foot of the bunk beds and the wall that was so narrow the locker had to be pulled out to be opened. On this low bench, Katherine had drawn her back to the wall and her feet up on the locker, a folded bit of woman tucked in a dark corner.

"What are you hiding from, Kathy?" Bob said in a voice loud enough that Anna watched the liquid in her mug shiver as the aftershocks struck its ceramic shores.

Katherine raised her head, her eyes invisible behind her glasses. "Just trying to stay out of the way," she said.

"You're not in the way," Robin reassured her. In such cramped quarters, they all were in the way all the time.

"Bob once carried me," Katherine blurted out. "He carried me up five flights of stairs." Her voice had an edge, as if she was making a point.

"Hey, careful, my head will get too big," Bob said with the first show of humility Anna'd seen.

"I don't really remember it," Katherine went on. "I was out cold."

Bob laughed and Katherine shrank back into her self-made cave.

Anna's thoughts sank to the lake bottom, how deep the silence had been, how like crystal the water, how the sand had seemed to go forever, never disappearing in the distance but merging with it, the two becoming one, how she had sensed she would be the lake when she breathed it, how she had come to want to breathe it, not because she wanted to die, or because she had to, but because she knew she teetered on the brink of something vast and a part of her was excited to step off that brink and experience the vastness.

ARRAYED IN THE FRILLY APRON, Bob started dinner. Onions frying in butter smelled of home and safety and warmth, but for once Anna wasn't hungry. Her fingers loosened around the mug she held, but it didn't fall into her lap, spilling the dregs of her drink. Other hands lifted it from her. Robin. Anna hadn't the energy to open her eyes, but she could smell the biotech. Like onions and butter, Robin smelled of life and rich earth, of young plants pushing up after the rain, meadow grass when it's crushed underfoot.

Soft hands touched her face, brushed the lank hair from her forehead. *Gray,* Anna remembered: red and gray, salt and cinnamon. Robin stroked her cheek and Anna felt the silky whisk of her ancient orange tiger cat Piedmont's tail, followed by the rasp of his tongue, a tongue designed to abrade flesh from bone. *Robin,* she reminded herself, *calluses, hardworking hands.*

"I am so sorry," Robin whispered. A kiss or a tear settled on Anna's cheekbone.

"De nada." Anna's lips moved, but if they made a sound she was asleep before she heard it.

ANNA SHOULD HAVE slept like the dead—or the very nearly dead—but she was troubled by dreams and the revenge of muscles she'd abused. Her legs flinched and quivered and sent mixed messages to her brain, unable to decide whether they were hurting or bored. She wasn't asleep when the beeping started.

Either Robin shared Anna's insomnia or was a light sleeper. She wriggled out of her sleeping bag and went to the radio receiver on the table.

"Which one?" Anna whispered.

"Between Intermediate and Richie, about a quarter of a mile from where you went in." She clicked on her headlamp. Using its light, she began pumping the Coleman lantern. Colemans worked. They'd worked forever, lighting places electricity would not. But they were noisy machines, clanking in the preparation and hissing like a thousand angry snakes when lit. Katherine and Bob woke up.

"What is it?" Katherine asked, her voice fogged with sleep.

"We've trapped a wolf," Robin told her. She was already pulling on her ski pants.

Anna swung her legs, bag and all, over the edge of the bottom bunk and sat up.

"You're not going," Robin said.

"I'm going," Anna replied. She stood up and fell down. "I'm *not* going," she admitted from the floor. "You're not going alone," she insisted.

They both looked at Bob. He stared back at them. The Coleman was not a cosmetic light, and he looked pasty and scared. "I'm not Superman," he said in a tone just short of surly. "I've already saved one of you today. Leave the fucking wolf in the trap till morning."

"It could die," Robin said and sat in the straight-backed kitchen chair to put on her mukluks.

"I'll go." This was from the top bunk. Anna, who had stayed on the floor rather than risk the humiliation of collapsing again, looked up at the researcher. The angle was bizarre; she was looking through Katherine's stocking feet up between her knees where they bent over the edge of the mattress to a head small with distance. Katherine was as frightened as Bob, and probably nearly as tired, but she meant to go.

Courage and bravado, Anna thought. It sounded like a TV cop duo. Anna sucked it up and tried again to rise. She made it to hands and knees, but the room spun, and she coughed till her chest ached with the spasms.

"Get in bed," Robin said. She picked up a radio from the table and called Ridley. He radioed back immediately. Robin told him about the motion detector going off.

"If Anna's not up to it, take Bob with you," Ridley said.

Bob moved back, legs still in his sleeping bag, and leaned against the wall, folding his arms over his chest.

"It's a fool's errand," he said.

"Bob's done in," Robin said into the mike.

There was a long moment of crackling silence, then Ridley said: "I think there's an old pair of skis in the cabin. You go, take the jab stick. If we've got a wolf, just put him out and set him free. He should wake up and get moving before he freezes to death. You can reset the trap tomorrow. Keep me posted."

The jab stick was what it sounded like, a long stick

with a syringe on the end, loaded with ketamine and xylazine. A trapped wolf was jabbed with it. In five minutes or so, the animal would go down long enough for the study team to do their work.

The skis and poles were stowed in the rafters. Robin had them down in a minute and was prying off the bindings with a butter knife. "No boots," she said when Anna asked. She dug in her backpack and pulled out a roll of silver duct tape. "Voilà!" She began taping the toes of her mukluks to the skis.

"Radio and flashlight," Anna reminded her as she jerked open the cabin door, skis with the unfilled boots over her shoulder.

"Got them."

The door slammed shut. Life had gone out of the cabin. Anna and Katherine and Bob wavered in the hissing light of the Coleman, ghosts left behind in an empty house.

"This study should be shut down," Bob announced. "Border security for sure, but it's run without any attention to the safety of the scientists. If they haven't figured it out in fifty years, they're not going to. Wolves eat moose; moose eat grass—how hard is that?"

"Moose don't eat grass," Anna said. "Moose eat trees."

"New DNA," Katherine said. "It might be a big deal, Bob." This was the second time Katherine had stood up for herself. Anna liked it. Bob didn't.

"They can't shut the study down now," Anna interjected to deflect whatever barb Menechinn was going to throw at his assistant. "New information. Maybe a hybrid."

Bob dropped that line of conversation and launched into a lecture about how personal safety was number one with professional big game hunters. Anna didn't hear it; she was listening for the radio.

She didn't have long to wait. Robin radioed Ridley. Anna turned the volume up.

"I'm here," the biotech said. She'd covered the miles in a startlingly brief time and didn't even sound out of breath. Anna remembered she'd spent most of her life on skis, racing and shooting. Anna wished she had a rifle with her tonight.

"What have you got?" Ridley asked.

"Nothing." Now she sounded breathless. "The trap and line have been torn all to hell. Whatever was in the foothold ripped free. The metal is bent and there's blood everywhere."

"Get out of there," Anna whispered at the same moment Ridley said: "Get out of there."

The radio went silent.

14

B ob talked. Anna listened for the radio. Katherine sat lost in thoughts Anna could only guess at. More than twice the time it had taken her to ski to the trap site elapsed. Robin did not return. Anna called on the radio and got no answer. The second time she radioed, the biotech's voice came back. Robin was almost to the cabin. She did not say what had kept her.

Anna didn't ask. The night was clear and full of stars. Robin was an excellent cross-country skier. Had it been Anna, she might have taken time to be free of others and in her natural element. Maybe Robin had done the same.

RIDLEY RECALLED THEM to Windigo. Robin skied out at first light and sprang the traps.

The next front had yet to arrive; the sky was clear and there was no wind. No one was sorry to be leaving Malone Bay. The meager comforts of the bunkhouse were palatial compared to the tiny cabin.

Anna had lost her mittens, her pack was ruined, the straps slashed and her clothing was still wet. Robin had lost one of her jab sticks and Katherine couldn't find her scarf. Other than that, they were in one piece.

An hour after sunup, the warm buzz of the supercub rolled over the tin roof and they started down to the bay. Anna flew out first. She was still coughing and there was not a part of her that didn't hurt, but she had walked to the airplane without falling over. She took that as a good sign.

ANNA'S TOUCHING NOSTALGIA for the bunkhouse vanished as soon as she opened the door and the reek of death slapped into her senses. The wolf had thawed.

By one o'clock, the team was reassembled, and Ridley declared the animal was ready for the necropsy.

"I'm going to miss this old boy," Jonah said as the wolf was transported from the kitchen to the carpenter's shop. "He was just beginning to smell good enough to drown out the smell of Ridley's feet." The pilot had to shout. The front had arrived with a vengeance. Snow was in a frenzy; naked branches of the trees creaked and whistled above them.

They carried the carcass on a tarp held at four corners by Ridley, Jonah, Katherine and Anna to the carpenter's shop, a twenty-by-fifteen-foot building behind the trail crew's bunkhouse. Designed for seasonal summer use, in January it was as cold as a deep freeze and used as such. Bones and bags of scat and urine, a half-eaten head of a young moose, the older moose head, with its windigo antlers and other delicacies, were wrapped in plastic and piled on the tool bench next to the wall.

A metal folding table, the kind used in church halls for potluck suppers, was in the middle of the room, samples from Robin's last expedition piled on one end. The wolf was placed on the table and the five of them gathered around. They looked like a band of homeless people, worshipping a long-awaited meal. At Ridley's suggestion, they'd all put on old clothes; at the suggestion of an icy Mother Nature, they'd donned many layers.

Ridley opened the wolf's jaws. "They must have a good dental plan," Anna said, startled by the clean, white, perfect teeth.

"Wolves' mouths are amazingly clean," Ridley said. "If a tooth gets broken, you'll see some brown at the edges; otherwise, they're like this guy's." He pinched the animal's tongue between thumb and forefinger and pulled it out to do a sweep of the throat. Short of a giraffe's, the wolf had the longest tongue Anna'd ever seen, cartoon long. Teeth, tongue and jaws: beautifully designed equipment for the work of staying alive.

"Let's open him up," Ridley said.

Anna was expecting a scalpel, but he pulled a steel knife with a six-inch blade and heavy hilt from one of his torn pockets. He smiled at Anna. "Vollwerth and Company, sausage makers over in Hancock. German made."

Jonah and Anna rolled the wolf onto its back and held it steady while Ridley slit the skin from throat to anus, then began to peel back the hide.

"You can see bruising or wounds better on the underside of the skin," he said. "They show up as dark red blotches or punctures." He stood back and Robin photographed the denuded animal.

With its hide partly peeled away and the sinews and ribs exposed, it bore an uncanny resemblance to a werewolf in transition from man to animal. A scene from *An American Werewolf in London* exploded in Anna's brain.

"See there?" Ridley pointed with the business end of the knife. "You can see where a rib has been broken and healed. That's fairly common. Moose will fling them against rocks, bash them against trees, anything to get them off."

Robin moved around the table and took several pictures of the rib. No bruising was apparent. "No defensive wounds," Anna said. She'd thought that once the hide was off, there would be evidence of damage incurred prior to the killing bite.

"Maybe our wog is the Arnold Schwarzenegger of wolves," Adam said and laughed, but none of the rest of them did. Bob snorted to indicate he had not been given the creeps, but Anna noticed he glanced out the shop's window as if concerned some inhuman force might hear his mockery and take against him.

"Governor Wolf," Jonah said.

"Subcutaneous fat?" Katherine asked.

"Not enough to collect." Ridley adjusted the shop light over the table, a light better suited to interrogating suspects than dissecting them. With the tip of his knife and his fingers, he pulled and pricked beneath the skin where it folded down over the paws and sides. "This time of year, with the moose population down, we don't see much fat on these guys."

Katherine cut out a sample of muscle tissue with a scalpel, the shiny, precise instrument looking delicate and civilized next to Ridley's sausage knife. She put the tissue into a glass vial with alcohol.

Ridley inserted his knife into the hide at the throat to make a lateral cut.

"Hey," Bob said, showing his first real interest in the proceeding. "Don't ruin it. And don't peel the skin off the head."

Ridley looked at him. His eyes went as dead as the wolf on the table. His hand tightened on the knife till the rubber glove he wore was pulled taut as a second skin over his knuckles. Anna thought he was going to cut Menechinn and she had no intention of trying to stop him—nothing against Bob Menechinn, just not a guy she wanted to get in the way of a knife for.

"I'll be careful," Ridley said and smiled. Anna got the feeling the smile was not a good sign. He turned his attention back to the wolf and made the lateral cuts in the hide. As good as his word, he did it conservatively and with precision, doing as little damage to the pelt as he could. When the cut was complete, he took two of the four corners in the X he had made and opened them like the pages of a book.

The wolf's throat wasn't shredded by repeated attacks from different angles the way most wolf-on-wolf kills were; it was ripped deeply four times. The tears went through an inch of hide and muscle. Two cut across the wolf's aorta, and two were near the carotid, in a distorted mirror image of the killing punctures.

"We got any tigers on this island?" Jonah asked. Nobody said anything. Whatever had attacked the wolf had a bite pattern close to twice the usual size wolf's.

"Any number of scenarios could have led to these marks," Ridley said. "Let's move on."

They did but a sense of the eerie, of the windigo screaming down out of the north woods to devour human flesh, remained. A hybrid, Jonah's wog, causing havoc in the wolf population wasn't impossible. Gray wolves mated with red wolves, red wolves mated with coyotes. There'd been a case in California of a seal/sea lion hybrid suffocating the female seals he tried to mate with because of his size. On the sunny summer beaches of California, dealing with creatures of the sea when one was on dry land didn't carry the psychological impact of a slaughtered wolf on an abandoned island in winter.

One of the reasons humans tended toward insanity was the weight of fear they carried. The blessings of storytelling, the handing down of knowledge and warnings, had a flip side. People carried the collective fears of their history, the biases of those long dead, the paranoias of other ages.

Anna flashed back to her college days. It had been raining hard; she'd been sitting in her sister Molly's kitchen, doing something or other. There was a horrific clap of thunder, the lights went out and the grandfather clock in the living room began striking midnight. Without bothering with coat or umbrella, she rose from the table, slipped out the back door and ran to a friend's house. She wasn't so much scared as wary; the setup was there, the cues were in place, she'd seen the movie half a dozen times. Should life mirror art, she didn't want to be in the kitchen in the dark when whatever was coming for her arrived.

She shrugged off that same feeling now and concentrated on the necropsy.

Ridley cut through the thin wall muscles covering the abdomen and exposed the internal organs. Since the wolf was fresh, the organs were identified and preserved for histological work. When an animal was partially decomposed, the organs turned to mush and the thin tissue samples required were unusable. Ridley lifted out the intestines and stomach. Small pieces of the liver and spleen were taken for DNA work.

Anna served as surgical nurse, handing the organs to Katherine, who identified, preserved and labeled them. Robin photographed each step. Jonah made wisecracks, and Bob watched.

"The pluck," Ridley said, the business of dismemberment apparently cleansing him of residual heebie-jeebies from the initial wound discovery. Reaching up under the ribs, he plucked out lungs and heart as a single unit.

Other than the bite on the throat, they found no other cause of death.

They completed the necropsy: salvaging bones, chopping off paws to preserve the small tarsals and metatarsals, breaking the rib cage to wrestle it free of the cavity. Bones would be macerated by boiling or, the preferred method, because it didn't dry the bones out, buried in soil in screen envelopes for slow decomposition of tissue.

This scientific butchering was grim work and Anna wasn't accustomed to it. Mated with the ambient weirdness of the throat wound, the oversized tracks and, most nerve-racking of all, being forever in the company of people in a small space, she found the necropsy depressing. And unsettling. A knot formed in her chest, and she wanted little more than to get away, get out into the woods. Caves and closets weren't the only threats for claustrophobes.

Ridley excised the muscle mass with the puncture marks. "Usually we don't need to do this," he said as he handed Anna the bloody chunk. "The wog bite—or whatever—makes it interesting. The lab in Michigan might be able to make something of it. My wife works there." A hint of pride touched his voice, warming it past the merely clinical. "She specializes in animal forensics."

Anna hadn't known such a discipline existed, but it made sense. There were animal DNA labs—she'd used one in Oregon, when she was working a case in Glacier.

"Bite patterns, tracks, fur—just like CSI," Ridley said.

But without criminals. However vicious an animal attack, it was neither a sin nor a crime, to Anna's way of thinking. Even when done with malice, it was without evil. One had to know what the taking of life meant before taking it could be elevated to the status of true evil.

"A married man," Bob said. "Any kids?"

"Not yet," Ridley said.

"Maybe when you stick closer to the den in winter she'll pop out a litter every spring. More fun than cutting up wolves." Bob grinned and winked at Anna. Having saved her life, he seemed to think he owned it. She wondered what he would look like with a plastic bag tied tightly over his head.

"Fuck!" Ridley jerked his hands out of the wolf and held his left cupped in his right, the knife trapped between them. The palm of his rubber glove was filling with bright, new arterial blood.

"I'm an EMT. Can I help?" Anna said, instantly forgetting Bob. Over the years, she'd said it so many times it was as instantaneous as "God bless you" after a sneeze.

Ridley kept his head down, his eyes on the blood welling in his glove.

Face averted in the growing dimness, hidden behind beard and mustache, he could have been thinking of anything from killing to Captain Kangaroo and Anna wouldn't have been able to see it. "Ridley, are you okay?"

He nodded without looking up and held out his hand. The gesture put Anna in mind of the pen-and-ink drawing in her childhood book of Androcles and the lion, the great beast's paw held up so that the thorn might be removed.

Anna handed the chunk of wolf neck to Katherine, peeled off the surgical gloves and pulled on a clean pair, then bent to examine the damage to Ridley's hand. A squeak, a tiny sound like that of a newborn kitten fighting for a nipple or the last sound of a mouse meeting a trap, distracted her. Hands dripping gore in front of her like a zombie in a B movie, Katherine looked the cliché of someone who's seen a ghost: her skin had paled and her lips gone slack. Behind the oversized lenses, her gentle eyes were so wide that white showed beneath the irises.

Having spent the afternoon elbow-deep in flesh and bone, Anna had a hard time believing Katherine was going faint at the sight of a little fresh blood. She wasn't. She was looking past Ridley, his wound beginning to drip human DNA into the carcass of the wolf, at Bob Menechinn. His heavy face had gone from flab to granite.

Frozen meat, Anna thought. The image jarred her.

Whatever was communicated with that stare was over in a heartbeat. Bob was all amiability again; Katherine's head was bent industriously over her collection equipment. Jonah started a long involved joke about the Sisters of St. Regis's Convent and House of Prostitution. Anna looked down at Ridley's hand in hers. An odd feeling of being once removed from the world came over her, the way it did when she had a bad cold, and, though she could hear perfectly well, she felt deaf; the way she felt in dreams when she needed to cross a busy street and her legs were lead.

"May I?" she said and carefully took the German knife from Ridley's hand. Despite the wound, he'd not let it fall. Using it, she cut his glove away. He'd gashed his palm, a bad cut, but blood had welled into the gash and she couldn't tell how bad; she couldn't see clearly.

The way she felt when the optometrist put belladonna in her eyes.

The room hadn't filled with fog; it was four o'clock and the sun was almost down. The white that had blinded the window when they arrived had turned to gray. The work light over the table created more shadows than illumination.

"We need to go inside," she said. "I need more light."

"We're about done anyway." Ridley finally raised his head. His skin wasn't pale but flushed, and, rather than having the vague alarm of shock, his eyes were so alive he looked feverish or half mad.

"Jonah, would you help Katherine finish up?" he asked. The control in his voice was so at odds with the heat in his eyes that Anna put a hand on the back of his neck. It was not cold or diaphoretic; if anything, it was a degree too warm.

"What are you doing!" he demanded as he pulled away from her.

"Checking your skin temp," she said. "Ready to go?"

As they left, they could hear Jonah: "Fakes an injury to get out of mopping up the really disgusting parts. I thought I'd taught that boy better . . ."

Anna half filled one of the metal basins from the water on the woodstove and washed and disinfected Ridley's hand in the kitchen sink. "So what's with you and Bob?" she asked, since she held him captive. She'd cooled the water from the stove with the drinking water in the second bathroom. Using the dipper, she ladled it over the cut.

He flinched.

"Sorry. Did I hurt you?"

"Not too bad."

The cut was deep but not long. "You don't seem to much like Bob," she prodded.

"He's not a real likable guy," Ridley said.

"Why did you want him to do the study evaluation?" She closed the gash with butterflies and patted his hand dry with paper towels.

Ridley took his hand back though she'd not yet bandaged it. "He came highly recommended," he said curtly.

The conversation was over but Anna'd found out a great deal. Aggressively avoiding a topic broadcasts just how emotionally charged that topic is. Why was a mystery, but if the snow kept up she was going to need something to do to pass the time for the next five weeks. And it would keep her mind off whatever it was with very big teeth and very big feet that was stalking the island.

She retrieved his hand and wrapped his palm with narrow gauze to keep it clean, then released him into the wild, wondering if, like Androcles, she'd made a friend. He went to his room and closed the door. Anna put her coat back on and headed for the carpenter's shed. The play being enacted in the shop might have a plot closer to *Saw III* than *Hamlet,* but it was the only show in town.

It wasn't the only soap opera, however.

Muffled in the saber rattle of winter branches and the fierce drive of the wind, and cloaked in the growing dusk, Anna was nearly on top of Bob and his graduate student before she saw them. They didn't see her. Anna didn't hide exactly or eavesdrop exactly; she just didn't call attention to herself.

Katherine was crying. "He was such a beautiful wolf."

Anna heard the words wailed on the wind, then the storm took the rest. After hours of slicing and dicing, pickling and bagging, all of a sudden Katherine was mourning her wolf. Bob said something, then Katherine hit him. She didn't slap or punch; she hit his well-padded, parka-clad chest with her fists the way helpless heroines in old movies did.

Bob had seen the movies too. He caught both of her wrists. He wore heavy gloves; Katherine was bare-handed. Anna tensed, waiting to see if she would have to intervene. Observing the escalation of violence was drummed into park rangers. Katherine could hit Bob all she wanted—she wasn't doing him any damage—but should he, with his height and weight advantage, strike back, he had to be taken down. Anna had no idea how she would do that. It would be like taking down the Pillsbury Doughboy on steroids.

Katherine jerked free and ran. In seconds, she was out of sight behind a curtain of snow and a scrim of trees.

The little drama had been played out within ten yards of the kitchen door against the glamorous backdrop of the outhouse. Bob didn't chase after Katherine; he turned and plowed toward the bunkhouse. Anna faded back into the trees and turned her back. The parka she'd bought off the Internet for this excursion was white, the ski pants black. Unless he was looking hard, Bob wouldn't see her.

Bob closed the door behind him. Anna continued to the shop. Mopping up blood and guts with a fistful of newspapers, Jonah was singing: "A spoon full of sugar makes the medicine go down, the medicine go down."

The wind snatched the door from Anna and banged it open. "Is everyone on this island insane?" she asked.

"All but for me and thee, and I have my doubts about thee," Jonah replied. He had small, even teeth, and when he smiled the hairs of his cropped white beard bristled out like the whiskers of an interested cat. It was hard not to smile back but Anna managed.

"What is going on around here?" she demanded.

"Unless I observe things from two hundred feet above-ground, they don't make much sense to me," Jonah admitted cheerfully and shoved the mess into a garbage bag. "Katherine was doing her thing. Bob split for the house. 'Wine time' comes earlier in the north, I guess.

Then Ms. Huff starts sniffling and snuffling. She jams half a dozen vials of blood-filled vacuum tubes in her pocket and runs out after him."

"Robin?"

"She left between the two. Headed for the bunk-house, I guess. Even our delightful, delicious bi-athlete wouldn't want to go out in this weather."

Anna ignored the "delightful, delicious" and helped him with the cleaning up.

DINNER, THE SACRED COOKING RITE presided over by the lead researcher, didn't happen. Ridley took his laptop into the room he shared with Jonah. Robin climbed into her sleeping bag for a nap. Bob took a coffee cup of boxed red wine and two peanut butter sandwiches into the room he shared with Adam and closed the door.

Being alone, or what passed for it in cabin fever country, hit Anna like a couple of Xanax on an empty stomach. Her shoulders dropped an inch, her lungs filled and she realized she'd been clenching her jaw most of the day. There were some for whom being with others of their kind was energizing. For Anna, it was as if her fellow human beings sucked the marrow from her bones if incarcerated with them too long. To a majority of felons serving time in the federal penitentiaries, the threat of going to prison did not—and, should they get out, would not—deter them from a life of crime. Even as a little girl, for Anna the mere thought of being locked in with people, having her life regulated by others, had been enough to keep her from pocketing so much as a penny candy at Idaho's Grocery.

In the unpeopled space, her mind unfolded like the wings of a bird kept too long in a small cage and her body relaxed into the fatigue left over from her dip in Intermediate Lake. She stretched out on the sofa nearest the fire and slept.

When she awoke two hours later, she was still alone, and she felt better than she had in three days. She sat up straight, settled her shoulders and commenced to find at least a few answers.

Ridley had a laptop, as did Katherine and Bob, but there was another computer, an old clunker that the biotechs who rotated through each winter had for their use. Anna got online and Googled Robert Menechinn. He was born in Canada and started his academic career in Manitoba. He'd gotten his B.A. at the University of Manitoba. He'd gotten an M.A. at the University of Winnipeg. Where the Ph.D. was obtained wasn't mentioned. All three degrees were in education, nothing in the natural or zoological sciences. The first connection with wolves was at the University of Western Ontario. When he was a lecturer there, he had taught "Education in Green" to students working on a project studying wolves. The "Green," Anna surmised, meant ecologically hip, how the neophyte researchers could teach others about their work.

From Ontario, he'd gone to the University of Saskatchewan, from there to New York, then to Virginia

WINTER STUDY | 189

and finally to Bethesda, Maryland, where he now taught "Education in the Sciences" along with several other classes that barely qualified him to lick the wolf scat off Ridley's mukluks when it came to a wilderness study of actual animals.

Anna could see how he might have gotten his name on one government list or another. He was a self-promoter. Every award or commendation he'd ever received was on every Web site that mentioned him. As a fish, he was too small to warrant such coverage. He'd had to provide the information unasked. More likely one of his graduate students did it for him. That could have impressed some government flunky sufficiently that Bob was put on the list for the ISRO evaluation, then Ridley recommended him. *Someone recommended him,* Anna amended. Ridley had simply taken their bad advice.

She leaned back and stared at the screen without seeing it.

Menechinn was forty-six; he'd gotten his B.A. at twenty-five. In a couple of decades, he'd worked in eight colleges and universities. Had this been a Park Service résumé, and the star of the piece not at least a deputy superintendent by the end of the story, she would have read it to mean Bob was a troublemaker or had severe adult-onset attention deficit disorder. It had the earmarks of an employee that nobody wants the trouble of firing so he is given rave reviews to get him passed up to be somebody else's problem.

Anna Googled Ridley Murray.

Ridley was a golden boy, commendations from all

and sundry, awards, and enough papers published to satisfy the greediest university.

Jonah Schumann's name came up twice, once in a newspaper article when he'd been hired by the wolf/moose study and once as a Web site, schumannairalaska.com. In summer, Jonah ferried hunters to camps on wilderness lakes in Alaska.

Robin wandered into the common room. "What happened to dinner?" she asked sleepily.

"I guess we're on our own." Anna closed down the Internet. She'd been sitting hunched over a hot computer so long her head had settled between her shoulders like a turkey vulture's. She pulled her bones back into alignment. "Want to heat up the leftover casserole?" Robin looked dubious, as if she'd dine on bits and scraps rather than cook. "I'll do it," Anna said. "You can keep me company." Robin's company didn't grate on Anna. There was a quiet center to her that people seldom achieved, and never before the age of forty. Maybe it was the unusual childhood, traveling the world, skiing and shooting in competition, before she was out of high school. Parts of her seemed arrested in an age of innocence, others world-weary yet without judgment.

Chicken-and-pasta casserole heated, Anna spooned it into bowls, and they carried their makeshift supper back into the common room. Sitting side by side on the couch like strangers on a bench waiting for the same bus, they ate by the warmth of the fire. Anna's ravenous appetite had returned. She marveled at how good the simple fare tasted and wondered if she could take seconds without being rude. The fierceness with which her body craved carbohydrates stunned her; when food was put before her, everything else faded away.

Wolfing it down. She was eating as a wolf would eat.

An image of the half-skinned animal on the table in the carpenter's shop, the graphic lines of muscles and the coarse thick fur making the carcass look human and inhuman, wolfish and monstrous, flared behind her brow bone. Then Ridley's hand, tight and bloodless on the hilt of the sausage knife, Katherine striking out at Bob, Jonah with his tiny, perfect teeth, singing as he slopped up viscera.

They were all becoming werewolves.

Perhaps after dinner she would go out and get in some first-rate howling. Short of a sauna and shampooing her hair, it would feel better than anything she could think of.

"That's weird," Robin said.

Anna looked up from her food, her mouth too full to speak.

"I've never seen it do that before."

Anna swallowed. "What? Seen what do what?"

Robin set aside the dregs of her casserole, stood and walked to the picture window. Uncurtained and without blinds, at night it worked as a one-way mirror. All Anna could see was the reflection of the living room and Robin. Things were sufficiently off balance that had the biotech, like the classic undead, cast no reflection, Anna doubted she'd have been surprised.

"The ice rime," Robin said. "When it warms up enough to snow but is still below freezing because of the wind or whatever, ice rime builds up on the trees, sometimes does a kind of crystal thing on the glass of the windows. But this is like . . . I don't know what it's like."

Carrying her bowl, Anna rose and joined Robin at the window. Eye level, about halfway across the pane, precipitation was turning to ice on the glass but not all in one place. As they watched, the ice crystals formed a vertical line, then a horizontal, then, as if spread by the gusts of wind, many straight-line segments began to appear.

"I've never seen anything like it either," Anna said.

"I better get Ridley. He'd kill me if he missed this." Robin backed away from the window, and Anna heard her soft tread as she crossed the common room. More lines appeared, joined others to create angles. They were beautiful. So close to the glass, Anna could see the crystals as they formed, each a tiny shard of the universe.

"Holy smoke!" came Robin's soft whisper, followed by Ridley's voice, angry and quiet.

"If this is a joke, you are off this island as soon as it clears."

"It's not a joke," Anna said. "We were eating and the ice started to form in geometrical patterns. There must be a fault in the window glass or something."

"Step back," Ridley said, his voice as flat and sharp as the blade of a knife.

"I doubt it will break," she said. "Not if it's held all these winters."

"Step back, God dammit."

Anna stepped back.

The ice lines had come together to form two words: "HELP ME."

15

"Help me," Robin whispered.

"Anytime," Jonah replied as he followed Ridley into the common room. "Who's been writing on the glass?"

"Nobody," Robin said. "It just appeared."

Bob joined them. Jonah pointed to the window. "Writing," he said. "It just appeared."

"By magic?" Bob sneered.

Anna didn't have a better explanation.

"Help who?" Robin asked.

"Me, obviously," Bob said, sporting his signature wink.

Adam was safely—if not comfortably—ensconced in the Feldtmann fire tower. Bob, Ridley, Jonah, Robin and Anna were in the bunkhouse.

"Katherine," Anna said. "Where's Katherine?"

Katherine Huff had been gone four hours. No one had noticed. Anna might have, but the door to Katherine's room was shut and Anna'd assumed the researcher was sulking, sleeping or licking her wounds from her spat with Bob.

Grabbing a flashlight, Anna went out onto the deck. Below the ghostly writing on the window, the snow had been trampled to ice rubble where Adam had been fetching armloads of wood for the stove. If there were new tracks, they blended with the old.

Anna shined the beam on the steps. They had nothing to tell her. Whoever had crept up to write the eerie note had left no tracks. That didn't mean the writer was a thing of air and mystery; it only meant he or she had been careful. The storm blocked the moon and stars. Far enough from cities to be free of light pollution, the night was blind black. Driving wind harried the snow until the flakes were small and mean, stinging skin and eyes. It wouldn't take an Eagle Scout—or an Apache scout, for that matter—to come and go, unnoticed and untraceable.

She, Anna thought.

This had the earmarks of a woman scorned seeking revenge or attention. How the trick was played on the glass, Anna couldn't guess, but surely a woman who played with DNA would know enough about chemistry to manage it. Mentally Anna brushed off her annoyance. She'd never stooped to such a trick, but she'd sure as hell fantasized about it a time or two.

She returned to the window. The words were still

there, limned in ice. Beyond the glass, she could see the dumb show of the three men talking, shaking their heads, gesticulating, walking short distances only to walk back. Without the pseudologic of words, they looked mad as hatters, each locked in his own world where he was king or jester or god.

A crazy-making current was running through the island. That a wog had manifest, a windigo died at their feet and a wolf been slaughtered didn't completely account for it. The unreasoning fear of children raised on fairy tales where wolves had an overweening penchant for evil trickled under saner thoughts. David Mech, Rolf Peterson, Ridley and a dozen other wolf researchers had spent decades debunking this myth, but there was no rooting out the ogres of childhood.

Fear was the yeast stirred into the mix of human dysfunctions, a catalyst that could spin them out of control. Fear was the difference between neurosis and insanity. Ridley detested Bob Menechinn for endangering his livelihood, his status and his study. He hated him for being ignorant and having power over the educated, being worthless but out to destroy the worth in other's lives. Ridley tried to hide the worst of these emotions, but even the beard and the mustache and the startling intelligence couldn't mask things all the time.

Yet Ridley had been the one to bring Menechinn to the island, had, in effect, given him the power of life and death over careers and learning.

Katherine was cowed by her mentor but had pounded his chest, however pathetically, and run away. Anna would have suspected a love triangle; it wasn't cliché for no reason. NASA, trailer trash, Rhodes scholars: it didn't matter, love—or what passed for love in the tabloids—made people dangerous. Katherine's first love was a wolf; perhaps, like a Freudian version of "Little Red Riding Hood," she was waiting to be devoured or rescued from a prolonged childhood by a handsome ax-toting woodsman.

Jonah drifted untouched by the Sturm und Drang as he flew untouched by the earth for much of his life. He'd been Winter Study's pilot for eighteen years; Anna'd seen a picture of him, slipped into the plastic cover of the daily log, when he was in his forties or early fifties. One assumed he had a life the other forty-six weeks of the year—Anna'd seen the Web site—but he never spoke of it. Never spoke of a wife or a home or kids or his other job. Never shared anything even remotely personal. He defended his internal landscape with jokes.

In the dumb show being played out on the other side of the glass, Jonah was slightly apart from the fray, leaning in the doorway to the kitchen, his arms folded over his chest, a slightly bemused expression on his face.

Robin had retreated to a low, narrow plank bench along the rear wall. Whether or not she brought anything but the TNT of youth and beauty to this stew, Anna didn't know, but Robin was affected by the uneasy atmosphere; Anna saw glimpses of it on her face occasionally before she escaped into the icy embrace of winter with the ease of one born of the union of a snow leopard and a polar bear.

Anna and her mother before her and her grand-mother—a fighting Quaker Democrat and a flapper—were feminists. Much of her life, Anna had worked in a male-dominated world. She would defend the right of any woman to do the same, but she was realist enough to admit women made things more complicated, more volatile. Not because women were stupid or incompe-tent but because their presence often made men stupid and incompetent.

Like Menechinn. Except she doubted he was stupid. Arrogance was a form of stupidity because it caused elective blindness. Bob Menechinn might be a fool, but there was nothing wrong with his brain. Anna hardly knew where to start thinking about him. He possessed too many degrees in education to actually know any-thing yet had the supreme confidence that he knew it all. When he smiled—which he did too much—he had a way of pulling his chin in and letting his cheeks rise to cover his eyes that suggested he was holding back, strik-ing a pose the way a penny-ante lawyer will when he thinks he's got an ace up his sleeve. Menechinn believed himself to be a ladies' man. The ladies, with the possible exception of Katherine, were unmoved.

"HELP ME" was fading, dimming out the same way it had appeared, line by line, in reverse order. Before hypothermia drove Anna back into the confines of the bunkhouse, she touched one of the rapidly vanishing marks. Her fingers were so cold from gripping the flash-light without gloves, she couldn't feel anything.

Ectoplasm, she mocked and went inside.

Bob either didn't think his run-in with Katherine was important enough or, conversely, was too important to share.

Anna played tattletale.

"She was crying," she finished. "She struck out at Bob, then ran. I don't think she was in any shape mentally to plan an adventure."

"Katherine was fine," Bob said blandly.

" 'Fine' is weeping and running off into a blizzard?" Anna asked.

"Snow was making her contacts go nuts, is all. She wanted to get back to the bunkhouse in a hurry, is my guess. You've been watching too much daytime television." And he winked.

One day you'll shoot your eye out with that thing, Anna thought.

They made a perimeter search of the housing compound, Anna and Ridley going to the left from the bunkhouse, Robin and Jonah to the right. Bob stayed by the radio.

And the fire. And the wine, Anna thought as she slogged through blind-black, bitter weather. A walk that should have taken ten minutes took twice that. The four met up at the bottom of the compound near the road down to the lake. Even with flashlights, they could scarcely see.

"We're not finding anybody tonight," Anna said. "We're liable to lose ourselves." She told them of her thought that Katherine was hiding, playing games.

"If she is, it's the last game she'll ever play," Ridley

said grimly. "She'll freeze to death." He was shouting. They were all shouting to be heard above the wind. Their puny noise did little to dent the immensity of the night and the storm.

"There are places she could survive," Robin said. "If she broke into permanent housing, she might find blankets. Or, if she took some, she could make it in a shelter for a few hours."

"Good," Anna said. "Ridley, you guys take the permanent housing. Robin and I will do the lean-tos. Then we're done for the night."

Ridley started to protest but Anna overrode him. He wasn't versed in search and rescue. Anna was. "We can't search in this. Period. It's too risky. We wait till daylight."

"Okay," Ridley said. "You're right. Come on, Jonah. You two be careful." Ridley was one of those rare leaders who only choose to lead when they are in their area of strength. Maybe this once Anna's first impression had been right, maybe he was a terrific man.

"Lead on," Anna said to Robin and, feeling trollish and lumpsome, stumped down the road beside Robin's fairy-stepping form. At the orange fuel tanks, they turned onto a smaller trail leading toward Washington Creek campground. The ugly monument to fossil fuels was invisible in dark and snow, but Anna could feel it being hideous all the same.

Lean-tos—screened-in sheds for campers—were scattered along the bank of Washington Creek above the harbor, about a ten-minute walk from the housing area.

"It's hard to believe a rational woman would spend the night freezing in an open shed when her toasty bed is so close," Anna shouted.

"Thermal wimp," Robin accused good-naturedly.

They shined their lights into every shelter. As the cold, dusty emptiness of one lean-to after another whispered of summers dead and winters lasting forever, hope dimmed. Had the missing woman been Robin, Anna would have been more optimistic. Robin was acclimatized, winter was her friend and she was accustomed to physical hardship. Robin wouldn't panic.

Katherine was none of these things.

Katherine was also not in any of the employee housing.

ANNA SLEPT FITFULLY, wriggling like an uneasy larva in her down cocoon. The single bed was adequate most nights, but this night she kept waking to find she'd squashed herself against the wall or was perilously close to falling off.

Robin didn't sleep much better. Anna could hear her thrashing about. Once she leaped from her bed, dug through her rucksack—at least that's what Anna assumed; the dark was impenetrable—clunked a found object down on the desk at the bed's foot and squirmed back into her sleeping bag. Or maybe Anna only dreamed she did.

Her dreams were thick and convoluted, dragging images from unrelated drawers and cobbling them together into stories Harlan Ellison couldn't unravel. She woke, thinking she heard the howling of coyotes on her mother's ranch. The call of a loon dragged her from sleep. She woke again to wretched disappointment, finding she was not in Paul's arms but curled up like a sow bug on a strange bed.

The sun didn't so much rise as the snow, still falling but with less vehemence, grew gray. There would be no search from the air. Breakfast was quick. Each person would take a radio and a different trail. Ridley attempted to call in to dispatch in Houghton, Michigan, to alert them to the situation, but radio contact, always sketchy, had been obliterated by the storm and the phone lines allowed more static than language. He e-mailed.

As they were dividing up the trails for the search, Adam dragged in. He had the body type Anna associated with the cowboys where she'd grown up and, later, the die-hard wildland firefighters: long muscles and bones, big knuckles, wide shoulders and skinny legs. The kind of men that can just keep on working, keep on digging firebreaks or building fence or riding line as if their lanky bodies were made of sterner stuff than mere flesh and didn't burn as much fuel as other humans.

Adam looked like he'd finally run out of gas. No longer held at bay by the strength of his personality, age dragged down his cheeks and made pouches beneath his eyes.

"You look like hell," Ridley said without sympathy.

"Yeah, well, freezing your butt off all night, then hiking nine miles in deep snow before breakfast, will do that to a guy," Adam snapped, and shrugged out of his coat.

"Don't get too comfortable," Ridley warned.

"Katherine's gone missing," Anna told him.

Adam put his coat back on.

"Grab some food," Ridley said, "then search the Hugginin Trail loop. That'll free Jonah up to stay near the airplane in case the weather breaks."

Bob announced he would stay at the bunkhouse near the radio. In case Jonah flew and they needed to coordinate, he said. Given the missing woman was his graduate student and, at least on her end, there seemed to be a proprietary interest, he didn't seem overly anxious to help find her. "Recheck the permanent-employee housing and check the maintenance buildings at least," Ridley said. He didn't bother to disguise the scorn in his voice. "She might have broken into one of the equipment sheds if she was upset enough."

Bob turned his face slightly away. Maybe Katherine's going missing had hit him harder than Anna'd given him credit for. Before this, Bob might have goldbricked out of fear of wild beasts or plain old sloth, but he wouldn't have bothered to look guilty about it.

"What did you and Katherine fight about last night?" Anna asked bluntly.

His shame, or whatever it was, vanished, replaced by the tucked-back smile of false bonhomie. "We didn't fight. I don't fight with women."

He didn't wink. Anna was making progress.

There, snow was deep enough for skiing. The best

skier, Robin, was given the Minong. It was the roughest trail on the island, running as it did along the broken crest of glacial ridges. Anna had skied a little, she'd seen others—people who were good at it—ski, but she'd never seen anything like Robin. It was as if the snow conspired with the skis to carry her effortlessly like *Winged Victory* into battle.

Ridley would cover the Greenstone Trail. Because of the shortcut from the housing area to the head of the trail, if Katherine had found a trail and not just stumbled off into the bushes the Greenstone would be it. He pushed off. Ridley's style was more prosaic than Robin's, but the power in his legs and his familiarity with wintry things was apparent.

Anna took Feldtmann Lake Trail. Adam had returned to Windigo that way, but he'd been traveling fast in bad light, not looking for a sign. She considered taking the one remaining pair of skis, but, in the end, she laced on her Sorels. She wasn't proficient enough on skis not to wear herself out with them.

In full winter regalia, passing through a snowy landscape, her suit bulky and her face peeking out through a bucket, the wheeze of her breath and the squeak of her boots all that penetrated to her muffled ears, Anna felt cut off from the natural world.

Isolation exacerbated by a sense of being crowded. A neurotic wouldn't know which way to flinch.

When she was a ranger on Isle Royale, she'd hiked the Feldtmann many times. It was easygoing, running over small hills and occasionally a basalt outcropping high enough to afford views of the lake.

Easy.

Except the cold was a wall. Sweat ran beneath the parka, while her toes, fingers and face burned like frost was gnawing on them. She unzipped her coat and pulled off one glove—the equivalent of sticking a foot out from under the covers to cool off. Taking Robin as her example, she tried to embrace winter but kept finding herself trudging along without thinking much and seeing even less. On a search and—it was still to be hoped—rescue, this was bad.

In frustration, she pulled off hat and balaclava. The cold hurt, and she wondered if Paul would still love her if the tips of her nose and ears turned black, but the sense of being bundled into helplessness diminished. At least she could hear the rat-tatting of the woodpeckers and the chittering of squirrels.

Life had come back while she wasn't paying attention. She tilted her head back and looked at the sky. The snow had stopped. The clouds were still too low for Jonah to take the airplane up, but they looked like they might lift in an hour or more. The thought of backup—or an audience to witness her weakness—gave her usable energy and she pushed on in better spirits.

Another two hours elapsed before she reached Feldt-mann Lake. It was too far. A woman running from a bad exchange with her mentor/tormentor, or whatever Bob was to Katherine, didn't run nine miles on the proverbial "dark and stormy night." Either she didn't want to be found or she'd gone off trail. Still, like the postman, Anna made her appointed rounds. When she got tired, she had to remind herself to drink. The body didn't give the same clues in a Michigan winter as it did in summer in the south.

She didn't have to remind herself to eat. The pathetic little peanut-butter-and-honey sandwich was gone before the morning was out. By noon, she was so famished she wondered if she could catch a squirrel and force it to give up the location of its stash.

She saw a red fox, woodpeckers, red squirrels, chickadees, wolf tracks, moose tracks and what looked to be martin tracks. Nothing to indicate Katherine had been this way.

Ridley radioed in. He'd skied ten miles up the Greenstone and seen nothing but two half-starved moose and more wolf prints.

Robin radioed in soon after. She, too, was turning back. She'd skied as far as Lake Desor, a brutal jaunt for a lesser person, and was still talking without gasping. Robin had seen nothing. Not so much as a fox.

Nobody could raise Adam.

"Battery must have gone dead," Ridley said drily.

"Yeah." For a man supposedly in charge of the physical plant, he seemed to be developing a penchant for being out of pocket and unreachable.

The sun didn't show its face, but the wind dropped to nothing and the sky lightened. When Anna was halfway back to Washington Harbor, she heard the buzz of the supercub.

Half an hour later, Jonah found something. Color, he said. Like a piece of clothing thrown off, and a disturbed area in a cedar swamp between the Greenstone and the Feldtmann. He couldn't see much, just that there was color on the snow where there shouldn't be, and it was the same gold and barn red as the old parka Katherine had been wearing at the necropsy.

No place to land that was any closer than the super-cub's tie-down on Washington Harbor, Jonah circled low and slow to see if he could get a rise out of anything in the trees around the scrap of gold and red.

Anna radioed Ridley. "When you get to the bunk-house, bring the Sked, a body bag and flashlights. Where's Robin?"

"Two miles out," Robin's voice came back over the air.

"Head down the Feldtmann," Anna told her. "I'll mark where I go off trail."

Jonah circled till he spotted Anna, then waggled his wings and led off trail toward the scraps of color. She followed like a baby trumpeter swan following an ultra-light.

The find. Scraps of color. Anna suspected they no longer went to rescue a victim but to recover a body.

She'd never have said it aloud. Bad juju.

16

Following Jonah's lead, Anna made it to the cedar swamp in forty minutes. At every moment, she expected to be overtaken by the skiers but was still solo when Jonah made his last transmission: "See that rise ahead of you? Got a big nose of rock sticking out of it and trees like nose hairs?"

"I got it," Anna radioed back.

"The body is right beyond that. Trees'll clear out and there'll be a rock about the size of a refrigerator, then you turn left. Can't miss it. Wind's coming up. I've got to head back."

Jonah had said "body" out loud. Out loud and over the radio. The breach of tradition gave Anna a shiver akin to that of an actor when the Scottish play is mentioned by name or peacock feathers are worn on stage. Till they knew for sure Katherine was dead—and that this was Katherine—time had to be considered of the essence. Close on quarter till four, wind rising, and fatigue dragging her steps, Anna had no choice but to keep on, but she was not averse to a little company at this point.

"Where is everybody?" She didn't whine, but she felt like it.

"They're coming," Jonah promised. "They got held up leaving the bunkhouse."

Anna wondered what in the hell could have held them up. Cell phones didn't work on the island, the radio was out, the island was socked in so seaplanes couldn't come and go.

Maybe somebody dropped by. Given recent events, that thought bordered on the sinister.

She topped the rise by the nose, spotted the refrigerator, half slid down and turned left as she'd been directed. Jonah said, "You can't miss it," and he was old enough and wily enough not to say that unless it was true.

In swampy areas, cedar trees fell like jackstraws, one over the other, the living with the dead, branches entangled. During the growing season, the swamps were water filled and choked with undergrowth. In winter, they were navigable, but just barely. Fresh snow cloaked the branches of the upright trees and filled tiny ledges in the bark. Downed trees, fallen willy-nilly, made a lumpy quilt, protecting the living trees' roots. Snow hid where one deadfall crossed another, and maybe three more below that, till walking through was like negotiating an icebound jungle filled with Lilliputian tiger traps.

Traversing a cedar swamp in the snow was just

begging to have an ankle broken or a knee sprained. Anna forced herself to slow down. Becoming a second victim was too humiliating to contemplate. A gust of wind knocked snow from branches down her collar, and something else that brought her to an abrupt stop, head up, sniffing the air like an animal. She'd caught a whiff of the odor she'd noticed the night they followed the wolf pack down to the harbor. A death-and-worse smell she'd associated with the stench of Algernon Blackwood's windigo, the horrible odor that heralded its coming. As before, the smell was snatched away before she could be sure she hadn't conjured it up from an overactive imagination.

Then the "find" was in front of her. A body.

Parts of a body.

The reason Jonah had been able to spot anything from the air was due to small creatures, probably foxes, which had worried and dug until they'd uncovered the arm. Not Katherine's body, just her arm, still in the sleeve of her parka, her ungloved hand a stump of chewed fingers. At least Anna assumed the arm was Katherine's; it was wearing her coat.

The sleeve of the parka wasn't the only color in the naturally black-and-white landscape. There was no blood on the ground—or, if there was, the snow had covered it—but on the trunks of the trees leading away from the severed arm was iridescent orange paint applied with a spatter brush. The neon color was so screamingly out of place, Anna had a moment of pure confusion as her brain tried desperately to make sense of the phenome-

non, flashing through traffic cones, construction saw-
horses, vandalism, police tape, confetti, graffiti, trail
blazes.

A macabre vision of the severed arm blazing a trail to
the body it was snatched from played through her mind.
She shook it off, the way a dog shakes off a bath, and
skirted the area where the arm lay, palm to the sky, fingers gnawed to the knuckle bones. At the first of the
orange-daubed trees, she stopped. The neon dots were
crystalline. She pulled off her glove and pinched a bit of
the stuff up, rubbing it between thumb and forefinger.
Body heat melted it, leaving a trace of red on her skin.

She didn't sniff it or taste it. Blood was said to smell
metallic, but she could never smell anything unless there
was a lot of it and it was getting ripe. Still, she was sure
it was blood. The spatter patterns formed when Katherine had fought whatever had taken off her arm. For some
reason, the interaction of blood with the intense cold
turned it Halloween orange.

White cedar trunks, bright Pollock-like paintings in
blood orange, black of the branches overhead sketching
a white sky: the scene was stunningly beautiful.

Until she saw Katherine.

The body was facedown, head shoved partly under a
log as if Katherine had tried to burrow away from her
attackers. The back of her parka was torn, tufts of down
leaking out rents that ran shoulder to hip where claws
had dug to get at the chewy center. Strands of light
brown hair mixed with the tatters of cloth and goose
feathers. The fur that ringed the hood of her coat was

ripped away, as was half the hood. Blood, not orange but black as tar, glued the mess together. From the waist down, she was clad only in Levi's. Her ski pants had been shucked off of her, as a man might shuck an ear of corn, and for the same reason. The light down trousers had then been torn to pieces, played with until there was little recognizable as clothing but the suspender buckles. The Levi's were surprisingly intact but for the bottom of the left leg. That had been chewed to a mess of string and blood. The foot was gone.

Anna had to fight a bizarre urge to run. Mostly she liked the dead: they were quiet, undemanding and never complained if they were dropped on a carryout. Because the teeth of hungry little creatures had busily uncoiled the mortal coil had never bothered her. Human bodies were as dried leaves, acorn husks, snake skins: a thing of no import any longer left behind.

Katherine bothered her.

She concentrated on breathing in and breathing out and making excuses: *The light was unsettling—dim and slanting and yellow-gray—cold carped on the bones, undermined body and spirit, the natural world behaving unnaturally, claustrophobic living conditions, discord in the human pack.* The list of reasons did little to stop liquid fear coursing through her veins because reason wasn't the root of it. Ghosts, yetis, skin walkers, vampires, zombies, gremlins, wogs and windigos—six million years of campfire stories—were undermining the rationale of everyone on the island.

"Get a grip," she growled and looked around the

rest of the clearing. Focusing past the mutilated arm, she began to see other disturbances in the snow. Over an area about five feet in diameter, animals had been digging. Where they'd dug were bright orange stains. She saw the foot, boot torn off and bones showing where the flesh had been eaten away. In another depression in the snow was a hank of light brown hair clotted with black. Mostly whatever had stained the snow—fingers, flesh, a toe—had been carted off and eaten elsewhere.

Little guys, foxes and ravens and rodents, had feasted. But the little guys had not torn a full-sized woman to pieces.

"Anna!"

She twitched so hard it hurt her neck. Being startled pissed her off and being pissed off was a lot better than being tired and scared. "It's about damn time you got here," she hollered. "Where the hell have you been? What in God's name could have held you up on this godforsaken island?"

Ridley, following her blasphemies, came through the tangle of downed trees with more grace than she had managed. Behind him was Robin and, beside her, Bob. That was what had held them up. Anna realized she was about to get out of line and scaled back her anger.

She thought to warn them, to say: "It's bad" or "Pretty grim scene" or "Take the women and kids back to the house," but instead she just waited till Robin and Ridley noticed the digging, the arm. Then, like a tour guide from hell, she pointed out the various pieces.

Bob waded in and started brushing snow away from the arm. "Leave it," Anna snapped. "I don't want the scene compromised."

"Wolves killed her," Bob said. He started in with the brushing again, and it bothered her that he was uncovering the arm.

The arm, for chrissake. It was cut off. It was hamburger. Anybody who wasn't Bob would have brushed the snow from Katherine's face.

"Wolves may have torn her apart," Anna said in a tone she considered reasonable. "We don't know what killed her. I need you to stop that."

He looked up at her desperate or dangerous or scared. Anna didn't think it was grief.

He was digging up her *arm. Her fucking arm.* Anna was having trouble getting past that.

"Another front is coming in," Ridley said. "We're going to lose the light in an hour or so."

Another dark and stormy night. Anna was getting that clock-striking-midnight-as-the-power-goes-out feeling again. "Whatever we miss won't be here tomorrow," she said. "It'll be somebody's dinner."

Robin took up photographic duties. The constant flash became a freakish punctuation to the finds, the pieces of what had once been a young woman.

A young woman murdered by her first love, the wolf; when the snow was swept from the body, it became clear she had been killed by a wolf or wolves. Her throat was torn out, her head connected to her body only by her spine. The damage was fierce but incomplete. The body had not been eviscerated, the face was intact, the coat, though badly torn, was not stripped from the meat.

"Odd," Anna said, and: "Wolf."

"Wog," Ridley said.

"It was a pack of wolves," Bob said, his voice as plummy and certain as if he were reporting the six o'clock news.

"If it was wolves—natural wolves, pure wolves—it's the first time in recorded history it's happened in America," Ridley said. "What's your take on this, Menechinn? If it was wolves, do you get to open the island year-round so Homeland Security can arm all the parkies and, between creel checks and wake-in-no-wake-zone citations, Ranger Rick can save us from the Canadians?"

Ridley asked as if it were a real question, as if he cared about Bob's answer.

"Homeland Security can shut down your little pissant operation anytime," Bob replied with the same big tucked-in smile he bestowed on everything, and Anna wondered if he liked making Ridley miserable or was simply incapable of empathy.

"Not if this is a wolf kill," she said. "Led by a wog or not, every wildlife biologist in the world will be lobbying to keep the study going. Scientists can't stand an anomaly."

"Doggone it, where is Adam?" Ridley demanded. Apropos of nothing that Anna could follow, he transferred his anger from Menechinn to Adam Johansen. "Radio him again," he ordered Robin and, turning his back on Anna and Bob, took the camera from the biotech and began photographing the scene.

Bit by bit, as it was recorded by the camera, they brought together what was left of Katherine Huff.

As they had at the necropsy, they worked as a team. This time Robin and Anna handled the corpse, carefully brushing away the snow, and Ridley photographed it in situ. Anna didn't know what Bob Menechinn was doing other than wandering around, staring at the ground, digging here and there.

"Wolves don't do this," Ridley said when the body parts were uncovered and accounted for. "They just don't. We were talking about this the other day. There's upward of two thousand wolves in Minnesota. They eat moose and deer and sheep, when they can get them. They don't hunt down and kill humans."

Anna was studying the scene in an attempt to reconstruct the incident. "Look." She took one of the flashlights Ridley brought. The sun must have been close to setting. The light was fading and sky, air and earth were a uniform gray. Holding the flashlight at ground level, she sent the beam across the surface of the snow. Ridley squatted on his heels and followed the line with his eyes.

"You can see where she crawled, trying to get away." Anna played the beam across a faint but discernible trough that had been cut through old snow, then filled with new. "And there she tried to pull herself up on a tree; tried to save herself. Then she goes down again there."

"Wolves don't behave this way," Ridley said doggedly.

"See where the bark is shredded on the downed trunk? She must have tried to crawl beneath it, and the wolves tore at it till they got her out. The marks are too big for anything else."

"They don't do this," Ridley said but he sounded more confused than convinced. "They just don't."

Anna didn't argue with him. She knew the wolf statistics. Western parks debated them endlessly as the subject of reintroducing wolves heated up.

"It'll be dark before we get back," Ridley said and stood. "Bob! Make yourself useful." To Anna he said: "We'll package the remains for transport. You and Robin look around a little more. We've got ten minutes, then we've got to move."

A foot of new snow could hide a lot of sins. There was no point in searching any areas that hadn't been disturbed by scavengers. The clearing where the body was found was not so much a clearing as a flat space where the trees had opted not to fall for one reason or another. It was scarcely six feet on a side. Beyond that, they were again in the giant's game of pick-up-sticks.

Anna followed Katherine's back trail. Five or six yards into the tangle of trees, she found a place where the snow had been dug down almost to bare earth. Shreds of fabric were scattered around the dig.

"Robin," Anna called. "Bring your light." Robin came lightly, gracefully, annoying Anna with her ease of movement in this hostile environment. "What do you think?" Anna asked, pointing out the fabric. "Backpack? She must have gone back to the bunkhouse before she ran off. That changes things. To what, I haven't a clue."

The pack, what was left of it, was of dark blue canvas,

a relic from before high tech went into the backcountry. The anachronism was jarring. Katherine was a state-of-the-art woman. The wolves had attacked the pack with a fury that struck Anna as almost personal, the way a deranged person will defile an object belonging to someone they hate.

Radios came to life; Adam calling from the base radio in the bunkhouse. "My batteries went dead," came through a storm of static. "Where is everybody?"

Ridley was the one who answered. He told him briefly of the body. "You may as well stay where you are," he said. "There's not much you can do now." Ridley's tone made it clear that there had been a good deal he could have done earlier if he hadn't been AWOL.

"Ten-four," Adam said. The Park Service had gone to plain speech years before, but people clung to the codes.

Handing Robin her flashlight, Anna carefully widened the dig. Shards of black plastic were embedded in the snow. "Film canister?" Anna wondered aloud as she collected them into a baggie and handed it to the biotech. She swept the snow clear of a broken glass vial, the snow around it dark with blood.

"Jonah said Katherine pocketed vials of wolf blood before she left the carpenter's shop," Anna mused. "Maybe that was a factor in the attack." Shading her eyes from the flashlight, she looked up at Robin.

The biotech's face was puckering the way a small child's will as it readies for tears. Her eyes had dilated more than the coming dusk could account for.

"Get me something to bag this in," Anna said to distract her from whatever thoughts were breaking her down. Robin did as she was told, but she didn't speak, and her movements lost their fluidity. Twice she stumbled over downed trees. The second time, she fell. When she regained her feet, she stood where she was as if she'd lost her way.

Delayed shock at the grisly scene and hypothermia would both account for the behavior. Maybe winter had finally turned on Robin. Anna left the hole she was excavating. There was no need to go on collecting "evidence." The wolves would never get their day in court. Anna'd been doing it out of habit. She left the scraps and buckles and took Robin's arm.

"Come on," she said quietly. "Help me get the Sked ready." Holding on to Robin, Anna clambered through the obstacle course of the swamp to the sled Ridley had towed from Windigo. Robin's knees buckled and she went down on all fours, head drooping, hair painting the snow.

"What happened?" Anna asked as she pulled her to her feet.

Robin didn't answer and Anna didn't push it. Opening wounds was best done in a controlled environment.

"Did you find a cell phone?" Bob called. "They belong to the university and I'll have to pay for it."

That's what he'd been doing, digging here and there. He was looking to save himself a few bucks. The callousness struck Anna like a snowball hitting ice. Too tired to bother turning her head in his direction, "No phone," she said.

By the time they got Katherine's remains stowed in

garbage bags—if the park had a body bag, Ridley didn't know where it was—and strapped into the rescue Sked, it was full dark. Wind from the northeast, bringing the promised front, had picked up and the temperature was falling.

Anna had to help Robin on with her skis. In the morning, the woman had worn them as if they were an extension of her body. Now she fumbled with the locks, unsure of how they worked.

"Hang on," Anna said and patted her leg awkwardly. "We'll be home in no time. Don't think too much." Robin said nothing.

Anna held the light for the others as they strapped on their skis, then helped Ridley into the harness attached to the Sked. The only one without skis, she would follow behind to free it if it got hung up on anything.

Now that the distraction of the corpse and its attendant parts was over, Anna was feeling every mile and minute of the day as well as the day before's fight to get clear of the ice of Intermediate. Fatigue pressed on her till it was all she could do to keep her head up.

Robin went first, carrying one of the flashlights. Anna didn't like her leading, but she didn't want her bringing up the rear either. At least in front, if she went down, they'd see her.

Bob followed in Robin's tracks. Anna was surprised how good he was on skis till she remembered he'd been born and raised in Canada. Ridley was third, carrying the other light and pulling the body. Anna fell into place at the tail of the train.

They'd not been on the move for fifteen minutes when the Sked tipped between two stones at the base of the outcropping with the stone nose. Anna was grateful. She was at the end of her strength and needed the short rest. "Hold up," Ridley called to the others, then stood silently in his traces like an old horse. None of them spoke. Anything that came to mind to say was too grim to share.

The narrow metal sled had ridden up on the right side over a rock beneath the snow until it was close to tipping over. Anna caught up the few yards she'd fallen behind and knelt to right it. Both knees cracked as she went down and she wondered if she'd have to push on the ground like an old woman to get up again. Bracing herself, she lifted and pulled on the left edge of the aluminum sled, sliding it back onto level ground.

"You're good to go," she said.

"Go, Robin," Ridley called.

Anna stayed where she was, the energy to rise eluding her for a moment. She'd heard about people wanting to lie down and sleep in the snow but had never understood the allure of it till now. She was gathering her strength to rise when she heard something in the trees to the left of the trail. Intermixed with the sighing of the wind was the sound of stealthy movement, whispering over the snow purposeful and stealthy, keeping pace with Ridley and the others.

They were being stalked.

17

The flicker and cut of the flashlights were ahead of her. But for these theatrical sharps of light, snipping images from perfect dark, Anna could see nothing. Three feet from where she knelt, the hounds of hell could be waiting, tails wagging in anticipation, and she'd not see them. She closed her eyes to shut out distraction and felt her universe extend on a plane of sound waves. Wind sighed, gentled from its earlier shrieks. Branches of trees discussed the small doings of the creatures beneath in whispers of snow falling from overburdened limbs and the snicker of bark on bark.

Nothing else. The stealthy slip and pad of predators had stopped. Or was never there. Ears swaddled in fleece, brain in fatigue, eyes in darkness: imagining sneaking noises was not beyond the realm of possibility.

With a grunt that she was glad none of the young and

agile heard, Anna pushed to her feet and trudged on. Ridley had reached the top of the small knoll. He wasn't a whole lot bigger than Anna, not more than five-foot-eight or so, and slight of frame. He had skied twenty miles before he was called to the body recovery, yet his movements remained fluid. Anna envied him for a few steps, then let it go. She hadn't the strength to waste on nonessentials.

"SWITCH OUT!" Ridley hollered.

Anna woke with a start. She was on her feet, she was in position behind the Sked where she was supposed to be, but she'd been walking in a trance. Thirty minutes had elapsed. Ridley and Robin were switching out. Robin would pull the Sked for half an hour, then switch with Bob, so no one got overtired.

As Robin made her way to the rear of the line, Anna knelt in the snow, glad the darkness was there to cover what might have looked more like a collapse than a controlled descent. Light smashed into her face and she threw up an arm to protect herself.

"Sorry," Ridley said. "How are you doing?"

"Good," Anna said. "I'm doing good."

"Eat something," he said.

"Good idea." That got the flashlight and his attention off of her and she slumped back into her clothes. She didn't have anything to eat and, for the first time in what seemed like forever, she wasn't hungry. Or, if she was, she was too tired to chew and swallow.

Ridley escaped the harness and buckled Robin into it. Robin had never towed a Sked before, but she'd skied a thousand miles with a pack and a rifle on her back so Ridley didn't bother with much in the way of instruction.

When they'd done, he shined his light over the harness and the Sked, checking that the lines were still secure. "Where's your light?" he demanded suddenly.

"Bob took it. He wanted to go first."

"Bob took it," Ridley said. "God damn him. Here, take mine. God damn him. God damn Adam," he said and pushed into the darkness toward the wavering speck of light that was the purloined flashlight.

"What's with Ridley and Adam?" Anna asked.

"Who knows," Robin replied. Her voice was hollow, as if part of her said the expected words while another, greater part of her was someplace else. Someplace where nightmare was the special of the day.

"How are you doing?" Anna asked. "My strength of ten men is down to about eight-point-five," she admitted. "Are you okay?"

"Bob took my light."

The biotech was crying. Anna couldn't see it but tears were breaking in her words.

"Let me pull the Sked for a while," Anna said, wondering if she could make good on the offer.

"No."

Maybe it would be good for Robin to keep working, keep moving, so Anna didn't argue with her. She didn't get up either. In a moment she would, she promised herself.

The wind stopped, the trees ceased their muttering and silence as cold and deep as an ice cave poured down. Into that silence came the sound Anna had heard before, stealthy movement in the trees to their left. Robin heard it too. In the glow of the flashlight, Anna saw her head jerk as if on a string; she uttered a strangled cry and began to swing the light in erratic arcs across the landscape. Suddenly illuminated, and as suddenly vanishing back into the dark, trunks and white and rocks flashed by, and for a second Anna felt as if she were falling.

Whether a curious moose, a band of squirrels or a slavering wog was with them, they couldn't stay where they were. Ridley and Bob were already out of sight. Without light, Ridley couldn't come back to help them; all he could do was follow Bob's flashlight the way a lost ship follows the flashing of a buoy. Shaking her head to clear it, Anna blinked a few times. "We better get going."

Without a word, Robin put her weight behind the harness and pulled. From her kneeling position, Anna pushed on the back of the Sked, breaking it free of where it had frozen to the snow while they'd stopped. A crack, a lurch, and it was moving. A crack, a lurch, and Anna was on her feet moving as well. Robin covered more ground than Ridley had, either not so considerate of Anna slogging behind or more anxious to get back to the main trail and then the bunkhouse.

Anna lifted one foot, then the other, and stayed upright, but the Sked drew away little by little. When the body, the biotech and the light source were several yards ahead, and traveling ever faster, Anna swallowed her pride and called out.

"Hold up. You're killing me."

The light stopped. Anna's breath sawed in her ears as she plowed through the snow. Reaching the Sked, she fell to her knees. She hadn't spent so much time on her knees since she went to Catholic school. It crossed her mind that a little praying might not hurt anything. With the wog and the munched-up graduate student, the slithery noises and the gigantic paw prints, all she could think of was the dyslexic who stayed up all night worrying about whether or not there was a dog.

She laughed shortly, and the bark of sound made the ensuing silence deeper. Through the thick, black quiet came the distinct crack of a twig snapping and a swish as of a tail sweeping over the snow. Not squirrels; two ounces of rodent didn't snap twigs. Not a moose; moose were not subtle creatures.

"Stop it!" Robin screamed. Anna squawked, scared half out of her wits by the sudden cry. At first, she thought Robin was yelling at her—fatigue and stretched nerves made the best of women into shrews—but she was yelling at the dark and the trees, at the wog and the windigo, the ice and the night.

The biotech, so seemingly strong and untiring, was breaking apart. *Delayed reaction,* Anna thought. It had to be; the woman was cool efficiency itself first when photographing the slaughtered wolf, then assisting with the packaging of the slaughtered researcher. She'd held up till near the end. Then she'd started unraveling.

"It's okay," Anna said. "We're going to be okay." With a huge effort but no grunt, she stood without using her hands to push herself up. "Let's go. It's nothing. The wind plays tricks."

"It isn't nothing," Robin hissed at her. "It's not fucking nothing!" she yelled at the dark. She began thrusting the flashlight beam into the trees, stabbing, as evil Nazis did with bayonets into haystacks in old movies.

Anna made her way to the front of the sled, the *mush* of her boots through the snow covering whatever sound the followers in the woods might have been making. She pried the flashlight from Robin's fingers. "We'll walk together," she said. "If the Sked hangs up, I'll go back. Come on now."

Robin's tears metastasized; she sobbed, snot running from her nose, tears freezing in opaque droplets on her cheeks.

"Pull," Anna said.

Through thick down gloves, Anna felt her hand being taken. Robin had reached out and taken it, two puffed, oversized hands, neither of which could feel anything but the pressure of the other, clinging together in the dark.

"Ridley!" Anna yelled. "We could use some help back here!"

There was no answer. Like a will-o'-the-wisp, Bob's stolen light had led Ridley astray. Ahead was only darkness and silence.

"Fuck them," she said cheerily. "We're better off without them." She squeezed Robin's hand in what she hoped was a reassuring manner and tucked her other arm through the harness rope where it stretched down to the Sked. She could take some of the weight off the younger woman's shoulders, literally if not metaphorically.

For twenty minutes, they labored on without speaking. Twice the Sked caught on downed tree limbs and twice Anna trudged back to free it. The act of pretending to be stronger and braver than she was helped. How long she could run on this low-octane fuel, she didn't know. Robin had stopped crying and went forward like a skiing machine. Her face, when Anna caught glimpses of it in the reflected light, was filled with such bleak hopelessness it was scary. Drawing breath, Anna was about to shout for Ridley again—not that she thought he'd answer but just to make a fierce noise against the darkness—when something beat her to it.

The howl of a wolf ululated through the frigid night, leaving not a ripple; a round, perfect sound that too many stories and too many movies imbued with the absolute distillation of terror. Anna felt the hairs on her body stand on end as her skin tightened. Her mouth was suddenly dry, and she wanted nothing more than to run away, leave Robin and what was left of Katherine to appease whatever it was, wolf or wog or the ancient eater of flesh the Ojibwa told of.

In the falling-apart arena, Robin beat her to the punch. She dropped like a stone, gloved hands over her ears, knees up under her chin, then rolled over into the fetal position. The flashlight hit the snow and disappeared into the powder, leaving only a glow where it had gone under.

Anna retrieved the light and crouched down, one arm across Robin. "Shh, shhh," she murmured automatically. "It's just a howl. They howl to say hi. That's all." Without being aware she was doing so, Anna was talking to the very little part of Robin, the part that covered her ears and curled up and hid under the covers when the monster was in the room. The adult Robin knew more about wolves than Anna did.

The howl came again. This time it had a sorrowful, almost questioning tone. Anna would have been hard-pressed to describe it, but on the musical glissando, where the singer carried the notes skyward, there was a longing.

"Wolves won't hurt you," Anna said, patting Robin. "Wolves don't eat people." Then she remembered what they pulled behind them in a trough of tin. "Anyway, they don't eat when they're full," she muttered.

"Come on," she said, changing tactics. "Up. Get up. We're moving." She uncurled Robin and forced her hands away from her ears. "Stand while I untangle you."

When the harness and the pull ropes were straight, Anna gave the front of Robin's parka a tug, much the way she used to give her horse Gideon back in Texas a tug to get him to go.

Robin didn't budge. She turned her head as if she heard something besides the howling, a call from the woods that was above the frequencies humans could hear. For a long time, she stood, staring, and a cold more severe than winter crept deep past Anna's bones and into her brain.

"We've got to go." She'd meant to say the words in a normal way, a comforting, leaving-the-mall-before-traffic kind of way. What came out was a squeak that would have emasculated the tiniest vole. She said it again and had a better result.

If Robin heard, she showed no sign. She showed no sign of knowing Anna was close, so close her fists were doubled in the front of her parka.

"They've decided to kill," Robin said.

Her voice held the same note of sorrow as the howl.

18

Anna would have thought any self-respecting werewolf or wog would have taken Robin's show of weakness as an invitation to come to dinner, but, after she'd cried out, the slithery, sneaky sounds of their uninvited escort ceased. Robin didn't bounce back. Youth and strength and athleticism went out of her. Her skis tangled and tripped her as if she were the rankest novice. She stumbled and fell, and each time it was harder for Anna to get her up. Finally Anna removed Robin's skis, stowed them on the Sked and put the harness on her own shoulders. To keep the biotech close, she insisted Robin keep one hand on the lead rope and help.

Help was the word Anna used to try to break through the walls that had formed around the young woman's brain and were suffocating her body. Robin had lost even the strength to close her fingers tightly enough to keep her hand from constantly falling away from the rope and her feet from slowing to a stop.

The flashlight began to brown out. Ski tracks leading back to the main trail were filling with blowing snow, becoming harder and harder to follow. Wind carved up the storm and slung freezing snow at them from every direction. Anna's eyes watered and the tears froze her lashes together. The drag of the Sked on her shoulders grew heavier. Her feet turned to chunks of concrete in leaden boots the size of canoes.

Ridley never came back. Then Anna forgot she'd once hoped he would.

There was a place in her about the size of a softball just behind her sternum. A surgeon or MRI or X-ray would never find it, but it was where her center of energy resided; the tiny machine that had to be kick-started at the beginning of every hike, revved up when the natural laziness of mankind wanted to crawl back into the hammock. Muscles could be tired or weak or cramping, and she could push on as long as that motor kept running.

Whatever it was—will, stubbornness, pride—ground to a stop.

The Sked hit the back of her knees and she went down on all fours. Robin stopped beside her the way an old dog will stop when its master does.

"Fucking Ridley," Anna gasped. "Fucking Bob." The fetal position Robin had adopted was looking pretty good. Being devoured by beasts wasn't looking all that bad either.

She tried to push herself up. Her arms buckled as if

the bones had been boiled to the consistency of over-cooked noodles and she fell face-first into the snow. She tried to find her feet and couldn't. Her fingers, around the grip of the flashlight wouldn't close.

"Robin!" she yelled. "Help me."

Robin looked down into the sepia pool of light where Anna struggled. The biotech said nothing. Her face showed no emotion, not even recognition.

"Help me up, God dammit!" Anna snarled. "Do it or we both die."

"Don't die," Robin whispered. Anna barely caught the sound under the sawing of the wind.

"I will fucking die and so will you if you don't help me." Anna's language was deteriorating. Fleetingly she wondered if she used it to shock Robin out of her trance or because she was just that fucking tired of the whole fucking mess.

Something got through. Robin leaned down and extended a hand. Using the woman's strength, Anna pulled herself upright, then began fumbling at the harness buckles. "Let the dead bury the dead," she said. "Or eat them. I don't"—she was going to say "fucking" again, but it wouldn't afford the anger she needed, just indicate how desperate she felt—"much care," she finished.

Without the Sked dragging her down, Anna felt almost strong for several yards, then exhaustion slammed back so hard it shut down her mind. She held tenaciously to three things: the faint tracks in the dimming circle of light, what it would do to Paul if she froze to death and the cuff of Robin's sleeve. Anna could abandon the dead, and, once or twice, she'd turned her back on the living. Leaving Robin would be tough to get over.

The world shrank till even Paul could not fit in it. Only the circle of light and her hand clamped on Robin's parka. Soon, Anna knew, one or the other of these would go; she would lose Robin or they'd lose their light. Anna managed to slide her hand up and close it around Robin's wrist. If she was lucky, it would freeze there.

"Keep walking," she whispered to the biotech. "Help me out here."

Help me. The words that had formed on the window glass of the bunkhouse. They'd not saved Katherine. Had her spirit come and written them with the cold fingertip of the dead after the wolves had savaged her?

Help me. Help me. Help me. Anna let the chant move her feet. Lift on *Help.* Down on *me.* Lift on *Help.*

"The walking dead."

Anna had not said that. She'd not said it in her mind and she'd sure as hell not said it aloud. Jerking Robin's arm, she stopped and shined their pitiful light into the younger woman's face.

Robin hadn't said it. Robin was the walking dead.

A groan pushed through the dark and the wind. The beam of the flashlight wasn't strong enough to penetrate more than a few feet, but it was strong enough to pinpoint her and Robin. Anna clicked it off.

"At first, I saw, but now am blind," came the voice. Then: "Don't tell me your batteries are dead." Then an "Uff!" and "I sound like an old man."

"Ridley?" Anna tried.

"Did your batteries go dead?"

Anna clicked the light back on and shined it down the trail. First the tips of skis, then the man came into the circle of illumination. "Why are you here?" she asked. She would have shouted at him but hadn't the energy for anything more than mild curiosity.

"Bob got ahead of me. It was too dark to catch him. Without a flashlight, I'd have killed myself trying to stay on the trail. So I waited for you."

The flashlight fell from fingers gone suddenly numb. The butt of it stuck in the snow, sending the light up beneath Anna's and Robin's chins.

"Holy moly!" Ridley said. "You okay?"

"Is this the Feldtmann?" Anna asked.

"Yeah. What happened to the Sked?"

Anna had to chip each thought out of the ice of her brain. Putting them in words took even longer. A thousand years ago, Jonah had led her off the Feldtmann Trail. She'd been on her way back, about three miles from the bunkhouse.

Three miles. Ridley had on his skis.

"Here." Anna picked up the light and gave it to him. "Ski back. Fast. Bring the snowmobile."

"The Park Service . . ." he began, then stopped, undoubtedly realizing it would be easier to explain using an engine in the wilderness than the death by negligence of a visiting District Ranger.

"Sit tight," he said.

"Don't stop to kill Bob," Anna managed. She put her

arms around Robin and together they sank to the ground. Anna could have propped her back against a tree and unfolded her aching legs, but she chose to sit up straight in the middle of the trail. This was not the place to get too comfortable.

ROUGH PAWS WERE SCRAPING at Anna, pushing her back and forth, dragging her from the first warm, light, pleasant place she'd been in what was beginning to seem like forever. She'd been in front of the fireplace in Paul's house in Natchez. There'd been a huge blaze and her husband's arms were around her, and she was just settling down to a wonderful rest. Then the paws.

"Come on, sleeping beauties. Don't want to wake up dead, do you? Wakey-wakey—well, I don't have eggs and bacon, but I've got coffee. Hot coffee."

Anna pushed the hands from her. A jolt of fear woke her up completely and she began shaking Robin. "Jesus. Right out of the textbooks," she said when she saw Robin open her eyes.

Saw it.

There was light. Adam was hunched over them, his skis making him awkward, a bright light on a band around his head and another on each arm.

"Where's Ridley?" The question sounded so pathetic it embarrassed Anna, but she couldn't make sense of anything: how long they'd slept, if it was tonight or tomorrow night, who, if anybody, had been eaten by wolves or wogs or Jack Frost.

"I passed him coming out," Adam said. "Soon as Bob showed up back at the bunkhouse all by himself with a cock-and-bull story about 'getting things ready' for when the rest of you arrived, I knew something stunk."

With a couple of expert movements, he unlatched his skis and stepped out of them, then swung his backpack down and began rustling around in it.

"Ho, ho, ho," Anna said stupidly.

Adam smiled. "Like Santa with a bag of toys," he said.

That wasn't it at all. Tall and covered with lights, he reminded Anna of a Christmas tree. Or the spaceship coming down in *Close Encounters of the Third Kind*. Her mind would not track; she had the attention span of a gnat; inside her cranium, things made a degree of sense, but when she tried to put that sense into words it didn't work anymore.

Adam took out a thermos and Anna remembered he'd said "coffee." To drink coffee would be as close to heaven as a woman with a checkered past would get. Hot coffee. Anna could almost feel it in her mouth, pouring heat into her.

"This'll help," Adam said and handed Robin a steaming cup. Anna wished he'd given her the first cup; she wished she was evil enough to snatch Robin's from her. She would have given a year's salary just to smell it but the wind took the steam and the perfume. Robin raised her hand to take the cup. Her fingers wouldn't move and the cup fell into the snow. Anna wanted to cry.

The next cup he held to their mouths for them. A sip for Robin, a sip for Anna, just like the old days when nobody was afraid of catching diseases, when the offer of a swig out of one's water bottle wasn't considered creepy. The coffee was as good as Anna had known it would be. Her body was too far gone for a small infusion of heat and caffeine to do much for it, but her mind sharpened. Even Robin's face took on a bit of life. When they could hold the cups without endangering themselves, Adam went again into the pack and brought out a box of six Hershey bars.

Dormant hunger raged through Anna and she took half of one in a single bite. It was beyond good. The gods didn't dine on nectar; they ate Hershey's chocolate, milk chocolate with almonds. "Canonize Hershey," she said sincerely through a third bite.

By the time Ridley roared back into their night following the beam of the snowmobile's headlight, Anna and Robin had enough strength to climb on behind him. The seat was designed for only two riders. The chocolate had raised Anna's spirits to such an extent, she offered to wait for the second trip. Ridley and Adam saw something in her and the biotech that made them veto the suggestion. Robin was squeezed in the middle and Anna on the back of the seat. Using bungee cords he carried in his pack, Adam lashed both of them to Ridley.

Little of the ride back registered with Anna. The life of the candy bars and the coffee was short-lived. The trail wasn't made for machinery and the ride was bumpy. Ridley seemed to waver back and forth between the need for speed and the need for safety, and each waver carried a bump at one end or the other. Mostly Anna hung on and tried to keep her face behind Robin's shoulder so the cold wouldn't scour it off.

Finally they drove out of the woods and onto the graded road. Anna was too tired to be grateful. When they reached the bunkhouse, she couldn't get off the snowmobile. Jonah was out as soon as he heard the machine coming up the hill, bare-handed, in his old ragged flannel shirt, his boots unlaced. He hadn't taken time to more than grab his wool cap and shove his feet into his mukluks.

"Ovaltine is on," he called. "We'll get you warmed up. I fired up the sauna. Food, heat, hot drinks. We'll make new women of you. Not that I'm complaining about the old women, not to suggest you are old, Ranger Pigeon. I doubt you are much older than I am." While he chattered, he helped take the bungee cords from around the three of them. Ridley let him. He wasn't as spent as Anna and he hadn't been hit emotionally as Robin had, but the man had skied over thirty miles among other things and he didn't seem anxious to take on any unnecessary tasks.

Anna tried to get off so Robin could move and managed to only flap her arms feebly. Jonah put his arm around her and lifted till, between the two of them, she was standing, if unsteadily, on her own.

"Give Ridley a hand," Jonah said, just as if Anna was capable of doing so. Because he treated her like she was able, she found she almost was. As she tottered to the front of the machine, Bob Menechinn emerged from the bunkhouse, hat and gloves on, coat zipped up.

"I had the snowmobile warmed up and was about to come looking myself," he said as he clomped down the snow-covered steps from the deck. "Then Ridley beat me to it. Supper will be ready when you're ready to eat it. I made beef stew. That ought to stick to your ribs." He hustled down and elbowed Jonah out of the way to tend to Robin.

"Honey made it," Ridley said.

"Whatever," Bob said. "It's hot and ready."

"You heated it up. My wife, Honey, made the stew." Ridley lurched from the machine without any help from Anna and faced Menechinn. Bob had both arms under Robin's armpits and his hands on the front of her coat.

Copping a feel. Anna shook that off. As many layers as they all wore, all anybody would feel would be fleece and goose down.

"Well, let's get in and eat it before it gets cold," Jonah said.

Ridley stepped in front of Menechinn and the difference in their size was apparent. Bob outweighed the lead researcher by a hundred pounds, if not more. Still, Anna would have put her money on Ridley, if this had been a betting match. Ridley pulled off his thick glove, and, for a second, Anna thought he was going to slap the other man's face with it in classic challenge fashion. Instead he poked Menechinn hard with a slender forefinger.

"Honey made the stew," he said. Ridley didn't yell or

curse or threaten, but there wasn't any doubt, at least not in Anna's mind, that he was dangerous.

Bob must have sensed it too. He backed down, and Anna doubted it was out of consideration for the feelings of the other man.

"I just heated it up," he said. Anna heard the fear in his words and saw it in his face. So did Ridley. Bob tried for his smile but his face wouldn't cooperate. Then he saw the scorn in the faces around him. It was a replay of the night in the tent when he'd freaked out. Anna wondered who he'd use to build back his self-esteem now that Katherine was dead.

"Robin, you must be about frozen to death," he said and, curling himself around the biotech, he led her into the bunkhouse.

"Tell Robin to stay away from Bob." Katherine had said that the day before she died. Anna wondered if ghosts felt jealousy.

Or if the warning had nothing to do with affairs of the heart.

19

Anna found the strength to eat two large bowls of Honey's stew. Usually Robin ate with a healthy appetite, replacing the calories her work burned by the thousands. Tonight she stared at the bowl as if it were a crystal ball too muddy to show the future. When Anna would remind her to eat, she would take a bite. Bob decided to assume mothering duties and all but spoon-fed her, till she stood abruptly and left the room.

He started to follow.

"Sit down," Anna ordered. "You haven't had dessert yet."

Menechinn reared back, pushing out his chest and pulling in his chin, and glared around the table, searching for support. The message was in Jonah's eyes and the rigid way Ridley held his butter knife:

Eat cake or die.

Anna took another mouthful of stew. A woman had to keep her strength up.

Adam made it back as the cake and ice cream with chocolate sauce was being dished up. "What took you so long?" Ridley asked when Adam came into the kitchen. The question was not friendly. Adam's coming to the rescue was canceled out by the fact that, had he been there in the first place, no one would have needed rescuing.

"I went back for the Sked," Adam said mildly. "It wasn't all that far. Maybe three hundred yards from the trail." He dished up what was left of the stew, took a spoon from the deep-fat fryer with the clean flatware and settled in the chair Robin had vacated.

Three hundred yards. Every cell in Anna's body would have sworn it was closer to six or seven miles. So strong was the feeling, she might have argued the point, had she not been distracted with more important matters: watching to be sure Jonah put enough chocolate syrup on her ice cream.

"I put her in the carpenter's shop with the wolf," Adam said as he slathered a piece of bread with peanut butter.

"She would have liked that," Bob said gravely, and all of them stared at him for a moment.

"That she will, Bob. I know how much she meant to you." Adam spoke in the same mild way he had when Ridley snapped at him. It was impossible to tell if he mocked Bob or sympathized with him. Anna chose mocked. Bob chose sympathized.

"She did, Adam. Thank you. There's been a distinct

lack of feeling around here. Robin's the only one who seems to care and she's being left to isolate herself."

Jonah clunked a full plate of cake and ice cream in front of Bob.

"GENTLEMEN AND GENTLE LADY, it is time to get naked," Jonah announced. He rose from the table and returned shortly with a plastic bucket, which he ceremoniously gave Anna.

"I'll see if poor little Robin wants to sauna," Bob said, pushing his chair back from the table. "Lord knows, it would do her good."

"Allow me," Anna said sourly. "It so happens I'm going that way, being it's my bedroom and all."

Bob did his pulled-back smile.

Sauna was a tradition in the north. On Isle Royale, during Winter Study, it took on its early importance; it was the most efficient way to get clean in a cold climate where there was no running water. Anna'd thought she was too tired to do more than fall on the bed, but the promise of deep heat and a shampoo revived her sufficiently that she could return to the room to get her towel and soap.

Robin was sitting on her bed, staring at her hands.

Anna sat on the bed opposite, no more than five feet between them.

"What happened?" she asked simply. Normally the shock of seeing a chewed-up corpse might account for a young woman's imploding, but Robin had not gone catatonic at the sight of the dismembered body. It had been later, while the body was being packaged, or shortly thereafter.

"We—" Robin began, then stopped. The decision to keep a painful secret was clear on her young face. Robin wasn't a practiced liar. "I don't know," she said. "I've got to work some things out."

Anna waited, giving her time to talk if she changed her mind. That she was speaking at all was a giant step forward. "Okay," Anna said. "Come sauna."

"No." Robin tipped her head farther down and her hair fell around her face.

"You smell like Ridley's feet," Anna said untruthfully. "Take your clothes off. I'll wait for you."

Robin stood obediently and stripped, as did Anna. Wrapped in towels, Robin in her mukluks and Anna in her clogs, each with a plastic pail, they left the room. Naked as the day he was born, Jonah was in the common room.

"Pure sex," he said and slapped a wiry thigh frosted with white hair. "You girls control yourselves."

Robin actually smiled.

"Even worn down as we are, it'll be tough," Anna said.

Jonah dashed out ahead of them.

They left through the door of the working kitchen. Snow fell into Anna's clogs as they hurried through the narrow band of trees between the outhouse and the building next to the carpenter's shop that housed the sauna. Wind snatched at their towels and whipped Robin's hair with such fury that strands of it stung across Anna's cheeks and she let the younger woman go ahead of her. They ran the last ten yards.

In the small anteroom was a single bench and a row of pegs. Three towels already hung there. Anna and Robin added theirs to the line, put their footwear on the bench and, pails in hand like children going to the beach, went inside.

The sauna was built of fragrant cedar and heated by a cast-iron potbellied stove. Benches rose in tiers on two of the walls. The stove and a woodpile took up part of the third. On top of the stove was an iron tank filled with water heated to just short of boiling. To the left of the door was another tank with cold water. A single candle placed on the lower bench near the cold water lit the room.

Candlelight made the walls golden brown, the corners fading into darkness. Jonah and Adam sat side by side on the top bench, arguing good-naturedly about whether Matt Damon or Leonardo DiCaprio was the greatest actor of the twenty-first century. Ridley was standing by the cold-water tank filling his bucket.

Oddly enough, the sauna, close and dark and hot, never struck Anna as claustrophobic. A small, dark room filled with naked male strangers, yet it had never felt threatening.

A sauna was the closest thing to a womb a person could find. In the north, where the tradition was untainted with the fear of nudity that most of the U.S. labored under, men and women took saunas together. And for the length of the sauna, they were fraternal twins, or, in this case, quintuplets. Jonah made no sexual jokes. No one exchanged loaded glances.

Anna climbed to her favorite place, the corner nearest the stove and closest to the ceiling. In its dark embrace, she pulled one leg up, hugged it and put her chin on her knee. Haloed in candlelight, Ridley stood, working shampoo through his hair. Unbraided, it was past his shoulders and dark brown untouched by gray. His body was beautiful, shoulders wide and legs strong, the muscles corded from use, nothing artificially bulked from the gym. The graceful, delicate hands were echoed in his small feet.

Anna watched him without thought, the way she might rest her eyes on a cat stretching in the sun simply because it was beautiful. Adam scooted down and Ridley filled his bucket for him. Between Anna and the light, Adam was limned in gold that ran in ripples through the muscles of his arms and stomach. Long and stringy, he coiled himself like a spring, washing the bottoms of his feet. When Ridley returned to the bench, sliding in beside Anna and dropping his head back against the cedar, Jonah joined Adam, dippered water into his bucket from the hot and the cold till it suited him, then poured it over his head. The old pilot was hewn down to bone and gristle. White beard and body hair glistened in the candle's flame till he seemed shrouded in a thin fog. Anna drifted for a moment, dreaming of feisty silver dragonflies with rimless spectacles on their multifaceted eyes.

"There's only one thing missing," said the dragonfly. Anna blinked and focused. Jonah, clean and scrubbed from white to pink, was addressing those on the bench.

"Bob?" Ridley asked.

"What makes that the most ridiculous thing Ridley has said in his entire career under my tutelage?" Jonah asked his audience.

"Nobody misses Bob?" Adam suggested.

"Gold star to the man on the top shelf," Jonah said. "I shall provide what's missing. It is always left to the pilot." He opened the door to the antechamber widely enough to stick his arm through, then pulled something into the sauna. "Voilà!" he said and held up a six-pack of Leinenkugel beer.

Anna found the energy to raise her head. "You are the handsomest man on the island," she said sincerely and was rewarded with the first bottle.

Heaven is constructed of small things, and Anna was grateful to have a bit of it that night.

Nobody did miss Bob and Anna chose not to wonder where he was, why he would miss a chance to clean up.

Why he would give up an opportunity to see Robin naked.

Robin washed her hair and body. The girl had as close to a perfect figure as Anna could imagine, and she loved the way the brown hair, heavy with water, slithered familiarly over the square shoulders as Medusa's pet snakes might have. Unless the men with whom they shared the sauna moved in rarer circles than Anna thought they did, they probably hadn't seen a woman's body that exquisitely made either. Perhaps because of this, or because of Robin's youth and their genuine affection for her, or perhaps because the sauna demanded

it, they never infringed on her privacy by the smallest notice or attention. Between sips of beer, Jonah lathered his
head again. Ridley poured water slowly over it so the pilot
could rinse effectively. They chatted about the weather
and when they might get in the air next and the need to
haul more fuel up for the generator.

*Bob Menechinn would have poisoned the very air and
water.*

Not to mention that Anna never ever wanted to see
him naked. On the ice, she had felt him to be capable of
watching her die without lifting a finger. Yet he had
saved her life. She felt he was indifferent—or pleased—
that Katherine Huff was dead. Yet he had expressed sorrow. Half a dozen times, she had felt he was passively
stalking Robin. Yet he had never done—or even said—
anything improper, or at least nowhere as improper as
Jonah. She finished her beer. Her chin was back on her
knee, her eyes were half closed.

"Would you like me to wash your hair?"

Robin was looking up from below, the gentle glow
from the candle stealing fifteen years from her face and
touching her cheeks with clear amber. Molly, Anna's
older sister and a psychiatrist in New York City, had once
told Anna there were only two things mental health pro-
fessionals could agree on for the cure of depression: exercise and helping others.

"Thanks," Anna said, unsure whether she accepted
the offer for Robin's good or because she had doubts
about whether she could hold her arms in the air long
enough to work up any suds. Where the harness of the

Sked had weighed heaviest, her shoulders felt like melted wax. Come morning, they would hurt like hell.

She sat on the lower bench and did nothing while her head was doused and rubbed and soaped and rinsed. Had she been a cat—a water-loving cat—she would have purred.

"Hey!" A hand caught her arm. She'd fallen asleep under Robin's kind ministrations and would have tipped over had Adam not caught her.

"I think I'm fully baked," she said. "I'm heading back."

"Do you want somebody to walk you to the bunkhouse?" Adam asked.

Anna did not. Being sleepy after stew, beer, sauna and playing in the snow for fourteen hours did not constitute frailty. She left them sweating on the wooden benches and slipped into the anteroom. Steam rose off her body in lazy wisps and curls. Under the light of the forty-watt bulb, her skin glowed pink. She slipped her feet into her clogs, wrapped her towel around her and opened the door to the world.

The wind had grown neither fiercer nor kinder but continued to fret the island with snow-filled gusts. Snowflakes whirled and dashed through the light, but whether they were new from heaven or snatched up from the nearest roof for this occasion Anna couldn't tell. Bitingly clean air entered her lungs, and she no longer felt quite so tired. With windchill, the temperature couldn't have been more than a degree or two above zero yet she was not cold. This was a phenomenon of the sauna she'd not experienced to such an extent before. A feeling akin to invulnerability came over her. For the fun of feeling it completely, she walked a few yards from the light. In the darkness, near the carpenter's shop, she dropped her towel and turned her face into the wind. For a minute, it was close to flying.

Then it was cold.

She was turning to run for the bunkhouse when she heard a metallic *clunk*. Nature made a myriad of noises and could mimic most sounds men made. Metal on metal wasn't one of them. Rewrapping herself in her pitiful scrap of terry cloth, she held her hand over her eyes in hopes of blocking the sting of the snow. The shop was the only building at this end of the housing area.

Forgetting she wasn't in uniform, wasn't armed and did not have to check out things that went bump in the night, she walked the three yards to the carpenter's shop, opened the door and switched on the light.

The fetid reek of the windigo's breath hit her. Bob Menechinn was hunkered over the Sked. The garbage bags that had served as Katherine's shroud had been removed. Not torn or cut off, neatly removed and set to one side. On top of them were Bob's gloves. The parka Katherine had died in was unzipped and folded open.

The image of a werewolf eating human flesh smashed into the view of man and corpse and Anna's tired mind reeled. A gust of wind snatched the towel from her. The icy tongue of the windigo slid over her butt and up her spine.

20

D oing a little corpse desecrating in your spare
time?" Anna asked.

"I was saying good-bye."

"You couldn't say good-bye with her parka zipped?"

"I was looking for the cell phone." Bob rocked back
on his heels, and Anna could see the first shock of her
appearance wearing off.

"You were looking for the cell phone in the dark,"
Anna said.

Menechinn raked her with his eyes, trying to use her
nakedness against her. She chose not to notice. She
couldn't help but notice what Mother Nature was doing
to her backside. The wind was as a cat-o'-nine-tails
against her bare flesh.

"What's with the light?" was called across the wind.
Adam. He had left the sauna and noticed the shop light

on. In seconds, he was behind Anna, serving as a wind-break. He retrieved her towel and handed it to her. Anna wrapped it around her body and was surprised what the addition of this paltry protection did for her courage.

"Hey, Bob," Adam said.

Bob stood and dusted imaginary snow or dust from his coat front. Moving deliberately, he took up his gloves, looked piously down on what had once been his gradu-ate student and moved his lips as if in prayer.

Adam stepped so close, Anna could feel his bare chest against her back. The gesture wasn't sexual and she wasn't offended. The body heat was welcome.

Finished, Bob turned to them and, pulling on his gloves, said, "Katherine and I were closer than just teacher and student."

Anna felt a shiver down her spine and realized it had nothing to do with her nervous system. The muscles in Adam's chest and abdomen flinched, as if he'd taken a rabbit punch.

"We're sorry for your loss," Adam said, his words like splintering wood in Anna's ear. The cliché, made famous by a thousand TV shows, struck her as thinly veiled mock-ery, but Bob took it as his due.

"Thank you again, Adam. Ms. Pigeon seemed to think I was practicing cannibalism. Or black magic." Bob smiled briefly. "It's okay, Anna. You've been through a lot in the past few days. More than the rest of us. You're excused a bit of overreaction. I'm glad you cared enough for Katherine to be upset."

"I'm freezing to death," Anna announced without

too great a degree of hyperbole, slithered around Adam and hurried back toward the sauna. The heat of its dry fire had been sucked away. The sense of safety she'd enjoyed in her corner of the womb was gone. What remained was fatigue so deep and cold so sharp, she could scarcely walk. Mostly she wanted to crawl into her sleeping bag and slide into delicious unconsciousness, but, with her reserves burned away, she knew she would never be able to warm herself. If she didn't take the sauna's heat to bed with her, she'd be cold all night.

Ridley was the only one still inside. The sauna was cooling as the fire was no longer stoked, but up near the ceiling there was still plenty of heat Anna could store in her bones.

Ridley opened his eyes. His long dark lashes were covered in tiny beads of moisture that rivaled the glitter of a Vegas showgirl, till he sat forward and lost the light.

"What?" he asked with the intuition of a man used to trouble.

Anna told him.

"Jesus!" He leaned back again but the angle was wrong and the magic of the eyes didn't manifest. "You know he's here to shut the study down, don't you?"

"Can he do that with the wolf's behavior so off?" Paradoxically, now that she was getting warm, she was beginning to shiver.

"He's an idiot but he can probably do what he wants. Or what he's told," Ridley said. "He wouldn't know one end of the wolf from the other if it bit him on the rump."

Rump.

Anna's brain caught at the word, a nice, round friendly word. Paul said things like that, his language never degenerating into cursing or obscenity. One day, she would have to clean up her vocabulary . . .

"Adam must have been out of his mind."

"Out of his mind," Anna echoed. She had no idea what Ridley referred to and no energy to pursue it.

"Seemed to think he was God's gift to science. Some of the people on the list were real scientists. None of them were any good—government hacks—but at least they'd seen a microscope at one time in their lives."

Ridley wasn't really talking to her; he simply needed her there that he wouldn't be crazy enough to be talking to himself. Anna lay down on the top bench and stretched out; something there'd not been room to do before.

"Bob's your basic prostitute; he screws whoever the man with the paycheck tells him to screw. Homeland Security wants the border parks open year-round. Bingo! Bob discovers the longest-running, most highly respected and—get this—popular study in the country is a piece of garbage."

That was the last sentence Anna heard. Vaguely she was aware of Ridley shaking her awake, of walking back through the snow with his arm around her shoulders, of sliding into her sleeping bag and—in the morning, she wasn't sure she hadn't imagined this part—of Jonah saying: "Good night, sleep tight and don't let the bedbugs bite."

SHE WOULD HAVE LOVED to sleep the clock around, if for no other reason than, in her dreams, she didn't have roommates, she had a husband. Nonetheless, twelve hours was sufficient for knitting up the raveled sleeve. At ten-fourteen, she awoke, tiptoed from the room, lest she waken Robin, and wandered into the common room. Where the harness had pulled across her shoulders was aching and the backs of her calves were stiff and painful. Other than that, she was in surprisingly good shape.

A fire was burning in the stove, as it was every morning. Anna suspected elves, wanting tiny mukluks, till she found out Jonah got up at five every morning to check the weather, built up the fire, then, if there wasn't going to be any flying that day, crawled back into his sleeping bag to emerge a couple hours later with the rest of them.

The common room was uninhabited. She could hear men's voices in the kitchen. Her parka was on the drying rack by the stove, as were the felt liners of her boots. Salvaging her gear, she dressed and slipped out the front door. The sky was still at the level of the treetops and the wind from the northwest was bitter cold, but it hadn't the fury of the previous night. Temperature too low for proper snow; flakes, tiny almost to invisibility, drifted sharp as shards of glass in the air.

Gray light, a world without three of the primary colors, clothes that swaddled and bundled out of doors, bodies and smells that swaddled and bundled indoors: winter wrapped a web around Anna. Without the rising of the sun and the rotation of the stars, time had taken her prisoner, and everything seemed endless, as if she'd done it a thousand times before and, like Sisyphus, was doomed to go on doing it for all eternity.

Pushing through new drifts between the outhouse and the sauna, she wondered how the prisoners sent to work camps in Siberia survived. She had warmth, good clothing, plenty to eat, a place to sleep—Winter Study was not a place of privation; it was a place of simplicity. Yet the suffocating timelessness disoriented her all the same. She reminded herself never to do anything to annoy the Kremlin.

The door to the carpenter's shop was closed. Fresh tracks marked up the snow. Great big tracks: Bob.

She opened the door and remnants of the stench she'd thought she'd dreamed were there to greet her. Katherine's body hadn't been put back into the garbage bags; they were smoothed neatly over her where she lay in the Sked. The severed foot was wrapped in plastic the way it had come from the scene. Bob had not seen fit to expose it in his worshipful frenzy. The hollowed-out remains of the wolf and its bagged organs were on the table in the center of the room.

The story of the wolf who had invited Katherine to go with him into the snowy woods came back to Anna. The wistful look of longing as Katherine told the story of the meeting. The final scene from *Wuthering Heights,* the version starring Laurence Olivier, unfolded in Anna's mind: Heathcliff and Cathy walking together into a snowy distance. In Anna's version, Heathcliff was played by a wolf.

Shaking the vision off, she lifted the bags off the body. For reasons known only to wolves—perhaps the way Katherine had wedged herself beneath a downed cedar before she died—but for one gash on her forehead her face was largely unmarked, yet it was not pretty in death. Freezing temperatures and rigor had set it in a mask of agony, a scream sculpted in flesh. The parka had been zipped.

Bob had returned early this morning and tidied things up. Or finished what had been interrupted the previous night, then covered his tracks.

Anna unzipped it, then sat back on her heels.

Looking for a cell phone.

What a crock.

Cell phones didn't work on the island. There wasn't a tower within hitting distance. Cell phones hadn't existed when Anna was a ranger on ISRO, but now the fact they didn't work would be a huge plus in her opinion. No hikers or boaters chattering away with their pals in the office while the glory that was Isle Royale rolled by them unnoticed.

Bob was looking for something, though. He'd been searching for it at the scene while the rest of them were packaging the remains. He'd left them, speeding off with the flashlight, because he'd found whatever it was and wanted to hide it before they returned, he'd not found it and wanted to search Katherine's room or he was a lazy piece of shit and decided it was "wine time."

He might have been searching the body as he'd said. If he'd had a flashlight with him, it hadn't been on when Anna arrived in all her naked glory, but that didn't mean he hadn't used it earlier.

Staring at the dead woman's face but without seeing it, Anna put herself back in the sauna and retraced her steps to the carpenter's shop. Memories of the night before weren't sharp. There'd been too many things dulling her brain.

She left the sauna. She flew with the wind. She heard a clanking sound—probably the Sked banging into the metal legs of the workbench under the window. She opened the door and turned on the overhead light.

Without the wind raking her back and Bob's eyes her front, Anna was able to see more clearly in memory than she had at the time. Bob Menechinn had been on his knees. His butt had been in the air and his head down, hiding that of the corpse. That's why Anna had the sudden thought he was eating it.

The time for rescue breathing was long past. Had he been kissing Katherine? Love lost and good-bye and rest in peace with Baby Jesus, like Bob claimed?

Or did he like making love to dead women?

That was a gruesome thought. Though, should Anna ever have to have sex with the likes of Menechinn, it would be preferable to be dead at the time.

Shuddering out of that mental place, Anna turned

her attention to cause of death. Wolf, certainly, but wolves weren't what had taken Katherine to the cedar swamp in the first place, nor, did Anna believe, had they taken the researcher down. The tracks at the scene, those that hadn't been totally obscured by snow, told the tale of a meal, not a hunt.

Anna got a pair of latex gloves from the box Ridley had left on the counter from the wolf necropsy and turned back the stiffened edge of the shredded trouser leg. A splintered femur thrust through the tattered flesh— broken, snapped, not gnawed through. A considerate beast of some sort had licked the bone clean.

Katherine had probably stepped in one of the swamp's natural traps and broken her ankle. Maybe the pack was hounding her, but it seemed more likely she'd broken her ankle and the pack had come upon her. Wolves could have smelled the blood from the compound fracture. There were vials of the dead wolf's blood in her pocket. She might have smashed them against a stone or the bole of a downed tree.

If they were in the area, the wolves would have smelled it. But wolves smelled blood all the time: crippled moose, injured pack members. Every meal was served up with the smell of blood. All summer long, they smelled the blood of tourists, scraping and blistering and cutting themselves with cooking utensils. It wasn't like chumming in shark-infested waters; at the scent of blood, wolves didn't go into a feeding frenzy. The odor of humans was enough to send them running.

The only thing that made much sense was a confluence of events: Katherine breaks her leg, wolves come upon her, she reeks of fresh blood—hers and theirs—and they kill her.

Reeks.

The breath of the windigo.

Smell, the most primitive of the senses, flooded Anna but brought with it no memory, only the knowledge that something was unutterably wrong.

21

Anna returned to the bunkhouse, let herself in the unused kitchen door, took Katherine's sample-gathering paraphernalia and carried it back to the carpenter's shop. There she began the painstaking process of collecting and preserving trace evidence.

She wasn't sure what she was looking for. A smoking gun maybe, though the murder weapon was clearly tooth and claw. Could be she was bored or paranoid or suffering from the madness of the Far North, but she couldn't shake the feeling that Katherine's death was not accidental, not entirely. Nor could she shake the feeling that Bob had something to do with it. But, then, she seemed pretty anxious to pin something on the Homeland Security guy and couldn't be trusted to be objective.

She swabbed and preserved and noted. What struck her most forcibly was how little trauma there was. Researchers hypothesized the size of a wolf pack was determined by how many animals could fit around a kill. When wolves brought down an animal, they surrounded it and ate it warm, often alive—for a while. *Canis lupus* were designed to eat *en famile* and efficiently; an adult wolf's jaws exerted fifteen hundred pounds per square inch, about twice that of a German shepherd and five times that of a human being. A mature wolf could gnaw through a femur in six or seven bites. Speed was also in their nature. They might be the most ferocious of predators, but they weren't nearly as focused as ravens when it came to scavenging. A single raven could carry away as much as four pounds in a day, meat cached in the branches of a nearby tree for later consumption.

Soft, small-boned, Katherine would have been torn to pieces in minutes. Yet the corpse was relatively undamaged: a foot torn off, throat slashed, arm severed and hands eaten. The rest was superficial damage. In a starvation winter, when moose were scarce, the wolves would not have left fresh meat of their own volition. They had to have been frightened off the kill.

Something had scared the wolves away, then didn't eat the body itself. The noneating, scary thing vanished before the snow stopped falling. Either that or it traveled in such a manner it left no tracks.

Anna rose to her feet and stomped to get the circulation moving. The stiff-soled Sorels were not made for kneeling. Or walking. Or fashion. They were simply designed to keep feet dry and toes from turning black. Dead wolf parts to one side, dead woman to the other, clapping and stomping in true zombie-jamboree fashion, Anna cast back to the night Katherine had been killed.

She couldn't even be sure Katherine left the shop intending to confront Bob. Nature might have called; Anna did come upon her near the outhouse. Bob might have waylaid her for some reason and they'd gotten into a fight. She might have run into Bob accidentally and taken the rare moment of privacy to unload on him about something that had been on her mind for a while.

Again Anna knelt and began searching Katherine's clothing. In the right front trouser pocket was a tube of Chap Stick. In the pocket of her parka was a handkerchief; not the great square of cotton of the present day but a smaller square of linen edged with crocheted silk. Anna had carried one very like it down the aisle when she'd married Paul, the "something borrowed." Her sister, Molly, inherited a box of them when her husband's mother died. They weren't the sort of thing one carried into the wilds to mop the frozen mucus from one's nose and eyes.

Hoping the delicate handkerchief had given Katherine comfort, Anna tucked it into a paper evidence bag. If there was organic matter on it, paper would preserve it better than plastic. That done, she did a thorough frisk of the body. A lump in the lining of the parka brought on the familiar rush any cop—green or blue—got when they were onto something.

Excitement dwindled as she discovered it hadn't been covertly sewn into the lining like smuggled jewels but fallen through a rip in the pocket. She worked it up the fabric to the light of day. Blood; one vial of wolf's blood had not been smashed.

Had Bob been looking for the cell phone like he'd said or was this what he was after? That made little sense when there was enough wolf meat in bags on the tool bench to glean any number of samples. Anna slipped the tube into an envelope, dated and sealed and initialed it. In every case, the chain of evidence had to be preserved: who collected it and anyone else who accessed it had to be recorded. One link in the chain broken, one unauthorized moment out of the chain, and an attorney would say the evidence could have been tampered with and was inadmissible.

Anna wasn't sure there'd been a crime. She wasn't even acting under color of law. Her jurisdiction was in Rocky Mountains in Colorado. It did not extend to a park in Michigan. Still, she worked with precision and strict adherence to the rules.

When she'd finished, she wondered what the hell she was going to do with her neatly labeled packets. There was no place to lock up the stuff. In the Visitors Center–cum–ranger station there would be an evidence locker, but the NPS wouldn't have given Ridley a key. Besides, Anna wasn't sure she trusted Ridley. At this point, she hardly trusted herself.

There was the storeroom off the common room between her bedroom and Bob and Adam's, a narrow, windowless room full of cobwebs and outdated backcountry gear. She dismissed it. Little used as it was, it was accessible to anyone who was interested. Besides, under normal circumstances, freezing organic matter would render it worthless. Since this had already been frozen, it would do more damage to thaw it and subject it to the possibility of refreezing.

A few minutes of rummaging about and in the rear of the shop, at floor level beneath a workbench, Anna found a partially rotted board; she could see the shallow crawl space beneath the shop. An old toolbox, rusted but still mouseproof, was pressed into duty as an evidence locker. She placed the box in the hole, then covered the opening with paint cans.

There was a bit of Nancy Drew about the entire episode that appealed to her. How serious could a situation be if the lead investigator was hiding metal boxes under the floorboards in old sheds?

Lunch was being consumed when she returned to the bunkhouse. Dinner was the only planned meal. Lunch was peanut butter and jelly on toast—or on biscuits, if there were any left from the night before. Adam wasn't in attendance. Ridley was but wasn't particularly chatty. The weather—or the threat of losing his vocation and avocation at the whim and will of Bob Menechinn—had left bruise-colored smudges under his eyes.

Anna pulled out a chair and sat down. Ridley nodded politely and passed the bread and peanut butter. She was hungry, but not with the insatiable, almost desperate hunger of the first days.

Katherine is butchered and you are sated. The

thought jarred her. The ravenous nature of the island jarred her.

Bob sat in his usual place, looking larger than he had the day before.

A tick filling up.

Given to black humor and a certain dark turn of mind, Anna was accustomed to thoughts better not expressed in groups, but, what with eating and being eaten—the whole food chain thing spelled out in gobs of flesh and strawberry jam—the words, rising unbidden, had a sinister cast, as if she were going mad. Or the world was.

Not superstitious by nature, she considered taking it up, as she chewed, staring at the table. There was no harm in protecting oneself against things that didn't exist. What could it hurt to carry a rabbit's foot? Other than the rabbit.

"I'm going to practice my cross-country skiing," she announced as she dusted the crumbs from the table.

"Take a radio," Ridley said.

Bob smiled, a half smile that said: *I saw you naked.*

I Know What You Did Last Summer fluttered out of a box in Anna's brain and she smiled back, not at Bob, at the silliness of the teen-scream B movie. A touch of the gory knife and the dripping hatchet must have shown. Bob stopped smiling and concentrated on eating.

TEN YEARS OR MORE had passed since Anna'd been on skis and she hadn't been much good then. Over rough patches where Robin would fly and Ridley power through, she would have to take her skis off and carry them; still, it would still be quicker than hiking. The only boots she had with her were the Sorels. There was no way the fat toes would fit into the bindings. Having learned from Robin's ingenuity at Malone, she grabbed a butter knife and popped off the bindings and affixed the toe of each boot firmly around the ski with duct tape, leaving her heels free. Not ideal, but it would suffice. The remainder of the roll of tape she shoved in her pack.

The gentle, curving slope where the road led down to the water gave her time to establish a relationship between feet and skis, hands and poles. By the time she passed the pier, she was moving with a modicum of confidence.

Following the Feldtmann Trail to where she'd cut cross-country was easy. Snowmobile tracks cut deep. The trail from the Feldtmann to where Katherine had fallen was harder, but the drag of the Sked and the holes left by Anna's boots had yet to be completely eroded by wind or filled by new snow. Ski tracks were mostly gone. Occasionally she'd see the stripe in the snow or a pock where a pole was driven in, but she would have been hard-pressed to stay on course if they'd been her only map.

Adam had said it wasn't too far to where she'd abandoned the Sked. It wasn't. Unburdened, rested, on skis and in the light of day, the trip took less than an hour. The cheekiness of time irked, then disoriented, her. Déjà vu telescoped, collapsed into two dimensions, as if she'd walked out of the living room in her house in Rocky and into the bath, the connecting hall suddenly not there.

The nose hill, the nose-hair tree, the refrigerator rock: Anna shed her skis and waded into the cedar swamp.

The neon orange patches where animals had unearthed tasty bites of researcher were erased by snowfall, but the trees were still startling in their neon spatter. Anna pulled her balaclava off and stood quietly, sending her senses out to taste the forest. Wind blustered through the tops of the trees but without malice; a teasing shake of bare branches, a rattle of dead leaves that had refused to fall in autumn. The air smelled clean and new; there was no lingering odor of the windigo, to speak of unspeakable things. She felt only the amiable curiosity of red squirrels.

Following the trail blazed so conveniently in blood, she worked her way out from the clearing.

She'd learned to track in the desert. A land of snow was very like a desert, and she found she could read sign tolerably well. Working slowly, she followed the spatters and the now-almost-obliterated mark where Katherine had crawled—or been dragged—from the swamp. She found the hole she and Robin dug, excavating the backpack. The bottom had filled in till it was just a large dimple in the snow. Anna pulled a pasta server she'd lifted from a kitchen drawer out of her backpack and used it to rake around the area. Gloved hands packed snow rather than lifting it, and it was too cold to use bare fingers.

Sieving turned up bits of blue canvas, one soaked with what Anna presumed was either wolf blood from the broken vials or human blood from the researcher. On fabric, there was none of the cheery traffic-cone orange; the blood had gone dark and hard. Anna had no idea of the chemistry involved, but, no doubt, one day an enterprising researcher would get a hundred-thousand-dollar grant to study the phenomenon.

Near ground level, she found a blue canvas strap. One end was intact, the buckle still in place. The end that had originally attached to the backpack was ripped. Either it had been torn from Katherine's back or been ripped in a game of tug-of-war between woman and wolf or wolf and wolf.

Or woman and scary noneating thing.

Anna rose to her feet and looked for the next spatter of orange. Snow humped over downed wood, and the swamp resembled a rumpled giant's bed. Half the trees were alive, erect above the snow, and half in a deadly tangle beneath it. Contours and cave-ins could be the mark of human intervention or snow cover interacting with gravity, temperature and the various levels of piled trees.

Anna had been hoping for a bit more blood. She'd seen the wolves taking down a moose. There had been a lot of blood. Wolves and moose hearts pumping at top capacity, wolves slashing, moose fighting back with hooves and antlers. Blood had flown in every direction.

Here there was little for a tracker to go by. Maybe because Katherine hadn't the physical strength to fight a predator that didn't weigh much less than she did and her clothing soaked up fluids from her wounds.

Without its bizarre coloration, Anna might have missed the next spatter. Seven orange drops in a neat arc stood out at snow line against the pale bark of a downed cedar.

With careful steps and her pasta-serving spoon, Anna worked Katherine's back trail. Fifty yards into the tangle of downed trees was a six-by-eight patch of snow that was sufficiently disturbed that the drifting had not completely concealed it. Digging was deepest in a crotch formed by two dead limbs. Around this patch was a wide area of lesser dimpling, the paw prints of wolves.

If they were paw prints. The windigo carried its victims so high and so fast, their feet burned away to stumps, and the prints they left in the snow were more like hoofprints than human tracks.

"Cut it out," Anna said aloud. An "inner child" was all well and good, but the little buggers could be a real pain in the ass when it came to scary stories.

Starting at the outer perimeter of the circle, she began clearing snow away. Within a foot of where the branches came together in a natural snare, she found a patch of frozen urine. It was human; a fragment of wadded tissue paper lay next to it. Katherine had been trapped long enough to need to relieve herself, and her leg was not yet broken. The compound fracture would have rendered her too crippled and in too much pain to have squatted neatly.

On the same imaginary ring around ground zero—the

foot trap—Anna found a flashlight, an unused emergency flare and a water bottle, half full and frozen solid as a brick, and a pack of Juicy Fruit. Katherine might have run madly into the woods, but she had returned to her room, or had this pack cached elsewhere, and come prepared.

Anna rocked back on her heels, wondering what a small, emotionally upset researcher from Washington, D.C., would rush out in the dark with a flare and a pack of gum to do. Did she plan to get lost to punish Bob but wanted to hedge her bets? Did she stage the fight with Bob to establish a reason to run off that wouldn't incriminate her?

In what? And why didn't she use the flare? Any late-night-movie viewer would know to strike the flare to keep wolves away. Whatever Katherine's reasons, it was here that the rucksack was wrested from her.

Not having evidence bags large enough to accommodate flashlight and flare, Anna stowed them in her backpack. A little more digging turned up the cell phone Bob worried about. Anna knew pretty close to nothing about cell phones. For much of her career, no one had such a thing, except for the crew of the Starship *Enterprise*. In the years since they'd become commonplace, she'd worked in places too isolated to get service. Paul bought her one, and, because she'd promised she would, she kept it in the car when she traveled between Colorado and Mississippi. A couple of times she'd gone so far as to turn it on. Once she'd even needed it, but the battery had gone dead and it had been demoted from glove compartment to trunk.

This phone appeared to be a fancy machine, many buttons and symbols, all in Lilliputian scale. The viewing screen was black. Because her phone worked this way, Anna took off a glove, then pushed END to begin.

Nothing.

She pushed TALK.

Nothing.

When her fingers got cold enough to cause pain, she gave up and slipped the phone in her pocket. The batteries could be dead or frozen. Probably both. Menechinn wanted the phone to save the cost of replacing it. Whether he was being petty or not, Anna knew she would put it down the outhouse rather than give him a moment's satisfaction. Since he'd saved her life, Bob had that effect on her.

Sitting on one of the limbs that had captured and held Katherine till death came on night's paws, Anna considered what she had found. Not much. And she didn't have a lot more time. She'd gotten a late start and had no intention of reprising her long day's journey into night, dragging a corpse and a zombie, not even with two flashlights and an emergency flare.

Putting all of the "not much" together, she fleshed out a story. Katherine had run from the housing area for reasons of her own. Maybe to conduct an activity she wanted kept secret or to make Bob sorry for whatever he had done. The flare in the pack suggested the activity might have something to do with signaling. Homeland Security had sent Bob to ISRO presumably because it was a hole in the border through which anything could leak, especially in winter when it was deserted.

Signaling offshore smugglers? Terrorists?

Anna laughed, surprising herself with the noise. Evildoers deciding to do evil in Lake Superior in January were a self-culling gene pool. Based out of a city, Homeland Security personnel might not know that. Provincialism wasn't just for the provinces anymore.

The facts were: Katherine had left Windigo, then intentionally or accidentally gotten lost. She'd gotten caught in the cedar swamp. Wolves found her. Contrary to natural behavior patterns, they decided to devour her. At some point, she remembered her cell phone and tried to call out. She fought to free her foot and her ankle snapped. That might also have been when the vials were broken. Blood from the compound fracture, blood from a dead wolf, frenetic noise and preylike thrashings: hard for any self-respecting wolf to resist. The foot comes free. Katherine drags herself or is dragged by wolves to the killing ground.

Then her ghost flits to Windigo and writes "HELP ME" on the window glass.

"I guess we solved this one," Anna said to a red squirrel, who, thinking her a bump on a log, had settled nearby to munch on a ration of fall's harvest. The little rodent squawked, scurried up the nearest tree and disappeared around the bole. Two seconds later, it reappeared on the other side and scolded Anna for her impertinence.

"I'm sorry I scared you. I thought you knew it was me. Hey, thanks." Looking at the squirrel, she noticed a set of tracks coming in at an angle on the far side of the tree. They looked like boot prints. Had she not been half expecting them, Anna would have written them off to the vagaries of tracking and weather. Overlapping moose prints often resembled a human track. Wolf tracks scoured out with the wind fooled the eye in the same way.

Most of the tracks had been obliterated. All she could tell was, they came from the west, the direction of the bunkhouse, which meant nothing. In rough country, only the crows fly as the crow flies. Creeping and climbing and scooting on her butt, she worked her way through the swamp in concentric circles out from the existing prints.

Nearer where the body was found, at the foot of an evergreen tree, branches full of needles and keeping out much of the snow, the tracks ended. The owner of the boots had stood, back to the tree, and watched the slaying or the body or both.

It was the watcher who had frightened the wolves from their kill.

22

Anna skied home in the last of the afternoon. By the time she'd stowed the items she'd collected beneath the shop floor, the last of the light had gone. The cell phone she kept. If the battery warmed, it might have enough power to at least let her see to whom Katherine made her last call.

Though it was after dark when she returned to the bunkhouse, no one had radioed to see if she were alive or dead. No one seemed to have the spirit to care. Cabin fever had become epidemic. Ridley worked at his desk in the room he and Jonah shared. Adam lay on the sofa, sleeping or pretending to. Bob's door was closed, and Jonah, for once uninterested in company, sat in the dim light of the common room's overhead light, dividing his time between watching Adam, as if trying to guess his weight, and staring at a well-thumbed *Newsweek*. On the table by the magazine was a mason jar with an inch of red wine in it. Number 2787, Anna knew. Ridley, Jonah and, before he retired, Rolf Peterson drank their evening libation—served by Jonah—from mason jars. Each knew which was his personal jar from the number stamped in the glass. Wolves were not the only creatures whose evolution was affected by isolation.

Divested of her many layers and dressed in dry, if not clean, clothes, Anna stood in front of the woodstove amid racks of drying underpants and socks. The fever was upon her as well; she didn't know what to do with herself. She wished she could call Paul, but she'd have to do it from the public phone in the common room and, since the storm moved in, the connection was so bad it was exhausting to try and converse. E-mail was a possibility, but Internet connection was patchy at best.

"Did Ridley get through to report Katherine's death?" she asked of the room in general.

Jonah answered. "E-mailed. Got one back. As soon as it clears, the Forest Service will be here with the Beaver. Everybody goes."

Bob had gotten his way, to a degree. That was the reason for the spiritual collapse of the Winter Study team. This season's work was over unless Ridley could talk the Superintendent into relenting. Given the manner of Katherine's death, it would be easy for the NPS to simply never reinstate the study. The high-profile nature of the research cut both ways. An ISRO researcher's death by wolf would be big news.

"When do they think the weather will break?" Anna

tried to keep the note of longing from her voice, but getting off the island was looking like a reprieve from a life sentence in a refrigerated lunatic asylum.

"Another front's coming down from Canada. Three days, maybe a week. We've been here as much as two weeks without the Beaver getting in to bring us provisions," Jonah said. "Too dangerous to fly in this stuff."

Adam opened his eyes. "Three days?" he said. There was a note of alarm in his voice, as if three days was either not enough or too much to bear.

To Anna, seventy-two hours seemed an eternity. A week, a death sentence.

Adam closed his eyes again.

Silence descended again, punctuated by sneaky pops and hisses as fire consumed wood. Jonah went back to reading and watching Adam. The easy camaraderie was breaking down. Ridley didn't laugh at Jonah's antics and Jonah seldom indulged in them. Ridley distanced himself from Adam; Jonah watched him, and Adam took every chance he could to go off by himself.

Another week of this and Anna was going to get seriously cranky. In the twenty-first century, people assumed that nothing could stop rescuers, but, as advanced as technology had become, weather could shut it down. She thought of the climbers who died on Mount Hood in 2006. Storms were too severe for the search-and-rescue teams to do their work.

Mother Nature had sold them out and Old Man Winter held them hostage. No risks would be taken for a body recovery of a woman killed in an accident.

Anna wished she were in Natchez, Mississippi, cutting back the roses in Paul's front yard.

Paul's front yard. Anna had been on her own so long she wondered if she would ever lose the mental habit of thinking of "Paul's" and "hers," never "ours." When she referred to "his" house, he would invariably take her in his arms and say "our house." When they married, Paul truly did give "all that he had and all that he was" to her. Much as she would have liked to do the same, Anna was not made that way. A core of her remained unshared, a fortress she retreated to when she needed to marshal her internal forces.

The outer shell of her parka was dry to the touch. She lifted it off the rack. Turning the coat inside out to dry the lining, she felt a lump in the pocket. The vial of wolf's blood; she'd forgotten to put it in the toolbox evidence locker. By now, it would have thawed. Stowing it beneath the carpenter's shop would only serve to re-freeze it and what little value it might have would be lost. She left it where it was.

The blood samples Katherine had carried with her to the cedar swamp stuck in Anna's brain: burrs under her saddle, stones in her shoe. Crimes—or accidents—told a story. The protagonist did something for a reason and the result was the incident. When an action occurred that didn't fit in the logical unfolding of the story, Anna couldn't leave it alone. People who lied were invariably caught eventually because the lie never completely worked with the rest of the story.

It was possible that the blood samples didn't fit into

the story because they had no relevance. Katherine might have pocketed them with the intention of doing tests when she returned to her kitchen/lab.

Katherine had fiddled with wolf parts nonstop for the better part of two days. The kitchen was filled with racks of vials containing samples of tissue, blood, bone, stomach contents, hair, ticks, mites and other marvelous things. What tests could be left to do? Why not use the blood she'd taken before the wolf was moved to the carpenter's shop?

Leaving the heat of the stove and the oppressive peopled emptiness of the common room, Anna went to Katherine's makeshift DNA lab. With its single bed shoved in a corner and the haphazard piles of a storeroom used by many and organized by none, the kitchen was bleak.

The PCR was in its travel case on the counter, the record book beside it. Anna opened the log and read what she could understand of Katherine's notes. The researcher had not written anything she'd not discussed with the rest of them, no illuminating secrets.

As Anna closed the log, *The Shining* unreeled behind her frontal lobe, the scenes where Jack Nicholson grinned his I-am-one-crazy-bastard grin. Was she growing paranoid and delusional in a snowbound building? No secrets, no plots, no ulterior motives or sinister intent, just a mix of strange bedfellows trapped in a very strange bed with one claustrophobic hypervigilant law enforcement ranger?

Anna put the book back precisely the way she'd found

it. The log's owner would never be back to notice; she did it from habit. Methodically she checked each of the various samples in their vials and packets. No seals were broken, no envelopes slit open, no papers in disarray.

Wog DNA wasn't what triggered Katherine. For a scientist, a find at that level of idiosyncratic bizarreness was tantamount to a cat finding a real live mouse full of catnip. Something she'd discovered during the necropsy precipitated her mad dash into the woods. Anna walked to the window and stared past her reflection in the dark glass, trying to see around the corners of memory to that precise moment.

Ridley's hand was cut and bleeding. Anna handed Katherine the chunk of meat from the wolf's throat. Katherine mewled like a newborn kitten lost in its mother's fur. Shortly thereafter, according to Jonah, the researcher pocketed the blood samples and ran out of the shop.

Jonah *said* she'd pocketed the samples and run out.

Feeling anxious but not knowing why till she realized she was half expecting another message to appear on the window glass in spectral words, Anna wondered what Jonah had to gain by the lie. He could have slipped the vials into Katherine's pocket; he could have said she'd run out when she'd merely strolled, but Anna couldn't come up with one moderately rational reason why he would do so.

The old pilot was as attached to Ridley as a father to a beloved son. Lately he had been watching Adam the way he'd watch a dog bitten by a rabid skunk. Jonah had no use whatsoever for Bob but didn't appear to harbor the hatred of him Ridley did or the schizophrenic anger and obsequiousness Adam displayed toward the man.

Anna gave up. She took the tube of blood from her pocket and stared at it. It was just a sample from a dead wolf, and there were plenty more where this came from.

Maybe.

Maybe the importance of the vials was in the fact that there weren't more. Would Jonah have reason to tamper with vials of blood, then switch the doctored versions for the real samples when Katherine wasn't paying attention?

"You're reaching," Anna chided herself. Even a diabolical, dyed-in-the-wool, honest-to-comic-book professional nemesis had to have means, motive and opportunity. Unless Jonah was the great professor he played at being when on a roll, such a convoluted methodology was uncharacteristic.

Anna decided to quit stirring in her brain and Katherine's lab before she began making up crimes just to keep herself amused. What she needed was a good book.

"Hey, Ridley." Anna leaned in the doorway of his room. His back was to her, his long, delicate fingers poised on the keyboard of his laptop, hair loose and shining around his shoulders. He looked the very image of Christ Jesus without the halo and the white nightgown.

When he turned, the renaissance artists' vision of Jesus vanished. Rings of purple beneath his eyes had deepened since breakfast and his winter-white skin looked coarse and loose. "Hey," he replied. Weariness flattened his voice. Anna snuck a look past his shoulder to see what he was working on. Unoffended, he followed her gaze. "Yeah," he said. "Yet one more defense of the study. Fifty years we've been at it. Fifty years of watching and what we know is, we don't even begin to know what we don't know about wolves and their relationship to their prey. Yet every bozo with a dog and a high school diploma knows it all. David Mech says one thing, Rolf Peterson agrees; I back it, and some NPS brass says: 'But the girl who sits next to me in homeroom thinks . . .'"

"'You've got vision, and the rest of the world wears bifocals.'" Anna quoted Butch Cassidy.

Ridley's eyes went hard, and it occurred to her he would have been five or six years old when the movie came out. Chances were good he'd never seen it. And he certainly hadn't memorized the good parts, as a percentage of her generation had. As far as he was concerned, he'd offered her a glimpse of himself and she'd mocked him. Anna wished it wasn't so but knew if she tried to explain herself it would make things worse. It always did.

"I need the key to the ranger station," she said instead.

"Sure. The lights aren't on. The generator serves only the housing area. What do you need?"

"A book," Anna replied. "The Visitors Center must have a library of some kind." The Visitors Center and the rangers' offices were located in the same building, the beautiful new facility overlooking Washington Harbor.

"Not much of one," Ridley said as he rummaged through the top drawer of his desk. It was full of pens, paper clips and other detritus that Anna thought would have taken more than a couple weeks to amass. "Reference stuff, is about all there is there."

"I've finished the *Newsweek*," she said drily.

Ridley laughed, and she was glad he chose not to carry a cross moment further than necessary. "The key is somewhere in this mess, but I don't know where. Adam!" he hollered.

Looking like a man who's been awaiting a call rather than someone roused from sleep, Adam appeared soundlessly in the doorway beside Anna. So soundlessly, she started when he spoke.

"Yeah?"

"Give Anna the key to the V.C. She says she's read the *Newsweek*."

"Already?" Adam cocked one eyebrow in a way that made Anna think of her high school principal, Sister Mary Corinne. "You've only been here a week."

"Speed-reader," Anna said.

Adam reached into the front pocket of his jeans and took out a small ring of governmental-looking keys. It was Ridley's turn to cock an eyebrow, but, not being gifted in that department, he managed a mere wrinkling of the forehead. Years in the wilderness or small isolated communities to inform her, Anna knew Ridley thought it peculiar that Adam carried keys. Nothing—or nothing they needed—on the island was kept locked. When he'd first arrived, Ridley unlocked the buildings they

would be using and left them that way. There was no
one to lock them against. The V.C. was only locked because it was unnecessary to the study.

In summer, with the exception no doubt of employee housing—NPS people were notoriously trusting—buildings would be locked at night against visitors
with larceny or vandalism in their souls. The major
thieves on the island in winter were the mice, and few
locks deterred them.

Ignoring the skepticism, Adam removed a single key
from the ring and handed it to Anna. "The door jams,
so don't let it fool you. When you turn the key, it's unlocked. After that, brute force is your best bet."

For the length of time it took her to walk through
the common room to her own room, Anna entertained
the wisp of a fantasy that she could just zip out to the
V.C. and zip back; that she didn't have to put on her
heavy socks, ski pants, fleece overshirt, balaclava, gloves
and boots. Like the Sun King's Versailles, much of one's
time in the frozen north was spent dressing and un-
dressing.

Outside, the temperature was minus seventeen. With
the windchill, it was closer to minus forty. A jaunt to the
outhouse was scarcely bearable. Without gear, the quarter mile to the V.C. could prove deadly.

THERE WAS NO WINDCHILL. The wind had stopped,
and the forest felt as if it were holding its breath, the
island in stasis, waiting. Despite the fact she'd been

steeping her brain in boogeymen and monsters of the id, the waiting didn't feel threatening, merely a stillness through which Anna moved, a moment out of time in which her breath was stilled as well. The good version of death without the annoying part where one died.

This frozen idyll was ended when she heard a shuffling in the dark beyond her flashlight and, before the beam had rooted out the squirrelly culprit, her mind had shown her a slavering, long-toothed, red-eyed wog skulking in the night.

"Damn!" she whispered. Being frightened of being alone in the woods pissed her off. The woods, the wilderness, were where she hid from the monsters of the populated world. To become prey, even in her mind, was intolerable. Despite the prickling of her neck hairs and the cringing along her spine, she forced herself to walk slowly and deliberately down the trail.

By the time she stood on the wooden porch of the V.C., stomping the snow from her boots, she was cold to the bone. Clumsy in gloves, she inserted the key, turned it counterclockwise, and exerted the recommended brute force. The door came open so easily, she fell backward, stumbling over her big feet and landing on her rump with a grunt that would have done a wild boar proud. For a moment, she lay there, staring into the blank sky. It crossed her mind that this was the perfect opportunity to wave arms and legs feebly, experience the worldview of a topsy-turvy beetle. That insight into the insect mind might be the most enlightening experience she'd have on ISRO. Sloth, not an innate sense of human dig-

WINTER STUDY | 287

nity, decided her against it. She rolled over, got to hands and knees, rose and started in the open door.

Halfway across the lintel, a cry stopped her. Not a breath of wind, not a decibel of sound pollution, the voice cut into her eardrums with the force of a slap in the face.

"Is somebody there? Is somebody there? Help me! If somebody's there, help me!"

Bob.

It was fucking Bob.

23

Bob had left the door open and caused Anna to fall on her keister. Now he wanted her help. God knows, with what, and Anna didn't much care. Had she been a lesser person, she might have turned and slipped into the night from whence she had come. For the time it took for her heart to beat twice, she considered that perhaps, as an act of humility, she should become a lesser person for one evening.

Switching off the flashlight, she stepped quietly into the Visitors Center. Stale air, marinated in winter, harbored a chill that the outdoors, fierce with life even at forty below, could not attain. Inside cold, like inside dark, was harsher and scarier than anything under the moon.

Instinct—or antipathy—dictated she keep her whereabouts in question. Without moving, without making a sound, she waited for Bob to call again. Thick and slow and glacial, silence flowed around her till she felt if she didn't move she would suffer the fate of the mastodons, encased in living ice for millennia. Gliding as best she might in the clown-sized boots, she moved from the door to the right, where an open, half-spiral stairway led up to a viewing area.

The main room of the Visitors Center was at least thirty by forty feet. Tall picture windows gave onto a view of Washington Harbor. To the west side of the windows was a skeleton of a mature moose, reassembled and displayed in a glass box. Beside it, trapped in an eternal howl to a mate long dead, was a wolf preserved by the art of taxidermy.

Anna'd seen the displays the first day when she'd looked in the windows. That she could see them now surprised her. Above the level of the trees, the white of the harbor ice and the white of the sky cast a faint silvery light.

"Is anybody there?" Bob's voice emanated from the offices on the opposite side of the building. He didn't sound particularly panicked for a man who had been hollering for help moments before. Anna said nothing. Dead, cold air settled more firmly around her.

A minute passed, two: he didn't call again and didn't come out. She started across the hardwood floor. Ski-pant legs whistled together, big boots creaked and snuffled.

"Who's there?" Bob called.

Yeti didn't sneak, she thought sourly as a beam of yellow light raked down the hall and shot by her.

Anna switched on her light. "Anna Pigeon," she said,

and Bob's beam blinded her. "Get that damn light out of my eyes. What's the problem? What are you hollering about?"

The instant he moved his light from her face, she aimed her flashlight at his. His eyes were bright, virtually twinkling, and his skin had a rosy glow. His balaclava was crunched down around his neck, but the hood of his parka was up as if he'd dressed for the cold in a hurry. With those jowls, it couldn't have been comfortable.

"You look fine to me," Anna said. A groan and a thump came from down the hall.

"It's not me; it's Robin," Bob said.

Sick fear washed through Anna on a wave of nausea. "Lead me to her," she said. Bob started to speak, but she cut him off: "Now." The flashlight beam on his back, she followed him down the short hallway. Years of experience and training told her she should have listened to what he had to say, but Bob managed to tap directly into a deep vein of irritation.

"What happened?" she meant to ask, but it was a demand.

"Robin's been pretty upset since Katherine's accident," Bob replied, his voice warm with concern.

"And?"

At the end of the hallway, he turned right. Anna quickened her steps; she didn't want him out of her sight. He stopped in the last doorway, the corner office with a view of the lake. A plastic nameplate, printed with DISTRICT RANGER, was in a faux-brass holder to the right of the doorframe.

Blocking the entrance with his bulk, big on a bad day, bigger still with the down coat, he said: "Not everybody can handle violence with your aplomb, Anna." He used his nice-fellow voice, but the intent to insult was clear. Anna was not insulted. With guys like Menechinn in the world, she was liking the idea of violence better and better.

"Robin," she called. A retching sound trickled on a moan from the dark room.

"Step away from the door," Anna said.

"She's been drinking pretty heavily," Bob said. "I think she started sneaking it not too long after you left for your ski outing."

"Move away from the door."

"Aren't we the officious little woman," he said, but he moved.

The office reeked of wine. Robin was on the floor, her long legs curled up, knees under her chin. She was hatless and her hair fanned out around her head. Damp strands stuck to her face.

Half her attention on the young woman, half on Bob's hulking shadow, glimpsed in stripes and washes as the beams of their lights moved, Anna knelt. "Robin, it's Anna. Can you talk to me?" she asked gently as she pried open one eyelid, then the other, and shined her light in. Both pupils reacted sluggishly. Dilation could have been caused by drugs or darkness. Robin's skin was cool to the touch and diaphoretic. Any number of things could account for that.

"I went out for a walk," Bob said. "When I came by

the V.C., I heard noises and came up to see what was going on. I found her back here with a box of the wine she'd taken from the bathroom fridge." He played his light to the box of merlot on the floor a few feet from Robin. A mason jar was tipped over next to it, a stain spreading on the carpet. "I was trying to get her up and take her back to the bunkhouse, so she wouldn't freeze to death, when I heard you come in."

Anna flicked her light to his face. He threw up an arm as if the beam was a blow. With the cut of shadow, she couldn't read his expression.

"Yeah, well, here's your chance."

Between the two of them, they got Robin to her feet and out of the Visitors Center. The trail from the bunk-house to the V.C. and dock was swampy in summer. A wooden walkway, two planks wide, had been built to keep foot traffic from tearing up the muddy ground. Snow hid the planks, rendering the path tricky in much the same way the downed trees made traversing the cedar swamps tricky.

"Better let me carry her," Bob said. "You walk ahead with the light."

Anna hated that idea. Hated the idea of Bob doing a good deed, hated the idea of Bob touching Robin, hated the idea of being helped and hated the idea that she didn't have the strength to carry the girl herself.

"Thanks," she said, wondering what it was about Bob—or about having one's life saved—that was so irri-tating. "Watch your footing."

Bob picked Robin up easily. The biotech was tall, but

slender as a blade of grass. "Go on ahead. I can light your way better from behind," Anna told him. This was marginally true; with an effort, she could shine the lights around him.

As she followed in his tracks, the size of the man, the unconscious woman in his arms, the flickering of the two flashlights, brought to mind a dozen derivatives of King Kong and Frankenstein; the beast, lumbering from the torchlight, the damsel clutched to his chest.

Anna opened the door to the bunkhouse and Bob shouldered in with his burden. At the computer on the rear wall of the common room, Adam glanced over his shoulder. Then he was on his feet. Anna didn't see him gather himself and stand—one moment, he was sitting; the next, standing.

Jonah stood as well. "Ridley," he called without taking his eyes off them. "Get in here."

Bob didn't put Robin down on the couch or move toward her room but stopped a moment to savor the spotlight. "Drunk as a frat boy on Friday night," he said.

"Robin's drunk. Passed out. Drunk," Adam said tonelessly, his face gone the color of ashes, his hands knotted in fists at his sides, knuckles hard-boned and sharp.

"Yep," Bob said. "I guess this wog business was getting to her. I, for one, will be glad when the Forest Service gets us off this island. Sooner is better."

To Anna's amazement, the permafrost that had replaced Adam's skin melted and his fists uncurled. "I'm glad you were looking after her, Bob. She's a good kid." Adam reached to take the unconscious girl. His arms were as stiff as a Hollywood mummy's.

Bob wasn't about to have his prize snatched away. Anna stepped in before they started fighting over Robin like dogs over a bone.

"Jonah," she said as she pried Robin from Bob's embrace and draped one of the girl's arms across her shoulders. "Would you mind making a pot of coffee?"

"I'm on it," he said.

Supporting the younger woman, Anna began their stumbling way to the bedroom. Bob and Adam followed. She stopped, braced Robin against her hip, turned and held them with her gaze for a moment. "When the coffee's done, ask Jonah to bring it to me."

They didn't recognize the dismissal.

Anna made it clearer. "Go away."

Having no idea how much Robin had consumed, what her tolerance was or if she was on any other drugs or medications, Anna had no intention of letting her sleep until some of the effects wore off. At a guess, besides the wine she had taken a barbiturate of some kind. Tranquilizers or sleeping pills from her mother's medicine cabinet secreted away for emergency meltdowns. If her system was too depressed, sleeping could push her from unconscious to dead. Coffee, poking, prodding and making witty conversation were all Anna had in the way of antidotes.

She settled Robin on her bed, back against the wall, legs out straight. Like a Raggedy Ann, Robin's head cocked to one side and her arms limp, palms up. Twice she blinked, then her eyes opened preternaturally wide. The beneficent image of Raggedy Ann was replaced by that of Chucky. The illusion lasted long enough for Anna's adrenaline to spike one more time.

"You're in our room. You are safe," Anna told her. "Whatever demons are chasing you will have to come through me. Can you tell me how much you had to drink?"

Robin didn't answer. Her eyes drifted closed and she mumbled, "Demons."

"No demons," Anna said with obnoxious good cheer, her voice pitched sharply enough to penetrate the biotech's fog but not to carry beyond the closed door. "How much did you drink?"

"Drink," Robin parroted. "Ish." Fingers numb with whatever was in her system, she began fumbling at the hem of her sweater, unable to clutch it hard enough to lift the wool over her head. "I'm wet."

"You have wine spilled on you. That sweater is soaked in it. You smell like a wet dog," Anna told her. "A wet, alcoholic dog." She moved to help Robin off with her sweater and she batted at Anna.

"No. No. No." Each was a single, pitiful cry, as if against an inevitable and familiar evil she was helpless to stop. Anna sat back down. Women who had been raped or sexually abused, either as adults or as children, occasionally exhibited a fear of having their clothes removed by anyone else, even an EMT or physician. Most overcame the instantaneous terror, at least enough to hide it when they were sober. Drunk or drugged or distraught, it often resurfaced.

"You're okay," Anna said. "When you want help with your clothes, you tell me. Till then, I'm going to sit right here and make sure nobody bothers you."

"How's our girl?"

Fucking Bob. "Go away."

With a jolt of guilt, Anna remembered Katherine had told her to keep Robin away from him. At the time, she'd written it off as the hissing of a jealous woman. Now she heard it as a warning. Bob had been eyeing Robin since he'd hit the island. Would he be evil enough to rape a young woman, mentally unstable from shock, who had gotten drunk?

Not raped, Anna thought. Had rape occurred signs would have been evident. A wave of relief, startling in its intensity, buoyed her up. Robin was, in some indefinable way, the essence of innocence. Not the coy, shy innocence the Victorians peddled but the fearless innocence of young wild things.

Robin's hands, palms up to either side of her thighs on the mattress ticking, twitched like cats' paws do when they dream. They stilled, and Anna saw not Robin but Katherine, the stumps of her gnawed fingers, the torn mess of her palms.

Anna had walked in on Bob, in the dark, on his hands and knees, over the corpse. Katherine's parka was unzipped. The thought Bob had been sexually involved with the body had crossed Anna's mind in a stampede of cloven hooves.

Katherine dead, Robin dead drunk. There were men who liked women to be objectified in this ultimate way.

Anna shook her head the way a dog with a sore ear will shake trying to rid itself of a pain it cannot stop or touch. America had changed radically from when she was a girl. Women—girls—had gone from the under-represented in numbers and inferior in ratings to the majority and the best rated in a huge number of areas: college, graduate school, medicine, law. A woman had been Secretary of State, a woman Speaker of the House, a presidential candidate. Women were mayors, governors and university deans. No longer was it said that girls weren't as smart as boys; now the focus was on how the system had failed the nation's sons.

That's what had changed.

Rape was what hadn't changed.

Women were in the military and they were raped by their fellow soldiers. Girls were in college and they were raped by their fellow students. Rape crisis centers had sprung up and rape counselors. Yet it was still ignored in the most essential way: people in power didn't want to touch it lest they get their hands dirty.

This was true in the armed forces, corporate America, universities. And in the National Park Service. A friend of Anna's had been raped; she'd been working seasonally as a fire technician. She'd been struck down and raped by an NPS employee, a permanent, someone close to the Assistant Superintendent. Anna and the woman's parents convinced her to report it.

The rape was never turned over to law enforcement. Higher-ups in the park talked to the victim, offered to set up "mediations" between her and her rapist that they might learn to work and play well together. The rapist was not fired. The crime was treated as a spat between roommates rather than as a felony assault. NPS employees raping seasonals wouldn't be good PR.

And maybe she was lying. Maybe she was exaggerating. Maybe she had it coming.

That was the unsaid, the way otherwise-decent men and women could refuse to help and still think themselves good people.

"Arthritis."

Still limp as a rag doll, Robin was staring at Anna. "Arthritis," she said in an eerie monotone a thread above a whisper.

Anna'd been cracking her knuckles and clenching her jaw.

"Thanks." She shook out her hands and let them hang loosely between her knees. Bone and muscle ached. "Drink some coffee."

Anna helped with holding the cup and raising it to Robin's lips. "Not bad," she said when only a tablespoon or two slopped on the ruined sweater.

"My mom made this," Robin said.

The sweater was a classic pattern, deep chocolate with a band of white reindeer marching single file across the chest and the back. "It's beautiful," Anna said. It had been, before the wine stained the reindeer the creepy color of cheap stage blood.

Robin bent at the waist to take off her knee-high mukluks and fell over sideways on the bed. Anna made no move to help her till the young woman asked for assistance. Having set her back up in her Raggedy Ann pose, Anna unlaced the soft boots and worked them off.

"There." Robin pointed at her sock-clad feet.

"What?" Anna didn't see any damage. The socks weren't wet and the skin beneath radiated body heat.

"Mom knitted my socks for my feet. They fit better than any other socks."

"Wow," was all Anna could say. "Beats baking cookies all to hell."

"All to hell."

Anna helped her to another sip of coffee, then took a drink herself. The long day was beginning to wear on her.

A tap at the door was followed by the pilot's grizzled face. "More coffee?"

"Food?" Anna asked.

"Coming up." The door snicked shut.

Another tap quickly followed. "Robin?"

Bob.

"Go away."

Jonah brought them each a bowl of beef-and-pasta casserole and more coffee. The food fortified Anna, and the few bites she could be induced to take seemed to help Robin some. Finally she asked Anna to help her remove the wine-soaked sweater.

As the fire was banked and others went to bed, the bunkhouse stilled and cooled. At ten, the lights went out; Jonah had shut down the generator for the night. Had Anna been sure Robin was loaded on booze, and only booze, she would have let her sleep it off and been grateful to do so. As it was, she lit a candle and propped herself next to the biotech where she could nudge her awake for at least another hour or two till her system wasn't so depressed.

To keep them both from falling asleep, Anna began asking questions. In the next ninety minutes, she learned that Jonah was seventy-three years old, Ridley's wife was probably a bona fide genius, Gavin, Robin's sweetheart, loved Proust and classical guitar and the early works of Andrew Wyeth, had wonderful hands and thought Isle Royale was America's last chance at saving Eden, that Adam had been married but his wife had committed suicide, slit her wrists and bled to death in the bath while he fixed the sink in the dressing room not ten feet away, and that Rolf Peterson had great legs.

By eleven-thirty, the candle was burned to a stub, and Robin was waxing fairly coherent. Anna watched her get undressed and slip into her sleeping bag. Her clothes didn't look as if they'd been messed with and there was no bruising visible on arms, back or thighs. Reassured, Anna blew out the candle.

Before she crawled into her own sleeping bag, she turned the lock on the bedroom door. Without the heat from the stove, the room would be cold, but at least she would know no one was watching them as they slept.

24

nna had hoped to plummet deep into the land of Morpheus as her roommate had done. Sitting, talking by candlelight, it had been all she could do to keep from falling asleep midword. Now her legs twitched and her mind raced and she couldn't get comfortable.

To stop the racketing thoughts, she focused into the night, hoping its deep quiet would creep into her soul. The bunkhouse groaned and popped in a satisfied manner as it cooled. Robin snored softly, something she never did sober.

Now that Katherine slept in a black plastic shroud on the floor in the carpenter's shop, the room across the hall was empty. Anna could move in. It would be a simple matter of dragging her sleeping bag and pillow fifteen feet to another single bed and another bare mattress, but her usual need for aloneness had given way to the comfort of safety in numbers. Even if that number was two, one of whom was semicomatose.

Jonah or Adam might take the room. Adam, probably. When he was in the bunkhouse and not on the couch, he shared a room with Bob. Anna couldn't figure out that relationship. Adam seemed to want to be Bob Menechinn's friend one moment and showed nothing but contempt for him the next.

Bob, as the axman from Homeland Security, wasn't in much of a position to make friends. Anna doubted if he fared much better when he was elsewhere, then wondered what it was about him that set her teeth on edge. When a person—or a situation—brought out a strong sense of unease, she'd learned to pay attention to it. A thousand "tells" were broadcast every minute: a tic, a wince, a smell, a shadow, a draft, a flick of the hand, a door ajar. The human senses experienced them all. The human brain registered them. The human monkey mind, clamoring with the shouting littles of life, was lucky if it recognized one or two. The message from the gestalt trickled down in intuition, gut feelings, geese walking on one's grave, déjà vu. There was a reason or reasons she didn't trust Bob. She just didn't know what they were yet.

A shivering ululation cut into her thoughts, reminding her that she had been seeking to quiet their flames, not fan them. A wolf's howl embraced rare magic; sound transforming into pure emotion, the kind that exists beneath the level of language. Train whistles had it. They touched a chord in the human breast that echoed a longing for things unknown. For Anna, the sound of a cat purring or the tiny thunder of their paws racing over hardwood floors had the power to cause instant, unthinking delight, but that might not apply to everyone.

Train whistles and wolves howling seemed to be universal in their ability to pass through the paltry defenses of civilization to the more fundamental primitive heart of people. Anna loved the sound, loved the pleasurable shivers it sent up her spine. At least until she remembered the wog, the pack coming through the housing area, the attack on Katherine.

Giving up on the idea of sleep, she slid from her sleeping bag and into Levi's and a sweatshirt. It occurred to her as she completed this abbreviated toilette that, should an unfortunate incident befall her, she would be found without underwear, clean or otherwise. She'd be careful not to get hit by a truck.

Lighting her way with a battery-powered headlamp secured around her brow with an elastic strap—the preferred headgear of the Winter Study team from ten p.m. till sunup—Anna found the kit Katherine had used to extract blood from the wolf. Two of the eight vacuum tubes remained. She took them both, returned to the bedroom and put the headlamp on the table, facing away from Robin.

The biotech was deeply asleep, but her breathing was even and twelve breaths per minute so Anna wasn't unduly worried. In fact, she hoped the girl was far enough out she wouldn't wake up when the needle plunged into a vein in her antecubital site. Robin did flinch, but she didn't wake. Anna watched as first one vial, then the second, filled with rich, dark blood. She'd neglected to bring a bandage, so when she'd finished she folded Robin's arm over the ruined sweater.

The blood should have been drawn hours before, but Anna had other things on her mind. Tomorrow morning, when she could get Robin's permission, would be too late. She hoped it wasn't too late already. Pocketing her purloined hemoglobin, she left the bedroom. The door locked only from the inside, and she locked it before she closed herself out. If need be, she'd bang until Robin woke to let her in.

In the faint glow from the fire, Anna donned the necessary layers of clothing and then laced up the Sorels. Her body felt heavy and tired, but she ignored it. Till she could shut down her mind, her body was going to have to lump it. Another wolf's howl threaded beneath the doors and around the window glass, and she stopped to listen. This call sounded closer, and she wondered if she was a fool to be heading out into the woods alone. Even having seen Katherine's body, Anna harbored a belief that the wolves would not attack her. She felt that way about mountain lions and bears as well—about most wild animals in parks where she'd worked. The major exception was the alligators of Mississippi. They, she was sure, would like nothing better than a bite of Pigeon meat.

Her sense of safety with other carnivores was based on nothing factual. It was a powerful and totally illogical feeling that they knew she loved them and would leave her untouched. Aware it was irrational, and probably born from watching too many animated Disney films as a kid, Anna was careful never to test this notion. She wasn't testing it tonight. Given a choice, she would have waited till daylight, but she wasn't sure how long the blood sample would be viable.

Trudging along in tracks—hers and half a dozen others, several of them being moose—she reached the head of the trail to the V.C. A shape shifted beyond the tree line; not a visual shape, a sound, the squeaking the snow made when crushed, the peculiar, dry Styrofoam sound.

Moose, she told herself. Moose, like deer, were curious and would come to see what was happening. Hunted only by the wolves, moose on ISRO had little fear of people and often wandered through housing areas, campgrounds and by the sundries store.

Anna walked into the woods. Trees, naked with winter, closed around her like a barbed-wire fence. The flashlight cut swaths through the black: tunnels of white tangled with twisted branches and gray-scaled tree trunks. The fear that had been with her earlier on her first ill-fated trip down this hill returned.

"Damn!" she whispered.

At each step, she began to think she heard the faint echo of snow being compressed in the trees alongside the path. She stopped. The echo stopped. Hard as she listened, as far as she tried to push her senses and her flashlight beam into the darkness, it was impossible to tell whether she was being stalked, followed or was hearing things. Panic stirred beneath her sternum, not the fear that motivates action or caution but the unreasoning whine of buzz saws in childhood nightmares.

Turning out the light, she let the fear have her, let the panic throb on violin strings out of tune, sirens and screeching tires on concrete. When the first wave had passed, leaving her feeling light-headed and breathless, she spoke to the darkness, within and without.

"Being scared is beginning to bore me. Do what you have to do and I'll do the same." Speaking aloud in the frigid darkness was oddly daring; a wild act of sanity enacted in a classically insane way. It reminded her many things were a choice. Fear, to a great extent, was a choice.

"I'm headed to the Visitors Center," she said to her monstrous, malevolent or imaginary friend. "If you need to devour me, or whatever, I'll be in the back offices."

She thought she heard a snuffle or a smothered laugh trickle back through the thick underbrush. It was so faint and quickly aborted she couldn't be sure it was anything more than the scrabble of a raven's claw on a branch.

The building housing the V.C. and the ranger station was not locked. The key was on the chest of drawers that served her and Robin as bed table. Stopping before the double glass doors, she stomped the snow off her boots so the first seasonals to arrive in summer wouldn't have too great a mess to clean up. Once inside, she closed the doors behind her. The mindless fear was gone, but if a wog did wander the island seeking human flesh there was no sense in tempting furry fate.

She went to the District Ranger's office, stopped in the open door and automatically swept the light switch into the ON position. No illumination was forthcoming. In the second it had taken her hand to push the switch, she'd remembered it wouldn't work. Finishing the sequence made no sense, due to lack of electricity, but she pushed the switch down again in the OFF position anyway.

Searching by flashlight had its advantages. Able only to see the three-foot-by-three-foot spotlighted area, the eye was not distracted. Occasionally Anna'd turned the lights out when there was electricity to burn and used a flashlight to concentrate her mind on details.

The box of merlot was on the floor where they'd left it, the overturned mason jar nearby. Anna shined her light on the bottom: number 4427. Adam's. Robin did well in the largely male world of wolf research by keeping as much under the radar as a beautiful young woman can hope to. In the days Anna had known her, she was careful not to call attention to herself and did her best to fade into the woodwork when others did. Breaking the tradition of the mason jars was out of character. If she'd been sufficiently drunk, she might not have noticed she was taking Adam's jar—or noticed but been beyond worrying about consequences. Robin might have taken Adam's glass for spite. Had she been a silly young woman, Anna would have considered that she could have taken it for love, the island equivalent of wearing the boy's letterman's jacket, but Robin wasn't silly.

Fingerprints could be lifted from the jar. Several were

apparent in the beam of the flashlight. Robin's would be on it; Bob's, probably. Maybe Adam's. The only print that would be telling would be the print of the human version of the wog; someone on Isle Royale who shouldn't be. Anna bagged it. At the rate she was collecting evidence of crimes that might or might not have been committed, the crawl space under the carpenter's shop would soon fill up.

Taking her time, she followed the yellow circle of light around the office. A few items had been left on the desktop when the island was closed to the public in October and the District Ranger went back to Houghton: a stapler, a plastic box with a magnetized opening half full of paper clips, an empty in-basket and a bright pink pad of Post-it notes. These were lined up neatly beside the many-buttoned phone.

Robin hadn't done the bulk of her drinking in this room. Not even a naturally graceful bi-athlete could get that totally pissed without disarranging a few things, spilling a few drops.

The office chair was overturned; the five starfish legs, each with a wheel on the end, did their best to trip Anna as she moved around the desk. Chairs of that design weren't easy to tip over. Robin must have collapsed into—or onto—it and carried it down when she went to the floor.

Tracing the three points she'd found of interest, Anna moved the light from the wine box to the mason jar's position to the overturned chair.

Robin had not been holding the merlot when she fell.

Rectangles half full of liquid didn't roll as far as the box was from the chair. The mason jar was a distance from both chair and wine box. Robin might have dropped them—jar, then box—then collapsed in the chair. Bob might have moved them.

Anna crouched down and shined her light along the fuzzy tops of the close-cropped carpet. A flat, square package an inch or so on a side was beneath the desk. Lying on her belly, she fished it out. A condom, the package unopened. Unless District Rangers in other parks led far more exciting lives than they did in Rocky Mountain, or a couple of enterprising seasonals, waiting for the last boat off the island, managed to find a key and take advantage of the office with the view, this belonged either to Robin or Bob. Either way, it suggested a rendezvous had been planned. If the condom was Robin's, Anna doubted Bob was slated to be the wearer.

It was not beyond the possibility that, as Bob struggled to help Robin, a condom he'd not thought of in years but kept handy in his wallet at all times like an ever-optimistic high school jock tumbled out and was kicked beneath the desk, but it wasn't a scenario Anna was going to put money on. Bob brought the condom because he knew Robin was drunk and an opportunity to take advantage might present itself. Or Robin had been intending to meet with a lover and Bob had spoiled it. Maybe Adam's jar was on scene because Adam had been on scene.

Anna shook her head as if an invisible jury watched

from the hall. Adam had been on the couch all evening, front and center in the common room, as if he wanted it to be seen that he was in the bunkhouse.

Anna sealed the package with its tidy ring in the center between two hot-pink Post-its and slipped it into her pocket. In movies, law enforcement fought dramatic, complex evils. In real life, that was seldom the case. Law enforcement was the endless slogging through the ooze and slime of run-of-the-mill evil, evil so ordinary, so interwoven with the threads of people's lives, that to root it out tore the victim and the community apart while the monsters shrugged it off in true monstrous fashion. Molestation, wife beating, incest, date rape, statutory rape, gang bangs at frat parties—all the nasty, dirty crimes—damaged the victims again when "justice" was perpetrated.

Anna had testified a number of times in her career and been to quite a few depositions. Defense lawyers were there to keep their client, innocent or guilty, out of jail. At any cost.

Prosecutors were there to put the accused, innocent or guilty, in jail. At any cost. Defense attorneys routinely boasted over cocktails of getting rapists or murderers or child pornographers off. It was a testament to their abilities. The excuse they made for shelving their integrity was the law school cant: they were making the state toe the line, make its case.

Most simply wanted to win.

The sound of metal sliding into metal blasted her musings with the jarring force of a shotgun being racked.

She switched off the flashlight and, trailing her fingers along the wall, moved rapidly to where the hall branched, leading into the Visitors Center's main room.

Stealth being impossible in full winter regalia, Anna turned on her light and swept the room before she crossed to the doors. Empty. No light came from outside, no person stood on the decking in front of the doors. Hitting the crash bar, she shoved, but the doors didn't give. She grabbed the handles and rattled. The dead bolt was engaged. The only way to lock it was with a key from the outside.

The only way to unlock it was with a key from the outside.

Switching off her light, Anna stepped away from the doors lest she make a target of herself. The one other door to the outside was at the opposite end of the hall from the District Ranger's office. Navigating mostly by memory and the occasional flick of her flashlight, she found it quickly. The bolt on it had been thrown as well, probably when the island was closed in mid-October.

Putting her back against the door, she stared down the dark hallway. The V.C. was built in the modern style: the windows didn't open. Climate was controlled even in the "wilderness," the vagaries of weather and the human need for fresh air shut out by glass and technology. Minutes before, she'd wanted to be in the building. Now, because someone—not wog or weird but a human, someone with a key and opposable thumbs—decided to imprison her there, she wanted out.

Bob Menechinn was her first thought. Ridley's key

had been missing. Bob or Robin could have lifted it from his desk and unlocked the Visitors Center. Robin was in no shape to creep back down and lock Anna in. She was also in no shape to defend herself from visitors in the night. Anna comforted herself with the thought that breaking down the bedroom door would rouse Ridley and Adam. The comfort was countered with the thought that Robin might open the door to whoever rapped on it.

Flashlight on, stealth forgotten, Anna ran down the hall, checking offices, in hope that somewhere a window had been made that would open, that in a mental lapse the architect had overlooked one small portal to the real world. Otherwise she would be reduced to shattering glass.

In the ladies' bathroom above the sinks she found a window that could be louvered out from the bottom, creating an opening ten inches high and thirty-six long. She shucked off her parka and boots, and the cold bit into her with sharp teeth. Standing on a sink, she dropped the clothes and flashlight and followed them out of the window, eeling through headfirst. The drop was more than man-high, but snow had drifted against the building.

Anna landed on her back in the drift. Pain would have been preferable to the blast of snow down her collar. Another minute was lost as she pawed through the snow in search of the flashlight and another while she pulled on boots and parka.

Running felt good. Tired muscles and weary soul

complained, but her body's need for heat and her mind's for speed soon quieted them and she plowed through the winter-quiet woods like a freight train, puffing and loud.

The housing area was still, the bunkhouse dark. Slowing to a walk, she turned off her light and let her breath return to closer to normal. Entering by the side door to Katherine's kitchen/lab, she stood a moment and listened. Peace prevailed.

Dressing in the snowdrift, Anna hadn't bothered with lacing her boots. She heeled out of the Sorels and slipped down the hall to the room she shared with Robin. The door was still locked.

"Robin?" Anna called softly and put her ear against the wood. The door was colder than it should have been. Heat from the banked fire in the woodstove sufficed to keep the bunkhouse at a fairly comfortable temperature even through the night. Anna knocked again. "Robin?" She called a little louder this time and knocked with a purpose.

Fear that she had let the biotech sleep before she should have took over and Anna shouted and pounded on the door to rouse her.

"What the hell is going on?"

It was Adam. At least somebody was responding.

"Robin," Anna answered succinctly and kicked hard beside the doorknob. No boots; the blow sent a stab of pain all the way up to her hip, but the door held.

"Here, let me." Adam was beside her, wearing boxer shorts and wool socks. He slammed his shoulder into the door and the lock gave way. A blast of cold air met them. Anna trained her light into the room.

The window over Robin's bed was wide open.

Robin was gone.

25

Anna turned her light onto the floor. Robin's parka, ski pants, socks—all her winter garments—were where she had let them fall when she undressed for bed. Anna spun, taking in a rush of the room. Closet door open, clothes as she remembered, Robin's rucksack on the table at the foot of her bed, her house moccasins peeked from under the bed, her pillow crushed between bed and bureau.

"Robin!" Anna shouted, crossed the room in two steps and leapt onto the bed. Cruel temperatures and black on black of forest and night met her like a wall. Her flashlight beam poked feebly into the scratch of branches, grabbing the white of snow and making shadows of it.

"Robin!" Anna yelled.

Ridley and Jonah crowded into the room, Jonah blinking behind wire-rimmed glasses and Ridley, hair

316 | NEVADA BARR

loose and clad only in long-john bottoms. Both wore
headlamps. They were so accustomed to the electric cur-
few, they donned them automatically. Anna suffered an
unsettling sense of being trapped in a coal mine adventure with two of the seven dwarves.

"Where's Bob?" she demanded. Jonah and Ridley
looked at each other in almost-comic confusion. "Adam,
was Bob in his bed when you got up?" Anna insisted.

"I fell asleep on the couch," he replied. "But he
should be. After the third time you told him to go away,
he went to bed."

"Check and see if he's there."

"I'm going to fire up the generator," Jonah announced and disappeared into the darkness of the hall.

"Yeah, thanks," Ridley said vaguely.

Anna echoed the thought if not the words. Fear of
the dark had never been one of her neuroses, but she was
thinking of adding it to the list. She was growing tired
of peering down narrow beams of light like a virgin in a
cheap horror flick.

"Where's Robin? What's the deal?" Ridley asked. Anger focused his words and, Anna hoped, his brain.

She gave him an overview of what she'd found in the
V.C., up to and including the condom. She did not mention that she'd been incarcerated there. Instinct told her
to save that revelation for another time.

"And you think the condom was Bob's," Ridley said.

"It wasn't mine."

Lights came on, startling her so badly she dropped her
flashlight. Adam was standing in the doorway, his head-

lamp turned off. Anna wasn't sure how long he'd been there, but it didn't matter. The information wasn't a secret she'd intended to keep. Since she didn't trust anybody, she had two choices: tell no one anything or tell everyone everything. She'd opted for the latter, so should anyone on the island besides herself turn out to be moderately sane and nonviolent he or she could help her watch the rest.

"Bob was in his bed," Adam said.

"You hear the bit about the condom?" Ridley asked.

"I heard. I doubt it was Bob's. The guy's not so bad when you get to know him." This was delivered in a voice so totally devoid of emotion Anna flashed on a group of POWs in the Iraq war who'd been tortured, then filmed mouthing anti-American sentiments by their captors shortly before they were beheaded.

"Get dressed," Ridley told Adam. "Tell Bob to get up and get dressed. We're going to need to get a jump on this . . . on whatever this is. Robin was stewed to the gills. She may have just gotten a sudden desire to go walkabout."

Anna hoped that was the case, but she doubted it. The men left, and she retrieved her flashlight. The window showed no signs of having been forced. Outside, near the bunkhouse, was a morass of tracks left by a moose that liked to scratch its back on the drainpipe from the gutters. No tracks left by bipeds; nothing that looked human.

Closing the window, she remained standing on Robin's bed. No track, no sign: that was not indicative of drunken meandering by a naked girl carrying a sleeping bag.

Robin had not left; she had been taken, spirited away, vanished into the night. There would have been a sort of poetic satisfaction if Anna could have gotten one more shiver out of Algernon Blackwood—the windigo was known for swooping down and snatching its victims bodily from their tents—but she couldn't quite picture the starved monster, lusting after human flesh, swiping a key and locking her in the V.C. so it might enjoy its midnight snack in peace.

Ridley called, radioed and e-mailed the mainland, begging for help as soon as they could send it. The radio failed. The phone was almost unintelligible. E-mail got through. ISRO's Superintendent promised Coast Guard, Forest Service, NPS search and rescue and law enforcement as soon as the weather allowed an invasion from the mainland.

That done, he and Anna divided the public area into three sections. Ridley chose to go alone. Anna would go with Jonah. Adam volunteered to go with Bob Menechinn. Anna suspected it was so they wouldn't have to go through the wretched moment when nobody picked Bob for their team.

As had been the case when Katherine went missing, they found no track or sign to indicate which direction Robin had been taken. Again they searched the perimeter. Again they searched the permanent-employee housing area. Again they searched Washington Creek campground. Again they found nothing.

Ridley radioed the order to return to the bunkhouse. Layers of cold-weather gear peeled off and dumped, they sat in the living room on the three sofas, like a family at a deathwatch.

No one was anxious to go to bed.

Leaning her elbows on her knees, Anna looked at the men with whom she'd been marooned.

She couldn't count the number of banal conversations she participated in where she was asked: "If you were marooned on a desert island, which book, man, song, tool would you want with you?" *The Complete Works of William Shakespeare,* Paul Davidson, "Amazing Grace" and a real sharp knife.

Finally marooned and she had none of the above.

Another opportunity squandered.

Ridley and Jonah looked much as they had for the past few days, only more so. The pilot's seamed face had lost its pixyish expression. Age dragged down his cheeks and dulled his eyes. Ridley was taking on the look of a lost soul. At each downward turn of events, he had stayed strong. Anna wasn't sure he could do it this time. Only Adam showed signs of life and hope. His face was no more animated than the others, but there was a focus and intensity where before there'd been raw energy. Like a seasoned soldier, he seemed relieved to finally be going into battle rather than waiting for it.

Bob Menechinn was the most changed. Robin's disappearance seemed to have gotten to him as nothing else had: not Ridley's hostility, not Katherine's death, not the wog or the windigo, not Anna's walking in on him—twice—being no better than he should be with a dead woman and a woman dead to the world.

Menechinn was a bit of a sociopath, she guessed. In Bob's mind, there was no Bob but Bob; other people were mere shadows, there to please him or be used by him or gotten around. An excellent government tool.

Following this train of thought, Anna realized Robin's disappearance, in and of itself, was not what was turning Bob's skin pasty or thinning his breath. Something had happened in the past few hours that had caused him to believe he was threatened. Adam might have told him Anna found a condom. She rejected that idea; Bob would just deny it was his. Even fingerprints wouldn't do it. There were a number of reasons he might have touched the package.

As the night wore on, she quit worrying about Ridley's ability to cope and began to worry about hers. Night closed tightly around the bunkhouse, the poor lighting in the common room inadequate to push it back past the mirror of the windows. Claustrophobia grew up through the cement suffocating her brain till she could picture herself running screaming into the night.

"I was locked in the V.C.," she announced suddenly and loudly. "Someone locked me in before kidnapping Robin." Her bomb fizzled. The men looked at her, faces devoid of emotion. If one of them had thrown the dead bolt, Anna couldn't have guessed it from their response— or lack of it.

"Or some *thing*," Adam said.

Anna shot him a weary look. "Bullshit," she said succinctly.

He shrugged.

Anna rose and began putting on parka and ski pants. If she didn't take an action—any action—the concrete and claustrophobia were going to seal her tight in their cold, airless vault.

"Where do you think you are going?" Bob demanded, rousing himself from his lethargy. He sounded angry.

"Out. Want to come with me?"

"You'd like that, wouldn't you?" he snapped. He glanced at Adam and then away. Whatever had been communicated was lost on Anna.

She stared at him long and hard. Bob was scared and it was making him mad.

Scared of her? If he was, so much the better.

"I'll go with you," Jonah volunteered.

Anna hadn't particularly wanted company. On ISRO, there clearly wasn't any safety in numbers, but, of all of them, she distrusted the pilot the least.

"Bring a flashlight," she said.

"I'll bring two."

They went out the front door and down the deck stairs. At the bottom of the steps, Anna stopped.

"What?" Jonah's head came up like a dog seeking scent.

"Nothing." Anna had stopped because she didn't know where she was going or what she intended to do when she got there. "Let's just breathe," she said, and Jonah laughed. For several minutes, they stood quietly, flashlights off, and drew clean air into their lungs. Wood-stoves were charming and functional but polluted the indoor air as surely as a band of two-pack-a-day smokers.

"Do we have a clue?" Jonah asked, and she appreciated the wisp of humor.

"I am clueless," Anna admitted. "Start over, I guess." She led the way around the bunkhouse to the window that let into her and Robin's bedroom. Without the distraction of many big-footed men milling about, Anna could see and think more clearly. Jonah stood back as she crouched down several feet from the area directly beneath the window and shined her flashlight beam across the snow, mimicking a setting sun.

"What's with Adam and Bob?" she asked, remembering the pregnant glance.

"Beats me," Jonah said. "Adam's a good guy. He's worked Winter Study a couple times before. Canucks tend to see the best in people. But Menechinn? Sheesh."

The moose that liked to scratch its back against the drainpipe had churned snow and earth into a mass of frozen clods and ice. With her light streaming almost laterally across the tiny field, Anna thought maybe she saw new prints. Maybe. Moose prints. She shined the light out in a circle from where she crouched. "Adam's Canadian?"

"I think he's an American citizen. He grew up in Canada, got married there and came to the States after his wife died."

"That was the wife who killed herself?"

"Where did you hear that?"

"Robin."

Nothing showed but the tracks they had made and several moose trails leading into the trees.

"Adam doesn't talk about it much. Evidently his wife had a miscarriage and went into a depression."

"Was Adam investigated for the death?"

"Like for murdering his wife? What are you thinking?"

"Nothing. Everything. Yeah, for murder, I guess."

"Probably. It's always the husband first in a thing like that. Anyway, it is on TV. So he must have been investigated, but it didn't amount to much. She'd left a note. She'd left a message on her therapist's phone, apologizing. She made a video, begging Adam to forgive her."

"'Do not go gentle into that good night,'" Anna said.

"'Rage, rage,'" Jonah said, startling her, then shaming her, with her own snobbery.

"We're done here," she said. Her knees cracked like rifle shots as she rose to her feet.

"Hah!" Jonah said. "Getting old is a bitch, isn't it?"

Her shame subsided.

Anna moved slowly uphill, following moose prints. The tracks coming down were shallower than those leading back up the rise. The moose had grown significantly heavier while under the bedroom window.

"You see that?" Anna asked and pointed out the disparity. "What could account for that?"

"Maybe the moose ate Robin."

Anna snorted, not a good idea when the air is below zero and the nose is chronically running.

"She could have ridden it," Jonah suggested. He didn't seem to be too concerned either way.

"What do you know?" Anna demanded, shining her light in his face.

"Cut that out, Dick Tracy," he complained.

"What?" Anna kept the light where it was. The lenses of Jonah's glasses flashed and the white of his beard glittered.

"I don't know anything," he said after a moment. "But you've got to figure Robin didn't go hop-hop-hopping away in her sleeping bag like a kid in a sack race. And there's more ways to make moose tracks than to be a moose."

"That's what I'm thinking. Did you happen to notice if the wog prints were always accompanied by moose prints?"

"Nope."

"Me neither. What do you want to bet?"

"I'm not a betting man."

"Me neither."

It was after midnight when Anna went to bed. She wanted to drag her sleeping bag into Katherine's room and close and lock the door, but she stayed in the room she'd shared with Robin. Like Mrs. Darling, she wanted to be there if Peter Pan returned the children he'd stolen, but she doubted Robin had gone with an immortal boy. And she doubted she was anywhere as magical as Never-Never Land.

26

A dam was asleep on the sofa, or appeared to be. Bob had long since retired to his room and Ridley and Jonah to theirs. Sleeping was usually something Anna was good at under stress, that and eating. Years hiking trails in the backcountry had taught her to sleep and eat every chance she got, the way animals did. When one's body was the only vehicle available to keep one's soul from drifting into the ozone, it behooved the driver to keep the tanks topped off.

Tonight was a glaring exception.

Muscle and bone sank gratefully into the hard embrace of the mattress. Fatigue washed over her mind, warm and soporific. Then the delicious sense of drifting into oblivion morphed into sinking under the ice in Intermediate Lake, and she fought desperately back to wakefulness. The nightmare version was more terrifying than almost drowning had been. In the lake, there had been little time for anything but staying alive. In dreams, there was all the time in imagination.

For reasons probably relating more to her sleeping habits than her near-death experience, she was naked in the water. The crippling cold wasn't a factor. Below her lay not the limitless new world she'd glimpsed at the time but the terrors children suffer in nightmares: being helpless and abandoned to a force so utterly evil, one never musters the courage to look at it; a force that would not have the mercy to grant the relief of death. Again and again Anna dragged her bare breasts and belly up an icy edge, serrated like a knife, kicking legs weak to the point of near paralysis, to fend off the black, sucking certainty of what lay below.

It didn't take too many repetitions of this nocturnal entertainment before she decided staying awake was a spiffy alternative.

She lay on her back in the dark and stared upward at a ceiling that she presumed was still there. In a lightless environment, the nothing above her eyes could have been two inches deep or gone on to infinity. The bedside lamp could restore the ceiling to its proper place; Jonah had left the generator running. He said it was in case of emergency, but it was for comfort, the knowledge that they could have light if they heard the stealthy footfalls of boogeymen creeping about. Or boogeywolves.

Bogus wolves, Anna thought. *Werewolves.*

Not the species of legend that morphed from seer-sucker suits to snouts but man posing as a wolf, taking on the imagined properties of the wolf: stealth, strength, ruthlessness, viciousness, love of slaughter for its own sake. It didn't take a trained psychiatrist to see the projection in that equation. Man gave the wolf all the dark bits of himself, then vilified the wolf.

Isle Royale's wog might or might not exist. It was said DNA didn't lie, but it had also been said pictures didn't lie until computers put the lie to that. What lied was people and they lied all the time, and for every reason under the sun. People lied with words and pictures, and, if it were possible, they would lie with DNA. Katherine could have faked the results for a reason that died with her.

Anna couldn't shake the certainty that why Katherine died was at the heart of the bizarre happenings, but the researcher had not been shot or stabbed or smothered. She'd been savaged by a pack of wolves. It would take more time and expertise than anyone on the island had at hand to fake that: tracks, scat, urine, wounds, fur and tooth marks.

Cause of death wasn't in question and death by misadventure didn't have a *why*. It had a cause: wrong place, wrong time, bad decisions, faulty machinery. *Why* needed motive and only humans had motives.

Anna turned her back on the crowding infinity of night above her and stared at the eternal nothing where Robin's bed had been when she'd turned out the light.

The heart of the issue was, why Katherine died.

Katherine had died accidentally at the auspices of wolves.

There was no way Anna could work that equation that didn't end up in the twilight zone.

Sensing herself headed in the same direction, she fumbled over the edges of the desk between the beds, found the light, switched it on and sat up, her sleeping bag tucked in her armpits. Reoriented in space, her mind back in her skull, she marshaled what she knew about Katherine.

Katherine met and fell in love with a wolf when she was three years old. Bob Menechinn was her graduate adviser. He had carried her up five flights of stairs when she was unconscious. Katherine had shown a desire to keep Robin away from Bob. She'd gone so far as to tell Anna to warn the pretty young biotech to stay away from him. Katherine was cowed by, in love with or frightened by her professor. She rarely stood up to Bob. The first time was in the camp between Windigo and Malone. The second was in the cabin at Malone Bay after Robin had gone to free the trapped wolf.

In the tent, wog or wolf snorting around outside, Bob had gone nuts, shouting and waving his headlamp. Katherine said: "Be quiet. You'll scare him away." Remembering the look on Robin's face when Katherine hadn't gibbered with terror—Katherine had been concerned about the monster—Anna smiled.

Did Katherine think it was her wolf lover come back for her after twenty-three years or more? In dog years, that would be one old lover. No, Katherine was not crazy; she didn't strike Anna as even particularly fanciful. She knew wolves and she wasn't afraid. Not then anyway. She'd told Bob to be quiet because she loved the wolf more than she did him.

Early on, Anna hadn't given Bob and Katherine as Bob *and* Katherine more than a passing thought. Lovers, married lovers, ex-lovers, jaded lovers were ubiquitous in every profession. Unlike wolves, humans weren't engineered to be monogamous. Considering it now, she didn't think Katherine was in love with Bob. Anna had found it impossible to so much as like the man, despite the fact he saved her life, but women often loved wretched men. Men loved vile women. In the infamous words of Woody Allen: "The heart wants what it wants."

During the Malone Bay adventure, Anna began to suspect that what she'd first taken for fear or jealousy on Katherine's part was barely controlled fury, the acidic variety that the powerless suffer, the kind that eats away from the inside.

Katherine had hinted Bob was withholding her Ph.D. Was that sufficient motive to hate? Probably. People hated without much provocation.

The second time Katherine contradicted him was when he'd said the study must be shut down; she insisted the foreign DNA was sufficient reason to keep ISRO closed winters, keep the study intact.

Protecting wolves again? Protecting scientific study? Anna wondered if Katherine had a greater investment in the island's wolf/moose research than she'd let on. Had she an interest that made it worth her while to fake the DNA results?

Katherine was all whispers and Bob all shouts, yet both of them were opaque, keeping their secrets.

The woodstove had been stoked later than usual and, though the door was closed, the bedroom was warm. Anna let her sleeping bag fall down around her waist. Pulling it back up to cover her nakedness, she realized that the window, curtainless and without blinds—a fact she'd never noticed before—was making her modest. No longer did she feel the safety of an uninhabited wilderness beyond the glass.

She switched off the bedside lamp and let the sleeping bag drop.

Drifting unanchored in the dark, she replayed Katherine. Bob introducing her the first night, Katherine ducking, hiding behind her hair. Bob asking her if they'd ever used ketamine, Katherine blushing and turning away. Katherine insisting on telling the others at Malone Bay that Bob was so strong, he carried her up five flights of stairs.

When she was unconscious. Anna turned the light back on.

Bob had carried Robin back from the V.C.

When she was unconscious.

Bob asked, "Have we ever used ketamine?" Robin lost one of the jab sticks loaded with ketamine and xylazine. Katherine fought with Bob after collecting the dead wolf's blood. Anna'd had trouble with that. Because Katherine had treated them as such, Anna guessed the blood samples were important but couldn't figure out why, given the work the researcher had done in the kitchen/lab before the wolf had thawed.

Anna had been assuming there were other samples from that wolf. There weren't, she realized. Blood had not been collected earlier during the external exam; the wolf and his blood were frozen. There were no other blood samples but those in Katherine's pocket. The dismembered wolf was blood dry and refrozen. Anna put the revelation that the samples were unique aside for later consideration and went back to Katherine.

Bob was with Robin in the V.C. before Anna arrived. Bob was with Katherine's corpse in the carpenter's shed, frisking—or fondling—the dead woman.

Anna wriggled free of her sleeping bag and, turning her back on the staring window, pulled on sweatpants and a turtleneck. She turned the light out again and, feeling her way from desk to door, opened it quietly, slipped through and into Katherine's room. Making no sound, she closed that door and shoved something soft under it, a towel, she guessed, then turned on the light. The black staring of the uncovered window startled her. Night and wild had always been her friends. Now both made her jumpy.

Katherine's laptop was on her desk, plugged into the wall to save its batteries. Once, when Anna wished to pry into the lives of dead or uncooperative individuals, she looked for paper: diaries, letters, notes; she listened to phone messages. Now she went straight for the laptop. Unless Katherine had a BlackBerry or an iPhone, the laptop would be where she housed her life when she wasn't using it.

Having unplugged the laptop, she turned the light out again, dragged back the bathrobe she'd thought was a towel, returned to her own room and completed the operation one more time in reverse. Then she covered the window with Robin's parka, shoving the sleeves into the grooves of the metal window frame to cover peepholes from the woods. There was probably no need for secrecy. There was probably no one out in the wee hours, peeking in frosty windows. But telling everyone everything hadn't worked. Anna was switching back to telling no one nothing.

The laptop wasn't password protected. The screen saver that came up was a photograph of Katherine and an older woman who looked so much like her, she couldn't be anyone but her mother or an aunt. The two women were laughing, the camera obviously held in front of them in Katherine's hand, as they yelled "Cheese!"

Anna clicked the START button and began methodically slogging through the files. Unlike paper files, computer files were snooper-friendly. There weren't mountains of paper to hide the molehills of information. Katherine's life was laid out and dissected as neatly as the wolf on the table in the carpenter's shop had been.

Number-oriented, Katherine kept spreadsheets of her personal finances. She earned barely enough to live on but was subsidized by a monthly stipend. From her mother, Anna guessed by the notes Katherine had typed beside two of the entries. She paid her bills by computer.

The usual cost of living was there: gas, water, electricity, food, insurance. Not surprisingly, Katherine spent about three times as much on books as she did on clothing and got her hair cut at a walk-in shop at the mall for ten dollars a visit.

She had been on the antidepressant Effexor for eighteen months. Half of America was on antidepressants, but Katherine had been given a hefty dose, 250 milligrams daily, plus .75 milligrams of Trazodone, an antidepressant and sleep aid. There were weekly payments to a Dr. Lewis. A psychologist, Anna assumed, from the regularity and frequency. Dr. Lewis's name had appeared at about the time of the prescription payments for the antidepressants. The month prior to the advent of the mental health expenditures was an entry to another doctor with the note "D&C" alongside it. Other entries in the medical expenses were marked "co-pay." This one wasn't.

Maybe an abortion.

Then depression.

Under the file named "Black Ops," Katherine had saved sixteen articles from newspapers and periodicals as ridiculous as *The Star* and as sublime as *The Journal of the American Medical Association* on the subjects of amnesia, traumatic amnesia, fugue states, repressed memory and multiple personalities.

The folder "Possibilities" contained short synopses of what Anna assumed were personal profiles from a matchmaking Web site. After each was written a number and a letter. Shorthand, possibly for the number of times they'd

334 | NEVADA BARR

contacted and the letter grade Katherine had used to rate the contacts. There were considerably more F's and D's than A's or B's. The last entry had been two months before the "D&C" entered into the medical bills. One of the A's or B's might have been the father of the D&C. Or Katherine might have stopped dating—or shopping—at the time she became pregnant. What, if anything, this had to do with her death by wild animal attack a year and a half later Anna couldn't fathom.

Under the file name "The Great Escape" were fragments of sentences, as if Katherine had been jotting down ideas or keeping a list.

THERE'S NO SUCH THING AS NEGATIVES ANYMORE.
IF MOTHER WAS DEAD, WHO WOULD CARE?
MURDER OR SUICIDE.
IF I WERE DEAD, WHO WOULD CARE?
MOTHER.
MURDER'S A DONE DEAL.
EVERYBODY'S ON THE NET.
WHO WOULD HIRE ME?
I WOULD DIE.

"Well, that's just cryptic as hell," Anna muttered. The list gave the impression Katherine was thinking of killing her mother or herself or her mother, then herself. The mother that gave her money every month. The mother she was hugging and laughing with on her screen saver.

THERE'S NO SUCH THING AS NEGATIVES ANYMORE.

The list that followed was nothing but negatives. "Everybody's on the Net," Anna read aloud. "Who would hire me? I would die."

She minimized that screen and clicked on a file named "Pictures" from the main menu. Given the propensity to save everything when space is measured in gigabytes, Katherine hadn't saved many photographs. Most were of animals, wild and domestic, that had been taken with more love than skill. There were a half dozen of Katherine taken with the woman on the screen saver, winter shots with mufflers and skis, both women smiling and laughing.

There's no such thing as negatives anymore.

Because few people used film. Katherine had been talking about digital photography. Anna returned to the list saved in "The Great Escape" folder. Viewed from the perspective of photography, it made sense.

There's no such things as negatives—in the classic stories of blackmail, victims had to buy back the negatives of incriminating photographs.

If Mother was dead, who would care? If Katherine was referencing compromising photographs this suggested, not that no one would miss Mother but that Mother was the person Katherine was most concerned about seeing the photographs.

What one didn't want Mother to see was usually sexual in nature. Though born from Mother's womb and because of her sexual congress with Father, girls— women—did not want Mom to see them in bed with some guy. *Or some girl,* Anna reminded herself.

MURDER OR SUICIDE.

Anna doubted the murder referred to Katherine's mother. More likely it referred to the man who had impregnated her. Given the list of graded Internet "Matches," it didn't appear that Katherine had any steady boyfriend. She might not have had a flesh-and-blood beau at all. The men in "Possibilities" could have been fantasies, a virtual love life.

IF I WERE DEAD, WHO WOULD CARE?
MOTHER.

Suicide was ruled out because of the devastating effect it would have on her mother. Katherine was thinking clearly enough to realize whatever the digital photographs contained, they would not damage her mother as much as the death of her daughter would.

MURDER'S A DONE DEAL.

The powerful emotion evoked by the concept of murder, with the other choice being self-annihilation, gave Anna the gut feeling that this line referred to the D&C, the death of an unborn child. Abortion was the word Anna would use. If Katherine used the word *murder* and still went through with the D&C to end her pregnancy, she had to have had a powerful motivation. The obvious one was that the child was terribly disabled or was a product of rape.

EVERYBODY'S ON THE NET.
WHO WOULD HIRE ME?
I WOULD DIE.

The rapist had sexually explicit photographs or videos of Katherine that he was threatening to put on the Web if she didn't . . .

What? Anna wondered. Katherine had no money. A graduate assistant, it was unlikely she had any power.

If she reported the assault? If she pressed charges? If she didn't continue to allow herself to be raped?

"Jeez, other people's lives," Anna whispered and shook her head, feeling suddenly sad.

Though prying eyes—should any be braving the night—had been shut outside, she closed the laptop partway and leaned her back against the wall.

The inferences she'd made from the list didn't seem connectable to Katherine's death. Blackmailers didn't normally kill their victims; it was the other way around. There was also the annoying but inescapable fact that Katherine had not been coshed on the head and tossed into a Dumpster. She'd been brought down by Middle pack or Chippewa Harbor pack. There was no way to be certain since the only one on the island who could have run DNA from scat was dead.

It was an accidental death. Anna announced this in her brain. The feeling that the death was key to the sickness of the island did not abate. Anna stretched her legs in front of her, flexing her feet in their thick wool socks, cracking her ankle bones. Till this moment, she'd not thought of Isle Royale as sick, but the word fit. Wolves, moose, researchers, all were suffering an illness not unlike the disease that must have swept through Salem before the witches were burned. Hatred and insanity were virulent and highly contagious. The infected lynched their fellows, gang-raped women, burned down buildings, saw the Virgin Mary in grilled cheese sandwiches and were beamed up to alien spaceships to have their innards probed.

The virus needed certain conditions in which to grow; its victims had to be willing to believe; they had to want, on some level, maybe even unbeknownst to themselves, to do what the virus would tell them to do. And they had to be greedy: for profit, for importance, for revenge, for entertainment, for adventure. Only the greedy could be effectively conned. One never read of Zen masters being taken in by scams. They didn't crave anything, and, therefore, con artists couldn't set the hook.

Ridley wanted to keep the park closed winters so the wolf/moose study could continue.

Bob wanted to open Isle Royale to the public in winter because he'd been paid to find a way to do that, if not in cash, then in future work. Travel writers and professional "experts" had to find what the client paid them to find. Honesty might be the best policy, but it didn't pay as well or get one invited back.

Katherine had seemed to want to keep the island open but was more concerned that Bob accept her thesis and pass it on to her graduate committee. At least until they'd come to a parting of the ways after the necropsy and Katherine had run off.

Robin wanted to keep ISRO closed in winter and the study up and running. She'd also seemed to want to be scared, the way teenagers love to terrify themselves with tales of the homicidal escapee from the insane asylum, Jason, Hannibal the Cannibal and countless assorted purveyors of horror.

Anna didn't know what Adam wanted. His vanishing acts seemed to indicate he wanted to be by himself, his words that he wanted to be of help to the team, his actions that he disliked Bob one day and wanted to be his best friend the next. Had a crush on Robin one day and was indifferent to her the next. Maybe Adam didn't know what he wanted either. Maybe he hadn't known since his wife died.

The wolves, the ice, the windigo, the weather, the very blood and bone of the island seemed to want them dead or confused or insane or gone. Wolves came so close, it was as if they wished to be near humans, wished to be seen. Wolves killed Katherine. Ice three inches thick, thick enough to ride horses across, broke in a mouth-shaped hole at the weight of one small woman. Snow blocked vision and wind tore at nerves and cold ate away at hearts.

If the wolves, wog led or otherwise, wanted the island to themselves winters, they'd probably get what they wanted: the unusual behavior patterns, the alien DNA and the oversized track sightings were sufficiently unique and exciting that the National Park Service and

Michigan Tech would fight to keep ISRO closed to the public from October to June and the study ongoing.

Ridley would get what he wanted for the same reasons.

Bob would not, but it wouldn't be through his annoying his employers with excessive truthfulness, so, in a way, he would. Anna doubted he cared about the study, the island, the wolves or anything but himself.

Robin was undoubtedly getting to be as scared as ever she'd dreamed.

Katherine would never get her dissertation published.

That left Adam, a widower or a murderer or both, a man who moved out of sync with the moods of the others.

ANNA CREPT INTO THE COMMON ROOM. The old computer, plugged into the wall for the use of seasonals, shined a single green, beady eye. The wood in the stove had been banked and a line of embers showed between two logs, casting enough light she could make her way without bumping into the furniture. Adam's outline darkened the couch, where he snored softly.

Stopping, Anna looked down at his recumbent form for a minute or more. Adam played possum; she'd figured that out. There was no way of telling if he played possum now. It didn't much matter, and, if he was playing possum, she had the satisfaction of knowing the visitation of a bedraggled middle-aged specter in the still of the night had to be giving him the willies.

She moved the chair in front of the computer at an angle so she could watch both the screen and Adam and clicked on the blue *E*. The island's Internet server popped up. They lived in a bunkhouse warmed by a woodstove, electrified by an old gasoline-powered generator, water brought up from the lake and an outhouse, and they were on the Internet. As she clicked on Google, it occurred to her that the odd thing was she didn't find it odd. As a kid, she didn't have television. It was all done with towers then, and she'd lived in a tiny town in a mountain valley where the reception was lousy. Now she took instant global communication from a remote island for granted.

She typed in "Katherine Huff."

Katherine had published in seven scientific journals, articles on DNA research in mammals, and sixteen magazines and periodicals, on the subject of wilderness education. On the latter, Bob Menechinn's name was listed first, with her as his graduate assistant.

The articles on DNA were painfully technical, written for other scientists and virtually incomprehensible to the uninitiated. Anna slumped against the back of the chair, feet thrust far under the table, chin nearly on her chest. She wasn't sure what it was she had leapt out of bed to seek in cyberspace. The mystery of who Katherine Huff was, why she'd been savaged by wolves, wasn't in journals. There wasn't anything else, no newspaper articles reporting murder or mayhem connected to her, no MySpace revelations or vanity Web site with pictures of her dog and a diary of her summer vacation in Europe.

According to Hollywood, savvy Internet users could find out everything right down to the subject's bra size and favorite food. Maybe in real life they could, too, but Anna wasn't on that level. Google and Wikipedia maxed out her cyberspace cunning.

Adam snorted from a snore into deeper sleep, his breathing more a vibration against Anna's mind than her eardrums. The light from the banked embers painted the angular planes of his face dull orange, his fancy mustache black as an ink drawing against it. The warm glow erased years from his face, the shadowed room the gray from his hair, and he looked no more than twenty. Supposedly he was an old hand at Winter Study, a friend of Ridley's, a Park Service renegade who traveled with ease between researchers and NPS staff. So Jonah had intimated. Anna had seen little of it. Adam had let Ridley and the rest of them down as often as not. When they needed him, he was nowhere to be found, and the batteries in his radio died and came back so often they could have had regular roles on *Buffy the Vampire Slayer*.

He shirked his work, then skied out in the dark when the body recovery went sour. Behind Bob's back, Adam praised, excused and mocked him. To Bob's face, Adam was obsequious and scornful by turns, the way a kid will be when forced to curry favor with a person he or she loathes.

Why would Adam need to curry favor with Bob Menechinn?

Anna typed "Adam Johansen" into the box on Google's home page. Seventeen hits. The front page of an old *Lassen County Times* had a photograph of him standing with three other men. They were dressed in fire-retardant Nomex and leaning on shovels. They'd been with the wildland firefighters credited with saving the tiny town of Janesville, California, from being burned. The rest were from local papers in Saskatoon. These were archival and covered the suicide of Cynthia Jean Johansen.

The first reported only the barest of facts. Cynthia Johansen, nee Batiste, a twenty-two-year-old senior at the University of Saskatchewan, had been in the bathroom of the apartment she shared with her husband of eleven months, Adam Johansen. The bath was separate from the sink area and she had closed the door. Her husband, a thirty-one-year-old freelance carpenter, had been cleaning the trap under one of the sinks. When he realized she had stopped speaking, he tried to get her to open the door. By the time he broke it down, Cynthia had bled to death from three deep cuts made by a man's straight razor, two to the left wrist and one to the right.

According to the school newspaper, Cynthia's best friend, Lena Gibbs, said Cynthia had miscarried two months prior to the incident and had gone into a severe depression. Gibbs said Cynthia had never talked about killing herself, but she had talked about being a bad person and suffered crippling guilt over the loss of the baby.

Twenty-two.

Anna slid farther down in the chair, the picture of a lowrider sans muscle car. Anna's older sister, Molly, had been born when their mother was twenty-three. This was not abnormal. The body wanted to reproduce at a young age, when the chances of conceiving and the mother living through the birth to care for her offspring were greatest. From Anna's vantage point, twenty-two seemed impossibly young to be dealing with college, marriage, pregnancy and miscarriage, yet women managed it without killing themselves—or anybody else. Often, younger women dealt with miscarriages better than their older sisters. Youth was resilient in body and mind. The future still held the possibility of many live births.

Anna wondered if Cynthia Jean's guilt was brought on or exacerbated by other factors. Drugs, maybe, or intentionally rash actions designed to end an unwanted pregnancy. An abusive husband had brought on more than one miscarriage. Because Adam's wife's death was ruled suicide didn't mean he didn't kill her; it only meant that if he did, he'd gotten away with it.

The next article, written the following day and on page two of the paper instead of page six, reported that Adam had been removing the sink trap because his wife said she'd lost her engagement ring down the drain. He told police that while he worked, Cynthia had talked with him through the door about how much she loved him and how glad she was he had given her a home and that the eleven months they'd been married were the happiest of her life.

The phone rang and he went to answer it. He said his wife asked him to stay and talk to her, but he said he'd be right back. The call was from one of Cynthia's teachers, and he brought the cordless phone into the sink area from the kitchen.

Cynthia wouldn't respond when he spoke, and the door to the bath was locked. He told the police and, later, the newspaper reporter that he thought his wife was mad at him for answering the phone when she'd asked him not to so he ignored her and went back to working on the sink, occasionally making remarks. He said he got angry, then worried, and that was when he broke through the door and found her.

Anna saw her husband, Paul, in her mind, felt him in her heart and couldn't imagine the kind of pain Adam must have suffered. That is, if he was telling the truth.

The only story she'd heard that was more tragic was the accidental death of a three-year-old who'd sneaked out and crawled behind his mother's Camaro to surprise her when she left for the grocery store.

Paul Davidson was a Christian, an Episcopal priest, he believed in a loving God. Paul was also Sheriff of a poor county in Mississippi. He saw suffering of the worst kinds, cruelty and ignorance, predator and prey on the human scale, and it was far more vicious than anything between wolves and moose. Anna's husband didn't believe in the magical thinking of God granting wishes, but he did believe in the importance of prayer. He didn't believe in pearly gates or Saint Peter or crossing the river Jordan. He didn't believe in any other hell than the ones found on Earth. He didn't believe in angels or ghosts or miraculous answers to prayers. Yet he believed he would be at one with his God when he died.

He believed Anna would, too, but she couldn't quite get there with him. She couldn't get her mind around a God who was purported to know—and care—about the ins and outs of human suffering. If there was such a watcher of the falling sparrows he—it was always he—was a bloodthirsty son of a bitch. Or he was a helpless son of a bitch.

Spending all eternity with either incarnation didn't appeal to her.

The next article she clicked on brought her upright in her seat. The headline read: "No Ring Found in Trap." Beneath it was a quarter-page color photograph of a young Adam Johansen on the front steps of a brick fourplex, carrying a bloody, naked woman. The woman's arms hung at her sides. Her hands were completely red, and blood trailed down the leg of Adam's khaki shorts and painted the side of his calf and the top of his running shoe. Cynthia's head was back in the classic Fay Wray swoon, but the woman in the photograph was either dead or soon to be dead. Long hair, brown or dark blond, streamed to Adam's ankles, the ends pointed and dark with water and blood. Anna could see the white paint on the doorframe behind Adam streaked from where the hair had been drawn across it when he carried Cynthia outside.

"It's a still from a videotape."

The voice was no more than six inches from her ear. Years of not responding to the machinations of people whose day she was ruining for one reason or another, Anna didn't leap out of her skin, shrieking.

"Did I wake you up?" she asked.

Adam leaned down, looking at the photograph on the screen. He was shirtless. Heat radiated from his skin. Threads of long hair trailed across Anna's neck like the tickle of spiderwebs walked through in the dark. Muscles at the corner of his jaw worked as he clenched and unclenched his teeth.

Fear on men smelled sour. Adam smelled of molten iron and metal ice-cube trays, red coals and rocks brittle with cold.

Adam reeked with a distillation of rage.

27

Anna sat perfectly still, her eyes on the picture on the monitor, and waited for the scalding anger boiling off Adam to dissipate. The back of her chair moved fractionally, the oak creaking as Adam leaned on it hard, using it as a lame man would use a crutch to push himself upright. The palpable heat of the man moved away from Anna's cheek and the sense of being on thin ice over a raging volcano abated. She clicked the BACK arrow, getting rid of the bloody photograph.

"I can't imagine anything worse than what you had to go through," she said. She didn't have to pretend to be sincere. If he had killed his wife, by the look of the young man in the picture it hadn't been nearly as much fun as he'd hoped.

"I didn't kill her, if that's what you're thinking," Adam said.

"The coroner ruled it suicide," Anna replied evenly. Adam was no longer breathing in her ear, his hair trailing over her shoulder, but he'd not stepped away either.

"Why are you looking at that?" Adam sounded more worried than angry at the breach of his privacy, or such privacy as remained in the instant-information era.

"Getting to know you," Anna said. "Since we're neighbors, let's be friends." She didn't take her eyes from the monitor, but she wasn't seeing. Every pore was opening to sense Adam: where he stood, how he stood, if he was dangerous.

His breath puffed out on a dry cough. The closest thing to a laugh he was going to make.

"You're a piece of work, you know that?" he said and, rather than leaving, pulled up another straight-backed chair to sit next to her, scooting it up till his knees were less than a foot from hers. He put his long forearms down on his long thighs and leaned in till their faces were close enough, Anna could see the tiny red rivers of blood from broken vessels in his eyes. "Do you think I took Robin? Is that it?"

His breath was hot, residual fire from the fury, and smelled sweet, as if he'd chewed a mint leaf. Anna couldn't back away from him without tipping her chair over.

"Adam," she said wearily. "You're crowding me. People crowd to intimidate. Could you either back off or do it in a more interesting way?"

Another cough of laughter. Anna considered whether or not she should go on the comedy circuit in the Catskills.

"Sorry," he said, sat up straight and smiled. It was a good smile, full of healthy teeth, and it went all the way to his eyes crinkling the corners. Anna believed he was sorry, that he'd not meant to scare her. It didn't mean he was a nice guy.

"Did you make Robin disappear?" she asked.

"Robin didn't need to be here this winter. She should have stayed home or waited tables in St. Paul." He rubbed his face. Both hands continued up until his fingers pushed his hair out in thick tresses. "We'll start the search at first light?"

The question took Anna off guard. "Yeah, I guess. Will we find her?" she asked pointedly.

He smiled again. This time, it didn't reach his eyes. "Who knows?" He rose and walked from the common room. A second later, Anna heard the door to his and Bob's room opening and closing again.

She couldn't tell if she'd just had an up-close-and-personal conversation with a backwoods John Wayne Gacy or not.

"Ted Bundy," she corrected herself.

In the minutes spent drinking the essence of Adam from the air as he stood over her half dressed and burning, she'd not tasted the sour warp of a psychopath. But, then, one didn't. That was why they got away with it.

Anna logged off. She wanted to rest, to sleep, but seemed to have lost the knack. She wanted to go outside, but she'd freeze to death in the dark. January's paltry eight hours of daylight depressed her. It was just enough to remind a person they weren't blind before it abandoned them for another winter's night. Because she could think of nothing more productive to do, she went back into Katherine Huff's room and stood staring at the simple dorm furniture. Two medium-sized duffel bags; all the personal gear any of them had been allowed to bring. There wasn't a lot to dig through, but Anna did it. Dirty socks and underpants were her reward. Since she'd taken the laptop, the desk was empty but for the cell phone charger plugged into the same outlet the computer had been.

Everything was so ordinary, so expected, at first she didn't realize what she was looking at. Modern conveniences had become as air; only when they weren't there were they noticed.

Why would Katherine have a cell phone charger out and plugged in when there was no cell reception on the island? Anna unplugged the charger and carried it back to her room, locking the door behind her. Katherine's cell phone was still in her day pack. She'd kept it, not as evidence but out of spite for Bob. Not particularly flattering but, as it happened, useful. Having plugged the charger into the wall, she connected the phone. A red light behind a dark blue plastic oval lit up. The oval had a star on it. Around the star, an elliptical circle was traced in silver.

It was a satellite phone. Katherine did have cell service. If she had it, Bob had it. Bob had been anxious to retrieve this phone. He'd said he'd have to replace it out of his own pocket if it wasn't found. At the time, Anna'd merely been impressed with his callousness. Now she wondered if he'd wanted the phone so no one would notice it was a satellite phone, know they had access to the outside world and one another.

Why wouldn't he want anyone to know that? Afraid they'd all make pests of themselves asking to borrow it? It wasn't as if they didn't know why he was on the island. Anna hit the CONTACTS button and scrolled down the list of names. None of them were familiar but Ridley's, with his work number at Michigan Tech, the Park Service office in Houghton and Bob Menechinn.

Without thinking why, she did it; Anna clicked on Menechinn and hit SEND. The warble of a loon called through the house. Quickly she pushed END. If Bob woke, if he looked, if he checked for missed calls, he would know the phone had been found. For several minutes, she sat still as stone and listened. There was no sound of doors or feet. Bob must have slept through the ringing.

A loon. The call of a loon in January.

The night Katherine had gone missing, Anna was awakened by the call of a loon. Since there wouldn't be any loons on the island for months, she'd thought it a dream, like the dream she'd had of coyotes on her mother's ranch. The coyotes frolicked in dreamscape, but the loon had been of this world. Bob had been called the night Katherine died. Katherine had died with the satellite phone in her hand.

Anna found RECENT CALLS and opened it. The last call was to Bob Menechinn.

Maybe he'd slept through that one too. There was no

way Anna could tell if the call had gone through or how long it had been but, even if Bob had missed it, presumably Katherine would have left him a message. Her last words. Bob never mentioned a message.

For a moment, Anna wondered if Bob had been the instigator of the mysterious "HELP ME" that had appeared on the window. The loon call of the cell phone had been after that by hours, but it was possible Katherine had phoned earlier, or he had phoned her.

If he knew she was in trouble, why wouldn't he have said so, led the rescue effort? When there was no physical danger to himself, Bob liked playing the white knight. If he didn't know, why wouldn't he have shared the message after the fact? Afraid they'd think he'd dropped the ball? Or was the message so vitriolic or damning, he didn't want them to hear it?

Reflexively, Anna looked over her shoulder, checking to see that the parka still covered the window. It did.

Not being a devotee of the cell, Anna'd not given it enough thought. But cell phones took pictures. They text-messaged, and did far more things than anything smaller than the Pentagon should be able to do. A person's cell phone was almost as rich an information trove as his or her computer. Anna hit MENU and began methodically deciphering icons, reading tiny print and punching buttons.

Katherine had not taken any snapshots of the wolves. Being crippled, then eaten, was evidently sufficiently entertaining that there was no need to record it. Anna couldn't tell if she had text-messaged anyone. She kept pushing arrows and buttons and hitting SELECT.

"Ish."

The phone also received photographs. The pictures Katherine had taken were of the same ski vacation as the photographs on the laptop, just different shots and poses. The photographs that had been sent to her had been unopened till Anna'd pressed buttons and pried her way into where they waited like evil beings in a dead-end alley.

There were five of them, but Anna suspected there'd been more. Katherine probably looked at the first few sent, then deleted the rest unopened. She died before she could delete these.

Katherine, nude, had been arranged on a bed. Her legs were splayed toward the camera. In the first photograph, there was a cucumber in her vagina and a carrot inserted in her rectum. The second picture changed only the objects used to rape her: a baseball bat and a green wine bottle. In the third, the photographer had gone to the effort of propping her head up and arranging her hands so she looked as if she had inserted the baseball bat herself.

"Jesus!" Anna breathed and closed her eyes. She had to swallow the sickness in her throat before she could open them again. Then it was another half minute before she could bring herself to look back at the tiny screen.

The fourth shot was a crooked close-up of her face with a man's erect penis shoved in her mouth. Her head was back, eyes closed and jaw slack. In the last shot, the baseball bat had been replaced by a man's fist pushed in up to the forearm. The man's face was not shown.

Katherine's was, every time.

"God damn!" Anna closed the phone and sat staring at it. "God damn!" she said again, shaking her head. Most of her adult life had been spent trying to put a stop to man's inhumanity to everything he could get his hands on. The news showed burned babies, mothers running screaming from bullets, dogs eating fallen men, bombs shattering homes and vehicles. In real time, snuff films every night in every living room in America played out in the name of Current Events.

Yet Anna could not get used to it. Paul had told her the day she got used to it was the day she lost her soul.

She opened the phone and pushed ten numbers in rapid succession. A ring, and two, three. It was very late or very early. Sane people in real places slept at this time of the night. "Please," she whispered. "Please."

"Yes?"

"Paul," Anna cried. "Paul, it's me," and she began to cry.

28

Ketamine stayed in the blood a relatively long time, as far as testing was concerned. Robin's blood would show traces of the drug for seven to fourteen days. One of those days was gone, and Anna didn't know how many more they would be weathered in on the island.

Skipping breakfast, she went, yet again, to the Visitors Center. The door was still unlocked. She wished there was a way to make sure it stayed that way while she was inside, but there wasn't. Indoors, it was so cold she couldn't see her breath. Frigid, superdry air would not fog.

The vials of blood—Robin's and the wolf's—were in her coat pocket. Though the man blackmailing Katherine had been careful to keep his face out of the pictures, Anna didn't doubt that it was Bob Menechinn. Katherine's warnings, the comments about using ketamine, being carried upstairs unconscious—it made sense. Ketamine was not only a cat tranquilizer and a club drug; it was also becoming the date rape drug of choice. The aftereffects often included amnesia, disorientation and paranoia. Three symptoms that made it extremely difficult for victims to successfully prosecute their attackers.

Bob—and Anna was sure it was Bob—had drugged Katherine, then photographed her in crude and mocking poses. These were the pictures that he'd threatened to put up on the Internet, the pictures that she didn't want her mother to see, the pictures that had made her want to die.

He intended to do the same thing to Robin. Robin wasn't drunk; she was drugged. When Anna had come upon him in the carpenter's shop, hunkered over the dead body of his graduate student, he had probably been looking for the cell phone. He also could have been indulging himself in a woman the way he preferred them: helpless and degraded.

Anger was racking up Anna's respiration rate. Inside her mittens, she clenched and unclenched her fists. Halfway through the main room of the Visitors Center she turned abruptly and walked to the floor-to-ceiling windows overlooking Washington Harbor. The sun had not yet risen above the hills. When it did, there would be no blue sky to greet it. Clouds touched the tops of the trees on Beaver Island, black and mysterious across the wide expanse of ice. As she watched the scene—devoid of movement, devoid of sound, of shadows—and slowed her breath and heart rate, letting the blinding anger clear from her vision, she began to see colors. The ice, slate and pearl, hinted of blues and lavenders so delicate they were wisped with imagination. Ink spikes of the trees on the shore harbored dark-dark greens, greens so close to black they shimmered in and out of vision like the hide of a whale deep in the ocean. Far out, where the ice stopped past Beaver and the open water began, were the barest touches of pink, iridescent and ephemeral.

In the night, the iris of the eye expanded to take in what available light it could to help clawless, blunt-toothed human beings live until morning. Perhaps in winter there was similar evolution, allowing the eyes to adjust to let in every scrap of color, so the fragile, neurotic creatures could stay sane to see another spring.

As Anna let the anger go, she knew she was terrified. She was scared to the bone that Robin was cached somewhere, drugged insensible again and posed for pictures like those on the cell phone in Anna's pocket. There were few places she could be hidden, unless death by hypothermia was part of the plan. Dead, a victim couldn't accuse the rapist. Katherine wouldn't be testifying anytime soon. Was that why Bob had said nothing when she'd called? Had she outlived her usefulness, and, when she got into trouble the night she ran off and called him for help, he just quietly turned over and went back to sleep?

Gutless, Anna thought in disgust, but the theory worked with what she knew of Menechinn. So did the date rape scenario. Bob had the means and opportunity for drugging Robin and raping her. Robin's jab stick, loaded with ketamine, had gone missing from Malone Bay cabin. He had the means to remove her bodily from the bunkhouse. He had carried Anna two miles and Katherine up five flights of stairs. Anna didn't think he had the means to stash her anywhere on the island and still keep her alive. Therefore, he didn't kidnap her. Or he didn't mean for her to live.

If Bob wanted her dead, Robin was dead. She wouldn't have to be taken any distance at all. A couple yards from the bunkhouse would be sufficient. Dump her naked in the snow, cover the body with powder and branches. She would have been dead of cold before anyone noticed she'd been taken. Robin Adair had shyly crept into Anna's heart and the thought of her murdered brought back the rage she'd been working so hard to lose.

She shook it off.

She needed to test the blood; she needed evidence before arresting Bob. "Proof," Anna said. "Woman, then wolf."

Holding on to what shards of peace the winter scene had given her, she turned from the window and stumped quickly across the hardwood floor, dynamic movement thwarted by the fat rubber boots and thick down.

In the back hall next to the DR's office was law enforcement's storage room: narrow, windowless and lined on both sides with adjustable metal shelves. Unlike many NPS storage rooms, it was neat and well organized. ISRO evidently had excellent seasonal rangers. On the top shelf were two briefcase-sized satchels, the standard field drug-testing kits used for years by police. They contained vials of various chemicals. Drugs were mixed with these liquids according to a key on the underside of the lid. The reaction gave the officer an idea of what she was dealing with. They were designed to find out what a drug was, not who was taking them, and were of no use to Anna.

In the District Ranger's office, where the light was best, she found what she needed, a gas chronometry–mass spectrum device, GC/MS. Boxy and white, it looked vaguely like a blood pressure machine, the kind in grocery stores near the pharmacy. Before 9/11, there wasn't a GC/MS in the entire Park Service. Now they were becoming almost commonplace, and they weren't used to test criminals. Using hair, urine, saliva or blood, they drug-tested employees, particularly law enforcement.

Ketamine, "Vitamin K," the cat tranquilizer, wasn't on a standard tox screen, but that would change. Once used exclusively by veterinarians, it had made its way into the pantheon of club drugs because of its euphoric and hallucinogenic properties. Several years before, Anna had taken a trip with "Lady K" against her will and without her knowledge and enjoyed neither the high nor the apparitions.

Ignorance stopped her in front of the GC/MS. She'd seen it operated exactly twice.

"Fuck!" she whispered. Then with more vehemence: "Fucking fool!"

None of it mattered: there was no electricity, no power. She couldn't turn the machine on. A detail she'd overlooked in her mad dash down the hill.

Modern conveniences were as air: expected.

"Damn!"

She turned and ran from the office, down the hall and up the hill through the snow. By the time she reached the carpenter's shop, she was puffing and sweating. Without waiting to catch her breath, she began pawing through the plastic-wrapped packages of wolf parts on the table. "Okay, Katherine," she muttered to the corpse at her feet. "Give me a hand here. What was it set you off? I can't test the blood. Maybe you could with your fancy PCR, but I can't, I made a royal fool of myself in the V.C. If a tree falling in the forest can be a fool. So what was it? What did I hand you? You squeaked like a rat. Skull? No. Paws? No. Bigger.

"This." Anna laid her hands on the square package that contained the excised flesh from the wolf's throat, the meat Ridley had preserved because of the size of the bite pattern that killed the wolf. "Hey, it's all coming back to me," Anna told the dead woman. "Bob mouths off. Ridley cuts his hand. I pass this gob off to you. I'm examining the knife wound. You squeak. I turn. You look like shit. It's this, isn't it?"

Without waiting for a reply, she set the package on the counter beneath the window and began prying the stiff plastic away where it had frozen to the tissue sample underneath. "Okay," she said when she'd peeled the cube of wolf and set it on the counter where the light was strongest. Like any frozen meat, the excised neck flesh had become featureless, pale, the folds and hollows settled while the meat was warm, then frozen in a chunk. "If the dead speak to the dead, do your stuff," Anna said to the corpse. "Otherwise, I don't think this guy is going to tell me anything."

Neither Katherine nor the bit of deceased wolf spoke.

What Anna was looking for wouldn't be in the bite marks. Those had been probed and examined by Ridley and photographed by Robin. It was what they missed that gave Katherine the squeaky pallor. Bending close over the rock-hard neck muscle, Anna turned it slowly between her gloved hands, examining every inch of the flayed neck. On the back, near what would have been the wolf's left side, halfway between ear and shoulder, was a tiny dot of silver metal, the broken-off end of a needle.

"Got it," Anna said to Katherine. She found needle-nose pliers in a drawer beneath the counter and pulled the metal from the neck. It wasn't a needle; it was the dart used when an animal is shot with a tranquilizer gun. Katherine had stood up to Bob after the necropsy for the same reasons she'd found the courage to do it the other two times. He was endangering her beloved wolves.

"Darted it, then opened its throat and it bled out. The wounds made to look like a huge bite pattern," Anna said. "The wolf was murdered." Lost in thought, she turned the splinter of metal in the gray light. Bob had said to Katherine: "We've used ketamine before." Bob had found the animal and he had stomped around it so much there was no hope of finding any tracks. Then he'd claimed the body for "research."

"You thought Bob did it, didn't you? Killed the wolf so the big game hunter could have the head and pelt for his wall. You knew Bob used ketamine; you knew because he'd used it on you."

29

Having cached the broken tip of the tranquilizer dart with the rest of her Nancy Drew collection in the rusted toolbox under the floorboards, Anna walked back toward the bunkhouse. Stillness was absolute. Air and cold melded to form a quantifiable mass, a solid that could be moved through without disturbing a single atom, a vacuum that held matter inside. Anna's steps grew shorter until finally she, too, was still: a rock, a tree, a single mote of ice.

"That doesn't make sense," she said. The words fell into the motionless universe, leaving no ripple. "Katherine, if Bob killed the wolf, why would he make the neck wound interesting? 'Interesting' doesn't get the study shut down. It goes against his interests. Bob never goes against his interests." Momentary sadness drifted across Anna's mind; she wished she hadn't voiced her doubts out loud, intimated Katherine had run to her death for nothing. Except that Bob had made her life intolerable.

"Talking to dead people," she said to the gray that knitted branches together above her head. "At least I'm not seeing dead people." Still, she didn't move.

Whoever had shot the wolf had made the bite marks so it would appear as if it was killed by a giant beast. It was possible that the animal was tranquilized by one person, then another person happened along in the dark with a pointed object and thought, "Boy, wouldn't it be funny if . . ." But Anna doubted it.

Flying back from Intermediate Lake the day she and Jonah saw Chippewa Harbor pack kill the old bull, she had seen a wolfish shape in black, a neat circling of nose to tail, as if a monstrous dog slept in the snow beneath the boughs of an evergreen, just the shape viewed from the air. She thought of the great deception in World War II when the British had salted England with cutouts of Spitfires and barracks without walls so that, seen from the air by German planes, they would look to be an army amassing for an invasion at Calais, while the Allies moved ahead with plans to land on the beaches of Normandy.

Huge paw prints in all the right places, never perfectly clear and always accompanied by moose prints, as if Bullwinkle had been adopted along with Romulus and Remus. A hard object shaped like the hoof of a moose and affixed to the bottom of snowshoes would work. Each step would leave the mark of the hoof; no sign of the human above it. Giant paw prints were easy enough, pawlike shapes on the end of ski poles. With the wind and the drifting snow, even an experienced tracker wouldn't be able to tell they weren't made by a genuine wolf.

Anna hadn't been able to.

The marauding animal that had terrorized their camp up by Lake Desor had snuffled like a bear, pawed at the nylon walls like a dog and left no paw prints. When Katherine hadn't been scared, Robin had snorted—almost a laugh. Because she had known the "wolf" wasn't a wolf? It was Robin who sent Anna and Bob to the side of Intermediate Lake, where there were giant paw prints neatly laid in to lure the unwary trappers to the center of the weird ring in the ice where Anna had fallen through. Then Robin had apologized repeatedly. "I'm so sorry," she'd said. "It shouldn't have happened."

Anna's dream of the night before came back; her naked chest scraping over the serrated-ice edge. She remembered, as she'd slid under the lake, how the ice had been striated vertical marks of white against the gray of older ice, and she remembered grabbing Adam's day pack before he ran for the supercub to leave Malone Bay with Jonah, how heavy it was.

"What's in this?" she'd asked.

"Books," Adam said.

Not books. A drill and spare battery packs and bits. The ring in the ice had been made by a drill, holes weakening the layer, water oozing up through them creating the ridge.

The trapline torn up by an animal so powerful, the

metal of the foothold trap was bent; Robin had reported seeing that. She'd gone to check the line by herself and she hadn't brought the trap back with her.

The wog was a hoax. The hoax had turned deadly. First Anna had gone through the ice, then Katherine had been killed.

As always, that was where Anna came to a wall: Katherine had not been killed by a human being; she'd been savaged by a pack of wolves.

"Damn," Anna said and mentally set aside the researcher's death.

Robin with her love of the island—what was it her boyfriend had said? The last hope for the soul of civilization? Ridley with the most to lose: vocation, avocation and summer cabin at one blow; Jonah, with his loyalty to Ridley; Adam, for whatever reason, maybe just the hell of it—were all of them in on it? Would one of them kill a wolf, a ranger and a researcher to make the island sufficiently interesting that the Park Service and the Michigan Tech would fight Homeland Security over the issue of opening it in the winter months? Anyone in Winter Study could have darted the wolf. The pack was on the ice for several days, and everyone was proficient with the use of tranquilizer guns.

Robin had been in the tent the night of the marauder, but Adam or Ridley or, possibly, Jonah could have followed them. Without the heavy packs that slowed the Malone Bay adventurers, it could have been done, round-trip, home by midnight.

If they were willing to kill, why didn't they just kill

Bob and be done with it? That's what Anna would have done. *With pleasure,* she thought, remembering the pictures on the cell phone.

Maybe they had tried to kill Bob, but he had answered the call of nature, and Anna toddled out onto the ice alone. If so, they—whoever *they* were—were awfully cavalier about collateral damage.

If the point of the hoax was to make the study indispensable, killing Bob wasn't the wisest course. There was nothing so easily replaced as a government flunky. Kill one and ten popped up in his place. And accidental death by drowning wouldn't make Homeland Security any more likely to leave ISRO alone. Katherine had a personal reason to want Bob dead, but Anna couldn't see how she could have seduced Adam—or anyone else— into drilling the ice in the short time she'd been with Winter Study.

"Move," Anna told herself and began trudging toward the bunkhouse again.

The men—all men; the women were vanishing at an alarming rate—were seated around the table in the kitchen.

Over the years, Anna had arrested quite a few people, taken them in for everything from annoying chipmunks to kidnapping and murder. She had arrested men and women and, once, just to make a point, a child. There were a few gaps in her repertoire. She'd never arrested an Asian and, as far as she knew, she'd never arrested a Jew or a Quaker.

It had been her intention to arrest Bob Menechinn,

but, as she took in the Breakfast Club, she couldn't figure out how to go about it. There was no place to incar-
cerate him. Should he decide he didn't wish to be
arrested, there wasn't a damn thing she could do about
it without backup and Adam, Jonah and Ridley could
not be trusted. One, some or all were perpetrating a
fraud on the federal government—which she wasn't sure
was a bad thing—and were willing to kill innocent
women and female park rangers to do it—which she was
sure was a bad thing.

"Hey," she said amiably as she banged the snow off
her boots on the lintel. "Any coffee left?"

"Hey yourself," Adam said. "On the counter. Good
and hot." No one else acknowledged her words or entrance.

Ridley bent over the stove, stirring the inevitable oatmeal, his shoulders rounded as a crone's, his long fingers
looking thinner than they had twenty-four hours before, the knuckles outsized, as if arthritis had taken him
overnight. Jonah was droning on about disrobing "Mrs.
Brown" as he took the cozy off the sugar bowl and began spooning brown sugar into an empty bowl. There
was no ribaldry or playfulness in the Mrs. Brown story
this morning. The old pilot spoke in a monotone, an actor who's forgotten his character and lost his audience.
Bob had taken his preferred chair in the corner against
the wall. The first time Anna had seen him there, she'd
thought of him as enthroned. Now "cornered" was a
better description.

Adam was a stark contrast to his fellows. He burned

again but with a new fever. Not rage, Anna decided as she poured herself a cup of coffee. Excitement. Adam couldn't sit still; he positively bounced in his seat the way a little boy will when an adventure is in the offing. A wonderful adventure. Adam was having a problem keeping joy from busting out all over.

"What are you so happy about?" she asked as she took her place at the end of the table, the de facto "Mom" spot. "Are we going to find Robin?"

Ridley turned from the stove. "Does he know where Robin is?" he demanded sharply. "Adam, do you know where she is?"

"I just have a good feeling, is all," Adam said. "We could do with a little optimism around here for a change. I, for one, would rather believe she's alive somewhere than dead in a snowdrift."

Anna cocked her head to one side, trying to hear through the tension that thrummed in the sinews of the room.

"Chipper," she said. "Adam, you sound downright *chipper*."

Ridley stepped across the small space between the four-burner stove and the Formica-topped table where the rest of them sat over empty bowls like Goldilocks's ursine victims. The thin, bony hands grabbed the front of Adam's shirt and Ridley hauled him half out of his chair and held him suspended with wiry strength. "Do you know where Robin is?" he whispered, a hissing of steam from overheated pipes.

Anna lifted her coffee cup off the table to protect the

precious liquid from the inevitable scuffle to follow. She needn't have bothered. Adam didn't rise to Ridley's anger.

"Rid, I'd never hurt Robin. You know that. If I could bring her back right now, I'd do it. Let me go, Rid." The last was said almost sadly, and Anna remembered that the two men had been friends for years, a fact that had been easy to forget from the interactions she'd observed on the island.

Ridley lowered Adam carefully back into the kitchen chair. "Sorry," he said and went back to stirring the oatmeal. If he didn't pay attention, it was going to be the consistency of library paste, but Anna knew better than to offer to take over for him. Age-old customs were not suspended merely because hard times came. People needing reassurance tended to cling to them with ever-more tenacity.

They ate quickly. Though no one but Adam seemed anxious to start the search for Robin, it was tacitly agreed that it would be wrong not to seem anxious. Anna didn't want to search because she didn't believe she would find a living woman, and the photographs on Katherine's cell phone had put her more in the mood for revenge than body recovery. By the way Ridley's once-lovely skin sagged around his eyes and pulled so tight across his mouth that dints of white showed on either side of his nose, Anna suspected he was holding on to control with his fingernails. A man of order, this chaos was unhinging him. *Ridley would search,* Anna thought. He'd do everything he had to until he was too tired to lift a foot for another step, but she doubted he was thinking clearly. Without the thinking, the physical work of searching would not bear fruit unless he got luckier than seemed likely. For all his flirting with Robin, Ridley was Jonah's love; he was like an old woman with an only son. Until his boy was out of the woods, the wolves could have everybody else.

Bob was scared.

Adam took the bowls from the table and dumped them in the sink.

"What do you want us to do?" Ridley asked Anna.

"We have to search," she said and tried to keep the pointlessness out of her voice. Adam was right; they could do with more optimism. "Since she was taken in her sleeping bag—a winter bag, probably good to five or ten below—there's a good chance she survived." She drummed her fingers on the table and thought. "One of us took her, you guys know that, don't you? Or there's someone else on the island who has been screwing with our minds."

That sat in the air for a while. Ridley stared at Adam and Bob in turn. Adam played with a spoon. Bob's eyes were skittering around the room, as if he followed the path of a butterfly on Benzedrine.

"Which one of you found Katherine's cell phone?" he blurted out finally.

He'd seen the missed call from Anna.

"Are you still on that cell phone kick?" she snapped. "Just pay the two dollars."

"What . . ." Confusion passed over his face, then

cleared. "It's more than two dollars. Somebody found it."

"Leave it alone," Ridley said wearily.

"Maybe Katherine took it with her," Adam said. Had he used sepulchral tones, it would have been mocking at best and bad taste at worst, but he said it the way a grocer would say "four dollars a pound." Bob's face quivered like a pudding when the door slams.

Anna made a mental note to call Bob again soon.

"What do we do first?" Ridley cut across the others.

There was a story problem Anna'd had a hard time with in fourth grade. A farmer with a rowboat wanted to get his fox, his goose and his bag of grain across the river but could take only one at a time in his tiny boat. If he leaves the goose with the grain, she'll eat it. If he leaves the fox with the goose, the fox will eat her.

Who would try to find Robin, if she did happen to still be living, and who would sabotage the search? Who was the fox, who the goose?

The matter was taken out of her hands. "Bob and I will head up the Greenstone," Adam said. "Get your stuff, Bob. These guys are going to dither half the morning."

Since Anna couldn't think of any better arrangement she didn't argue. The five of them couldn't cover enough country to find a hidden woman. Or a hidden corpse. The only way they were going to locate Robin was if the kidnapper wanted them to or if Robin was alive and helped them find her. Much as Anna wanted the latter to be true, she didn't let herself get too attached to the idea.

Adam and Bob left to get their gear together and suddenly the kitchen felt bigger. There was more air to breathe and the walls moved back.

"Can you ski, Jonah?"

"I got the silver medal in skiing in the 1908 Olympics," he said.

"I knew that," Anna said and smiled to make sure she still could. To Ridley she said: "Why don't you and Jonah do Feldtmann. We've got nothing to go on except that she was carried out in a sleeping bag. That suggests whoever carried her had to travel on improved trails or he wouldn't get far. There's only a couple places on the island she could have been taken and kept alive: Feldtmann fire tower, Malone Bay ranger station or the cabin at Daisy Farm. Daisy Farm and Malone are reaches. They're too far."

"Why would anybody take Robin to Feldtmann?" Ridley asked. He wasn't asking Anna; he was asking the ether. Neither of them answered.

"What are you going to do?" Jonah asked.

Anna looked hard into the pale blue eyes behind the round lenses. "Why? Are you worried about me?"

"It seems the animals separated from the herd aren't living to a ripe old age this winter. *Riper* old age," he amended with a ghost of his old raillery.

"I'll recheck the housing areas and the lean-tos," Anna told him. "Anywhere else and we're just looking for a body."

"Keep your radio on, and keep it on you," Ridley said.

"Make sure your batteries are charged," Jonah added. "Adam's been having a heck of a time with his. A heck of a time."

Then Anna was alone in the bunkhouse. Every pair of cross-country skis was in use. The snow was eighteen inches deep where it drifted and nearly a foot where it didn't. Snowshoes hung on the wall, but with a foot to a foot and a half it was a toss-up whether they were more or less trouble than slogging through in boots. Had Anna meant to search, as she'd said, this might have bothered her.

What she meant to do was take the bunkhouse apart till she found out what the hell was going on. In the process, she dearly hoped to find out who took Robin. "Who" might tell her where the young woman had been stashed.

In time to find her alive was the thought Anna wouldn't let herself add.

30

Anna found exactly nothing. Bob's laptop was password protected, as was Ridley's. Neither Jonah nor Adam had a PC. Drawers and duffel bags produced the expected long underwear and dirty socks. Sitting on the floor of Bob's room, his duffel bag between her knees, Anna was swamped with helpless rage. Snatching up the emptied satchel, she flung it. It bounced off the side of the bunk and smacked her in the face, a stinging cut high on her left cheek where the luggage tag struck.

The bag was old and worn; the leather around the tag had grown stiff and cracked. Anna looked at the offending object: PROFESSOR MENECHINN, UNIVERSITY OF SASKATCHEWAN. Bob was so lazy that in ten years he'd never bothered to change the address. "University of Saskatchewan," Anna said aloud. The name struck a chord, and she sat in silence waiting for the rest of the music to surface.

"They're both Canucks," Jonah had said of Bob and Adam.

"Cynthia Johansen, a graduate student at the University of Saskatchewan, lived with her husband, Adam Johansen, a freelance carpenter."

Not only were Adam and Bob Canadians, they had both lived in Saskatchewan and at the same time. Bob taught at the university where Adam's wife, Cynthia, went to graduate school. It wasn't a great leap to put Cynthia into one of Professor Menechinn's graduate courses. It was an even shorter leap to imagine him assaulting her.

Then Cynthia committed suicide.

Adam never recovered from her death.

Adam told Ridley to recommend Bob for the Homeland Security review.

Adam had been excited at breakfast, happy.

"Holy shit!" Anna said. Adam was going to kill Bob. He was going to do it today.

Without skis, she'd never catch them. She took the snowmobile. Hammering up the Greenstone, icy wind lashing her cheeks and scraping her skin, Anna more than once considered turning around, letting Adam do mankind a favor. A world without the Bobs was a tempting idea. Rehabilitation didn't work with guys like Menechinn. What he did wasn't just a crime; it was a character flaw, a rottenness within.

Still, she didn't leave Adam to his work. For one

thing, she liked to think of herself as a half-decent human being. Not to mention if the two killed each other, she might never find out what happened to Robin.

The Greenstone climbed gently at first, then rose precipitously with switchbacks that threatened to push the snowmobile into the trees to a rocky escarpment thrusting above the tree line. The slope on the western side of the island was forested. On the east, the ridge fell away precipitously, a sheer sixty-foot drop, to a flat narrow boulder field skirting the edge of a meadow.

Forcing the snowmobile to its limit, she built up sufficient speed that when she reached the ridge the machine leapt a foot into the air, banged down in a spume of snow and rushed toward the drop. Squawking, she jerked to the left. The front of the snowmobile jackknifed. The machine rose up on one ski in alarmingly slow motion, toppled over and shuddered to a stop as the engine died.

Ahead of her, through the veil of falling snow, stood two shrouded figures. Skis and poles were jammed into the snow like battlefield grave markers. This was where Menechinn was to meet with the fatal accident that had been awaiting him since he'd been brought to the island.

"Adam!" Anna yelled. "Adam, wait!"

"Go back," Adam called.

Anna wriggled off the machine, rose and stumbled a few steps as her numbed legs refused to carry her. Blood began to flow and she stomped her feet, but she didn't go any nearer to the men at the edge of the fall.

"Go back," Adam said again. Without the roar of the small engine, his words were clear, ringing in her ears like the tolling of a bell.

"Lord knows, I want to," Anna called back. "But I can't. You come with me, Adam. Bob can make his own way home. We've got to talk. You need to help me find Robin."

"Robin's better off where she is," Adam said. "Bob made sure of that."

In his uniquely dreadful winter gear, goose down poking out and the duct tape taking up more area than the nylon, Adam looked like *Robinson Crusoe: The Northern Saga*. He also looked crazy as a loon.

Anna moved closer. Menechinn was a yard or two from Adam, saying nothing and standing in a heap of clothes and flesh as if his bones had softened and could barely keep him upright. Hoods and balaclava hid his face.

"Bob!" Anna said sharply. He raised his head with the slow swaying of a bull too old and too blind to know where danger is coming from.

"Bob," he echoed, and his pulled-back grin creased his face above the folds of his neck scarf. With a hand the size of a club, he pawed off his hood, baring his head to the elements. His face was the color of new brick.

"What's wrong with him?" Anna asked.

"Tasting his own medicine," Adam said. "Go back. I don't want to hurt you."

"Ketamine?"

"His drug of choice," Adam said.

"You are doing this for Cynthia?"

"Cynthia is dead," Adam said. "This is just for me."

"For revenge?" Anna asked. "To even the scales? To get some of your own back? Like you said, Adam, Cynthia is dead. She's going to stay dead. Give me one good reason to go through with this."

"For fun." There was no expression on his face. It was as blank as if the executioner's hood was already drawn over his features.

"Okay," Anna admitted. "That is as good a reason for doing it as any, I guess."

"Doing what? What are we doing?" Bob asked, alarm creeping into the smear of happiness Lady K had put on his mouth.

"As much a fan as I am of fun, it's short-lived for the most part," Anna said. "With a first-degree murder rap, prison lasts forever."

"Go back," Adam said.

"Let me arrest him," Anna said.

"And then what? Cynthia can't testify. Robin can't. Katherine can't."

Adam's words were heavy, falling in flat chunks through the snowy air. Anna wanted to argue, tout the fierce and powerful justice of the law, but he was right. Bob would get off. Robin's blood would prove positive for ketamine if Anna could get it to a lab in time and if its freezing hadn't changed the chemical properties, but who was to say Robin hadn't taken it herself? The pictures on Katherine's cell phone were damning only to Katherine. They could be traced to Bob, but who was to say it wasn't consensual? Rape was hard to prove at the most obvious of times.

Institutions hated rape charges. This would be swept under the table by three powerful bodies: Homeland Security, the National Park Service and American University; well-meaning people wanting to keep the mud off their organization, wanting to keep their positions.

"Arresting him would be fun," Anna said finally, and a smile ghosted across his face.

"You drilled the ice," she said to keep his attention.

"I drilled the ice," Adam said.

"I nearly died."

"I know. Bob here always has to strut out front. I thought he'd be first on the ice. It's hard to grasp how complete a coward he is." Adam's attention left Anna and focused like a laser on Bob Menechinn.

"Go, Anna." He took Bob's arm. Menechinn tried to jerk away, but his movements were slow and clumsy. The drug had made him forget where his arms and legs were. He overbalanced and fell. He lay moving feebly, making a fat snow angel.

Anna took a deep breath and was immediately sorry as the cold burned her lungs. "You'll spend the next forty years of your life in a penitentiary. You'll get up when you're told and go to bed and eat and see the sun when you're told," she said. "You've lived your whole life out of doors, Adam. Let me take Bob back."

Adam's face didn't change. "I've spent the last ten years in prison," he said, watching Bob paddle at the snow. "Get up," he said to Menechinn.

Anna needed him to connect with her sufficiently so he could hear past his pain. "You said Katherine would never testify. You knew about Katherine?"

"I'd seen the look before. On the face of my wife before she died. The wolves saved Katherine the trouble of killing herself."

"Or you did."

"I had nothing to do with her death. Not one damn thing. I don't kill women."

"How about wolves?"

"The giant bite marks?" He smiled. "People will believe what they want to believe. I just helped it along."

"So you darted the wolf and stabbed it to death," Anna said coldly.

"An animal. The pound puts thousands to death every year. Fluffy and Bootsie and Socks. Don't get onto me about an animal."

Adam straddled Bob, took hold of his wrists and pulled him to a sitting position.

"You drugged me," Bob said without bitterness, a sense of wonder in his voice.

"How do you like it?" Adam asked, standing over him, hands still clamped around the bigger man's wrists.

"I don't . . ." Bob rolled his head over and squinted to bring Anna into focus. "Ranger Danger," he said and smiled. "You were going to kill me and now we'll kill you."

"I'm not going to kill you," Anna said. "I don't want to wait in line that long. Since you are going to kill me anyway, you might as well tell me: did you drug Robin?"

Bob leered. Snow was catching on his wiry hair and the fat of his cheeks where they pushed out beneath his eyes. "Adam said you were trying to frame me, Miss Ranger. Too bad you're a fool." His head rolled till Adam came into his line of vision. He had to let it flop back on his neck to look up at him. "Wearing a wire," he said conspiratorially.

"How much did you give him?" Anna asked.

"Enough," Adam said.

"You told him I was going to kill him or set him up?"

"Divide and conquer," Adam said. "Upsy-daisy, Bob." Using himself as a lever, he rocked back and pulled Bob to his feet. They were no more than two yards from the edge of the basalt shelf, yet the drop was practically invisible, the white of the snow melding seamlessly with the white of sky and ice. Anna knew it was there from her time on ISRO and the hike they'd made to Malone Bay. She doubted Bob had any idea he stood on a precipice. Adam turned Menechinn so he faced to the east over the cliff.

"Don't," Anna said. She didn't move any closer. If a tussle started, it wasn't going to be her who was nudged to her death.

"Bob, see there?" Adam pointed into the void where the white on white of weather created a blank canvas for the ketamine to paint on. "Robin wants to meet you there."

"Don't," Anna said again. "Bob, there is no *there* there. Adam means to kill you. You're on the edge of a cliff; step back."

Adam spun around. The dead look was gone from his face replaced by the fury she'd felt the night she'd seen the photograph of him and his dead wife. "Get the fuck out of here," he hissed, a whisper metastasized into a shout.

"Bob, do it, go. Anna will kill you. Run!" Adam shouted in Menechinn's ear. Bob began to lumber forward toward imagined sex and safety.

In the eternal second of the mind, Mary Shelley's Frankenstein, huge and shapeless in ill-fitting clothes, running into the arctic wilderness, played in Anna's mind, overlaid by Peter Boyle's singing "Puttin' on the Ritz"; monsters pieced together from the dead and given life by the insane. Bob was a monster; that she didn't doubt. She would never know what had made him or if there was true evil in the world and he had chosen his own monstrousness. Anna wouldn't have chosen to save him. She wouldn't have said she particularly wanted him saved. Her mind reacted to what he was with a cringing loathing she didn't care to examine.

Her body reacted from years of training. She threw herself forward in a flying tackle aimed at the backs of Bob Menechinn's knees. Big men had bad knees; the joints couldn't cope with the bulk, and most of them had played football at one time or another. Knee injuries were a small ranger's friend. Her right shoulder and side of her head smashed into him and the knees gave. Falling back and to the side, he crushed her right arm into the snow. Pain exploded in her elbow.

"It's a cliff, it's a fucking cliff, I was going off a cliff,"

Bob began yelling. Mad with the sudden realization of physical danger, he scrabbled backward. His knee ground over Anna's wrist and she cried out. A flailing hand struck her on the side of her head so hard her ear burned and roared.

"You're welcome, God dammit," she shouted as she tried to roll out of his thrashing way. On hands and knees, Bob scuttled through the deep snow, moaning and bellowing like a mad boar. He didn't stop till he'd reached the trees. There he pulled himself upright, using the bole of a tree, and screamed: "He tried to kill me. He tried to kill me." The litany didn't stop there, but Anna tuned the rest of it out and got to her feet. Snow and down padding had saved her serious injury. Her wrist still rotated, and, other than the misery of ice down her collar and up her sleeves, the dive didn't seem to have done any appreciable damage.

Adam was still standing near the cliff's edge, his feet inches from where the rock fell away.

"Why did you do that?" he asked softly.

"I don't know," Anna said. For a minute, they stood, listening to the scissor cut of the wind in the trees and Bob's lament. Snow came at them in spinning gusts, air currents made wild and playful where the earth dropped away to water.

"You know what he is?"

"Some of it. I think he drugged Robin. I think he did the same to Katherine, then raped her and took pictures to blackmail her into silence. I'm guessing he did something like that to your wife."

"Cynthia," Adam said.

"Cynthia," Anna gave Adam's memory the honor of a name.

"She was like Robin. Not raised like her or athletic like her, but with that innocence that doesn't wear off at thirteen like it does for most of us." Adam's gaze moved from Anna's face to where Bob clung to his tree, his moaning and cursing settled into a murmuring chant low enough they could sense the tenor but no longer had to hear the words.

"Cynthia had never been out of school—went straight from kindergarten through to her Ph.D. program. Her dad raised her by himself; only kid. Her mother died of appendicitis when she was barely walking."

Anna didn't know what to say and figured nothing was best. The talking was taking the action out of Adam for the moment.

His attention returned from the trees where Bob had run. "Cynthia thought men were nice," he said. "She thought they took care of women and children, saved kittens from trees and helped old ladies carry groceries to the car." A hint of warmth touched his voice and it no longer sounded of frozen harp strings.

"I hadn't thought of that in a while," he said to Anna and shook his head. "How could I have forgotten that?"

"Too busy hating?" she hazarded.

"It was something to do," he said, and most of the chill was back in the strings.

"Bob was her teacher?" Anna asked.

" 'Outdoors Education.' Two semesters."

Anna waited for him to go on, but he didn't. He drifted, his eyes moving slowly over her head as if he was reading a complex story in the gray of the sky above the basalt. Finally his gaze returned to Earth, to Bob, sitting now, his back to the tree he'd been hugging, his head back and his mouth open.

"Bob drugged her. He did it more than once. She didn't tell me till she got pregnant. She was ashamed. She was afraid she'd lose me, that either I'd never feel the same way about her or that I'd go berserk and tear his head off and spend the rest of our lives in jail. She couldn't tell anyone else. There were the pictures, and she knew what they'd do to her dad and me. Then she found out she was going to have a baby. I'd been on a six-week job in Manitoba when the baby was conceived. So she told me. Three days later, she got into the bath and cut her wrists.

"I wasn't with her when she died," Adam said, and, for the first time, Anna could hear tears in his voice. "I had to answer the phone. Guess who was calling."

"God damn," Anna said, the oxygen gone from the air.

"Yeah."

"I've got to take him back," Anna said. "I'm sorry," she added.

"I could kill you," Adam said.

"Maybe."

"Getting killed for the likes of Menechinn's crazy." Adam laughed, and there seemed to be genuine humor in it. "Shoot, getting a hangnail for the likes of Me-nechinn is crazy."

Anna said nothing.

"I guess wasting time trying to kill him is crazy too," Adam said. The thought or the laugh had gentled his voice, and he shook his head as he spoke.

"Maybe," Anna said.

"No maybe about it."

Slowly he raised his arms out to his sides, a man cru-cified on white. He cocked his head, smiled and stepped back into nothing.

31

Anna fell flat on the brink of the drop, arms out-stretched. The fingers of her right hand caught Adam's sleeve above the elbow and closed convulsively over the fabric. Then his weight struck her, and shoulder and collarbone smashed into the stone beneath the snow. The noise in her head was the cacophony of pain. A loud, sucking pop, and her ulna was torn from the socket. Crack of a dry twig: the collarbone snapping. She would have screamed, but cheese-thick agony blocked her throat.

"Don't let go," she managed in little more than a whisper.

A ripping sound sawed her eyes open. Her face was hanging over the cliff, her body spread-eagled on the edge. Her right arm, weirdly elongated, wrist showing between glove and sleeve, drew a straight line to Adam's arm, drawn rigidly above his head. Anna had not held on. No one could have stopped the plummet of one hundred sixty pounds with four gloved fingers and a thumb. Not even Anna. In a freak accident, her hand had jammed through the nylon of his ripped coat and her wrist was in a noose of duct tape he'd wound round the sleeve to keep it together. Had she wanted to, she couldn't have let him go.

"I'm pulling you up," she gasped. Breathing hurt where her collarbone had broken, but the pain in the dislocated shoulder made it seem like nothing and she snorted a laugh that turned to snot and mixed with the snow caked on her face.

"Damn you, Anna," Adam said. She couldn't see his face; it was gone below the tatters of his sleeve and her arm. For a moment, a moment that was made into a nascent eternity by the vicious firing of nerve impulses in the right side of her body, Adam said nothing.

Finally words floated up their conjoined arms: "Let me go."

"I'm pulling you up," Anna said. She doubted she could pull up a four-week-old kitten at this point, but there wasn't much else to hope for.

"You haven't the right. Let me go." He didn't sound afraid, only tired—so tired he could barely find the strength to speak.

Anna might have done it. People had a right to die if they wanted to. People had a right to die the way they wanted to.

"I can't," she admitted. "My glove caught in the duct tape."

"You are a piece of work," Adam said.

"Bob!" Anna yelled, an echo of when she'd called for him on the breaking ice. It yielded the same result. There wasn't enough expansion room in her lungs to try again, and she laid her cheek on the sleeve of her parka, the bare rock of the cliff edge where Adam's fall had scraped the snow away an inch from her eyes.

It was moving. Tiny increments of rock no bigger than sand pebbles were creeping past. Adam's weight was dragging her over. Kicking hard, she tried to drive her toes into the snow to anchor herself. The duck-billed Sorels pummeled down to the basalt but found no purchase. The effort accelerated the slip.

"Uh, Adam?" she said.

The grating sound that had opened her eyes after her shoulder tore sounded again.

"Adam? I was wondering if you could grab onto anything. I'm sort of sliding up here."

More grating. She slid another inch. Her nose was ripping across the basalt. Tears and snot and snow and fabric blinded her.

"You know, just anything. Maybe a branch or something?" she tried. "Once you've saved me and I've saved you, you can always jump again.

"Bob!" The guy was a pervert and a rapist and stoned out of his mind, but he was strong as the proverbial ox. "Bob!"

She slid farther, the skin of her chin peeling off against the sharp rock. Her eyes cleared enough, she could see down her arm to where her wrist bent, the duct tape wound around like a manacle.

Wedging her free hand heel first into the snow beneath her chin, she pushed till the bones in her good shoulder cracked. Muscles wrenched at the collarbone, forcing the shattered ends farther apart, and she screamed. The slipping stopped.

"Adam? Let's die later. Give me a hand here, okay?"

Grating. Metal, it sounded like, and Anna dared hope he was doing something constructive, maybe driving a fingernail file into the basalt like a piton or carving a foothold with his belt buckle.

"Anna?"

"I'm here," she said. "Where the hell else would I be?"

"On a three count, you pull. Got that?"

Anna nodded, feeling the ice and stone cut her face. "Got it," she managed.

"Anna?"

"I got it, for chrissake! Count already."

Adam laughed.

"I'm glad you're having fun," she snarled.

"One . . . two . . . three." There was a tearing sound as Anna pulled, digging her knees in the snow and pushing with the heel of her hand. Adam flew up over the cliff, sailing into the air, as she fell back on her butt and heels.

Not Adam. His ripped-up old parka. He had unzipped it and slid into the arms of his wife. Or the devil.

Anna flung herself back in a belly flop on the top of the escarpment. "Where's Robin!" she yelled into the white void. There wasn't even an echo. Adam lay shattered at the bottom of the rock face, coatless, his red flannel shirt a scrap of color in the landscape.

Life isn't for everybody. Robin Williams had said that. Life wasn't for Adam. When his wife had died, he had his hatred to sustain him. Had Anna let him kill Bob Menechinn, she knew he would still have stepped off the cliff. Without Bob, Adam was lost.

"Damn you," she whispered sadly.

Bob.

Presumably he was still tripping at the foot of the tree. Rolling onto her side, good arm beneath her taking the weight, Anna curled her legs into the fetal position. There wasn't as much pain as there had been; the cold was numbing her. She'd been still too long, and an injury burned heat. Using her elbow as a lever, she pried herself up till she was kowtowing to the east, forehead on the ground, injured arm throbbing. For all the motion her arm had, her right sleeve might as well have been empty. She sat up on her heels, the bones in her shoulder and chest dragging like knives across the soft tissues inside her body. For half a minute or more, she could do nothing else. She hadn't even the strength to breathe. When breath came, it was in a cutting gust of icy air that set her to coughing. The coughing threatened to tear her collarbone from its damaged moorings.

Finally the coughing wore itself out, and she took careful sips of oxygen. When she could bear to move again, she unwound her neck scarf and laid it over her knees. Catching up the cuff of her right sleeve with her left hand, she lifted it, as a mother cat lifts a kitten by its scruff, and laid it over the scarf. With her left hand and her teeth, she managed a rough sling, and the pain lessened slightly.

"What in hell did you think you were doing?" she muttered. "Let people die. World's overpopulated as it is. Christ."

This last comment was in reference to the snowmobile. In the flurry of shared confidences, bone breaking and premature death, she'd forgotten she'd tipped it over. Whole, healthy, she could have wrestled it back onto its skis. In her present condition, even finding a lever big enough to shift this part of the world was going to be a Herculean task.

Bob.

He was still sitting, head atilt, mouth agape, a mute old hound trying to bay at the moon. Anna attempted to lift her butt off her heels and get one of the platypus Sorels out in front of her so she could stand. All she managed was a rocking motion that set the nerves in her shoulder and arm jangling. Pain was a good motivator. Death was better. If she stayed where she was, she'd die of hypothermia. Bob would die as well, but that wasn't a particularly motivating factor. Her grunt of effort turned into a shout as she forced herself up to one knee.

Her shout roused Bob. He rolled onto all fours and

swayed back and forth, his eyes never leaving her. For an instant, she thought he was going to charge like a grizzly, and the fear of being torn apart by teeth made for grinding corn sent a jolt of fear through her that brought the bile to her throat. His eyes focused, and he pulled himself to a standing position, using the tree he'd been taking advantage of since he'd fled the cliff's edge. Upright, he looked no less like a grizzly and no more like a man.

Blinking the image away, Anna tried to rise. She failed.

Bob Menechinn walked toward her. He was unsteady on his feet, but she thought his eyes were clearer. If Adam administered the ketamine awhile before Anna arrived on scene, the stuff might be wearing off—or at least wearing thin.

"Give me a hand up, if you would, Bob," Anna said, hoping normalcy would beget normalcy. She stuck out her good hand. Bob reached down and grasped it firmly. Apparently without effort, he drew her to her feet.

Anna started to thank him, but he kept right on drawing her, pulling her into his chest and belly.

"Easy, easy, Bob," Anna said. "Enough. Enough. Back off, God dammit." Her face mashed into his parka and his arm crushed her bad shoulder into him. He held her like a lover, his other hand groping down her side, under her arm.

Fighting a revulsion that made the pain pale by comparison, Anna jerked a knee toward his groin, stomped his instep and scraped his shin with the side of her boot.

It was like struggling in a dream. Thick-layered clothing swathed them both, and she fluttered like a moth in the soft and killing folds of a spiderweb.

His big hands crawled over her body, pulling at her clothes. Then he stepped back and shoved her hard in the chest. Anna landed on her rear end so hard that, without the padding she'd just been cursing, she would have broken her tailbone.

He held up a rectangle of black and waggled it back and forth. He'd been frisking her for her radio. As she watched, he carried it to the cliff edge and threw it over.

She didn't ask what he was doing. She had a bad feeling; she knew. He plucked the skis out of the snow one by one, then the poles. They followed the radio over the escarpment.

Displaying the same ease with which he'd lifted her, Bob set the snowmobile to rights. The key was still in the ignition.

"You scared?" he asked.

"Pardon?" Anna asked politely, hoping to get him to come closer to her. What she would do, should she succeed, she had no idea, but there was nothing she could do from thirty feet away, and she knew, if she could rise again, it was going to take a while.

"You heard me," he said. He threw a leg over the seat of the snowmobile and reached for the ignition key.

"Yeah," Anna said to stop him leaving. "Sure, I'm scared. What kind of an idiot wouldn't be scared."

He sat back and smiled. She couldn't remember seeing a smile uncoil as slowly as Bob's did. It came over the lower half of his face, then rose to his eyes in the malicious sunrise of the day of Armageddon.

"You and Robin thought it was pretty funny when Ridley's pet monster was pawing at our tent, didn't you? Smirking like teenage cunts at a sleepover. Let's see you smirk now. Come on, one little smirk. What's the matter, ice got your tongue?"

Anna stared at him. Adam was dead, Katherine killed, Robin missing and this was what Bob was thinking of: that two women had seen him panic.

"Smirk," Anna said.

"I think it's pretty funny," Bob said, his smile still in place.

Anna's legs were hurting. Soon they would stop hurting. They would be completely numb. Then standing would be a bitch. "Okay," she said. "I can smirk. What's it worth to you?"

"Maybe a ride back to the bunkhouse. Maybe nothing."

"Deal," she said. "I'm only going to do it once. Get your fat ass over where you can get a good look," she said nastily. The insult moved him off the machine. Anna's left hand was shoved in her pocket. She worked it out of its glove.

"Women want balls now, that it? Fast-tracked into jobs you can't handle. Scraping babies out of your cunts because you fuck everything that moves and don't want to be mamas. You don't want to wear the pants. No, that's not good enough for you, is it? You want to have the cock. No more pretend. No more strapping it on and fucking your girlfriends. A real cock. You think you can take it right off a man, don't you?"

Bob was working up a good head of steam. The euphoria of the cat tranquilizer was double-edged, and the dark side was rising. He stopped eight or ten feet from her.

Too far.

"Well, I wouldn't take yours," Anna said scornfully. "Size does matter."

Bob stepped into her, almost straddling her. He grabbed her hood and jerked her head up. His fist went back.

And Anna's went up. Bare-knuckled and hammer-hard, she punched up into his crotch. Her fist buried itself in cloth and soft flesh. Bob screamed and fell, crashing down on his side, his gloved hands between his legs. Scooping up snow, Anna flung it in his face, curled her fingers into claws and launched herself at his eyes. Her shoulder cracked again as she bounced into his chest, and she knew she'd broken the floating end of the collarbone. Her vision blacked at the periphery.

Bob backhanded her. As easily as a grown man would throw a cat off, Bob knocked her off him. One hand still on his privates, he crawled away. Confused by the ketamine and the sudden assault, he took a minute or more to get his bearings. Then he stood and went back to the snowmobile. From beneath the seat, he took out a spanner used to tighten the tractor treads and started back to where Anna lay on her back, holding her arm across her chest.

"Bob, you're not guilty of murder, but you kill me and you will be," Anna said rationally—or as rationally as she could from a supine position. *Maybe I should have tried the rational approach before he'd gone for the spanner,* she thought, but that was blood under the bridge now.

"I'm not going to kill you. You're going to have an *accident*." He grabbed her right boot, jerked it off and pulled her sock down. Holding the bare foot against the snow-covered rock, he smashed her ankle bone with the wrench.

Through the haze of misery that followed, Anna heard the snowmobile motoring down the Greenstone.

Winter was going to do Bob's dirty work for him.

32

For a while, there was nothing but the blinding pain and the knowledge that she could not save herself; that she couldn't walk out. Had the thought of losing to an idiot like Bob not been anathema, Anna might have given up. Instead she opened her eyes; she sat up. With her uninjured hand, she hooked the boot Bob had jerked off and put it back on her foot. If one was going to die, it was important to die with one's boots on. Soon the ankle would begin to swell. Then even the bulbous Sorel wouldn't fit over it.

Put ice on it, Anna thought and almost smiled.

The glove she'd removed, the better to bust Bob's balls, was still in her coat pocket. Wriggling her fingers like so many eels, she worked her hand into it. Then she sat, exhausted by the pain, wishing she believed in God that she might convince Him to get back into the smiting business. Without a radio, there was no one else she could call upon.

For what seemed an eternity, she sat in her broken bones and cooling blood and thought about Paul. It had been so good to talk with him.

On Katherine's satellite phone.

"Thank you, Paul," she said. The phone was in her pocket. She'd been carrying the wretched thing since she'd found it. Fumbling, twice dropping it, she got it out and again exposed her fingers to the cold. In CONTACTS, Katherine had the number for the Park Service offices in Houghton, Michigan. Anna pushed the SEND button and mashed the phone to her ear.

"Our offices are open from eight-thirty to five, Monday through Friday."

It was Saturday. Anna jabbed 411, and, sitting crippled in the snow, made her way through the ether, into space, through a satellite and down to the National Park dispatch office. As clearly as she could, she told the dispatcher her situation. "Radio Ridley Murray," she said. "Tell him what I told you. Tell him he needs to bring the Sked. I'll hold."

A scratchy muttering startled her, till she realized it was her radio, and Adam's bleating from the bottom of the cliff. Three more times, they bleated.

"He's not answering," the dispatcher said. "I'll keep trying."

Anna closed the phone and stowed it back in her pocket. In a bit, when she was sure she had no more time, she would call Paul and say good-bye. *How weird will that be,* she thought, and heard her pathetic last words to her husband being replayed on the six o'clock news all over the country.

She could call Bob, tell him all was forgiven, she was in a serious smirking mood and would he come fetch her home.

That thought festered for a minute.

"Bob, you bastard, you are coming back for me," she muttered suddenly. Action gave her hope and hope gave her courage and courage gave her the strength to lift her crippled leg and lay the damaged ankle on top of the sound ankle. Using her own body as a Sked, she inched herself backward with her good arm till she'd reached the side of the outcropping where the Greenstone descended into the trees. A dead branch provided her with twigs she could break free with one hand. Having snapped them into suitable lengths, she shoved them into her boot between the sock and the thick felt lining.

The ankle stabilized, Anna could stand. The branch that had kindly given her its twigs was as big around as her arm and no more than eight or ten feet long. A lesser branch, perpendicular to the main growth, sprouted from near the end. The whole didn't weigh more than thirty pounds—forty, at most—yet shifting it with one hand, her weight on one leg, was a circus act that might have been amusing to an audience of sadists.

Whimpering and grinding her teeth because she couldn't seem to stop herself, she dragged the longest, sturdiest part of the branch across the Greenstone Trail where it came into the open on the basalt ridge. Wind, carving up over the escarpment, had taken much of the snow from the rock. Where Anna laid her branch, it was scarcely six inches deep and powdery. Using the feathery end of a pine bough, she whisked the powder over the wood.

It was a lousy job. She moved with tedious slowness; her tools were crude and wielded with one weakening arm. A Boy Scout, a rank green Cub Scout, could see the branch and the attempts to cover it, if they were paying attention. Anna kept on. It was better than sitting and freezing to death, and if her Rube Goldberg, jury-rigged, half-baked plan failed, as it probably would, at least the sweat she worked up would hasten her freezing to death adventure when the time came.

The blueprint of her plan was simple and finished in five minutes: the branch lay across the head of the trail, its tip buried in the snow, the end where the smaller branch grew out at a right angle from the main branch, resting on a flat stone a foot and a half high. The bough she'd used for a broom leaned against the wood where it angled up out of the snow.

"It's good to have a plan," she said and wondered if she was getting hypothermic. One of the first symptoms was mental confusion. She remembered that from her white-water rescue training in the Russian River in California. It had been winter; the water rushing down from the Sierra was cold. The instructor had also said a person with hypothermia could not raise their arms over their head.

404 | NEVADA BARR

Anna raised her good arm over her head.

"Hope you weren't full of shit," she said to the by-gone instructor. Straddling the main part of the branch that crossed the path, she sat on the rock. She rotated the L-shaped offshoot upward till it was vertical and running parallel to her spine like a skinny chairback.

Having gotten as comfortable as she could with bro-ken bones and a four-inch branch under her behind, Anna dug the cell phone from her pocket, pulled off her glove with her teeth, found Bob Menechinn's number in CONTACTS and pushed SEND. It rang four times, then went to voice mail.

Anna didn't leave a message.

She stopped, just stopped. She didn't move or replace her glove or close the phone or pray or curse or plan. She barely even hurt. At best, the plan had been frail, ab-surd; she'd known that when she blew the last of her re-serves on it. Like Adam's hate, it was something to do when the alternative was unthinkable.

There wasn't another plan.

Try and stay alive till Ridley decided to answer his ra-dio. That could qualify as a plan, but to stay alive till the cavalry came one had to keep one's body temperature above eighty-six degrees so the organs didn't start shut-ting down. To do that, one had to move, and Anna couldn't, not enough. Isometrics might give her a little time; they generated a modicum of heat. But the trauma to muscles, grating over splintered bone as she tensed and relaxed, would undo any benefit the exercise might have.

Coward. Anna tried to goad herself into action, but

there was no action to take. The peace she'd glimpsed at the bottom of the lake would have been nice, but it had apparently been induced by oxygen deprivation. All she felt now was frigid depression tinged with a sour note of self-pity and a terrible guilt at the misery her death would cause her husband and her sister. Dying because a pervert banged one on the ankle with a wrench and absconded with the snowmobile wasn't the sort of death that comforted the living. Defusing a nuclear bomb about to explode in a nursery school full of crippled kids—that would be a good death. Saving a busload of nuns from a fiendish death at the hands of ninja assassins would be a decent death. Stepping on a land mine while carrying the last man in the battalion out of enemy territory would be a nifty death.

This one was going to suck for everyone concerned.

It was time to call Paul.

Anna stared at the tiny miracle of the phone.

A wolf howled.

Maybe I'll get eaten, she thought and was somewhat cheered by the prospect of not dying alone.

The wolf howled again, and she realized the sound was coming from the phone in her hand. Bob's ring tone was the call of a loon and Katherine's was the howling of a wolf. What else? Anna squinted through the rime that had built up on her eyelashes at the screen. *Bob.* He must have heard his cell, stopped the snowmobile, and seen Katherine's number.

The plan was back in place; frail, absurd, but up and running.

"Hallelujah!" Anna whispered and pushed the button lighting up with green. "Bob." She blew the name out on a soft, long breath, the cliché of the call from the great beyond. Paranoia, guilt and ketamine were on her side. She heard a sharp intake of breath from the other end.

"Katherine?" came a choked voice.

Anna's lips made it all the way to a smile this time. "Cynthia," she breathed in the same long, hollow tone. "Cynthia."

"Bullshit," Bob said, but his voice was shaky and uncertain. Anna said nothing, just breathed gently into the mouthpiece. A whining sound interrupted, and she realized he was turning the ignition key to start the snowmobile again. She wasn't going to get the chance to lure him to the cliff top with apparitions.

"Dickhead," she said sharply, "I'm not dead. I've got Katherine's phone, pictures, notes on the blackmail and your name's all over it. I'm calling everybody I can think of to tell them the good news. Give my regards to the boys at San Quentin when you get there."

She hung up. The phone howled again. *Bob.* She ignored it. Having replaced her glove, she scooped snow over her boots and lap as best she could with one hand and a shoulder that attacked its host every time she moved.

Zach, her first husband, had been an actor. One of the things he loved most in the theater was waiting in the wings to go on. Quiet, in the living dark of backstage, he said he knew he was where he was supposed to be, in a space only he could occupy; he knew who he was and who he could be. He could be as brilliant as Laurence Olivier, as graceful as Nureyev. The audience might come to its feet in wild applause when he finished his monologue. In the wings, all things were possible.

The shriek of the Bearcat came into the edge of her hearing. Bob hadn't gotten far. As high as he was, he probably could barely keep the machine on the trail. Anna pulled her white hood down over her eyes. She wedged her good hand underneath the branch between her knees, bent forward and, showing the trail the top of her head, she waited.

33

The growl of the snowmobile grew reassuringly louder. Anna focused on the noise to keep her mind from drifting. There would be just the one chance and it was slim. If she failed, she would be joining Adam at the bottom of the cliff. Closing her mind to the distractions of her body, she used the racket to marshal the energies remaining to her. The roar filled her head, and she directed it down her spine and into her good leg, down her uninjured arm and into the working hand until she thrummed with vibrating energy.

The engine pitch changed. Bob was making the last hairpin turns, climbing the switchback to the ridge. Anna repositioned her fingers beneath the branch and pushed her butt against the offshoot running up her back.

There was a final burst of horsepower and the snow-mobile came into view. Bob hunkered over the handlebars, thick shoulders rounded down, face raw with cold and wind. He was still bareheaded.

His ears will be frozen off, Anna thought with grim satisfaction. Win or lose, Bob would have something to remember her by every time he looked in the mirror.

He reached the short, steep climb before the trail opened onto the basalt shelf.

The snowmobile ate up the last ten feet with startling speed. Every cell in her body screaming in protest, Anna threw herself back against the upright branch, simultaneously pulling on the one between her knees. Her back slammed against the limb. She felt it give, her weight forcing it back. As she went over, she saw a line of gray bark rearing up from its lair in the snow, the butt caked in white, a shaky pole levered up over the trail.

Her back struck the stone. The tree branch across the trail wrenched violently to the left. The limb jerked from her hand, tearing her glove half off. Her body hurled to the ground beside the rock. Torrents of hurt poured through her, and she wished she had state secrets that she might shout them from enemy rooftops, anything to stop the vicious knives inside her skin. Vision dimmed at the edges. She fought to stay conscious. To pass out now would be to waste all the trudging and weeping this sojourn into physics had cost.

Like a turtle peeking out of its shell, she craned her neck and lifted her head.

Idling unevenly, the riderless machine nosed into a copse of balsam firs munched by hungry moose till they were the size of bonsai trees. She couldn't see Bob, but he had to be close by. Her wish was that he was dead or dying, but she'd used up the standard three just getting him to answer the phone, bring back the snowmobile and let himself get knocked off of it with a stick. Dead was too much to hope for. The lever had been long enough to take his head off, but she didn't think she'd managed that. It might have caught him in the shoulder or the chest. If it hadn't and had only fouled the skis of the snowmobile enough to dump him, he was probably unhurt.

In which case, Anna was dead.

"Not dead. I'm rising, rising, rising," she whispered to herself, and she pushed up with one arm till she was on hand and knees. The repetition of words swam through her brain with Ellen DeGeneres's voice and the face of the blue fish she brought to life in *Finding Nemo*. Comforted by the nonsense, Anna kept on. Standing didn't strike her as possible at the moment. Leaning back, she lifted the broken ankle and stacked it on top of the other, toes down. "Ouching, ouching, ouching!" she whispered as she settled the splinted boot across the back of the other. Feet crossed, a travois of bone and sinew, she dragged the bad foot along behind as she inched forward one knee at a time, one hand for balance. "Creeping, creeping. I'm creeping creeping, creeping."

The changing mantra in the spirit of a gay blue fish kept her moving. The snowmobile was less than four yards from where the limb had swept her off her rock. Four yards wasn't a great distance. One hundred forty-four inches was. When she had reached "Whining, whining, whining," and was less than a body length from the Holy Grail of vinyl, plastic and horsepower, she saw Bob Menechinn.

He was on his side across a downed trunk a foot in diameter. Legs and butt were on the side away from Anna—a small blessing but worth counting—one arm was outstretched and his head was pillowed on it as if, as he'd lifted a foot over the log, he'd fallen asleep midstep. The down of his parka was ripped out in a puff of white that Anna first mistook for snow. The branch had caught him in the shoulder. The down was tinged with red; not as much as she would have liked but enough to indicate damage. Bob had been thrown off as she had been thrown from her rock. His body spun in the air, and he landed with his head pointed toward the Bearcat.

Anna dearly hoped this meant he suffered great injuries. Good sense and personal preference dictated she crawl over and bash in his skull with a hard object while he was safely unconscious. Unfortunately her injuries would not allow her the additional fifty feet that dictate would require.

Menechinn groaned. Or maybe it was Anna who groaned. She didn't wait to figure it out. "Moving, moving, moving," she whispered and dragged herself the last three feet to the idling snowmobile. The seat was no higher than her sternum when she raised herself onto her knees, but it seemed an impossible distance and for a moment she knelt before it as if in prayer, her mind in confusion. In order to travel, she'd stacked her useless limbs in a pretzel-like configuration, and the logistics of getting herself into the saddle baffled her. She began at the bottom, lifting the broken foot from the opposing ankle, then pulling her knee up. Using the seat for leverage, she managed a standing position, turned and sat on the snowmobile. Another few precious seconds were taken straddling the Bearcat, feet on the running boards, hand on the throttle. The only way to go was forward. She needed the open space on the rocky outcropping to turn around.

Gingerly she eased the throttle open. The engine revved, but the machine didn't move. She rotated it farther back; the skis broke loose and the snowmobile lurched, nearly unseating her. Then she was on the flat and moving slowly. Bob still lay across the downed trunk, his bare head on the snow.

Maybe he was dead. The thought cheered her as she maneuvered the heavy Bearcat in an awkward circle on the cliff top. A chore that was a moment's work to the able-bodied took Anna a painful forever.

By the time she got herself pointed back in the right direction, Bob Menechinn was standing at the head of the Greenstone.

The side of his face was a mask of blood and snow. His arms hung at his sides, the huge hands clublike. His eyes were almost lost in the flesh of his face, but the heat and hatred in them bored through the masking beef until they took up most of the space in the world. Moving with the creaking strength of rusted iron, he staggered into the middle of the trail.

Anna had neither the time nor the inclination for negotiating. She opened full throttle and, bent over the handlebars, engine and woman screaming, the snowmobile leapt forward. Banshees of flesh and metal, they shrieked toward Menechinn. The nose of the Bearcat struck him. With a crunch Anna hoped was bone, he fell. The Bearcat's skis jerked over his leg, jolting the snowmobile. Agony smashed into Anna's brain, and she clenched her hand on the throttle to stay upright. The Bearcat bucked free of the obstacle and stalled.

"Fuck, fuck, fuck!" Anna muttered in language no self-respecting Disney fish would use and pawed at the key with gloved and frozen fingers. An animal roar rose from Menechinn. In the tiny rearview mirror, Anna saw the hulk of him rising. Biting the ends of the glove's fingers, she ripped it off and turned the key. The engine came to life and she blessed Arctic Cat.

Then she was moving. The Greenstone took her. She was going to make it.

Without warning, the Bearcat slued to the left, the engine crying like a dying calf, as Bob grabbed onto the back, his weight forcing it to the left into the trees. Anna jerked the handlebars wildly, fishtailing down the steep incline, a moose—a dying moose—trying to bash the wolf from its flanks. The Bearcat sideswiped a tree. Gripping with her knees, as if riding an unbroken horse, she yanked the handlebars the other way and veered across the trail, gaining speed on the downhill run, and banged the other side into a chunk of rock. Bob let out a guttural shriek, and the snowmobile surged ahead, crazy with speed and freedom, hurtling down the narrow trail.

Vision blurred. Black trunks snapped at her face, white strobed till she couldn't tell where movement left off and hysteria began. Her injured arm fell from where she'd zipped it in a makeshift sling in the front of her parka and the dislocated shoulder tore at the muscles. She started screaming—or kept screaming—her noise melded with that of the laboring engine.

The trail switched back on itself in a hairpin turn, and Anna cranked the handlebars as far as she could. The Bearcat raised up on two skis, the nose fighting for purchase as it was jackknifed to the right. With a slam that brought the black of the trees and the glare of the snow into the tiny pinpoint of an old television going off the air for the night, the snowmobile righted itself. Anna forced her frozen fingers to back off the throttle.

The snowmobile slowed.

Then it stopped. For a long moment, Anna sat on the cooling machine, trying to find the energy to peel her bare hand from the throttle and turn the key. With the cessation of the cries of flesh and blood and the roaring of metal and fuel explosions, the silence was eerie, ringing. Anna listened to the echo of quiet fading into the inexorable softness of falling snow. True silence whispered in where the ringing had been. She drew it into her mind and into her lungs, let it touch the ruined parts of her body. The pain didn't lessen with the kiss of the quiet, but she ceased to mind as much.

She didn't want to move. Ever. Had she not been in love with Paul, she might not have bothered turning the ignition key.

Except to the Catholic God, it wouldn't have mattered either way.

The snowmobile was out of gas.

34

Anna did not get off the Bearcat. It would be no warmer, no more comfortable, lying in the middle of the trail, and she knew that was as far as she would get. She dug for the cell phone but it was gone, fallen from her pocket somewhere between being knocked from one rock and scraping Bob off with another.

No last, last, really last calls for the six o'clock news. No telling dispatch that if Ridley didn't answer his fucking radio, he should be shot on sight.

Bob might be dead, might be too injured to walk or he might be coming after her. Mayhem paraded through her mind: making a Molotov cocktail with her water bottle and the gasoline from the fuel tank, tipping the Cat over and using it as a bulwark for throwing rocks—or snowballs—peeling the decorative chrome-colored stripping from the chassis and planting the sharp metal strips beneath the snow.

As the engine cooled and she listened to the pings and clicks of metal assuming new shapes, her brain cooled with it. Thoughts of attack turned to thoughts of retreat, of crawling to a snowbank, sweeping her drag tracks out with a branch and burrowing deep into a personal igloo, of working the skis free of the snowmobile and fashioning a sled that would carry her downhill.

She listened past the pings, listened up the hill through the fog of snow. Bob wasn't moving. Had he been, she would have heard him. He had no stealth, only strength.

Cold, a living thing, a being as bodiless as gas, as all-pervasive as air, as cunning at finding every crevice and pore as water, insinuated itself past the fur around her hood, trickling beneath her sweat-drenched hair, then filtered through her fleece collar to slip an icy hand around her neck. Squirming like rats, it squeezed into her pockets and under the cuffs of the parka, up the legs of her ski pants and down into her boots. Winter's teeth gnawed on the flesh of her feet and tore at her chin and nose.

To take her mind off her troubles, she imagined the rats chewing up Bob Menechinn. Then she imagined the rats dead from consuming the poisons in his psyche.

After a while, the teeth weren't teeth anymore, the rats weren't rats. Winter had gone soft, touching her with kittens' paws, claws sheathed. A hearth fire started in her stomach and warmth radiated out as the soft pad of winter crept inward. Freezing to death was supposed to be a very nice way to die. But, then, she'd heard that about drowning and that had been a bust.

Not the drowning itself, she thought, mildly surprised that she could think philosophical thoughts while seated on a snowmobile. It was the *not* drowning that was so miserable, the choking and vomiting and scraping and coughing. Still, that first suck of water into the lungs had to be hard. Certainly the last few seconds before the first suck would be tough. There'd be that impulse to fight, to not breathe in.

Freezing to death had it all over drowning. Winter didn't want you to fight; she wanted you to curl down snug and warm in her bosom and die.

What a bitch, Anna thought. *I'd rather drown.*

Moving so slowly molasses would have beaten her in an uphill heat, she pulled up the leg Menechinn had attacked with the wrench and dragged it to the downhill side of the Cat. The key was still in the ignition. Having the sled stolen wasn't one of her worst fears. She tried to pull it out, but her frozen fingers couldn't execute the complex movements required. She cannibalized her right hand for its gear and put the glove clumsily backward on the five Popsicles she had, until the race downhill, considered her "good" hand. With the still-mobile fingers of her right hand, she teased the key out and managed to thread it into the lock between her knees below the seat. Maneuvering till she got her butt off the vinyl, she turned the key and the seat popped up. In the small storage space beneath was a plastic tarp, two flares, an old first-aid kit, the kind she used to carry in her backpack, and an army blanket.

Winter outfitters had lightweight high-tech blankets that salvaged body heat and harvested the heat of the sun with the efficiency of a *Dune* Freman's stillsuit. The Park Service had an army blanket. Anna wrapped it around her shoulders and lifted out the rest of the cache. The flares and first-aid kit she shoved into her jacket on top of the rude sling of a half-zipped coat. Working one-handed and moving her feet as little as possible, she put one edge of the tarp beneath her boots, then shook it like a bedsheet. The fold of the material billowed four or five feet away from her knees.

In the short time since Bob had bludgeoned it, her damaged ankle had swollen. This was good. The swelling filled the boot, and the makeshift splint of twigs became more rigid. Anna found she could stand and even walk a bit, at least as well as she had before the more recent topplings and batterings.

The remaining third of the plastic she draped over the snowmobile, creating a bivouac, with the tarp forming floor and ceiling and the Bearcat the wall. The rude tent would keep her dry and keep out the wind. With luck, and the army blanket, she would still be alive when Ridley got word where she was.

Anna lowered herself gingerly to hand and knees to wriggle into her den.

A low, piggish "Ungh!" ground through the sifting silence of the snow. Bears grunted that way. Boars did.

On ISRO, the only thing that made that sound was Bob Menechinn.

The grunting became staccato: "Ungh! Ungh! Ungh!"

Bob was running or maybe limping; the grunts were from pain, not exertion. Either way, he was up and moving. He was coming after her. Bob was always interested in saving himself. He'd be scared. Maybe he'd leave her alone, leave her to die of "natural causes" as he'd done on the cliff top. Unless he hadn't come across Katherine's cell phone with the damning pictures and messages—the one Anna no longer had—then he'd take her apart trying to find it.

Anna scuttled backward into the trees. She hadn't time or strength to cover much ground. A couple yards from the sled, she stopped and whipped the snow with the army blanket to help obscure her track. That done, she wormed beneath the low boughs of a spruce tree, pulled her knees up under her chin, spread the army blanket over her head, reached up and shook the bough, bringing down an avalanche of snow on herself. Theoretically, under the dark brown wool and snow, she would look like a rock. Army blankets put high-tech thermal wraps to shame when it came to disguising women as rocks.

Bob would kill her; he was that much of a rotter. But she was hoping he was too lazy and cowardly to go out of his way to kill her. She was hoping he would try to start the Bearcat, then leave without bothering to look farther than the plastic lean-to.

Hoping, hoping, hoping.

Anna stopped that chant before the gay blue fish could swim any further into her mind. Hoping was well and good, but it was better to focus on Plan B in case the hoped-for didn't manifest.

The grunts stopped.

She opened a tiny window in her wall of rough wool. Menechinn was not yet in sight.

A whuff gusted from up the trail, then regular panting and the crunch of boots on snow.

Pushing pain and fear out on a soft sigh, Anna stilled herself internally and tried to think rocklike thoughts. Behind the bough of the tree, in the purdah of wool, snow falling thickly, she was nearly blind. For a moment, it panicked her, as if to see was to be in control.

Poor eyesight is the least of your problems, she mocked herself. She had become as the littlest things in the wilderness. Concealment and cleverness, blending in and putting away acorns for an unseen winter, were the keys to survival. Bunnies and ducklings, chipmunks and sparrows, were not nature's big risk takers. Anna schooled herself to timidity and hugged her protective coloration around her.

A black square loomed out of the trees at the switchback. Bob was walking with a list as if gale-force winds buffeted him from the north. Either being bashed by a tree limb or being scraped against rocks had injured his left leg. The imaginary gale let up, and he staggered the other direction for a few steps, then went back to favoring his left side. Head injury or ketamine, or both, was affecting his balance. The goose down sticking out from where his jacket had been torn was a rich true red.

A nice color, Anna thought. His nose was white and waxy, as were his cheekbones and the tips of his ears. Gone to frostbite. They'd be black in twenty-four hours.

Black was a nice color too. Anna wanted to be around to watch parts of him fall off in painful and ugly ways.

"Ungh!" Bob saw the snowmobile in its blue shroud and began to run down the hill, his arms windmilling to keep him from falling. Spittle flew from his mouth and appeared on the snow in spots of red.

A broken tooth, a split lip, Anna told herself, not wanting to count on massive internal injuries bringing him down anytime soon. Bob braked his downward rush by slamming into the side of the snowmobile. The Bearcat rocked up, showing the tractor treads that powered the sled. Packed with snow, the treads looked like the maw of a beast with many rotting teeth. They bit down again, and the heavy machine creaked with the force. Bob continued to lean on the seat, supported by his arms, hands on the saddle.

Anna'd forgotten how big he was. His splayed fingers reached across the vinyl seat. His shoulders, rounded and padded, heaved like a walrus's back when it barks. Liquid ran through his gasps, the gurgling of lungs worked too hard in air too cold to process. The blood on his face had turned dark, forming into lumps that cracked to show the brilliant red of the new blood beneath as his jaws worked, trying to chew more oxygen from the air.

Drool fell from his lips to the seat and he pawed it up, surprised maybe at how much red was in it. Anna expected him to rip the tarp free, jump on the Bearcat, then go nuts when he didn't find the key in the ignition. Unless he was blind with desperation, he'd find it in the side where she'd used it to unlock the storage compartment, get back on the snowmobile and go through the whole fit again when he realized it was out of gas.

Bob did none of these things. Straightening, he looked around him, as if there might be prying eyes from the upstairs unit of the spruce tree next door. With an expression Anna could only describe as crafty, an overblown twisting of his face the way an actor's playing Fagin in *Oliver Twist* might when playing to the back row, he tiptoed around the sled. As in the sly moue of a moment before there was an element of exaggeration, of the theatrical, in the way he picked his big feet up, bending the knee, and put them down toe first.

A terrifying urge to laugh swelled inside Anna's lungs, a need to howl and guffaw. Partly the long tension, the waiting, but mostly because Menechinn was being funny. Very funny. Adrenaline born of the fear that she would give away her hiding place did nothing to quell the hilarity. Balling her hand into a fist, she punched her boot above the place Bob had so diligently applied the wrench. Searing pain cleansed her of laughter. Nausea and relief took its place, and she began to shake. Her teeth started to chatter uncontrollably, and she shoved the corner of her shirt collar between them lest the clatter call his attention to her. Her body trembled so hard, she could feel her skin touch the fabric of her clothes in a rapid pattern of waves and retreats. Belly and bowels and heart and spleen and liver shook inside of her.

Holding herself together, teeth clamped on the fleece, she watched Bob finish his half circuit of the sled. In front of the slit she'd been about to crawl through into her plastic lean-to when he'd announced his impending visit in porcine fashion, he stopped. Bending at the waist, he started to peek inside. A better idea came to him before he'd gotten his eye to the proper level. He straightened again, shuffled back three steps, took a running leap and came down, crushing the tarp to the ground. Demons took him then, and he stomped and kicked and jumped till the tarp was ripped free of the sled and mangled in the snow. Nowhere did it stick up more than an inch or so.

He had meant Anna to be inside.

He meant to trample her to death.

That was so rude. It had crossed Anna's mind that, at some future date, she would take a moment to feel guilty for all the evils she'd wished upon him. Now, should opportunity present itself, she would gloat. The shaking ebbed. Maybe she was getting better. Maybe that was her body's last attempt to shiver warmth into her, and her vital organs would start shutting down.

The fit of violence over, he stood in the ruin of the tarpaulin and looked around him, eyes narrowed against the snow, breath coming in wet gasps. He was so close, Anna could smell the sweat boil off of him. She envied his heat, his ability to move. She wasn't sure she could move anymore, that, if a time came when it would be safe to stand, she would be able to get up.

Tilting his huge head back, Bob sniffed the air. Less than three yards separating them, Anna could see his nares expanding and contracting the way a dog's will when it seeks scent. Fleetingly she wished Katherine's cell phone hadn't been responsible for the howls, that a pack of wolves had come to devour her. It would have been more civilized than dealing with Bob Menechinn. What with the killing and maiming and the nearly being killed and actually being maimed, along with the hallucinogenic effects of the ketamine, he had been stripped of the veneer of urbanity he cultivated. Even the coat of arrogance had been taken from him.

Bob's inner man was this stomping, sniffing brute, a beast that preyed on women, for whom the physical rape was merely the appetizer. Control by fear and humiliation was the main course. Hate rose from him with the sweat smell, hate and a darker odor. Shame, Anna guessed. Not for what he did; he was proud of that. Shame for not doing it well enough, for letting Anna and who knows what other women see him afraid, for whatever had been done to him that made him what he was, shame that every witness in the world who had seen it was not yet dead.

Suddenly Anna knew what the wild shaking had been about. She was scared to death of Menechinn. Occasionally there had been those who wanted to kill her. That she could understand. Occasionally there'd been those she'd wished to kill. The difference between her and the people she arrested was that she didn't do it. Violence was a passing thought, not a way of life. Violent people scared her, but they didn't terrify her, not like Bob did.

Bob didn't merely want her dead. He wanted her, like Katherine and Cynthia and Robin, disgraced, ruined, savaged. He wanted them shamed, their memory shamed and the memory of their deaths in those still living to crush out the life and sow their souls with salt that nothing green could ever grow there again.

Bob needed to annihilate women.

Burning holes in his too-fleshy face, his eyes scanned across the bough she sat beneath. They remained dead. He'd not seen her. Turning full circle, he began to whistle "Pop Goes the Weasel" under his breath.

Anna'd never liked the tune, and she'd never liked jack-in-the boxes. When the clown popped out, she did not squeal with childish delight; she smacked the clown down again.

Pivoting, he searched the circumference of their shared landscape. Blue tarp twisted beneath his heels and rucked up in a ridge around his boots. The big gloved hands opened and closed at his sides. The eyes passed Anna's tree again, lower down this time. The shaking started, and she fought it back with the clench of her jaws and the wall of her teeth and will. Another full circle, the volcano neck of blue plastic rose to his knees as he churned the fabric.

For the third round, he dropped his gaze to the ground. When he faced Anna's hiding place, his eyes followed the trail she'd not had time to completely erase; they followed it, climbed the branches and bored into the slit in the army blanket that camouflaged her.

His chin pulled back. The slow, tucked-in smile started, then metastasized.

"Gotcha," he said.

35

"Hi, Bob," Anna said. By rights, her voice should have been squeaky and high, the voice of a mouse being swooped up out of a meadow by a hawk, but the world-class screaming she'd indulged in trying to run Menechinn down with the sled, then hurtling down the switchbacks, had given it a nice brave, gravelly quality. "You should put a hat on. Your ears and nose are frostbitten. They'll rot away and leave black holes. Hard to get a date, once the ears and nose go." She didn't lower the army blanket. She didn't even widen the gap through which she looked at him with one eye.

Bob's smile pulled another half inch back toward his spine, his eyes momentarily invisible behind the slabs of cheek. Rictus apparently set in; the smile stayed exactly the same as the eyes came back out a fraction, and Anna had the weird feeling that she was watching the thing that was Bob Menechinn, the thing that wasn't human at all, peeking out from under the rock of his brow bone.

"Didn't your mother ever tell you if you make a face, it will freeze like that?" Anna snapped to make the thing go back inside Bob's skull.

"Did your mother ever tell you you're a fucking cunt?" he asked with the same razor-edged merriment he'd used with Katherine.

He had to be in pain. His brain had to be crashing from the cat tranquilizer. The parts of him that weren't past feeling the cold must ache with it. Still, it was clear he was beginning to enjoy himself.

Tucking her chin against her chest so the blanket wouldn't fall, Anna loosened her fingers where they clutched the rough wool over her face and let her hand slide slowly down her chest till it rested on top of the arm dislocated at the shoulder. "No," she said. "'Fucking cunt' doesn't ring any bells. Once in a while she called me 'knucklehead,' but I think she meant it in a loving way."

Bob seemed to suck her words through the screen of spruce needles and into his nose. Against the gray static of snow and clouds, his head was enormous, and Anna believed she saw it swell when her words were vacuumed into his brain. It bobbed, balloonlike, and she had to remind herself to stay in her skin, stay alert, when what she most wanted to do was close her eyes and let it all be a dream.

"What did Katherine say?" Anna asked conversationally. "The night she died, she called you. What did she say?"

"You think if you keep me talking long enough, somebody will come and rescue you?" Bob put his hands on his knees and bent forward, the better to peer into her hiding place. "They won't. The girl never gets rescued. Nobody fucking cares about you—any of you."

"That has crossed my mind a time or two," Anna admitted. The blanket started to fall away from her head and face. She clamped her chin down more tightly to hold it in place.

"Aaaaw," Bob crooned. "You're all shy and virginal now, got your blankie covering your face? Gonna hide under the covers?"

"Yes," Anna said. "Hiding under the covers never fails. Monsters can't find you under the covers. What did Katherine say when she called you?"

"She said, 'Anna Pigeon is a cunt.' Nobody likes you, Danger Ranger."

"It seems we have something in common after all," Anna said. "What did she say after the cunt proclamation?" A searing flare of agony fired her shoulder as she moved her damaged arm. Pride touched through the pain when she did not let her hurts show, not in her voice, not in any untoward disturbance of the blanket covering her from head to toe. The story of the Spartan boy, the stolen fox held tight to his middle, showing such stoicism the guard questioning him never suspected until the fox had eaten so far into the boy's innards that the kid died on his feet, flickered in her mind. Anna wished the story had ended better. The guard adopting the little boy; fox and the lad becoming fast friends, chasing goats together through the Grecian hills; maybe the fox saving little Timmy Tchopotoulis from some Greek variation of a well.

"Bobby," she said in her sharpest schoolmarm voice. "Tell me what Katherine said or you'll be in big trouble."

Bob blinked twice, his face lost all tension as if she'd slapped him. "She thought she'd broken her ankle," he said quickly.

"And?"

Bob was stoned and traumatized and a wretched excuse for a man, but he wasn't stupid. Two more blinks and he dragged himself out of whatever place Anna's authoritarian voice had taken him.

"Why do women ask so many questions?" he asked, his terrifying bonhomie back in place.

"For the sheer joy of hearing men talk," Anna replied. Wrestling with her metaphorical fox, she accidentally dislodged the blanket and it began to slip away from her face. "What else did Katherine say?" she managed before she caught it and held it between her teeth. Half her face was exposed, and the overwhelming relief startled her. Maybe women had to be raised in burkas before they could seem like protection instead of prison. The wool tasted of motor oil and its coarse fuzz drew the moisture from her mouth.

Bob shook his head from side to side as if trying to clear it. His hands slid from his knees up his thighs as he pushed himself upright. He was tiring of the game. Anna wondered how Scheherezade had managed to keep her train of thought going a thousand and one nights when a misstep meant her death.

She unclenched her teeth. The blanket slid a couple of inches down her chest but didn't fall off of her shoulders. The cold felt clean and good on her neck. "Katherine thought you'd killed the wolf, shot it with a tranquilizer, then cut its throat," she said, desperate to put off whatever was coming for another minute. "She figured you for the kind of guy who liked other people out cold, didn't have the balls to deal with the conscious—woman or wolf. At least that's what she said to me. 'Everything's big about Bob but his heart and his cock,' I think she said. Yeah, that was it, verbatim. Shrinkage: cold heart, shriveled cock. Makes sense, you know. Based in language: cockles of the heart, warm the cockles, cock—" Anna was babbling, but she was doing so in such a reasonable tone of voice that for half a moment she listened to what she was saying, thinking it might actually make sense.

"I told her it served her right," Bob snarled. "She said, 'Send somebody, you fat fuck,' and I threw her to the wolves. Literally," he said and laughed.

Anna wished she'd changed the subject before he'd gotten to the "fat fuck" part. Choking on the insult, his throat puffed the way a frog's will before it sings. In a second, he would realize he'd told Anna about it and thus been twice shamed.

"Not literally," Anna said, drenching her voice with

scorn. "Figuratively. *Literally* you hung up on her. *Literally* you did nothing. *Literally* you showed what a spineless, pathetic excuse for a man you are." The impromptu cowl fell from her shoulders, sliding down to pool behind her and in her lap. She made no attempt to stop it or retrieve it this time. "You don't rape women. That's way too scary for little Bobby, isn't it? You rape *unconscious* women. Whole different thing, Bobsie. Whole different thing."

Anna was finding it extraordinarily easy to go off on Menechinn. She didn't have to waste a moment's time thinking up horrible words to say, words she hoped would cut all the deeper for being true. Bob's face shook minutely, the way she'd seen it do each time a woman had the unmitigated gall to awaken him from his happy coma of Bobness. The miniature tsunami made him look young for a brief second—very young; the face of a toddler the first time Mommy punches him or Daddy burns him with his cigarette—and, for an even shorter second, Anna felt pity for him.

Not him, she told herself. *That little boy.*

To Bob she said: "Since we've been doing business together, I've been meaning to tell you what a pompous ass you are, with your pouffed hair and oily smile. Women have to be drugged to keep from laughing in your face. And a hypocrite! Sheesh! It would be scary, if it wasn't so obvious. *Expert.* Lord! You're a whore, Menechinn, a prostitute; you screw whoever hands you a dollar. This time, Homeland Security; next time . . . well, anybody with a buck and a quarter. You're not even a good whore.

You can't get it up personally or professionally. You're a limp dick.

"Your raping is like your killing: no balls in it. You rape women who are not there, and you're not there when you kill. You don't *literally* kill anybody, do you, Bobby boy? You *literally* do nothing. If you're going to kill me, you many-chinned fat fuck, you're going to have to do it personally, because, unless you do, I won't die.

"I. Won't. Die."

That was her best shot. She had been as vicious and mean and ugly as it was possible to be without using a thesaurus. Smiling in what she hoped was a damning and disdainful manner, she settled the last of her strength in her wrists and waited.

Through the curtain of spruce needles, she watched him, trying to read her future in his stance, the way his eyes seemed to grow larger as his face relaxed and the cheek flab melted in a grim facsimile of the melting of one of Madame Tussauds wax madmen.

She realized she was seeing his eyes for the first time. Her revulsion and his grin-narrowed gaze had kept her out till now. His irises were dark, but the color was indistinct: blue or brown or hazel, or all three mixed together. He wasn't more than five feet away, yet Anna couldn't have reported the color with any more accuracy than that. They were the color of old water moccasins, the thick, unpretty snakes that took on the greenish brown shades of the muddy water of the Mississippi ditches where they thrived. Like the moccasin's eyes, Menechinn's had a flatness. In the snake, Anna knew it to be myopia and dullness of mind. In Menechinn, she wasn't sure what it indicated but doubted it boded well for her continued good health.

Time wasn't in its petty-paced persona. It had ceased to be linear, and Anna watched Menechinn's face for a moment, then an hour, then a heartbeat. She waited for the look of sly craftiness to take it the way it had before he'd gone into a berserker rage and stomped the life out of the National Park Service's tarp. She waited for it to grow still and raw-beef red as it had when he'd walked over to slap her on the cliff top. She waited for the gleam of joy and triumph to come into his eyes as it had when he hefted the wrench to smash her ankle.

She was growing old waiting and yet scarcely more than fifteen seconds passed before the waiting was over.

Bob Menechinn's face crumpled and tears squeezed from the corners of his eyes. They froze before they'd traveled halfway down his face. His jaws yawned wide, rows of teeth bleached too white by the dentist's art appearing false in the black of his mouth. He ducked his head and brought his forearms up to hide his face like a child ashamed of its tears but too broken to keep them from falling. Maybe he had regressed to a childhood state, when he'd been abused. Maybe he'd had a psychotic break and thought Anna was his dead puppy, Spot or Toughie or whatever.

A better person might have felt sorry for him, but, as far as Anna was concerned, whatever hell he was going through was way too good for him.

Then he charged, head down, mucus and tears

streaming, and he crashed through the ephemeral defenses of her spruce bower and was on her. Though she'd been watching, waiting for it, the onslaught took her by surprise. Not even slowed by the tree branches, he came down in an avalanche of snow and rage, in the reckless flying tackle of a high school football player too young to know how frail the human body is.

Anna went over like a stone, Bob's weight pinning her knees to her chest, her hands trapped between thighs and breasts. Air gusted from her lungs and she couldn't get it back. Bob's hands scrabbled at her head, trying to work under the layers to her throat to strangle her. Hot blood or snot or spittle hit her face. Moans and grunts, expelled on breath like sulfur, burned her nostrils. Like a trapped animal, Anna howled. Then she bit. Catching his nose between her teeth, she clamped down and hung on. Bob roared and thrashed, his fists pummeling her head. But for the hood, she would have been knocked senseless. Salty liquid filled her mouth, streamed down her throat, but she didn't unlock her jaws. With a jerk, Bob freed himself. A chunk of his nose was still in her mouth. She spit it into his face. He reared back and her knees were free; her hands were free.

The flares were still clutched in her fingers. Striking one against the other, she heard the hiss of red fire and pushed them up into Bob's gut. The down of his coat took the flames, then he screamed high and wild as the fire cut into his body. Anna pushed them deeper. He rolled away, pawing at his middle. Then he was up and running. Crazed with the fire in his belly, he crashed into the trunk of a tree several yards away, then fell. Screams turned to cries and cries turned to silence. Finally the only sound was the hissing of the flares, ships' flares designed to burn underwater, under blood and flesh.

The smell of it sickened her. For a long time, she lay where she was, curled up like a sow bug, the taste of Bob Menechinn in her mouth and her mind. It was hard to remember why she lay like this, where she was and who she had killed. Presumably killed. Her eyes drifted closed and she began to fall. Through the rush of the canyon walls flashing by in her brain, she heard a growl. Bob had come to his feet, a human torch; he staggered toward her, arms outstretched, fire streaming from his hands.

With a lurch that triggered the pain in her shoulder, Anna came awake. Bob was where he had fallen. She'd gone to sleep. If she fell asleep again, she would freeze to death. More out of the habit of surviving than a force of will, she bunched her legs under her and, using the tree trunk, climbed to her feet.

Menechinn was dead. There'd be no last-minute rising from the jaws of death to make one last stand for the final scene. "Thankyoubabyjesus," Anna muttered. He lay on his side, his hands hidden in the melted, blackened ruin of his coat where they'd clawed at the fire consuming his insides. The front and back of his parka were tarry messes of bodily fluids and goose down and synthetic fabric.

For a while, Anna stayed, looking at the wreck that

458 | NEVADA BARR

had been, at least nominally, human. The sight of the damage she'd done didn't please or displease her. It had taken time and pain to hobble the few yards to where he'd finally collapsed, and she hadn't the energy to move away. She spit and spit again, not from disrespect—once one killed a man, there was little point in lesser forms of malice—she wanted the taste of him out of her mouth.

She also wanted his coat to keep herself warm, but hadn't the strength to wrestle the garment off the body. Much of it would be melted to his skin. Its value wasn't worth the calories it would take to harvest it. A story she'd read when she was a teenager flitted into her mind. To keep from freezing to death in a blizzard, a man had killed his horse, cut it open and crawled inside.

"Gross!" she said. She left coat and corpse unmolested. His radio had been melted, the leather case burned away, the buttons a mass of plastic still hot to the touch. Anna made her way painfully back to the Bearcat. Beyond hurting or thinking or much caring, she rolled herself in the army blanket, then the blue plastic tarp, leaned back against the snowmobile and let the winter coalesce around her.

36

I told you not to breathe into your sleeping bag."

Robin's voice drifted into Anna's cloudy brain and she smiled. Her face might not have moved, but, in her mind, she welcomed the young woman. It was good to have her company again.

A soft warmth crept under the bundling around Anna's throat, and she wondered if, unlike the depictions in literature and lore, Death did not have a cold and bony hand but one warm and open, a kind and relieving touch welcoming saints and sinners alike, taking away the pain of the suffering, the cravings of the addict, the sorrow of the bereft.

"She's not dead." The warmth receded, and Anna knew she'd flunked the test. Her bell wasn't tolling. Death had not come for her.

A new blessing came in its stead. The warmth that

touched so briefly at her throat spread over her face. "Anna, you're not dead," Robin's voice told her. "Since you're not dead, you have to wake up or you will be dead. Come on, wake up."

Anna opened her eyes. Robin's hands were on her cheeks, her face only inches away, so close it was hard to bring into focus. "You're not dead either?" Anna asked.

"Just hungover," Robin said.

It took Anna's cold brain a minute to put two thoughts together. "Ketamine."

"Yeah. Adam freaked. He was afraid what happened to his wife was going to happen to me. He got hold of Gavin and Gavin came and took me to Feldtmann tower."

"She only looks light," said a voice. Robin's face moved away, and Anna saw the speaker, a tall, slender, Byronesque man with the deep-set green eyes of a poet off-set by the square jaw of a pugilist.

"The wog," Anna croaked.

"I am the wog," Gavin said and smiled, a sweet blink of teeth and good nature. "Robin and me and Adam."

"Adam's dead," Anna said. The words should have meant more to her than they did. By the shock she saw in the faces of Robin and Gavin, she knew she had told them a horrible truth. To her, it seemed so long ago, hundreds of years. One didn't cry over history, didn't break down when telling the third-grade class that George Washington was dead, Napoleon lost at Waterloo or Atlanta was put to the torch.

"Bob Menechinn's dead," Anna said, to see if the news felt any different. "I killed him."

Robin and Gavin did not react with shock this time, just a minute freezing of the facial muscles. Robin put her deliciously warm hands back on Anna's face. "You poor thing," she said as Gavin said:

"Did you kill Adam too?"

Anna tried to remember all those thousands of years ago. "I don't think so," she said finally.

"I killed Katherine," Gavin said.

"You did not!" Robin cried.

"You thought I did."

Robin reached up a hand toward Gavin and he took it, his glove swallowing the slender fingers and palm.

"Put your gloves on," Anna said.

"I'll try Ridley again," Robin said and rose to her feet. "Dispatch has been trying to raise him for half an hour," she told Anna. "Gavin and I were out skiing. We called in as soon as we heard."

"Blew your cover," Anna said. She was too fog-brained to count how many laws and park regulations the two of them had broken, but it was enough to land them in jail or the poorhouse if the judge levied the full penalties and fines.

"You were in trouble," Robin said simply.

"Gloves," Anna said so she wouldn't cry and watched as the biotech obediently put her gloves back on before using the radio.

Gavin squatted beside Anna. He was graceful, the

towering length of him folding neatly, effortlessly. "Are you hurt?" he asked.

"Dislocated shoulder and broken or badly bruised ankle," Anna replied. Said succinctly, it didn't sound all that bad, not like it should have. She decided she'd keep the limping and weeping and whining parts to herself. Why not? The witnesses were all dead.

Gavin began a proficient physical check, starting with her pulse and body temp.

"EMT?" Anna asked.

He shook his head. "Eldest of seven," he said.

Robin interrupted: "Do you think you can survive a ride out on the Bearcat?"

"Out of gas," Anna said, and Robin went back to the radio.

"Hot packs. Tell him we need hot packs," Gavin said. As with Robin, his winter gear was worn and idiosyncratic. In place of a hood, he wore the same woolen tasseled hat Robin sported. They were probably the only two people in the world—other than the Lapps—who didn't look silly with reindeer on their earflaps and pointy tufts on their heads. "Who is the president of the United States?" Gavin asked, to see if Anna was oriented in time and space.

"The blue rucksack," Anna said suddenly. The old canvas day pack they'd found shredded at the scene of Katherine's death had bothered Anna. Like Anna, both Bob and Katherine had all-new gear. It was out of character for Katherine to carry a beat-up canvas bag. The affectation fit with Robin's boyfriend. "It was yours. You had scent lure, didn't you? To make the wolves go where you wanted them to."

"It was mine," Gavin admitted. "I forgot I had the canisters of lure in it when I left it with Katherine. I only meant her to have food and water while she waited for help."

"'HELP ME,'" Anna said. "On the window."

"Ski wax," Gavin said. "It grows opaque as it cools."

Anna said nothing. *If scribbling a magic message on the glass and vanishing into the night was his idea of rescue, he wasn't worth accusing.*

Gavin read the thoughts she chose not to express in words. "Katherine said she'd phoned Bob and he was arranging the rescue. She promised to keep our secret. She wanted Bob to look the fool, be discredited. I didn't think anyone was still at the bunkhouse. It seemed a good time to further the hoax," he said.

Anna closed her eyes so she needn't see the misery on his face. She'd had sufficient misery to last at least a few days if she was careful and didn't blow it all in one breakdown. Gavin's confession exonerated the wolves. Covered in scent lure, bleeding, running, flopping about in true helpless-prey fashion, no self-respecting predator could have resisted Katherine. Not and held its head up at the next carnivore convention. The poet in Gavin would have him suffer the guilt of Katherine's death. Had she more energy, Anna would have reassured him it was an accident, that Katherine had broken open the canisters in a fall or opened one not knowing what it was. Instead, she just sat with her eyes closed and listened to the crabbing of the radio as Robin clicked and talked and then, finally, Ridley Murray answered.

Anna roused herself to shout: "Ask him why in the hell he wasn't answering his radio!" That, at least, had been her intention. Instead, she heard herself whisper "Why didn't he come?" in the voice of a little girl, the one Bob Menechinn said nobody cared about, nobody would rescue. That little girl embarrassed Anna and she hoped her whisper went unnoticed.

"Ask Ridley what's kept him," Gavin said.

Gavin heard Anna's little-girl plea. Him, she didn't mind so much. He had the same feel as Robin did, as if the two of them were not quite of this world, raised in bubbles, maybe, or from another dimension where good always won out, the cream rose to the top and the poor were not always with you.

Undamaged, Anna thought and wondered how damaged she was.

"Ridley and Jonah are just leaving Feldtmann. I'll go back to Windigo and get gas. Enough to get you home," Robin said to Anna.

"I'll go," Gavin said.

"I'm faster," Robin said.

To Anna, Gavin said: "She is. Like the wind." He seemed proud of her, and Anna liked him for that too.

"It's too far," Anna said, thinking of how far Robin had already come that day.

Robin smiled. Ten miles on easy trails had probably not been "too far" since she was nine years old. "I won't be long," she said and pushed off with the sudden grace of a bird taking flight.

"I'm guessing an hour or a little more. Downhill with no pack, she'll make good time. Coming back with the gas can will take longer, but she doesn't need to bring more than a gallon at the most. Eight pounds. That's nothing for Robin," Gavin said reassuringly.

The blanket and tarp Anna had wrapped around herself for warmth were beginning to feel like a shroud and one that was shrinking noticeably. They had done their job, she was found alive, now she wanted out. "Unwrap me," Anna said.

Gavin looked alarmed, and she knew he was remembering the tales of finding people naked and dead of the cold. A rare but not too rare hypothermic reaction was to feel hot. In late stages, victims would sometimes take off their clothes and lie naked in the snow.

"I'm okay," Anna said. "No running naked for me. I've got to move. I'm getting crazy. Crazier. Can you reduce a dislocated shoulder?"

"I've never done it," Gavin admitted.

"Me neither. I learned it in EMT training. It looked easy enough. Align the arm, pull, snick back into place. One . . . two . . . three."

"Two sounds like it would be pretty painful," Gavin said.

"We'll numb the shoulder with ice first," Anna said, then: "Oh, hey, that's already taken care of."

Gavin laughed.

Unwrapping her was more of a job than she'd anticipated. Expecting to stay in her blue-and-brown cocoon for the foreseeable future, Anna'd rolled herself in the fabric more concerned with putting as many layers between herself and the elements as possible than with eventually getting free.

"Help me stand," she said, pushing away the last of the tarp. "I have to get up. Help me. Then we can reduce the shoulder."

Gavin put one arm around her back and gave her his other to brace herself against, so she could control how much pressure was on her shoulder and ankle, and began to draw her to a standing position beside the snowmobile. "Anna, maybe you should—"

"No," Anna interrupted him. "My arm is useless, numb. I've got to reduce it. I can wedge myself against the seat. You'll have something to brace against—"

"Anna, you'd have to take off your coat," Gavin said reasonably.

"No. Why would I?" Confusion was clouding Anna's brain. Instead of making her cautious, it made her desperate, angry.

"I couldn't see what I was doing. Where the lump was. Which way to pull to make it go back into the socket," Gavin said.

"I'll take the damn thing off," Anna snapped.

"You'd lose too much body heat, and it would hurt you too much unless we cut the coat off. It won't be long. Robin's fast."

Hysteria. Most of Anna wanted to give in to it, go

with it. Breathing slowly through her nose, she gained enough rationality to wonder what made the human mind want to spin over the edge, what evolutionary genius thought this would ensure the survival of the species. Maybe it was the flip side of being self-aware. Dachshunds had bad backs because of the long spine. People had craziness because of the big brain.

"I can wait," Anna said after a time. Gavin looked relieved.

"Let's keep you warm," he said kindly. He helped her to the seat of the Bearcat and wrapped her legs in the army blanket, then sat behind her and put his long arms around her. "Lean back," he said. "Consider me your sofa."

Menechinn was dead wrong. The girl did get rescued.

37

Gavin stayed at the bunkhouse. Crude as it was, it had amenities that put his camp in the abandoned fire tower to shame. He'd come to the island from Grand Portage, seventeen miles in a kayak, and had been living at Feldtmann for thirteen days, his only heat a camping stove and a cooking stove. Food and supplies had been cached there over the summer. The plan had been hatched by the biotechs when they heard Homeland Security was to evaluate the study.

They had stolen scent lure from a team of martin researchers to effect the wolves' movements. The props, the black silhouette of the gigantic wolf, the moose and wolf prosthetics to make prints in the snow, had been created by Gavin. The alien DNA was procured by Robin. A friend and fellow researcher in Canada had mailed her

WINTER STUDY | 449

a box of wolf scat. Robin simply bagged it up with the ISRO samples and delivered it to Katherine.

The simplicity of the plan impressed Anna. It would have worked, created a tidy little mystery, had Adam not joined the conspiracy. He'd discovered what they were up to on a trip past Feldtmann in late summer and was mildly amused. It was only when, at his urging, Ridley had requested Bob Menechinn for the evaluation that he had taken an active part.

Ridley had known nothing of the plot, a fact Anna could tell both annoyed and embarrassed him. He'd not even suspected until he and Jonah had gone to Feldtmann tower and noticed fresh tracks and turned off their radios, the better to sneak up on whoever was within.

ANNA WAS LYING on the sofa closest to the stove, enjoying being warm and relatively pain free. Jonah had expertly reduced the dislocated shoulder. Forty years of flying hunters into the Alaskan wilderness had made him a de facto combat medic. Her ankle was elevated, but she'd refused to put ice on it. Enough was, occasionally, enough. She was fairly certain it wasn't broken, the bone merely chipped and bruised. The result was the same: it hurt and she couldn't walk on it.

The bodies had been recovered by Robin, Gavin and Ridley and lay in the carpenter's shop with Katherine's. There'd been no more body bags and they were wrapped in cheery blue tarps.

Three dead, not counting the wolf. The surviving five members of the Winter Study team shared the warm darkness of the common room, the sun long gone, the only light from the fire in the woodstove. Jonah had turned on the generator, but no one, it seemed, wished to see clearly and the lights had been left off.

Those who remained alive on ISRO were all in the room. No one was talking. Anna was glad for the silence, for the heat, for the companionship and for the life that coursed through her veins. Never in her career has she been so close to dying and never before had she such magnificent reasons to resent it: Paul, a wonderful job, her sister, Paul.

The hopeless tangle of human relationships would have depressed her had she not been in a mood of gratitude. Menechinn had destroyed Cynthia and, in the process, Adam. Menechinn had destroyed Katherine and, Anna didn't doubt, her mother.

Robin and Gavin, in their heroic desire to save the wolf/moose study, might very well have ruined their lives and those of their families. Despite the ruination on her mind, Anna found herself smiling in the dark. The mental picture of them stomping about with moose hooves strapped to their boots, sprinkling trails of stink to manipulate the movements of the wolves, cutting out and placing decoys to be seen from the air, planting alien scat and generally sewing the seeds of a wonderful mystery delighted her.

She would love telling the story to Paul. Soon, a week at most, she would be with him, sitting in front of a fire, snuggled close, her life in front of her. A life she was determined not to lose to any fool that happened by with a penchant for evil and the will to carry it through. Soon Ridley would be back with his Honey, eating hot dish and preparing class lectures. Jonah would be up north, hauling wood and waiting for the next round of hunters. Life would go on. What happened at ISRO would become a legend to amuse visitors around the campfire.

Blue skies would be there again.

Except for Robin and Gavin.

The thought dimmed some of the glow of her gratitude.

"How bad is it?" Gavin asked, as if reading her mind.

"Bad," Ridley said. "I've told the NPS as little as possible, but, when the weather clears tomorrow or the next day, the island will be swarming with law enforcement."

"Could we go to jail?" Robin asked.

"Tampering with research would get you a slap on the hand," Anna said. "But your tampering contributed to the death of Katherine Huff. That could get you jail time."

The fire crackled. Jonah slid down in his chair like a teenager, almost horizontal, chin on his chest. Anna and Jonah were not innocents. Ridley, though young, was touched with world-weariness. Robin and Gavin had not considered jail, that what they were doing was a federal crime, that people could be hurt. Anna watched them from half-closed eyes. The two of them sat close

452 | NEVADA BARR

but not touching on the couch opposite hers. The light
of the fire painted their faces in translucent oranges and
yellows, erasing what faint lines of age and worry recent
events had carved there. They looked like children in a
storm, lost and lovely.

Gavin lifted his chin and the look was gone, replaced
by the clear courage of a man born to carry his weight in
the world. "I will make a full confession to whoever hears
these things. Robin helped me but the plan was mine, the
execution was mostly done by myself and Adam, and
Katherine's death is my sole responsibility."

Robin opened her mouth, no doubt to try and take
the blame from Gavin onto her own shoulders.

"Go for a walk," Jonah said abruptly.

There was a moment's startled silence, then Robin
said: "It's night."

"Go to your room, then," Jonah said.

Anna laughed and he gave her a dirty look. "Sorry,"
she said, though she didn't know what she was apologizing for.

"Go to our room?" Gavin said, confused.

"Yeah," Jonah returned. "Just go away and let us
talk."

"Let the grown-ups talk," Gavin said evenly.

Ridley jumped in before Jonah said anything else.
"Would you mind, Gav? You and Robin are . . . too
deeply involved as . . ."

"Criminals," Robin finished for him.

Ridley smiled sadly. "Exactly. Would you guys mind?"

Gavin said nothing, but he followed Robin as she left

the common room. They went into the bedroom Katherine had occupied and shut the door.

"What is it, Jonah?" Ridley asked.

"We've got three dead bodies. The NPS, Homeland Security and probably the state of Michigan are going to come down on us like a ton of bricks."

"Adam was a suicide and Katherine was an accident," Anna said. "I killed whatshisname. Maybe it won't be so bad after the first excitement dies down."

It would be bad; she just said it in hopes it would be true.

"Katherine's death wasn't an accident," Jonah said. "Gavin could have helped her get her foot free and hauled her out of there."

"He thought rescue was coming," Anna said reasonably. "It was farther back to Feldtmann tower than it was from here to the cedar swamp. Gavin said when he got there Katherine was expecting us at any minute. He couldn't have known we weren't coming, that good old Bob turned over and went back to sleep."

"Gavin could have radioed," Jonah said.

"Katherine had phoned. Why would he radio?" Anna asked. "Would you have?"

Jonah grunted.

"Me neither," Ridley said. "You don't expect people like Bob. That's why they win."

"Bob didn't win," Anna said.

"No," Ridley agreed. "No he didn't. You did what you had to. I hope you won't lose any sleep over it."

"Not a wink."

"Gavin and Robin might've torpedoed your career," Jonah said to Ridley.

"I don't think so," Ridley said.

"We're going to have to explain. There's too much. E-mails about the big tracks, the DNA. It's not going under the rug," Jonah said. "When it comes out, our little perpetrators are going to get slammed from every direction."

"Not if they're dead," Anna said with sudden inspiration.

Before Jonah could snatch up the kindling ax to defend himself and Ridley from her homicidal mania—which he looked ready to do—Anna went on: "Adam and Bob set it up. Bob to . . . what? What would be good?"

"Bob wanted to take over the study himself," Ridley said slowly. "Become somebody in research circles."

"Right," Jonah said. "Earn the big bucks."

Ridley laughed. Anna was glad to hear laughter. It had been a long time since she'd heard any that wasn't tinged with some poison or another.

"There's fame attached," Anna said. "You're somebody. Bob was nobody. People who knew him might buy that."

"So when did he bring in the goodies?" Jonah asked. "The paw prints and scent lure and doggy cutouts? It won't work."

"The windigo!" Anna exclaimed suddenly.

"Are you feverish?" Jonah asked, his concern genuine.

"No. Maybe, but that's not it. It just occurred to me

that was what I was smelling. The windigo is supposed to have this reek that announces its presence. I kept smelling a hint of it. I was smelling the scent lure. That stuff is the essence of all things vile. Dogs and wolves love it. Hah!" she said, pleased to have one more niggling question answered.

"So when did Bob stash his tools?" Jonah went back to his question.

"Adam did that," Ridley suggested. "Adam was doing it to save the study. Bob figured it out, took over and there was a falling-out. Bob kills Adam and is killed attacking Anna."

"And Robin and Gavin skip away hand in hand—no harm, no foul?" Jonah said.

"Why not?" Anna said. "Do you want to see them behind bars? Boy, would that ever make you a cold-hearted bastard. Why don't you just turn in Smokey the Bear and Woodsy the Owl and Ranger Rick for ecoterrorism?"

Silence returned. From Katherine's old room came the gentle murmur of Gavin and Robin talking. The thought of them going to prison, or even through the ruthless misery of the legal system, hurt Anna, an ache in her chest near where her heart was. Justice had been meted out already in the dribs and drabs of violence and insanity that Bob and Adam carried with them to the island. Evil had vanquished itself. What came now, if they let it come, would be politics. Politicians did not sacrifice themselves for the greater good, not if it meant losing their jobs.

She wanted to push Ridley and Jonah, to preach and to beg if need be, but she sensed it would be best to let them alone. So she waited. Finally Ridley spoke.

"We can burn the stuff they used for the hoax. There's time. And clean up Feldtmann tower. It's too cold for whatever law shows up to want to dig too deep. Too cold and too isolated."

Anna felt a surge of affection for the young man. The animosity he'd evinced toward federal law enforcement early in this adventure had annoyed her. Now she loved him for it.

"So we play God?" Jonah asked.

"People always play God," Anna said. "There's nobody else to do it."

And now a sneak preview of Nevada Barr's
newest Anna Pigeon mystery,

BORDERLINE

Available in hardcover from G. P. Putnam's Sons!

A leave of absence, "medical leave" the park was calling it. Anna wasn't sure what she called it. Maybe the end of her career. More than not knowing what to call it, she didn't know how she felt about it. Ambivalent was a good word.

"I'm ambivalent," she said to Paul.

Paul Davidson was her husband of less than a year and most of that spent apart. "Ambivalent is a good word," he said, echoing her thought. For a moment Anna just looked at him. He was the most beautiful man she had ever seen. White hair fell thick and straight across his broad forehead. There had been more blond in it when she first met him. Perhaps being married to her aged a man quickly. The white suited him, and the hard bright sun of a Texas spring burnished it to a fine gloss. Paul was fifty-seven, eight years older than she. He wasn't much taller, five-feet-eight in his socks—precisely the right height to hold and be held, to kiss and be kissed.

"Are you ready to do this? It's all adventure and parky," he said softly. The rest of the rafting group was in the middle of preparations peppered with laughter and chat as they loaded the raft with gear. "We could still do something else. Go to Italy. Hike the Great Pyrenees. Spend a week getting wrapped in seaweed and glopped in mud at a fancy spa."

"It's warm here and I'm not the boss," Anna said.

Paul kissed her gently. He was the best kissing man she had ever met. Most men thought they were good kissers, just like they all thought they were good drivers. Most were wrong on both counts.

"Stop kissing! You're setting a bad example for the children!" a girl shouted at them.

Though Anna could have finessed a trip down the river with other rangers, she and Paul had chosen to go with a commercial outfit out of Terlingua. Anna had wanted nothing to do with the green and gray, and it was one of those rare occasions she didn't want to be alone in the wilderness: She needed the distraction other people provided. This group of college kids—three girls and one boy, a boyfriend of somebody, Anna assumed—promised to be more distracting than bucolic. The girl who had shouted at them was a lanky nineteen-year-old, who was so thin her bones were held together only by the spandex she wore. Her dark hair was slicked back into a ponytail that stuck through the back of her ball cap. Cyril something. Anna liked her. She had a wide smile full of big teeth, and eyes so black the pupils were nearly lost giving her the perpetual look of a night-seeing cat.

Paul released Anna but held her hand as they walked over the stones to the raft. This trip was a luxury outing. Camp chairs and sleeping pads, coolers full of food and beer, folding tables, a portable fire pit made from the bottom of a metal barrel, a grill for cooking steaks, pots, pans, and tents had been stowed in the raft's midsection. Life jackets had been provided but no one bothered to put them on. Not yet. The guide, Carmen, a small woman of muscle and attitude, told them they'd need them later but here, where the water was flat and amiable, they could use them as seat cushions.

Carmen directing, the seven of them pushed the raft into the water of the Rio Grande River. They were putting in at Lahitas on the western border of the park and would float downriver through Santa Elena Canyon. In all her years in the park service, including time in northern Texas at Guadalupe Mountains National Park, Anna had never visited Big Bend. She had always meant to.

"What's with all the black SUVs?" one of the three girls asked. Her name was Lori, Anna recalled. She was the quietest of the group and looked to be the strongest which wasn't saying a great deal. These were urban children, raised on electronics and junk food. Their minds were sharp but their bodies could have used a lot more dodgeball and tree-climbing in their early years.

"Mayor of Houston is in the park. She's going to announce a run for governor."

"You'd think they'd show up in Priuses or Smart Cars or something," Cyril said. "Be all green in a park."

"Texas does oil," Carmen said succinctly. The raft was in knee-deep water and was twitching as if anxious to go with the flow.

"You hop in," Paul said and waited to see that Anna slithered over the side without incident before he climbed aboard himself. Anna had never needed anyone to take care of her, or never admitted she did, but she wasn't minding it. She was liking it and that surprised her. The surprise was followed by a twinge of guilt. Raised by hardworking parents, who had been just starting out during the Great Depression, the virtue of carrying one's own weight and incurring no debts had been drummed into her and her sister. Anna didn't buy things she couldn't afford and that included things that had to be paid off over time. Since Zach, her first husband, died she had more or less run her emotional life the same way: no debts incurred, no promises made for an always unsure future.

Paul, a classic with his gun and his Bible, had found a way to give and love in such a way that it actually seemed he did it because he liked to, because it enriched him, that virtue was, indeed, its own reward.

Anna caught his eye, hazel and full of life under the brim of a canvas hat. He winked at her and she was startled to think it didn't just seem, for Paul it was.

"This is the right trip," she said, putting her back into

her paddling until Carmen hollered that they weren't in a race.

The thundering emptiness that had taken her to the psychologist's office in Boulder, and the broken shards of thoughts and conversations that had come in its wake, began to lose ground to the great state of Texas and the wonders of the Chihuahuan Desert. The water in the Rio Grande was high, but, where the banks were low and the river could spread out, it didn't require much thought to navigate. Besides, thinking was Carmen's job. Anna didn't want any part of it. Fantasies, when the empty dark and the fragmented thoughts allowed her to have them, had run to quiet gardens in countries where no one spoke English, of severed phone lines and silence and no responsibility greater than pushing her hair out of her eyes and making coffee every morning.

The chatter of happy people little more than children and the wet, friendly lapping of the brown water against the sides of the raft soothed Anna. The sky was huge and deep, on the horizon towers of cumulonimbus clouds rose in great columns exploring every shade of white. Cane grass, growing out from the bank, fought a soundless battle for territory with the exotic giant reeds. The reeds had been brought from the Orient to serve as cattle fodder and had taken over. They had the lush yet hungry look of countries Anna had only seen in movies that were drenched in blood: *Apocalypse Now* and *Full Metal Jacket*. Larger and darker of leaf than the indigenous cane, they reached out far over the water, their stems so thick and interwoven that only the smallest of creatures could travel through them to the river.

They were voraciously beautiful, and, for once, Anna chose not to care what was indigenous and what was exotic, what was healing for the park and what harmed it. Later, if she felt truly wild and crazy, ultimately devil-may-care and irresponsible, she might try littering simply to see if she could do it.

"Why's the land all torn up on the left bank?" Cyril asked.

"They're putting in a golf course," Carmen answered. Her voice was carefully neutral; so much so that it left the listener in no doubt that she loathed the idea of the development.

A water-sucking, pesticide-drenched, whore of a golf course smacked down in the middle of the desert. Anna snorted. Only Tiger Woods in perfectly pleated trousers could make a golf course attractive anywhere. Even he might fail on the sere banks of the Rio Grande. *Not my problem,* Anna told herself firmly and put it from her mind with a deep breath. The air was so clean and dry she scarcely felt the need for inhaling and exhaling. Pure as it was, it felt as if it might permeate the flesh without bothering to trouble the lungs.

"It's not in the park?" Cyril asked.

"Nope."

"There wasn't a sign or anything," Cyril said. "You know, like 'Give Up All Hope Ye Who Enter Here.' Or 'Now You're in Parkland, Stop Having Fun.'"

"There used to be a sign but the river rangers talked

the NPS into taking it down. There's no need for a sign. It makes no difference to the river whose land it flows through. Technically all the land on the right is Mexico and all the land on the left is the United States. Since the border was closed eight or nine years ago, according to the law, if we drift over the center of the river and into Mexico then drift back into U.S. waters—we've broken the law."

Anna recalled a dustup over that issue years before. One of the river rangers was so incensed over the sudden closure he called the Border Patrol to come and arrest a bunch of lily-white college kids down from New York State to go rafting. He was trying to make the point that if it was illegal for anybody to do it, then the law should be enforced against Americans as well as Mexicans. What he succeeded in doing was pulling off a magnificent career-limiting gesture.

Anna put the border issues with the golf course. Not her problem.

Letting the talk of the others meld again with the chuckle of the water, she watched red-eared box turtles slide off their perches on stones and logs, hiding them-selves beneath the dark water. Red-eared turtles were as much an invasive species as the giant reeds, but today Anna wasn't going to hold it against them. Everybody had to come from somewhere and she appreciated that they allowed her to share their space with them.

"We'll be in the park after we round that bend."

Anna glanced back to see Carmen pointing down-river where the land began to wrinkle then reared up in

466 | NEVADA BARR

sudden bluffs, high and sheer and burnt-gold in the strong light. Leading up to—or falling away from—the crown of shale were ash-gray hills pocked with cacti. Here and there a splash of luminescent yellow-green or shocking pink sparked from a blooming plant.

"Cool," Anna heard the boy say. He had a nice voice. Mucho basso profundo and coming out of a rib cage that a big man could probably fit his hands around. The kid was nowhere near the size of the noise he made, at least not in breadth. He was paddling opposite Anna and she watched him for a moment, her paddle idle across her knees. Out of self-defense she bet he'd learned every skinny joke there was from turning sideways and sticking out his tongue to look like a zipper to having to run around in circles in the shower to get wet. He was at least six feet tall and weighed a hundred twenty to a hundred twenty-five at a guess.

"Are you and Cyril related?" Anna asked, seeing it for the first time.

"Twins," Cyril called from behind her. "I'm the pretty one. It's important that you remember that. I'm real sensitive on that issue."

"I'll remember," Anna said.

"Steve," the boy introduced himself in his marvelous voice.

"You should go into radio," Anna said before she realized it would be taken as an insult. He groaned. Evidently he'd heard that one before as well.

Being rude was shoved back to keep company with

the golf course and the border issues and the evil intruding grasses.

Not my problem, Anna reassured herself. Much of her life, when she'd chosen to think about it, which was not all that often, she'd assumed being lazy and irresponsible and self-centered was the easy way. Practicing it was turning out to be a lot harder than she'd thought. There was so much in the world to not care about, so much to blow off, brush off or otherwise put out of her mind. Clearly she wasn't going to become proficient in it at the rapid pace she had expected. Littering would be out of the question for at least a year or two. *Maybe gum*, she thought. In a few months she could begin training by spitting her gum out on the ground instead of carefully folding it in the slip of paper the stick came in and carrying it in her pocket until she remembered to put it in the trash or laundered it with the cigarette butts and pop-tops and other bits of refuse she was constantly picking out of the world.

"*Hola*," Carmen called. Anna pulled out of her mind to see a group of vaqueros on the left bank, three men on horseback and a half dozen scrawny cows. The rafters stopped paddling and the men on the bank waved. One of the girls, Christine, who despite being considerably overweight, wore the low-cut spandex shorts and high-cut spandex top that Cyril showed off to such advantage. A pale fold of fat rounded over the tight band. Anna hoped the girl had had sense enough to slather her soft, white underbelly with sunscreen before exposing it to the elements.

Christine took a camera from her dry-bag and began clicking pictures of the cowboys. A tall Mexican in a wide-brimmed hat that looked as if it had herded many cows over the years smiled widely then pulled a disposable camera from his belt and took a picture of the raft. The other vaqueros laughed, touched the brims of their hats respectfully, and kicked their horses into a walk as the raft drifted downstream of them.

"Wow," Christine said. "Mexicans. All we ever get are Puerto Ricans."

"Chrissie doesn't get out much," Cyril said. "She is from a small desert isle in the Atlantic Ocean."

"Staten Island," Chrissie defended herself. "And I do too get out."

"No," Steve corrected her. "Sometimes they *let* you out. It's a whole different thing."

"They're on the left bank. I thought the Mexicans couldn't cross the river and be in America because of the drug thing," Chrissie said. The raft took them from the last view of the vaqueros as they started pushing their small herd into the water to cross back to the Mexican side of the river.

"Nobody told the cows," Carmen said. "Technically they aren't supposed to come over to get them but the park kind of turns a blind eye. Once in a while the rangers will round them up and take them up to El Paso where they get auctioned off or slaughtered, I guess. Mostly they just let the vaqueros retrieve them. It's a whole lot cheaper than trucking them the length of Texas."

Silence didn't fall, but Anna tuned the talk out and put herself back into the natural world. Or tried to. The pit that had opened inside her altered the landscape. She could see it when she looked inward, a great black hole, wide and deep and without light, yawning like the mouth of an underground cavern. Around it the desert hills rolled away, the river wound by, the sky rose into the ether. She could see herself, small and fragile, on her hands and knees at the rim of the crater trying not to be sucked into the darkness.

"Weird," she said aloud and shook her head to free herself of the image.

"Are you okay?" Paul asked quietly.

Anna wasn't sure how to answer that, at least not if she answered honestly. "Fine," she told him.

"It will be," he promised.

Since she had known him, Paul had never broken a promise to her. Anna contented herself with that, and so she forced the pathetic image to crawl slowly away from the abyss on its hands and knees.

The
"STUNNING"
(*The Seattle Times*)
"EXCEPTIONAL"
(*The Denver Post*)
"SUPERB"
(*The New York Times Book Review*)

ANNA PIGEON SERIES
by Nevada Barr

Winter Study
Hard Truth
High Country
Flashback
Hunting Season
Blood Lure
Deep South
Endangered Species
Firestorm
Ill Wind
A Superior Death
Track of the Cat

penguin.com

Don't miss the page-turning suspense, intriguing characters, and unstoppable action that keep readers coming back for more from these bestselling authors...

Tom Clancy
Robin Cook
Patricia Cornwell
Clive Cussler
Dean Koontz
J.D. Robb
John Sandford

Your favorite thrillers and suspense novels come from Berkley.

penguin.com

"This is a Nevada Barr book through and through, with its careful examination of how humans interact with the natural world, and infectious fascination with nature and dense, resonant descriptions." —*The Miami Herald*

"One of the country's top mystery writers . . . one of our finest nature writers . . . Barr's strong, evocative writing richly explores the scenery as well as the characters and her sturdy approach will have readers putting on jackets as frigid winds blow through *Winter Study* as the suspense heats up." —*South Florida Sun-Sentinel*

"Barr skillfully uses archetypal images of the wolf to deepen the suspense, but ultimately it's the more sinister human who is truly frightening."
—*The Washington Post Book World*

"The blizzards, the dangerous ice, and the manhunts through the frozen woods are described with crisp, hard-edged beauty. And the wolves, those maligned 'ogres of childhood,' are magnificent."
—*The New York Times Book Review*

"Barr's sharp descriptions of the wilderness add a special kick." —*The Seattle Times*

continued . . .

"Barr deftly weaves a grand lattice of suspense as both humans and wolves act out of character . . . riveting . . . The tale is plausible, suspenseful, and, in the end, unexpected. The eminently likable Pigeon is a sassy, smart woman who will pilot you through a satisfying adventure." —*Star Tribune*

"You may want to switch off the air conditioner as you turn the pages of local author Nevada Barr's fourteenth Anna Pigeon adventure. It's that chilling . . . a harsh beauty reveals itself in this action-packed adventure offering chills of every kind." —*The Times-Picayune*

"Barr loves writing about challenges presented by water and weather, and she can make the most benign landscape seem fraught with danger. In *Winter Study*, you can almost feel the deep cold . . . Anna fights her way out of more predicaments in this book than ever before, including a heart-stopping entrapment on dangerous ice and a long sequence involving a snowmobile when, for the first time, I wondered if Anna was going to make it. *Winter Study* is fast-paced, intricately plotted, and filled with foreboding." —*St. Paul Pioneer Press*

"Barr's intense closed-room drama integrates winter's forces—blizzards and ice—with the psychological play of ghosts and legends . . . tremendously satisfying . . . Barr tackles human depravity head-on while introducing readers to this area's natural beauty." —*Library Journal*

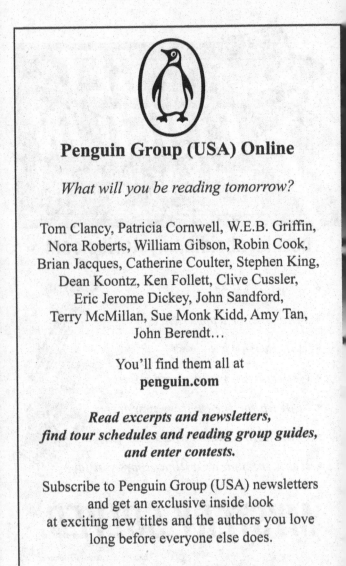